I0831906

GREATHEART
SILVER
AND OTHER PULP HEROES

AND OTHER PULP HEROES

PHILIP JOSÉ FARMER

Edited by Michael Croteau

Introduction by Garyn G. Roberts, Ph.D.

Meteor House

Greatheart Silver and Other Pulp Heroes

by Philip José Farmer

Meteor House and the editor would like to give special thanks to
Garyn G. Roberts, Ph.D., Paul Spiteri, Keith Howell, Win Scott Eckert,
and Jason Aiken for their contributions to this collection.

Meteor House
ISBN 978-1-945427-16-9
First Trade Hardcover Edition

Table of Contents

Fibers of Pulpwood Ran in His Blood
Philip José Farmer in the 1970s

Garyn G. Roberts, Ph.D.

Let's start cosmic—not World of Tiers, Riverworld, Dayworld or Wold Newton world building—but still cosmic. In recorded history and literary history, our best, most popular and pervasive, critically recognized, enduring authors are those among us who are the best read. They have made reading their passion, their vocation and avocation, and by doing so are familiar with language, motifs and storylines, world culture, and people. In this regard and more, Philip José Farmer was at the top of his class.

Now, let's look at this another way. What's the best strategy to become a successful writer? Read, read some more, read again, consider and embrace, imitate, interpret and expand, write, read some more—then repeat. Stephen King wrote, "If you don't have the time to read, you don't have the time or the tools to write." (King, 174) Philip José Farmer was a voracious reader. And it is probably safe to say that, beyond his personal experience and cultural inheritance, virtually all of his writing was inspired by reading—much of this pulp magazine reading.

Like Ray Bradbury (1920-2012), Philip José Farmer (1918-2009) consumed world literature, popular and pulp fiction, and popular culture as if it were going out of style. Few other twentieth century authors celebrated and incorporated other authors and story forms—in their own creative writing—as did Bradbury and Farmer. No one was (or is) better adept than Philip José Farmer at interweaving literary and popular culture history, and then providing an overriding narrative of his own. No one.

Philip José Farmer broke into the pulps in a big way in his early thirties. That first landmark contribution to pulp fiction, the novella "The Lovers," was not only featured in the August 1952 issue of *Startling Stories*, it was the subject of that issue's cover. Pulpwood magazines were print media of fiction that overlapped and followed the dime novel/story paper (1830s-1920s), and overlapped and preceded the paperback book (1930s to the present).

Pulp magazines were named for the highly coarse, highly acidic cheap pulpwood paper upon which they were printed. These publications were designed to be ephemeral, not meant to last. Over time, for some, but not all, "Pulp" became a pejorative not only for the quality of the paper, but for the quality of the fiction that splashed across these magazines' pages. This pejorative was a vast overgeneralization with inherent "truths" and "fallacies." Many of the world's most important authors of the past 130 years cut their teeth in the pages of pulp magazines. Many important narratives first found life on pulpwood pages. Never was there a time, before or since, when an aspiring author could, with dogged persistence, become published in widely distributed popular fiction. (Bradbury often claimed that he threw his first one million words away.) Editors and publishers were more often than not willing to provide detailed feedback, constructive criticism and suggestions for aspiring writers. These editors and publishers built stables of pulp authors that they called upon for years to come—tales of these relationships are documented many other places, and many of these tales are legendary.

Philip José Farmer did not belong to any "stable" of authors, though he had many professional colleagues and networked friends—he was in many ways a unique, independent voice. Farmer consumed pulp fiction from the time of his childhood between the two world wars until his passing in the early twenty-first century. At the end of the pulp era, Philip José Farmer was a bright light in the fading medium. Similar to the great Richard Matheson (1926-2013), Farmer began in the twilight of the pulps, helped usher in the pulp digest and paperback eras, and then eventually transcended and expanded all of these popular media.

(By the late 1930s and early 1940s—when the United States became an even more active participant in what would ultimately be called World War II—conservation of paper became critical to the war effort. For this, and for several other reasons, the pulp digest and popular paperback became viable alternatives to the pulp magazine. Ultimately, by war's end, the pulp magazine became too conventional and predictable in its product offerings and was being squeezed out in the popular entertainment field by burgeoning network television. The rise and fall of the pulpwood magazine is a fascinating history chronicled in other books, essays, and electronic sources.)

The Official Philip José Farmer Web Page (www.pjfarmer.com) provides a complete, detailed and definitive publication history of Philip José Farmer in the pulps, pulp digests, and hardcover and paperback books. This website also records Farmer's pulp tributes and pastiches, and his non-pulp literary pastiches. But to set some important context, the following PJF landmarks are noted here.

Philip José Farmer's first publications in the pulps are today legendary—even archetypal. Consider the following:

"The Lovers" *Startling Stories* (August 1952)
"Sail On! Sail On!" *Startling Stories* (December 1952)
"Mother" *Thrilling Wonder Stories* (April 1953)
"Moth and Rust" *Startling Stories* (June 1953)
"Daughter" *Thrilling Wonder Stories* (Winter 1954)

Pulp digests, primarily Fantasy and Science Fiction publications, provided an important market for Farmer's inventive and groundbreaking fictions during the post pulp magazine era. The author's early entries into these digests included:

"Attitudes" *Fantasy & Science Fiction* (October 1953)
"They Twinkled Like Jewels" *Fantastic Universe* (January 1954)
"The God Business" Beyond *Fantastic Universe* (March 1954)
"Rastignac the Devil" *Fantastic Universe* (May 1954)
"The Celestial Blueprint" *Fantastic Universe* (July 1954)

"The Wounded" Fantastic Universe (October 1954)
"Totem and Taboo" *Fantasy & Science Fiction* (December 1954)
"Father" *Fantasy & Science Fiction* (July 1955)
"The Night of Light" *Fantasy & Science Fiction* (June 1957)
"The Alley Man" *Fantasy & Science Fiction* (June 1959)
"Heel" *Worlds of Imagination* (May 1960)
"Open to Me, My Sister" *Fantasy & Science Fiction* (May 1960)
"A Few Miles" *Fantasy & Science Fiction* (October 1960)
"Prometheus" *Fantasy & Science Fiction* (March 1961)
"Tongues of the Moon" *Amazing Stories* (September 1961)
"Uproar in Acheron" *The Saint Mystery Magazine* (May 1962)
"How Deep the Groves" *Amazing Stories* (February 1963)
"Some Fabulous Yonder" *Fantastic Stories of Imagination* (April 1963)
"The Blasphemers" *Galaxy* (April 1964)
"The King of the Beasts" *Galaxy* (June 1964)
"Riverworld" *Worlds of Tomorrow* (January 1966)

And more. In the cases of "Rastignac the Devil" and "Some Fabulous Yonder," however, editors, without the author's permission, took a heavy hand and severely compromised Farmer's original tales.

By 1970, Phillip José Farmer began a series of pulp tributes and pastiches that are revered yet today. While other pulp heroes and characters appeared in these tributes, Mr. Farmer's favorite characters were Edgar Rice Burroughs' Tarzan and Kenneth Robeson's (Lester Dent's) Doc Savage. Among these tributes and pastiches are:

A Feast Unknown (1969)—Doc Savage and Tarzan;
Lord of the Trees/The Mad Goblin (1970)—Tarzan and Doc Savage;
Lord Tyger (1970)—Tarzan;
Hadon of Ancient Opar (1974)
Flight to Opar (1976);
Escape from Loki—Doc Savage (1991); and
Tarzan and the Dark Heart of Time (1999/2018)

There were other such tributes and pastiches of various lengths.

Introduction

In the early 1970s, Farmer published two extraordinary books. These extremely detailed and well-synthesized hard cover books are *Tarzan Alive* (1972) and *Doc Savage: His Apocalyptic Life* (1973). Both books, which have gone through multiple reprintings, are fictional biographies of Tarzan and Doc Savage respectively. Using the original books about each character, Philip José Farmer organized, crafted and supplemented life stories of these legendary pulp heroes. In the process, Farmer not only respectfully tied the longstanding legends together, he preserved and expanded the already existing scholarship on both characters. Farmer's research and documentation is top rate and ground breaking.

About this same time in the early 1970s, Philip José Farmer also produced several important non-pulp literary pastiches. Perhaps only tangentially related to our discussion here of the author's pulp tributes and pastiches, these are interesting to note. Each is an excellent novel. These include *The Wind Whales of Ishmael* (1971), Farmer's tribute to Herman Melville and *Moby Dick; The Other Log of Phileas Fogg* (1973), the author's celebration of Jules Verne and *Around the World in Eighty Days*; Farmer's *The Adventures of the Peerless Peer* (1974), a nod to both Arthur Conan Doyle's Sherlock Holmes and Edgar Rice Burroughs' Tarzan; and *A Barnstormer in Oz* (1982), a worthy contribution to L. Frank Baum's *Wizard of Oz* mythology. Again, there were more. I have taught *The Other Log of Phileas Fogg* and *A Barnstormer in Oz* in my university classrooms with great success.

All of this leads us to Philip José Farmer's pulp fiction collected in this volume, much of which had its genesis in the 1970s. Greatheart Silver was Farmer's amalgamation and celebration of the old pulp heroes. The synthesis of hero pulp tradition found in the three Greatheart Silver stories is nothing less than incredible. These three stories work on two distinct levels for two distinct audiences of readers. For that first group of readers, these stories are raucous adventures that stand by themselves. For the second group, the exploits of Greatheart Silver invoke romantic memories of 1930s hero pulps.

Originally, the Greatheart Silver saga appeared in Byron Preiss's short-lived, but wonderful 1970s pulp tribute paperback series released by Pyramid/Jove/HBJ Books, *Weird Heroes: A New American Pulp!* In 1982, TOR Books collected these stories in paperback form as *Greatheart Silver*. The first of these three stories, entitled "Greatheart Silver in Showdown at Shootout," debuted in *Weird Heroes #1* in 1975. The second, "The Return of Greatheart Silver," appeared in *Weird Heroes #2* (1975); and the third, "Greatheart Silver in the First Command," premiered in *Weird Heroes #6* (1977).

"Greatheart Silver in Showdown at Shootout" weaves literary genres and traditions in a most wonderful way. As this adventure opens, Greatheart Silver, is a First Mate for the Acme Zeppelin Corporation. World War I romanticism abounds—there are zeppelins, vintage airplanes and more that invoke memories of vintage pulp magazines with titles such as *Aces*, *War Birds*, and maybe most famously, *G-8 and His Battle Aces*. Ultimately, there is an epic Western-type shootout of villains and heroes that rivals the legendary shootout at the OK Corral.

For "The Return of Greatheart Silver," the second adventure in his pulp tribute series, Philip José Farmer again employs a subtitle. This time that subtitle is formatted very much like something people saw when they read old Nineteenth Century dime novels. The full title reads, "The Return of Greatheart Silver; Or, The Secret Life of Rebecca of Sunnybrook Farm." For "Greatheart Silver in the First Command," the third installment of this pulp series, Farmer uses the dime novel-like subtitle, "Or, Inglories Galore."

By the time the three Greatheart Silver hero pulp stories are complete, all kinds of popular culture and popular literature themes, images and characters are invoked including Glinda of Oz, the Shadow, Norse mythology, and so much more

"The Grant Robeson Papers" first appeared in *Weird Heroes #8* (1977). This was designed as an introduction for a new series Philip José Farmer envisioned. Unfortunately, Farmer only completed one of these proposed series stories, "Savage Shadow." In "The Grant Robeson papers," the editor (Farmer) explains that a wealthy collector paid Maxwell Grant and Kenneth Robeson to write stories using each other's characters—The Shadow and Doc Savage respectively. In the 1930s, The Shadow and Doc were the two most famous, popular, and prolific of Street and Smith Publishers' hero pulp line. Walter B. Gibson (as "Maxwell Grant") wrote the vast majority of the original 325+ *The Shadow* novels, while Lester Dent (as "Kenneth Robeson") scripted the vast majority of the 181+ *Doc Savage* stories. Of course, in the case of "The Grant Robeson Papers" Philip José Farmer is the real author.

Interestingly, Farmer was certainly acutely aware of the following situation. Not long after Street and Smith, and Gibson/Grant, launched *The Shadow* series with "The Living Shadow" (April 1, 1931 cover date), Lester Dent, in the summer of 1932 submitted his own *Shadow* novel entitled "The Golden Vulture" to Street and Smith. This later appeared as the feature novel of *The Shadow* with a July 15, 1938 cover date.

Something more about what is going on in "The Grant Robeson Papers"—The Shadow had more than one alias. While his most famous fictional alias is that of "Lamont Cranston"—probably the best known alias because of radio adaptations of *Shadow* stories—his first alias was that of aviator "Kent Allard." The "L*****C*******" referenced in "The Grant Robeson Papers" is easy to identify as Lamont Cranston. The "J*****D***" moniker is a little more difficult for those not familiar with pulp heroes prior to The Shadow and Doc Savage.

Frank L. Packard (1877-1942) was a prolific and popular Canadian author with lots of United States/New York City ties—including publishers. He wrote for the Munsey line and other magazines, and his serials for these magazines were often later collected as hardcover books. Among his rich background and accomplishments are his five Jimmie Dale novels—the first, *The Adventures of Jimmie Dale* debuted in 1917 (This story first appeared serially in 1914.) The "J*****D***" referenced in "The Grant Robeson Papers"—is Jimmie Dale. Dear Reader, if you haven't noticed yet in this writing, the author of this introduction is passionate and subjective about his love for Philip José Farmer and related pulp topics. With that said, Frank L. Packard was a tremendous talent and remains a great read. His books are treasures, and they are available, but since many of these were written and published in the teens and twenties, only the most dedicated pulp aficionados and scholars are aware of them today. Philip José Farmer obviously knew and enjoyed the works of Frank L. Packard. As a story character, Jimmie Dale, Alias the Gray Seal was a gentleman thief, a safe cracker, who was and is much in the line and tradition of E.W. Hornung's Raffles from the generation before him. As a pulp hero, Jimmie Dale was a generation ahead of The Shadow and Doc Savage.

"Savage Shadow," by Maxwell Grant, is the only Philip José Farmer story to fulfill the vision of "The Grant Robeson Papers." Like "The Grant Robeson Papers," "Savage Shadow" first appeared in *Weird Heroes #8*. In "Savage Shadow," Farmer makes "Kenneth Robeson" (the pseudonym/house name most often used by Lester Dent) the protagonist of the story. "Savage Shadow" is set in 1932, a most appropriate date since this is about the height of what would later be deemed "The Great Depression," and a prime year for pulp heroes—Maxwell Grant's *The Shadow* debuted in 1931, Kenneth Robeson's *Doc Savage* in 1933. The saga begins on a cold, windy December day of '32 on the 86th floor of the brand new Empire State Building, started in 1930 and completed in 1931. PJF knew New York City well; the 86th floor features a real-life and famous observation deck.) In many ways, including setting, characters and stereotypes, plotting and so on, "Savage Shadow" from start to finish reads very much like a classic Doc Savage story. There is also a very real sense of "Kenneth Robeson" as a writer. Throughout events of this adventure, the reader gets a real feel for what it was like to be a struggling pulp author in the early 1930s. "Savage Shadow" is an excellent story, and it makes the reader really wish that there had been more installments of "The Grant Robeson Papers."

"Skinburn" is a genre hybrid story which features "Kent Lane," a private detective who is the son of Kent Allard and Margo Lane. This Farmer "pulp" story first appeared in the October 1972 issue of *The Magazine of Fantasy and Science Fiction*. It was later reprinted in *The Book of Philip José Farmer* (DAW 1973, revised Berkley 1982), and then Subterranean Press' *Up the Bright River* (2010). Kent Lane is a private detective, and he goes to the doctor with a very Bradburyesque illness—in other words he, as the central character, has a physical malady similar to that of the protagonists in Bradbury's "The Skeleton" (*Weird Tales*, September 1945) and "A Careful Man Dies" (*New Detective*, November 1946). What an excellent—what do we call it these days?—"mashup!" Hammett/Chandler Detective Fiction, *Weird Tales* Dark Fantasy, Science Fiction, Romance all bound by the balances and justices of karma and the gods.

Philip José Farmer's fiction has always been rich in metaphor and literary allusion. No era of his work is fuller of such allusion than his 1970s pulp fiction. In his 1970s writing, Philip José Farmer provides many clues, many bread crumbs for his readers to follow. Herein, we, as those readers, are encouraged to further investigate specific pulp heroes, authors, legends, traditions, storylines, and so much more.

Philip José Farmer is like One-Eyed Willy in the 1985 movie, *The Goonies*. Farmer, like Willy, gives us the clues, shows us the way—fraught with perils and excitement—and leads us to treasure. He was unique, and in his own way, he was the best.

Thank you, Michael Croteau and all the great and dedicated people of the Philip José Farmer Society and Meteor House for including me in this important and excellent volume. I know of few, if any, Fantasy/Adventure/Detective Fiction/Science Fiction writers that have the dedicated, professional fans and scholars as those members of the Philip José Farmer Society. Meteor House is one of the very best publishers of Fantasy and Science Fiction working today. I humbly think Mr. Farmer would have been very proud of each of you.

What I already knew from reading Mr. Farmer's work through the years is that the author was sincerely great. In writing this introduction, not only am I reminded of this fact, I am once again searching out and reading everything I have previously missed by Philip José Farmer. This guy was good!

Notes

Farmer, Philip José. *The Book of Philip José Farmer*. New York: DAW, 1973; revised New York: Berkley, 1982.

----. *Greatheart Silver*. New York: TOR, 1982.

----. *Up the Bright River*. Burton, MI: Subterranean, 2010.

King, Stephen. *On Writing: A Memoir of the Craft*. New York: Simon and Schuster, 2000.

The Official Philip José Farmer Web Page (www.pjfarmer.com)

Preiss, Byron, ed. *Weird Heroes: A New American Pulp!* New York: Pyramid, #1 (1975), #2 (1975), #6 (1977), #8 (1977).

Greatheart Silver in Showdown at Shootout Or The Grand Finale

Author's Foreword

All Golden Ages end.

The great heroes and great villains of the pulp-magazine era would be old men, old indeed, if they were still living. But it's sad to think of them dying with their boots off, their careers uncompleted, decaying into senility, blind, deaf, noses running, salivating, dirtying their sheets, babbling of green fields. So it is only fitting that this tale have them end their days as they lived—in the glory of their youth.

This adventure contains a certain amount of levity, but any parodying is done with love. I hope all will pardon me. But, to be safe, I apologize beforehand to the following: Secret Agent Number One, The Avenger, The Black Bat, Captain Satan, Captain Zero, The Crimson Mask, Dan Fowler, Doc Harker, Doc Savage and his aides; Monk and Ham, Doctor Death, Doctor Yen Sin, Don Diavolo, G-8, Herr Doktor Krueger, The Green Ghost, The Green Lama, The Lone Ranger, Tonto, Nick Carter, The Moon Man, The Octopus, Operator #5, Pete Rice, The Phantom Detective, G-77, The Scorpion, Secret Agent X, The Shadow, The Silver Buck, The Spider, The Whisperer, and Wu Fang.

James Bond, Doctor No, Fu Manchu, and Sir Nayland Smith are not pulp characters. But they have all the characteristics of the heroes and villains who appeared on less expensive paper.

My apologies to them, too, along with my love.

Philip José Farmer, 1975

One

The Mad Fokker struck again.

Greatheart Silver had no idea that he'd soon be meeting the Mad Fokker. He knew about him, of course. The world had been hearing for six months about him and the gang that had been terrorizing the Southwest and California. Banks and loan offices were robbed, plutocrats kidnapped, dirigibles pirated, oil storage tanks drained, radioactive materials ripped off, army arsenals looted, and extortion practiced on a grand scale.

The Blimp Gang, as it was called, had some members who seemed to be scientists gone wrong. The cotton growers of the Southwest had parted with six million dollars because of the so-called Brain Trust of the Blimp Gang. The trust had developed a mutant, an insecticide-proof boll weevil which would be loosed unless six million dollars were chuted into a wild area in the Superstition Mountains. Government scientists had tested the boll weevils the gang had provided as proof of its boast. Sure enough. The weevils thrived on the most potent of poisons. The scientists advised that the money be paid. A few days later, the scientists had red faces. And most of them had no jobs. Though immune to insecticides, the mutations died soon after their first meal of boll. Otherwise, they were perfect.

The world, excepting the cotton growers, laughed. "Blimp" Kernel, head of the gang, undoubtedly laughed. His most famous aide, the Mad Fokker, must have laughed, too. But then he was always laughing. His high-pitched cachinnations terrified his victims as he robbed them, and they floated down to the pursuing police as he flew off in his tiny three-winged airplane.

The Fokker *was* mad. Everybody agreed on that. Who but a crazy man would land on a city street (after clearing it with a few bursts from his machine guns), run into a bank, rob it, and fly away at rooftop level? Who else would shoot up state police cars and helicopters just for sport?

Another great coup was the London Bridge Extortion Plot. The Mad Fokker put a note in a paper sack of horse manure, then dropped it on the head of the chief of police of Phoenix, Arizona. The note was cleaned and then read. It stated that the historical monument over Lake Havasu would be bombed unless two million dollars was paid. The authorities told the Blimp Gang to go to hell. Not a cent would be paid. Anti-aircraft guns and radar equipment were installed at London Bridge. Air National Guard planes were alerted to fly at a moment's notice. A regiment of National Guard, armed with heat-detecting missiles, was added. Come ahead, the authorities said.

Two weeks passed; nothing happened. The third week, during a rainstorm, the Mad Fokker attacked. He came in just above the lake surface, thus evading radar detection. Just before he reached the bridge, he zoomed up and over it, dropped a package, and fled, zig-zagging, a few inches from the water. The package opened up like a great white flower and burned, doing little damage. But the heat-detecting missiles, launched to catch the triplane, headed instead for the heap of thermite on the bridge. Moths to the flame. London Bridge flew apart, up, and then down.

The following day the Mad Fokker dropped another note in a paper sack, weighted with cattle manure this time, splattering the governor as he walked down the steps of the capitol building.

"NEXT TIME, PAY UP. NO BULL."

Greatheart Silver was thinking of this and laughing to himself. He was standing in the bridge of the AZ-8, midway through the second dogwatch. Before him Steersman Chesters sat in a chair in front of a control console. The steersman was smoking a cigarette and monitoring gauges, dials, and instruments, though he was not actually steering the great zeppelin. This was usually done by a computer, which also operated just about everything on board. Beyond the control console was the curving window of the bridge. This was not in a control gondola which hung below the fore, as in the old-type dirigibles. It was set within the hull, below the nose.

Ahead and below was the Arizona night. In a short time the lights of the Phoenix area would be seen. The zeppelin was already in its downward path toward the hangar. The air was clear and relatively still. The roar of the starboard and port motors was muted here; the loudest sound was the steersman humming to himself. Radar had reported that there was a storm forty miles to the north, but the airship would be in its hangar before the storm reached the Valley of the Sun.

The dirigible of the Acme Zeppelin Company bored through the night, carrying passengers and freight in no hurry to arrive at their destination. The atomic pile in its lead casing squatted within the center of the ship, silently issuing heat which was converted to electrical light and power.

Mr. Greatheart Silver, first mate of the AZ-8, was content, perhaps even happy. He had wanted to be a gasbagger ever since he had taken an overseas trip in one. He'd been ten at the time, and now he was thirty. In a few years, he would be eligible to pin on a captain's bars.

It hadn't been easy. His parents had died when he was seventeen, and he had had to get a football scholarship to put himself through college. On graduating, he had turned down offers to play professional football and had entered the officers' academy of the Acme Zeppelin Company at Freidrichshafen, West Germany. At the end of three years he had gotten his third mate's papers. Now, six years later, he was one step—a long one, true—from captain.

At the moment, he was thinking of home. This was a small and expensive apartment in the Great Hohokam Tower. His fiancée, Ms. Lassie Graves, with whom he shared the apartment, was probably feeding his birds right now. Then she would fix dinner for him, and they'd go to bed early. He had to rise at six A.M. (civilian time) to get to the AZ-8 at seven, an hour before take-off for the Pasadena port.

He visioned with pleasure his fiancée, a tall lovely blonde, bustling around the apartment. She might even dust off the big oil portrait of his great-great-great-great-great-great grandfather. This had been done by John Singleton Copley in 1772 and was, aside from its sentimental value, worth six hundred thousand dollars on the market. It showed a big old man with a large head, broad face, and white wig, clad in the velvets and lace of the period. The face was lined but merry and did not look at all like a buccaneer's. Yet the family tradition was that he had been a pirate who had escaped from a vessel taking him to England for trial and an inevitable hanging.

He'd shown up in New York with a bagful of guineas (doubtless stolen), and in a short time had become rich. The source of his wealth was reputed to be smuggling. He had added to it by marrying a young widow of an affluent Hudson River patroon. During the Revolution, he had become very wealthy through smuggling, which was at that time approved by the American authorities.

Along the wall were a dozen other paintings and blowups of photographs. One was of Thomas Jefferson, an even more distinguished ancestor of Greatheart. His descent from him had been through Sally Hemings, the quadroon mistress of Jefferson and half-sister of Jefferson's deceased wife.

Next to the president was Greatheart's great-great-great-grandfather, the Sioux warrior, Crazy Horse.

Near it was a photograph of his grandfather, a famous gunfighter of the Old West. The picture, taken when he was in his thirties, showed a handsome man with black hair distinguished by a tip of gray, like a tiny horn, just above each temple.

Greatheart was satisfied that he had let none of his forebears down. He might not be a pirate who'd terrorized the Spanish Main or a president of the highest distinction or the greatest tactician of the Sioux nation or a saddle tramp with the fastest draw in the Old West, but he had done all right. He was close to attaining his own goals, and his profession had a certain glamor to it.

Greatheart turned around, and his contentment gushed out of him like water from a ballast sack. By the entrance stood a semi-transparent figure.

It was a middle-aged man with a red-and-white striped jersey, crimson velvet pantaloons, one huge silver-buckled shoe, and brown hair, bound in a pig-tail. He was leaning on a crutch to compensate for a missing left leg. A large green parrot sat on his shoulder and screamed silent obscenities.

The figure jerked a thumb at the entrance, drew a finger across its throat, and faded away.

Greatheart had seen such apparitions before. Sometimes, it was John Silver. Other times, it was his Indian grandmother or Crazy Horse or his grandfather, Silverhorns Silver, or Sally Hemings. He didn't know why Thomas Jefferson never appeared. At first, when he'd thought that the figures were ghosts, he'd supposed that the president was too busy, wherever he was, to make an appearance. He'd transmitted his warnings via Sally, who was used to doing all the menial labor anyway.

Later, he'd figured out that they could not be ghosts. For one thing, his grandmother was still living. They were actually symbols projected by his unconscious mind. He had some kind of psychic sense which told him when a situation was going to change for the worse. His conscious mind didn't detect the danger, but his unconscious did, and it used the figures of his ancestors to alert him.

He whirled around just in time to see a light on the console begin flashing red and to hear a buzzing issue from beside the light.

"The skyhook!" he said to Chesters. "Why's it being let down?"

"I don't know, sir," Chesters said. "There's a UO on the screen, too." He indicated with a nod the blip that had appeared.

"Put it on DIST," Silver said. He strode to the console, flicked a switch, and said, "Skyhook room! What's going on?"

There was no answer. Chesters said, "It's a small airplane, sir. It must have come from beyond that mountain there. It's climbing toward us."

"Magnify," Silver said. On another screen the blip became a small single-seater aircraft with three sets of wings.

"The Mad Fokker!" Chesters said.

Silver did not say so, but he knew why old John Silver had appeared, why the skyhook room had not answered, why the hook was being lowered. The piracy of the AZ-10 and AZ-15 had started like this: Passengers who were members of the Blimp Gang had seized key points, the skyhook was let down, the Fokker's plane was fastened to the sky hook via the temporary hook-rig on it and the Fokker was drawn up into the ship, the crew was tied up, and the passengers' money and valuables were taken, along with the most desirable cargo. The AZ-10 had been landed first, but the AZ-15 was unloaded while aloft.

Three men, masked and holding automatic pistols, entered the bridge.

Two minutes later, Chesters and Silver were bound to chairs, taped so tightly they looked like mummies. Their mouths and eyes were also covered, but they had the use of their ears. Silver forced himself to repress the rage that sent the blood thumping through his head and drowned out all sounds but that of his frustration. The voices of the pirates were those of old men and, yes, one sounded just like the recording of "Blimp" Kernel.

Knowing this helped nothing. There had been no doubt about the identity of the gang.

Suddenly, a maniacal laugh burst in his ear. Then he cried out as the tape was ripped from his eyes. Before him stood a man of middle height, masked, wearing the helmet and goggles and uniform of a World War I AEF flying officer. His hands were gnarled, blotched with liver spots, and bulging with huge blue veins. Behind the goggles were thick spectacles, and behind them were two large watery gray eyes.

"Zo, *schweinhund*!" the man yelled in a brittle voice. "Traitor! You work for the Huns; you fly your *gottverdamt Luftschiff* over the U.S. of A., hah!"

His right hand slapped Silver across the cheek. Tears of rage trickled down Silver's high cheekbones, but he did not reply. The officers of the other zeppelins had been slapped and insulted by the madman, and the more they talked back the more they had been struck.

"I spent my youth serving my country as no one else served, and what did I get for it? Suppression of my identity, no public notice, private neglect, and then the bastards were so secretive about my record they lost it! They said I couldn't even get their measly pension! And I was put into an insane asylum! I, who had saved my country, the world, from its greatest perils time after time! Locked up with the crazies! *Ach*, the shame of it all!"

Silver let him rave, and finally Kernel spoke to the Mad Fokker in a soft voice, the words of which Silver could not hear. He strode out, and Kernel replaced the tapes on Silver.

He could not see what was happening, but the events were reconstructed later. As with the AZ-10, the AZ-8 was landed behind a mountain. Pima Control had detected the triplane and the AZ-8's change of course and notified the authorities. Helicopters had left the state police HQ and Luke Airfield, but by the time they arrived, the gang had dispersed. The zeppelin was drifting, its computer turned off, the passengers locked up, its crew tied up. At an elevation of one thousand feet, the Mad Fokker had disengaged his plane and flown into the storm sweeping southward. A few minutes later, the storm struck the airship. It also hit the choppers, which in any event could not have put men aboard the zeppelin.

The gas cells of the dirigible, punctured by the pirates, lost their helium rapidly. The AZ-8, at an altitude of five hundred feet, smashed into the side of a mountain.

Silver heard a rending of framework as the great rings and girders crumpled. And then he lost consciousness.

Two

The Acme investigators, the CIA, the FBI, the police, the reporters came and went. The pain stayed. After a while, the agony in the stump of his left leg eased off into something tolerable. But the agony of knowing that he was forever crippled would not go away. It haunted him even in his dreams: he was sitting on a sidewalk and holding out a hat for passersby to drop coins in while around the corner young women were laughing at him. And then he was arrested for begging without a license.

Lassie visited him three times. She cried a lot, but it was evident that the tears were caused by the prospect of marrying a one-legged man.

"Why did this have to happen to me?"

"I feel for you," he said. "So I release you. We're through, *kaput*. You only loved my body, Lassie. To you I was just a handsome face and a pair of great legs and the rest I won't mention. Anyway, I was beginning to see how shallow you were. I didn't want to admit it to myself, but I would have eventually. So, get out and don't come back!"

He was lying. He hadn't seen at all that her psyche was as thin as the skin on a dirigible. He'd been too much in love.

"I'll go because I think it's best for you," she said, blinking, the tears rapidly drying up, her makeup running. She looked like a sexy Raggedy Ann with about as much sawdust inside her but none of the compassion.

"Anyway, you have good medical insurance," she said, "and the company will give you a good pension. You won't have to work for a living."

"And I'm still a human being, even if not a whole one," he said. "And I have a brain. That's more than you ever had or will have."

"Up yours," Lassie said and stormed out.

Greatheart wasn't depressed. Instead of becoming melancholic, he became angry. This, his doctor said, was a healthy reaction. Depression was anger turned in on oneself. It was far better to project it at others, especially if they deserved it, as Lassie did.

Greatheart said, "You're a good doctor, Doc."

When Silver found out that the good doctor was now dating Lassie, he didn't change his mind about his qualifications as a physician. But he did think the doctor was a rotten human being.

"Love knows no ethics," Doctor Rongwon said. "Eros shoots his arrows where he will, and we defenseless mortals have no shields."

"You should have been a lawyer, Doc," Greatheart said. "A shyster instead of a quack."

"Always kidding," Rongwon said. "A good sign. And here's good news. Next week we start fitting you for your prosthetic leg."

"The better to kick you with," Greatheart said. The doctor, laughing, exited. Greatheart threw his ashtray and broke a picture. The nurse said that was a healthy reaction, too. "What about some healthy stimuli?" Greatheart said. The nurse, middle-aged but handsome, said, "You want me to play Jocasta to your Oedipus?"

"Everybody's too educated nowadays," Greatheart said. "No, I'm not looking for a mother image or incest. I just want some loving. Maybe I want to prove I'm still a man, too. Does that turn you off?"

"Ever since my husband died two years ago," she said, "I've been propositioned by nothing but old creeps. And I've turned every one down. I don't think you're a creep, and I could stand a little loving myself."

"It won't be a little," Greatheart said.

"I'll see you about half-past midnight," she said. "The night supervisor is my buddy and very *simpático*. We won't be disturbed. But you might have to fight her off later. She has eyes for you."

"The more the merrier," Greatheart said, and the nurse exited laughing.

His happiness didn't last long. Just after breakfast the following day, two police detectives entered his room. They didn't take long to get to the point of their visit.

"Your apartment was ripped off last night."

The burglary had been detected when the manager noticed that the door to Silver's apartment was partly open. He had reported this to the police, along with the information that the Copley painting was missing, the photographs and the furniture had been slashed, and the birds had been released out the windows.

Greatheart groaned and said, "You better question Ms. Lassie Graves."

Lassie, however, had a perfect alibi, if her friend wasn't lying. Greatheart thought he was, but there was no way of proving it.

The final blow was the discovery that the insurance on the Copley had lapsed the day before its theft. He'd left it up to Lassie to make the payment, and she had not done it. On purpose, no doubt.

"What else can happen?" he said to himself.

He found out after lunch, when the president of the American branch of Acme visited him. Mr. Micawber exuded joviality, but the small eyes above the big nose were disconnected from the hearty speech and the florid gestures of good fellowship. Mr. Micawber was the son of the founder of Acme, an immigrant from Australia who had started business in a small way. Roadrunner traps were his specialty, but these never seemed to work, and he had gone bankrupt in a short time. Then he had gotten a loan (from a Mafia loan shark, it was rumored), and gone into other lines. When he died, he had left millions to his only heir. Mr. Micawber owned many industries and businesses, but the Acme Zeppelin Company was his pride, the nearest thing to his heart, aside from his daughter. It was he who insisted that the symbol of Acme be a stylized roadrunner. This was probably to illustrate the humble beginnings of his fortune. Every one of his zeppelins bore on its upper and lower vertical stabilizers a huge roadrunner.

Mr. Micawber—who never just walked—swept into the room. With him were his omnipresent bodyguards and his beautiful titian-haired secretary.

"Don't rise, my boy," Mr. Micawber said. "We don't stand on ceremony."

Greatheart thought his words were ill-chosen, but a mere employee did not reproach the great Micawber.

"How are you, son?"

Silver opened his mouth to reply, but Mr. Micawber swept on. "Terrible thing, terrible thing! Two hundred million dollars lost when the AZ-8 crashed! Fortunately, we have insurance, and anyway there's no use crying over spilt milk."

Greatheart couldn't restrain himself. He said, "I wouldn't say that a hundred people killed and fifty badly injured are exactly in the category of spilt milk."

"They were insured," Mr. Micawber said. "One has to take the historical perspective on such things, not to mention the financial and fiscal. All flesh is doomed to become grass, or its equivalent, and in the economy of nature, in its statistical function, what's the difference if one dies now or later?

"Anyway, my boy, I'm not here to discuss philosophy—a time and place for everything and this isn't the time or the place. Now, we've been reading the reports of the piracy, and what I'd like to know, son, is if the reports are true?"

"You have my statement," Greatheart said. "I told the truth. What is this, anyway? What are you getting at?"

"It's this, my boy. When you became an officer of Acme Zeppelin, when you took the oath at Friedrichshafen, you swore to defend your honor, the honor of the company, and to hold its interests close to your heart. Closer, we might add, than your own."

"I don't remember saying that," Greatheart said. "And I memorized the oath; I can recite it to you letter-perfect now."

"In effect, we mean!" Micawber cried. "In effect, my boy! The point is that we have been considering the foul piracy of the AZ-8 and what might have been done to thwart it. There is some excuse for the AZ-10 being taken so easily, though not much, we assure you! There was no excuse for the AZ-15's ripoff, since, once warned, twice armed! Or is it forearmed? Anyway, the captain of the AZ-15 was discharged . . ."

"I thought he retired," Greatheart said.

"That was for public consumption, my boy. PR, you know, the backbone of the business. No, son, he was discharged, but even so he was given his pension. The company has a heart, believe us. Besides, he would have sued if he hadn't gotten it.

"But your case is different. You were the officer in charge when this regrettable business occurred, and so . . ."

"The captain is responsible, whether he's on the bridge or not."

"Don't interrupt, son. The captain is dead, as you well know, and so you as captain ex tempore assume the responsibility. And a captain who permits his charge to be so easily pirated is no captain of mine, son."

"I can't believe this," Greatheart said. "The captain died after the ship was taken. I was never in any sense the senior officer. Besides, what could I do?"

"You could have screened out the thugs posing as passengers and crew members. And if that failed, as it did, you could have resisted. Now, we are making no accusations . . . do you have that?" he said to the secretary, who was holding a tape recorder. She nodded, and Mr. Micawber said, ". . . no accusations. But there was undoubtedly complicity . . ."

"Get out, you phony bastard!" Greatheart shouted.

"A good officer never loses his temper," Micawber said loftily. "In any event, you are no longer an employee of Acme Zeppelin. For one thing, and this should suffice, the loss of your leg disqualifies you as an airship officer. You know the rules. As for a desk job, we think not, son. Trust is everything—trust and loyalty—and while we make no official accusations, or, indeed, unofficial, trust is in doubt and loyalty seems to have been lacking. Besides, you have just insulted me, and that is reason enough for your instant dismissal."

"You're branding me a crook without the slightest evidence!" Greatheart said. "You're crazy! And a crook, too!"

"You lack good judgment, as well as a leg," Micawber said. "No one talks to Bendt Micawber like that, son. So, I bid you adieu. But don't worry about your hospital bills or your prosthetic leg. The company honors its obligations."

Micawber swept out; his employees walked out.

Three

"You haven't got a leg to stand on," the lawyer said. "Oops, sorry!"

"Then old B.M. is going to get away with this?"

"We'd have to take it all the way to the Supreme Court," Seymour Sheester said. "And I doubt that it'd rule that Acme would have to hire you back. You do have a definite physical disability which might interfere with your ability to operate the ship and safeguard your passengers. As for Micawber's accusations, you have no witnesses of your own to that. The old man is crazy, and he thinks everybody's a crook because he's one. But he functions one hundred percent; he's crazy like a coyote. No, you don't have a case. What's worse, you can't get on another airship line as an operations officer. They have the same rule about disabilities. Besides, though there's no way to prove it, they will honor Micawber's blackball. Good business, you know."

"And all because I didn't commit suicide by resisting that gang," Greatheart said. "I hate that bunch of crooks, and I hate Lassie. But I hate Micawber even more."

"Hate buys no cookies," Sheester said cheerfully. He stood up, held out his hand, and said, "Sorry I can't do anything for you. What do you intend to do, by the way?"

"Well, I can't play football," Greatheart said. He shook Sheester's hand and then walked to the window. He stared out of it at a landscape as bleak as his future. Rocks and cactus and rattlesnakes.

After a while, he turned, slowly because it was only a week after his electronic leg had been fitted to the stump, and began walking slowly back and forth. At the tenth circuit, he stopped. A man was looking into his room. The man came in holding a bird cage and a slip of paper. The cage held two huge ravens.

"Put it on the table," Greatheart said, and he reached out for the receipt.

"You don't seem surprised," the attendant said.

Greatheart laughed and said, "No. My grandmother wrote me that she was sending them. She's too old to come see me. She's a hundred and one years old."

The attendant said, "She lives on an Indian reservation?"

"Grandma is a full-blooded Sioux. I used to stay with her during the summer vacations when I was a kid. It was great fun. I played with the reservation kids, and they taught me to speak Sioux. Grandma taught me bird language."

Seeing the attendant's brows go up, Greatheart said, "Grandma was a sorceress, or anyway she claimed to be. She had a way with birds, and she said I had her gift. Her house was full of birds, and birds were always hanging around the place."

He grinned and said, "No wonder she was called White Spots."

"You'll have to keep them in the cage," the attendant said. "If you wasn't in the rehabilitation ward, you wouldn't be allowed to have them at all."

Greatheart uttered some croaks, and the ravens, looking alert, croaked back.

"What'd they say?" the attendant said, grinning.

"Quote. To hell with the rules. Unquote."

The attendant said, "I gotta go now."

Greatheart opened the cage, and the big glossy black birds flew onto his shoulder and pecked softly at his ear.

"Let's see," he said quietly, "what'll I call you? We don't want to use your true names, buddies. No one's going to get your number. How about Huggin and Muggin? After the two ravens that sat on the great god Odin's shoulders?"

The birds croaked at him, and he said, "You like them, heh? O.K. Back into your cage. We'll obey the rules until I get this leg working, and then we're getting out, and we're going to make some rules of our own."

They croaked twice and flew back into the cage. Greatheart did not bother to close its door.

A month later, Greatheart Silver sat in the office of the manager of the Phoenix branch of Acme Security-Southwest. "Welcome aboard," Mr. Spood said. "Here's a toast to your career." He and Silver lifted their glasses of fine Kentucky bourbon and poured the amber down the hatches. Mr. Spood was always toasting something or other. Perhaps this explained the lack of security in his own office. It had been easy for Silver to let himself in, bypassing the electronic alarm circuits, and to reprogram the data and communications computer. When Mr. Spood's secretary had typed out an inquiry for validation of Silver's references the next day, she had received full confirmation. The central clearing computer in New York had replied—or seemed to—that Greatheart Silver's references were in order and that Mr. Micawber himself had taken the trouble to O.K. them.

"Tough luck about the leg and all that," Mr. Spood had said. "But evidently old B.M. thinks highly of you. And what he thinks highly of, I approve most heartily. If I didn't, I'd lose my job, haw, haw!"

Now he was saying, "Ordinarily we wouldn't hire a handicapped person, but then what the hell, you aren't really handicapped, are you? I saw what you can do with that electromechanical marvel of a leg. And those birds! Man, you're going to be a gem! Who'd ever think of private-eyeing with trained birds? Nobody'd suspect that a raven was taking pictures of them and transmitting their conversation? Right?"

"Right," Silver said.

"I'm putting you under the charge of Fenwick Phwombly. He's an old guy, older than he says he is. That dyed hair and those contact lenses don't fool me. But he's an excellent operative, though you may find him to be a little eccentric. Anyway, here's a toast to him and you and Acme Security-Southwest, sometimes referred to by employees in less happy moments as AS-S, haw, haw!"

"Here's to justice," Greatheart said.

Silver trained with Phwombly for two months before he was given the grade of Junior A-man. By then, Silver, who learned fast, had mastered more than the rudiments of investigation. Experience taught him much, but an hour listening to old Phwombly was worth ten years of practice.

Phwombly was very tall and somewhat stooped, which was to be expected of a man who had to be in his late eighties. He was half deaf but too proud to wear a hearing aid. His makeup almost concealed the wrinkles, and his huge curved nose had no broken veins, except in certain lights. His eyes behind their thick trifocal contact lenses burned as if he were only twenty years old. He was spry, too, except sometimes in the morning when his arthritis was "acting up." And sometimes, when he forgot himself, his natural voice issued from his throat. This was dry and brittle, but when it slipped by him, he would say, "Time to wet the whistle," and he'd pull a flask, a relic of the 1920s, out of his coat pocket.

If the flask happened to be empty, Greatheart remedied the lack. The hollow spaces in his leg were handy for carrying booze and salami sandwiches. They were handy for other things, too. But first things first.

"Greatheart, heh?" Phwombly said on being introduced. "An Indian name, no doubt, since your grandma is Sioux?"

"That's what everybody thinks," Silver said. "Truth is, it's of British origin, and it was given to me by my father. He was a great reader, and his favorite book was John Bunyan's *Pilgrim's Progress*. He named me after a character in it, Mr. Greatheart. He was the one who helped the wife and children of Christian after he'd deserted them."

"Yeah?" Phwombly said. "I missed John, though I read about his brother Paul when I was a kid. I didn't have much time for reading after 1914. Been pretty busy since. You might not believe it, son, but I was a big shot, especially in the thirties and forties. Wealthy, too. I had a private gold mine in Central America. My Indian blood-brothers supplied me with gold so I could carry on my battle with the evil that lurks in the hearts of men. I operated outside the law because that was the only way to get things done, to ensure that true justice triumphed. I was a quick-change artist, too, the best. Oh, Doc Ravage and the Arachnid and the Phantom Dick and the Punisher were good, but compared to me they were bumblers. I musta done away with a thousand or so crooks, high and low, though I was more humane than the Arachnid. He musta slain his thousands. In fact, between me and Doc and those others, I'm surprised that there were any criminals left in New York City. But no matter how many went to jail or died, their number increased daily. It was like there was a crook factory operating day and night."

"Social conditions breed them," Greatheart said.

"Social conditions, hell!" the old man said. "Didn't you ever read Sartre? That's one guy I read a few years ago when I was on welfare and didn't have anything else to do. Every man is responsible for his own fate, his own destiny, his own character. Social conditions are just an excuse to screw somebody. How do you account for so many rich men being crooks if social conditions make crooks?"

"Psychological conditions?"

"Then there isn't any free will. But I know, from my own experience, that every man has free will. I battled, and I lost. My Indians decided to rip me off, and they kept the gold for themselves. I was broke, and I was too old to get a job doing the only other thing I was good at. I was a great flier, you know, and the best damn spy—I don't care what they say about Agent 8-Ball—in World War I. I served the Czar in the first two years of the war, and he gave me a family heirloom, a ring worth thousands."

"Where is it?" Silver said.

"I had to hock it! When the funds from it ran out, I took odd jobs here and there. Then I went on welfare, me, that did more for my country, for the world, than any fifty men you can name."

"How'd you get *this* job?"

"I told the manager I'd turn him in as a drunk if he didn't hire me. So, here I am, back in the harness again. Though in a small way. There's a McDonald's. Turn in, time for chow. Me, eating at a hamburger joint, me, who once dined at the most expensive restaurants in Manhattan! Me, who belonged to the ultra-exclusive Cobalt Club!"

"Listen," Greatheart said, "You surely can't be . . . ?"

Phwombly burst loose with a mocking maniacal laugh that chilled Greatheart's skin.

"Yes, I'm the only one who knows the evil that men have in their hearts!"

Greatheart was stunned with awe.

Four

At 15:40 of a Thursday, Phwombly burst into Silver's office. "Forget about your reports! We've just gotten an assignment! It's what I've been expecting and what I've been longing for! Tomorrow and tomorrow and tomorrow craps on this petty pace . . . but no more, Silver! The day I've been waiting for is almost at hand!"

The old fellow was shaking, though Silver didn't know if it was from excitement or incipient palsy. Or both.

"Where and what is it?" he said calmly.

"It's the town of Shootout, and the Blimp Gang may be planning to rob it. And there will be others there, many others!"

Greatheart didn't press him for details. Phwombly was always reluctant to give out more than minimum information. He claimed that subordinates shouldn't know more than a piece of the plan. Then, if they fell into the hands of the enemy, they couldn't give the enemy much. Greatheart agreed that this was, in certain situations, a good policy. But it had puzzled him how it applied to the divorce cases and skip tracings that had been their only jobs so far.

He and Phwombly got their equipment together, loaded it into a motorhome, and drove out of Phoenix to the southeast. Shootout, he knew—everybody knew—was the scene of the famous Kayo Corral Gunfight. Marshall Watts Upp and his brothers, Doc Hyloday, and Basher Missters had shot it out with the infamous Clinton Brothers. The town was in the midst of its annual celebration of this event.

The motorhome was equipped with air-conditioning, a small laboratory, a smaller lavatory, bunks, a shortwave radio, TV, a kitchen, a bar, and a radar set. Silver drove while Phwombly sat at the bar and muttered of past glories. Then he broke into curses when Huggin decided to use his shoulder instead of the papers Silver had laid out for the ravens. "If you don't housebreak those .*!+& birds, I'll let them have it with both my .45's!"

"Don't swear around them," Silver said. "They've picked up enough bad habits already."

Phwombly went back to muttering while Silver tried to figure out what might be happening at their destination.

The bank at Buzzard Gulch, a tiny cowtown near Shootout, had been robbed that morning by the Blimp Gang. Since the bank was under the protection of Acme, Silver had expected to be sent there to investigate. Instead, he and Phwombly were going to Shootout. Maybe the boss believed that the bank there, also an Acme client, was the next target. He and Phwombly would try to lock the barn door before the horse was stolen.

But the old man seemed to have some inside information. He acted, almost, and maybe indeed, as if he were going to a long-awaited rendezvous.

Meanwhile, Silver's idea of getting into the Acme superorganization and exposing Micawber's crookedness didn't seem such a good one now. In his desire for vengeance he had overlooked the fact that it might take years to work up to a spot where he could get the goods on old B.M. Actually, he might never have the opportunity.

However, he did want to catch the men who were responsible for the deaths on the AZ-8 and the loss of his leg. He was now even hotter to get them than to face Micawber. And it looked as if he would be given the chance.

He did have one item of information which had slipped out of Phwombly. One night they'd been following a woman in a divorce case. The woman, Mrs. Spood, in fact, had gone into a tavern. Silver and Phwombly had taken a table close to her and to preserve appearances had had to drink a lot. Phwombly, after seven double bourbons, had started talking to himself. It was then that Silver learned the identity of the Mad Fokker. Phwombly, in his dialog with himself, had stated that the criminal had to be the man known only by the code name of 8-Ball. This man, once the foremost aviator and spy of the Great War—after Phwombly, of course—had done great deeds. He'd shot down more enemy planes than Richthofen and his whole Flying Circus, 1,238, to be exact, but he was given no official credit because of his espionage activities. Besides, it was well known that 8-Ball was insane, though usually quite competent, and that had to be kept a secret from the folks at home.

And so, when the Armistice came, 8-Ball was carted off to an asylum and locked up. He'd been seeing so many monsters, supposedly created by the great German genius, Herr Doktor Krogers, his mortal enemy, that he could no longer be ignored. His delusions had always operated in favor of the Allies, true. When he shot a bunch of German planes, which he thought were flying leopard-men or radio-controlled vampire bats, he was hurting nobody but the enemy. Now, though, it was peacetime and he couldn't be allowed loose. He'd be mothballed until the next war to save democracy.

The next war came, but the existence of 8-Ball was forgotten. The new generation of generals and paper-shufflers knew nothing of him. Besides, he was too old.

"That's the way they treat vintage heroes," Phwombly had muttered, the tip of his huge nose almost in his bourbon. "I don't blame old 8-Ball at all for escaping from his padded cell and taking to crime. What? Spend all his life in a puzzle factory? After what he did for his country? And what's he supposed to do after he gets out? Go on welfare, like I did? Yes, that's him all right. There's only one other man who could fly a plane like he does, and he's sitting at this table. So it must be him. Carry on, old fighter! Too bad I have to track you down and put you away again! But that's life! Duty calls! The minions of evil must pay through the nose, or whatever, for what they've done. But why? Ah, yes, but why?"

Either the booze, or the philosophy, or both, had gotten to him. He slumped over, and Silver had had to carry him out before the management called the cops. Mrs. Spood had run away with her lover to Mexico the next day.

Five

Shootout was a small village of about five hundred permanent population, most of whom existed on the tourist trade. Its business section was two blocks of buildings constructed to look as they had in 1881, when the famous gunfight had taken place. The city hall and the Canary Cage Theater were the only original buildings left. The Boot Hill cemetery (one dollar per customer at the entrance) was outside the town. It contained a number of wooden crosses bearing amusing commemorations of the sudden demise of citizens during its heyday:

HUNG BY MISTAKE.

MURDERED BY THE UPP GANG (put up by supporters of the villainous Clinton boys).

HERE LIES SOAPY SUE. SHE GAVE HER LAST FAVORS TO DEATH.

DEALT FROM THE BOTTOM OF THE DECK AND NOW HE'S IN THE BOTTOM.

DON'T LAUGH, STRANGER, AS I AM SO SHALL YOU BE.

STRUCK IT RICH BUT WAS KICKED BY A MULE.

Actually, most of the Hill's inhabitants had died of dysentery, syphilis, or liver cirrhosis, but these were not glamorous enough to be noted. And most of the graves were empty. The bodies had been moved to another location for sanitary reasons. What the tourists didn't know wouldn't hurt them.

Shootout this October night was a lively place, crowded with visitors, many dressed in Western costume, the streets decorated with flags and pennants and posters. Greatheart drove through the narrow pedestrian-packed street slowly to the other end of town and parked on the side of the road. Phwombly had phoned for reservations at various motels but had been informed that there wasn't a room available. If they had not had the motorhome, they would have been obliged to find quarters in Buzzard Gulch, seven miles away.

They washed up and then had a few drinks. Presently, they heard a car pull up by them, a door slam, and a voice call. Phwombly admitted a tall white-haired gray-eyed old man wearing thick spectacles. He was dressed as an old-time Western lawman. This was just what he was.

"Pete Ruse, sheriff of Buzzard Gulch," he said, extending a vein-ridged hand. After accepting a drink, he told them all he knew about the holdup in his hometown.

"I was taking my noon nap when they struck," he said. "I'm getting up there, you know, and now some people are saying I'm too old for my job. Hell, it coulda happened to anyone. Anyway, I heard the commotion and ran out in my longjohns. By then the Mad Fokker had taken off with the money, and his confederates—ain't any of you from the South, are you?—was ten miles away.

They was riding motorcycles. I radioed to the state police, but the Mad Fokker chased them down a gulch with his machineguns. The other Blimpers abandoned their choppers, they was stolen, anyway, and took off in the blimp. By the time the police copters got there, the blimp was gone. Probably deflated it, put it in a truck, and drove off to their HQ. That Mad Fokker, he's really something! He landed in a street that ain't wide enough for two Packards side by side, turned the plane to face the bank, let loose a couple of bursts, incidentally taking off the manager's toupee, ran in, took the money from his confederates—no offense if you're Southrons—and ran out. Slick as a baboon's hind end."

"We think the gang is planning to rob the bank here during the festivities," Greatheart said.

Ruse's eyes lit up, though not very brightly. "Yeah? We'll see about that! Pete Ruse always gets his man. I'm planning on retiring soon, and I don't intend to let those .*/+!ing as!*/! spoil my record! Whatta you say we go into town now and look things over?"

They rode back in Ruse's 1946 Cadillac, a collector's item which Ruse meant to sell to finance his retirement. Ruse parked by a fire plug. They got out, leaving the ravens sitting in the back seat on a newspaper, and started to enter a Chinese restaurant. Ruse stopped suddenly to stare at two old men on horses riding by. The one in front was a white man with long white hair. He wore a black mask and white neo-Western clothes. His horse was a beatup nag that must have been beautiful when young. Behind him rode an old Indian, a red band around his forehead.

"Hell, that *can't* be!" Ruse said. "Not the Long Ranger and Pronto! They wouldn't dare. They know I'm liable to be here! Naw! They must be tourists!"

Phwombly peered across the street, but the two riders weren't the object of his scrutiny. "That garbage truck!" he said, clutching Silver's arm. "Parked by the Hell For Leather Saloon!"

"What about it?" Silver said.

"Scorpio!" Phwombly said. "That S.O.B. uses garbage trucks in his operations! His headquarters was beneath an incinerator plant when he operated in New York!"

Phwombly rubbed his hands with delight—or he was restoring the circulation—and said, "Yeah, my theory's working out! They're all together now! Too old to do their foul deeds by themselves; too old to get respect from the young punks anymore! So they're putting their old white heads together!"

Silver was beginning to see what Phwombly had in mind, but he didn't believe it. Was the poor old fellow a victim of senility?

He pulled his partner into the Ga See Chow Restaurant. Pete Ruse followed them in. It was a large place, but it was jammed. The lights were dim, and the air was curtained and stinking with the fumes of tobacco, Acapulco Golds, and Tia Juana Merdas. Though it held at least a hundred customers, it was strangely quiet. Everybody seemed to be whispering, and even the clatter of silverware on plates was absent. The proprietor, an aged Chinese (and pigtailed!) told a waiter to bring out a table for them. This required that all the other tables be moved closer together. The customers got up and shoved their tables nearer to their neighbors, though their expressions revealed that they didn't like doing so. For a while, the place sounded as if a landslide was coming down on them. Then silence returned.

"I don't like this place," Silver said. "It makes me nervous."

"Are you kidding?" Phwombly said. "This is where everybody's hung out!"

Silver shook his head but didn't say anything. The old man was too proud of his knowledge of up-to-date slang.

They sat down, the backs of their chairs against those of the people behind them. The two Acme agents ordered chop suey, bird's nest soup, thousand-year-old eggs, and rice wine. Pete Ruse ordered a steak and beans. Phwombly stared at the ancient Chinese who was taking their orders. When the old man, who seemed hard of hearing, bent over near Phwombly, Phwombly sniffed loudly. After the waiter had left, he whispered to Silver, "Smell his breath? That's Doctor Sen Sen or my name isn't . . ."

He put his hand over his mouth to hush himself. Ruse said, "Who's Sen Sen?"

"One of the most dastardly villains that ever infected the fair face of earth, the athlete's foot of mankind," Phwombly said. "But did you pipe the proprietor? Notice the tall forehead and the green eyes behind those thick glasses? If that isn't the archfiend, Doctor Fyu-men Chew, I'll eat my hat."

"It might turn out to be better food than this stuff," Ruse said disgustedly as their orders were placed before them. Phwombly shushed him, and Ruse was silent until the waiter left. "Whatever these guys are, they're rotten cooks."

Phwombly cupped his right ear and said, "Crooks?"

"COOKS!" Ruse bellowed, and everybody in the restaurant leaped up, their hands under their jackets. They glared around and then, somewhat sheepishly, sat down. Phwombly got up and strode to the big counter on which the food was placed for the waiters. He peered into the kitchen for a minute and returned, looking somewhat groggy.

"The opium smoke's so thick in there you could get constipation just breathing it," he said.

He sat down, shaking his head. "It wasn't easy to see them through that cloud. But there they were. Doctor Terminal, Won Fang, and Doctor Negative, archfiends all, masters of men's minds, cooking in a chop suey joint! Enough to make you cry, and I haven't cried since I was five years old. Well, there *was* the time when my radio show was cancelled . . . never mind that.

"Anyway, one of them looked me in the eye, and I saw a gleam that bodes nobody good. And the one I thought was Won Fang, well, a big purple spider slipped out of his pocket while he was frying hamburgers. Won Fang used to breed mutated snakes and lizards and spiders, you know. Poisonous all. I'll bet that spider was left over from an old job."

He sat down, saying, "Don't touch the food until I check it out," he reached into his coat and pulled out a set of vials. While Phwombly mixed their contents in a water glass, which he'd emptied on the floor, Silver looked around the restaurant. Phwombly wasn't the only one testing the food.

Phwombly sat back with a sigh and said, "It's O.K. I didn't think they'd try to poison us anyway. Even *they* couldn't get away with that in a place like this. Besides, it'd attract attention from the local fuzz and maybe ruin their operation."

Ruse took a bite of the steak and said, "What the hell?" and spit the piece out onto his plate.

"Oh, yeah," Phwombly said. "The chemicals ruin the food. We'll have to order again."

"I can't afford to pay twice!" Ruse said. "You don't know how little I get paid! And what with inflation . . ."

"We'll put it on our expense account," Silver said. "Have another drink."

They waited a long time for the second order, because almost everybody had sent the first dinner back. Meanwhile, Silver listened in on the conversations at the tables. He pressed a button in his prosthetic leg, and a tiny antenna shot out of the irradiated plastic. It missed the minute hole he'd left in his trouser leg for its admission and tore a hole in it. He cursed—the pants were from an expensive Beverly Hills shop—and then he put a tiny speaker in his ear. This was attached to a slim wire which ran under his clothes to an attachment on his leg. It was disguised as a hearing aid, but he doubted it was fooling anyone. Almost everyone had hearing aids in their ears; the place could have been mistaken for a convention of deaf people. He leaned over and whispered to Phwombly that he should talk very softly.

"WHAT?" Phwombly said.

Silver wrote a note and handed it to him. Phwombly, after reading it, growled, "I already knew that. You think I'm wet behind the ears?"

It was necessary to point the antenna directly at the table to be eavesdropped, so Silver had to go through some strange contortions. But nobody acted as if they even knew of Silver's existence.

Phwombly reached out and put his hand on Silver's wrist. Silver was annoyed by his nervous tapping, and besides he didn't want people to get the wrong idea about their relationship. Just as he started to speak harshly to the old man, he caught on. Phwombly was tapping out a message in code. He wanted Silver to use Morse to tell him what he was hearing.

The other customers must have observed him. All of a sudden, almost everybody stopped talking, and wrists and palms were being fingered staccato. Pete Ruse, looking around, said, "Say, what kind of a place is this?"

Silver cursed again and pointed the antenna at one of the only two tables at which men were still talking. The diners there were dressed in gray flannel suits, white shirts, and black ties. It wasn't hard to figure out that they were FBI agents. Silver reported their talk and Phwombly tapped back, "Yes. And the three old geezers with the young punks are Dan Fooler, the greatest G-man of them all, Valiant Kilgore, second-greatest, and G-Double-7, third greatest. They must have come out of retirement for this. Kilgore, by the way, is Won Fang's archnemesis.

"Word's got around that all the big evil ones are here, all members of the Blimp Gang. Nobody told me about this, but then they know that I don't have to be told to know. It's the gathering of the clans, boy, the big roundup, the last stand, the grand finale!"

Silver swiveled to zero the antenna in on a group of dark heavy-set men eating spaghetti and drinking wine at a table in the corner. They were talking, but the language, though it sounded Italian, was almost unintelligible.

Phwombly came to his rescue. "They must be speaking a dialect, Chicago Sicilian. The big guy who's drinking Alka-Seltzers is Joe 'Sour' Lemono. He's the head of WAX, Western Auxiliary Board. That's the West Coast branch of the Mafia, which many claim doesn't exist, but I know, I know. I also know why they're here. The Blimp Gang has had the effrontery to muscle in on their territory, and WAX is here to rub them out. The grapevine says the dons, East Coast dons, are unhappy with Lemono, and if he doesn't come through, it's *finito* for him. In fact, those thugs at the two tables by his are from EBB, the Eastern Business Board. They're here to rub him out if he doesn't come through."

Phwombly rubbed his hands and said, "It's the big shape-up, all right."

He stopped and then noted excitedly, "Hey, that bunch in the opposite corner!"

"Use the Morse," Silver said.

Phwombly ignored him, saying, "Those guys must be the CIA.

See the gent with the white moustache? That has to be Secret Agent Ecks. No man has ever known his true face. Unfortunately, he's getting forgetful, and he can't recall it either. I say, 'What's the difference?' He never used it anyway."

"How'd you recognize him if he always has a new face?" Silver tapped.

"It's because every time I see him he has changed his features."

While Silver was trying to figure this out, three men entered the restaurant. One was almost seven feet tall. Though he must have been in his late seventies, he had a physique which wouldn't have disgraced Tarzan. Behind him came two men in wheelchairs. They were trying to get through the door at the same time but were wedged together. They were hollering insults and striking each other on the head with canes. The blows, despite their feebleness, were bringing blood. One old man was a thin fellow with the sharp foxlike features seen in cartoons of big-shot shysters. The other was incredibly hairy, massively muscled, and had a face that looked like a reconstruction of the Java Apeman.

The giant stood watching them, a look of long suffering on his handsome face.

"Doc Ravage!" Phwombly transmitted. "And his two aides, "Porkchop" and "Chimp," everybody calls them. Last I heard, they were in a nursing home. But Doc's brought them out for the battle of the century! I told you this is the big one!"

He quivered with delight.

The two very senior citizens suddenly quit caning each other. Their gnarled hands dived under the blankets over their legs. The blankets must have concealed some controls. Loud explosions deafened the diners, fire and smoke shot out of the rear of the chairs, frightening everybody, and the two vehicles surged forward. But the rockets propelling them only wedged them more tightly. In addition, they tilted forward and cast their occupants sprawling before the feet of the giant. He stepped forward, his face showing extreme irritability, and kicked one of the chairs. It flew out into the street, knocking down an old lady. He returned, picked up the two raving oldsters by their coat collars, one in each hand, and replaced them in the chairs.

These were somewhat crumpled, and he had to straighten the wheel of one with his bare hands. Muscles like piano wires bunched like coiling pythons under his bronzed skin and tore his shirt along the arms, around the chest, and on the back.

He went out to the sidewalk, helped the old lady up, wrote her a check—which she threw in his face—and returned to the restaurant. "You two punchdrunks make any more trouble," he said loudly, "and I'll ship you back to your knitting, cheating at cards, and feeling up great-grandmas! *I'm fed up!*"

The oldsters grinned shamefacedly and wheeled their chairs behind him as he walked majestically toward the proprietor. But Chimp banged Pork-chop once over the head with his cane while a table was being brought in. Doc turned around at the thud of wood on bone, looked at Porkchop, who had slumped down unconscious, and said, "What's wrong now?"

"He's getting old," Chimp said gleefully. "He's always falling asleep. Why, only the other day, he had this nurse backed up into a corner, what a peach, couldn't have been a day over sixty, and he started sawing wood while he was ripping off her dress. I had to finish it for him, haw, haw!"

"It's all in the head," Doc said, "which, from what I hear, is where you spend most of your time anyway. Shape up, Chimp, or be shipped back!"

The manager wiped the blood off the two, and Chimp revived Porkchop by throwing beer in his face. Porkchop straightened up, muttering, "Your Honor, this woman lies when she says I promised to marry her," saw Chimp's grin, and said, "Wait'll I get you!"

At that moment a scuffle broke out between a man with a heavy Russian accent and a man with a heavy English accent. Apparently, the fight had come about because of the closeness of the tables. Due to this, the Russian had mistakenly transmitted his message to the Englishman at the next table instead of to his own Russian partner. Whatever it was he'd communicated, he'd angered the Englishman. The latter was a tall gray-haired man with a deeply lined face and bloodshot eyes behind bifocals. The waiters hauled the two away from each other, and after some low-voiced exchange, the two bowed to each other and returned to their seats.

"Why," Phwombly said, "I do believe that's Jim Binde! Secret Agent 00-something or other, I forget. What's he doing here? Wait a minute! I know! One of those cooks must be Doctor Negative! He was supposed to have been asphyxiated when Jim dropped that load of guano on him. But I know he got out and escaped the atomic blast afterward, too! So, young Binde came here to chalk up the final score with his old enemy. And that explains why the Russians are here. That gray-haired guy he grappled is an agent from the terrorist organization. Used to be called SMERDE but now it's ISPANAZHNYENIYE. They're here to end an old feud, too. And that explains why the CIA and the FBI are here. They're keeping an eye on the foreign agents."

"What about that bunch of Chinese at that table in the corner?" Silver said.

"I should have known. They must be agents from the Hwing Ding, a Chinese terrorist group. They're here to pop off the arch-fiends Fyu-men Chew, Won Fang, Sen Sen, Negative, and maybe Terminal. All these S.O.B.'s gave China plenty of trouble, you know. And Ecks and Fooler are watching them, too, you can bet. Oh, boy, oh, boy!"

The waiter started to serve them, and they quit communicating. When he'd left, Phwombly brought out his vials again. Pete Ruse, whose stomach was rumbling, said, "You dummy! You'll have to order again!"

Phwombly glared at him and said, "I forgot I'd been served the first time. So much going on, you know."

"Let's get out of here," Ruse said. He shoved his chair back and stood up. "You ain't going to learn anything more. These guys are on to what's going on. There's a good steak house down the street. The smell of Chinese food makes me sick, anyway."

As they went out onto the street, two men entered the restaurant. One was a middle-sized white-haired man with thick spectacles. Behind them were two gray eyes that looked as cold as wintertime windowglass after a heavy frost. The man behind him was goateed and in the costume of a Kentucky colonel. A patent medicine bottle stuck out of a pocket of his coat.

Phwombly chuckled and said, "Dick Bendsome, the Punisher himself. And Doc Barker."

"For a minute, I thought Barker was Colonel Sanders," Silver said.

"He's put on some weight," Phwombly said.

"For Chrissakes, let's eat," Pete Ruse said. "If I don't eat regular, I get irregular."

Six

After dinner, the three drove back to the motorhome, which they then drove back into town. After Silver parked it by another fire plug, they settled down to observe the passersby. The windows in the rear and on the sides could be polarized with a push of a button, permitting them to see without being seen. The first thing they observed was a cop ticketing the motorhome for illegal parking.

"Don't worry," Pete Ruse said. "I can fix it."

Phwombly said, "There goes the garbage truck. Hey, if that isn't Scorpio himself driving it, I'm a dingbat! Look, his arm's dangling out the window, and his big ring's showing. I can see the scorpion on it from here. He used to wear a ring with an octopus on it, you know, and he called himself the Kraken. Then he lost the ring, or it was stolen, and he couldn't find another with an octopus on it so he bought one with a scorpion on it and changed his name.

"And, hey, there goes Dick Windworthy, the Arachnid. He's got on a good disguise, but he forgot to tell his helper, old Ram-Chandu, not to wear his turban. And he's also carrying his violin—takes it with him wherever he goes now. A dead giveaway. I heard he was so hard up he was putting on dark glasses and playing his violin on street corners while Ram-Chandu passed the cup around. Things sure aren't what they used to be."

Silver noted down the names and brief descriptions while the old man rambled on and on about the good old days. Once, Pete Ruse broke in with a discovery of his own.

"Cut me for a steer if that ain't Dude Onley, the Copper Kid! So he's here for the showdown, too! Look at him, a rambling wreck of a man who was as good as any mysterious avenger to ever roam the West righting wrongs. In his heyday he was called the Silver Simoleon. He'd put a silver dollar at the feet of a crook, and if the punk knew what was good for him he left the country."

Pete shook his head.

"Now he's called the Copper Kid. He went broke and he can't afford anything but pennies."

At the end of two hours, Silver had a long list of twenty positive identifications and a score of possibilities. There was George Luck, the Green Sheet, who'd been spotted because of a piece of green cloth sticking out of his pocket: There was Jed O'Hill, the Green Llama, once well known for his terrorization of evildoers and his bad spelling. After having spent some time in Tibet mastering the mystical techniques of the lamas, he returned to the States to use them on criminals. He always wore a long scarf which he used as a bullwhip, and he occasionally swallowed some radioactive salts which charged his body with several hundred thousand volts. Any crook who laid hands on him was electrocuted without due process of law. Once, he escaped from a dangerous cave by putting a light bulb in his mouth and illuminating his path.

There was Gary Adieu, Captain Lucifer, The Red Masquer, Donald Diabolo, the magician known as the Vermilion Mage, and Esteban Hatcher, the Luna Head. The latter was identified by the hat-box he was carrying. Phwombly said this contained Luna Head's robe and fishbowl-shaped metal helmet which concealed his features. Phwombly also tagged Richman Curtwell Van Debt, titled the Phantom Dick, and James "Bearcat" Guerdon, known as the Gargler.

"Hold on!" Phwombly said. "Can it be? Yes, it is! Another Englishman! Sir Daines Neighland Smythe, the foe of Doctor Fyu-men Chew! He's made up to look like a cowboy, but I'd know him every time. He always looks like Sherlock Holmes in disguise."

Silver decided he wouldn't ask how he knew that.

"And there's Secret Agent Operator No. 4 + 1," Phwombly said. "Note the ring with the skull cut on it? It contains a vial of poison gas. He also wears a rapier in his belt."

"Spotted 8-Ball or Blimp Kernel yet?" Silver said.

"I've never seen Kernel, not under that name, anyway. He must be one of the great ones, though, otherwise the other great ones wouldn't work for him. And I might not recognize 8-Ball. He's almost as good at disguises as I am. But I wonder where Herr Doktor Krogers, 8-Ball's great enemy, is? Surely he wouldn't stay away. Oh, oh! There goes Tony Winn, the Black Night Owl. Notice the dark glasses and white cane? He used to be blind but he secretly got a doctor to transplant a dead man's eyes, and now he just pretends to be blind. But *I know*! Say, what time is it?"

Phwombly had hocked his watch before he got hired by Acme and had never gotten around to redeeming it.

"Twenty minutes after midnight."

"No wonder I haven't seen Dirk Alone, Captain Nothing," Phwombly said. "He becomes invisible from midnight until dawn. It's a great help in combating crime, and it wouldn't hurt a bank robber, either," he added. Silver thought he detected an envious tone. "But it's a handicap, too. He obtained his power of invisibility accidentally, during an experiment with radioactivity. He has no control over it, and he's gotten into some embarrassing situations because of that. He's been jailed three times for getting caught in the ladies' room. But he escaped every time."

They decided to drive back to their out-of-town parking space and call it a night. Ruse accepted their invitation to sleep in the motorhome. After an hour of trying to get to sleep, Silver went out to Ruse's car and lay down in its back seat. The snoring of the two old men and the complaints of the birds about the snoring were too much for him.

Late in the morning, after shaving and showering, all, including the birds, ate Wheaties, toast and hardboiled eggs. Phwombly and Ruse followed these with Geritol, vitamin pills, testosterone, and Maalox, and after a while everybody was ready to venture into town again. While Silver drove, his partner cleaned his two .45 automatics and Pete Ruse checked out his trusty six-shooter. This was routine, but Silver became alarmed when Phwombly brought out a box of other armament. His eyes bulged as he saw in the rear view mirror the hand grenades, smoke bombs, M-20 automatic rifles, a 60-mm bazooka, a blowgun with poison darts, wire nooses, throwing knives, machetes, a carton of plastic explosive, tomahawks, bear traps, and an 81-mm mortar. From another box Phwombly brought out the ammunition.

"What is this, World War III?" Silver yelled back.

"It's for the good of the world," Phwombly growled.

"My God, what are we into?" Silver said. "What about all those innocent bystanders?"

"No one is innocent," Phwombly said, sighting an M-20. "Read Sartre."

"Come on!" Silver said. "If you can identify these crooks, tell the FBI. They'll arrest them, and that'll be it."

"For what?" Phwombly said. "They'd be sprung in an hour. You don't think any of those great brains have left any evidence behind them, do you? Or witnesses, either. And us few old timers aren't going to squeal. We're going to have the big showdown, finish it ourselves. We've always operated outside the law—most of us, anyway—and that's how we'll do it."

"That's the way I want it," Pete Ruse said, twirling the barrel of his revolver. "I ain't going to die in a drooling ward."

"But all those men, women, and children!" Silver said. "Think of the kids! How you going to get them out of the way?"

"The town'll clear out as soon as the shooting starts," Phwombly said. "We have to consider the good of all against the evil that might be done to a few. Somebody always gets hurt; it can't be helped. But it's justifiable."

Silver didn't reply because he could see the uselessness of argument. He determined that as soon as the motorhome was parked, he would go straight to the sheriff of Shootout. But the sheriff would have to call in the state police and the National Guard to handle this situation. And meanwhile . . . maybe he could get to Dan Fooler, Val Kilgore, and G-Double-7, the FBI men. No, that wouldn't do any good. They were retired, here in an unofficial capacity, and doubtless as determined as the others to ignore legal restraints.

"All right," Silver said, though it wasn't all right. "Are you planning to initiate this or will you wait until the Blimp Gang robs the bank? *If* they do, that is. Maybe they're scared off."

"Not them!" Phwombly said, snorting. "The way I see it, they'll make their try about two or three in the morning, when the streets are cleared. There are two days left for the celebration, so it'll be tonight or the next night. We better get some sack time today, because we're going to be up all night."

"You'll be in jail, if I have anything to do with it," Silver muttered. He stopped the motorhome by the same fire plug. The sheriff's office was only a block away. He'd go to it as soon as he thought of an excuse to get away from his partner. Looking out the windshield, he saw the giant figure of Doc Ravage making his way through the crowd. Behind him, bellowing insults at each other, came Chimp and Porkchop in their wheelchairs. Their heads were heavily bandaged, and Chimp must have suffered a recent blow in the nose, since it was taped over. Porkchop was wearing dark glasses, so the chances were that he had a black eye or two.

Silver stepped out and looked into the deep blue Arizona sky. "Oh, no," he said, and he turned to Phwombly, who was just stepping out of the vehicle.

"You're the only one who knows?" he said.

"That's right," Phwombly said, looking furtively around.

"If you knew that, why didn't you tell me?" Silver said. He pointed up at the three-winged airplane which was diving straight down, seemingly directly at them.

Phwombly said something but Silver couldn't hear him. The front of the bank blew out in a cloud of smoke and a pillar of noise.

While Silver stared, stunned, Phwombly dived back into the motorhome. He emerged a few seconds later, wearing a broad-brimmed slouch hat and a long black cloak. In each hand was a huge .45 automatic. The midmorning sun, caught on his contact lenses, made his eyes blaze.

"Bring the arms and the ammo!" he screamed.

"How could I carry all that stuff?" Silver said.

Pete Ruse jumped out of the door then, and he fell flat on his face. Cursing, he got up unsteadily on all fours and began feeling for his glasses, which had dropped off. Phwombly, stepping back to avoid the machine fire from the strafing Mad Fokker, put one heel on the spectacles. The glasses were broken, and so was Ruse's heart.

Silver hauled the protesting Ruse into the vehicle and got behind the wheel. He had to get the motorhome away. If the Fokker's bullets hit the ammunition in the box, goodbye Silver, goodbye half the town.

But the crowd, screaming, shouting, was running by and before him. The only way he could move was to run over a dozen people. One thing he'd say for them; they were certainly cooperating with the Fokker in his desire to clear the street.

Doc Ravage was loping along toward the Canary Cage Theater. Behind him sped his two aides. Each held in a hand a tiny submachine pistol while the other hand steered the chair. Evidently, the chairs were powered with electric motors; they had previously used their hands to propel them to conceal this fact.

They weren't going fast enough. The triplane, turning at the end of the street, had come back for another strafing run. Machinegun bullets, digging chunks out of the pavement, headed in a line for the wheelchairs.

Chimp, looking back, saw the inevitable. He shouted something at his partner. Flame shot out of the jet exhausts, and the chairs leaped ahead. Silver estimated they were doing fifty miles an hour when they veered off to the left, went out of control, bounced off the sidewalk, and soared through the big plateglass window on the front of the Chinese restaurant.

Doc Ravage looked out from the doorway in which he had taken refuge, saw what had happened, and came running. At the same time, Doc Barker, looking like a Colonel Sanders in pursuit of a chicken thief, ran after him. The bottle was out of his pocket, and it was evident that it held something more potent than snake oil. It had a soaked rag stuck in its neck, and Barker held a cigarette lighter in the other hand. Just as Doc dived through the window to rescue his aides, Barker lit the rag. He threw it after Doc, and suddenly flame and smoke issued from the window. Yells broke out then, and men poured out. Among them were three old Chinese, Doc Ravage, and his two helpers. The wheelchairs were bent but still serviceable, and the jets were flaming. They shot out through the doorway, passed the runners, hit the sidewalk on the opposite side, bounced, and soared through the plateglass window of a millinery shop. The explosion that followed littered the sidewalk with the EBB Gang and the wheelchair jockeys. Dozens of hats were still sailing like little flying saucers through the air.

By then the crowd had disappeared into buildings or the side-streets. Silver wheeled the motorhome around as Pete Ruse tried to step out. Pete hit the pavement and rolled over and over until he hit the sidewalk. There he lay, stunned, but still clutching his six-shooter.

Silver completed his half-circle and accelerated down the street. Holes appeared in the windshield, and bullets screamed by him. Straight ahead, moving toward him on a collision course, was the garbage truck of Scorpio. A dozen men stood on its fenders and in the dump, all firing at him.

Silver desperately zigzagged the motorhome, which did not respond with the speed of a passenger car. A tire exploded, and the bumping and the force pulling the steering wheel to one side told him he had better abandon ship. He dived out just as the truck rammed into it. The men on the fenders and in the dump were hurled out onto the pavement, and none of them got up.

A white-haired old man crawled out from behind the wheel of the truck. His face, not much to begin with, had not been improved by its contact with the windshield. Then Silver saw that the hideousness did not originate from his features. He wore a mask formed to represent the head of a scorpion. The mask had probably saved his face from being cut, though it had not kept him from being knocked half-conscious.

Silver, crouching, ran to him. The shadow of the triplane passed over him. The plane had almost hit the truck, making Silver wonder if it had been coming in for a landing but its pilot had been frustrated by the collision of the vehicles. Never mind. He had time to put Scorpio out of commission before the triplane could turn again.

Machineguns chattering and grenades exploding distracted him for a moment. He looked down the street and saw that the windows and doorways on both sides of the street bristled with flame-spurting rifles and machineguns. Something dark sailed up into the air, descended, and landed before the front of the Canary Cage Theater.

"Not another mortar!" Silver groaned and then was knocked flat by the explosion. The front of the theater collapsed in a black cloud.

Scorpio muttered something. Silver said, "What?" The old man rolled over, exposing a huge hypodermic syringe. Its needle was stuck in his left hip.

According to Phwombly, Scorpio used this to inject drugs into his victims. The drugs turned them into mindless monsters who murdered and mutilated at his command. Evidently, he'd meant to stick the needle into Silver. But on falling out he'd been, if not hoist by his own petard, needled with his own syringe.

"Get out of town," Silver said in Scorpio's ear. "And keep going until I tell you to stop. And don't obey anyone else's command."

"I obey," the old man said weakly. He struggled to his hands and knees and began crawling. Silver never did know how far he got. The triplane came back, the double line of bullets headed toward the motorhome. Silver ran as fast as he could with his mechanical leg, not very fast, and dived through an open window. He hit the floor just as the ammunition in the motorhome went off. The house shook, and the blast deafened him. Half-stunned, he rose and staggered to the doorway. The door had been blown off. So that was what had struck him, he thought dully. The smoke was clearing outside, and he could see the garbage truck across the street, lying on its side in front of the Hell for Leather Saloon. There was no evidence that there had ever been a motorhome, which was to be expected.

He also saw the triplane bouncing along on the street. The Mad Fokker had certainly cleared everything for a landing. Too well. Its wheels dropped into the big hole made by the explosion, and the fuselage, deprived of wheels, slid down the street. Its propeller bent and then fell off, and the three sets of wings were torn off, and the fuselage disintegrated. And there was the pilot, still holding on to the control stick, sliding along on his rear, smoke curling from the edges of the heels of his shoes and the bottoms of his pants.

Inertia being what it is, he finally stopped. His motionlessness did not last long. Impelled and propelled by the flames leaping from his pants, he leaped up and ran toward a horse trough and dived into it.

At that moment, the blimp appeared above the street.

Seven

Silver was too numbed to feel alarmed. But he did have a slight sense of joy when he saw his two ravens circling below the blimp. He had thought they had perished in the explosion. Evidently, they'd had enough sense to get out of the motorhome sometime during the fight. He wished he was with them.

The pilot rolled out of the trough and lay on the ground. His face was still concealed by goggles and a handkerchief. Then he got shakily to his feet and turned, exposing a big hole in his pants and a somewhat blackened posterior. Two men ran out from a nearby doorway, shouting, "Got you, Mad Fokker!" One was Secret Service Agent Operative No. 4 + 1. The other, in a scarlet mask, undoubtedly was the Red Masquer. The pilot staggered away down the street. No. 4 + 1 stopped and grabbed his huge belt buckle. Silver watched, fascinated. Phwombly had said that he carried a sword in his belt, though he hadn't explained how he could wrap a sword around his middle. But there it came, sliding out of the sheath of the belt. There went his pants, too, dropping down to his ankles. The sword had cut through the belt and the belt straps. No. 4 + 1's coordination wasn't what it used to be.

Two more men came out of a shattered store front. One was the man Phwombly had pointed out as the Punisher. The other was Captain Lucifer. The Punisher held a peculiar weapon, a combination gun and knife. It held one .25 caliber bullet, which the Punisher never fired to kill. Instead, he always creased his enemy's head in the middle of the scalp, stunning him. So much for good intentions. Whether it was because of impaired eyesight or shakiness due to age, his aim was somewhat lower than he had intended. The bullet skimmed the flesh of the exposed posterior. The Mad Fokker, stung out of his lethargy, increased his speed. Bullets fired at him, seemingly from both factions, accelerated him even more. He disappeared into the bank.

The Punisher and Captain Lucifer, both breathing so hard that Silver could hear their wheezes across the street, ran back for shelter. No. 4 + 1, holding his pants up with one hand, was a step behind them.

At that moment the Arachnid ran out of a drugstore. He had somehow found time to put on a disguise, but Silver recognized him from the ring he wore, a ring bearing a scarlet spider in alto relief. His face was made up to look like that of the Wicked Witch of the East after Dorothy's house dropped on it. It was supposed to scare his enemies, but Silver imagined that they were of sterner stuff than the run-of-the-mill crook. Besides, it wouldn't have looked out of place on the Bowery or North Clark Street in Chicago.

The Arachnid shouted, "Stop, Captain Lucifer!"

Lucifer turned pale and on his heel at the same time.

The Arachnid shouted, "I've been looking for you for forty-two years, you bum! I'm the one who thought of the idea of stamping a spider image on the foreheads of crooks I assisted to a bad end! But you took up the idea without giving me the slightest credit! You stamped your devil on crooks' foreheads! No more! You've had it, Captain Copycat!"

The two men grappled each other. No. 4 + 1 quit running, let his pants drop again, and opened the cover on top of his ring. From its hollow interior he took a tiny round glass, a green marble glowing in the sun, and he threw it after the Mad Fokker.

Halfway toward its target, it broke, undoubtedly struck by one of the many bullets flying around. A green cloud billowed out. It expanded to a diameter of about twenty feet, drifting back toward No. 4 + 1 and the two combatants. It dissipated rapidly, but it evidently was quick-acting. The three oldsters were as still and as green as cucumbers.

By then the blimp was directly above the bank. It halted there, turned against the wind, its single propeller spinning just enough to keep it stationary. A little car containing one man was being lowered at the end of a cable, the other end of which went through an opening in the bottom of the gondola. Men were shooting from the gondola; their target seemed to be the Ga See Chow. Of course, they had no way of knowing that part of their own gang was trapped in the restaurant.

Doc Ravage stepped out of the shadow of the rear portion of the Canary Cage Theater, which was somehow still standing. Coolly ignoring the bullets and curses hurled at him, he raised the little submachine pistol and pointed it at the blimp's bag. Evidently he meant to punch it full of holes and bring it down on top of the bank. But nothing came out of its muzzle. Either it was out of ammunition or it had jammed. Doc Ravage threw it away from him and went back into the Canary Cage Theater.

Meanwhile, Phwombly had appeared on top of a building half a block down from the theater. Ordinarily, he'd have been hidden from view by the false front of the building, but this had been blown off along with much of the rest of the structure. Phwombly had somehow managed to haul a mortar, no doubt captured from the enemy, to the top of the roof. Now he cranked its wide muzzle up, and then he was dropping the shell into it. Smoke and a loud noise came from it, and Silver glimpsed the missile as it went up in its sharp arc. The recoil of the mortar, however, must have been just enough to add the final straw to the weakened structure. The roof fell in, Phwombly with it, and the walls followed. Silver reached for his hat to remove it and place it over his heart. But he had lost it somewhere along the line.

The shell blew up behind the bank. The blimp bobbed from the impact of the shock waves and then settled again. The cable car passed out of Silver's sight, but a moment later it came into view again. The blimp was going to let down another man, the first having gotten out on the roof.

Doc reappeared, this time with a huge spear he must have gotten from the theater stockroom. He raised it above his shoulder, ran out into the street as bullets zinged by, and cast the missile. It soared up and up, a pretty good throw for a young man, let alone a septuagenarian, but it wasn't good enough. It dropped before it came within six feet of the gasbag. However, it wasn't entirely off the mark. It hurtled toward the man in the cable car, and he, believing that it was going to hit him, jumped. Since he had a twenty-foot fall, he was probably now no longer interested in the battle.

Doc ran back into the building, agony on his face, and holding himself just above his right hip. It looked to Silver as if he had badly strained himself. Was he out of it, too?

His eyes widened. Phwombly, covered with plaster dust, was crawling out from the wreckage. The old fellow was certainly tough. But if he didn't find shelter, he'd be mincemeat very quickly. Bullets tore up wood and bricks around him.

Silver's hair stood up on end. A groan had come from the back of the building. Cautiously, he went through the door and looked around the room. A man sat huddled against the wall under a table. Silver looked under it and said, "Captain Nothing, I presume? What're you doing here?"

"Waiting for midnight," Dirk Alone said. "I'll be invisible then. And invincible, too."

"Forget it," Silver said. "This'll be long over before then."

He looked up, and he gasped. An old Indian woman stood in the corner.

"Grandma!"

"What?" Captain Nothing said. His hand went toward his coat pocket.

White Spots was shaking her head and pointing at the man under the table. Then she drew her finger across her throat and disappeared.

Silver bent down swiftly and seized the old man's hand, which had just come out of his coat pocket. He twisted it, it opened as Captain Nothing cried out with pain, and a tiny lizard with a scarlet cock's comb and a pale green skin covered by pustules fell on the floor. But it turned, fast as the tip of a cracking whip, and sank two rattlesnakish fangs into the hand of its owner. Captain Nothing screamed once, slowly turned purple veined with gold, and slumped over.

Silver picked up a chair by its legs and brought the edge of its back down against the lizard's back. The pustules shot up inch-high needle sprays of a foul-smelling liquid. The stuff burned the floor where it fell and sent up a choking smoke. Silver backed away, waited until the lizard quit twitching and the air was cleared, and returned to examine the old man. The texture of his skin looked so peculiar that Greatheart tested it with his fingernails. Presently, he pulled off the plastic skin of the face.

"Doctor Won Fang!"

During the melee, the old Chinese had become isolated from the others. He'd quickly made himself up to look like Captain Nothing, no doubt hoping to fool, and so kill, any of his enemy who took refuge here. But he had never run up against a man with an unconscious that operated like a movie projector.

Silver explored the room and quickly found another body behind a pile of boxes. Old Valiant Kilgore, ex-federal agent, chief foe of Won Fang. The two had had the final confrontation here. Judging from the absence of any wounds except some scratches on his face, Kilgore had died of a heart attack. Then old Won Fang, exhausted, had crawled away.

Silver returned to the front of the building. The men in the gondola were still shooting, but firing elsewhere had ceased. Maybe, he thought, the others had run out of ammunition.

Silver stuck his head out of the door and whistled three times. The ravens quit circling and headed straight toward him. After they'd settled on his shoulders, and he had soothed them, he took a pen and a piece of paper from his pocket. He wrote a note on it, put it in Huggin's bill, and croaked softly at the bird. Huggin didn't want to carry out his mission, but Silver assured him that there wasn't any danger. Huggin squawked indignantly at that. Silver added, well, there wasn't *much* danger. Huggin flew away across the street at an angle and dropped through the opening in the front of the Ga See Chow. Immediately, an aged Chinese dashed screaming out of the restaurant. He screamed all the way across the street as he headed for the bank.

Silver stared in astonishment. He'd sent a note demanding immediate surrender. The town was surrounded by police and National Guardsmen, it stated, and those holed up in the restaurant didn't have a chance. But if they surrendered now, they might get some leniency. As for those in the blimp, they didn't have a prayer either. Air National Guard jets were just over the mountain. Within a few minutes, they'd be shooting the blimp out of the sky.

He'd signed the note with the governor's name. He hoped they'd be too rattled to wonder why the governor would transmit a message by such unconventional means.

But he'd forgotten about Doctor Negative's psychotic fear of birds. Ever since he'd been buried in that pile of guano, he couldn't stand even the sight of a robin. The appearance of Huggin had panicked him. It had also set off a chain reaction that was going to result in just the opposite of what Silver had planned.

Jim Binde, on seeing his archenemy dash out, had run after him. He carried only a knife, which meant that he, like most of the combatants, was out of ammunition.

Behind came a dozen Chinese and a moment later, from another building, the Russian contingent. The Hwing Ding were after Won Fang, or maybe their old foe, Secret Agent Binde. Or both.

The Russians were also after somebody. It might be the Hwing Ding, which they hated, or Binde, whom they didn't like either, or Won Fang, who'd given them a hard time during the post-Revolution years. Probably they were after all three.

And here came the rest of all those who could run, walk, or crawl. The FBI, the CIA, Sour Lemono and what was left of WAX, and the surviving great old ones. They were out of bombs and bullets, but they had their knives and special weapons and their hands and feet.

In the middle of the street, before the half-shattered bank, they met and mixed in the melee of the millennium.

Eight

Doctor Negative was the first to go. In fact, he had left before the final conflict. His heart had given out as he reached the pile of debris before the bank.

Jim Binde did not get long to congratulate himself. He was only sixty-two but looked eighty because of his incessant boozing and smoking. A few seconds after Negative dropped, alcohol and nicotine dropped their guillotine on Binde. He clutched his chest and collapsed beside his enemy.

The Copper Kid succumbed next, pennies spilling from his opened hand.

"Too many years of anticipation of revenge," Silver muttered to himself. "Too much excitement for hearts that had been stimulated by too much adrenalin for too long."

The old men were dropping like stocks in a Wall Street panic.

There went Doc Barker, making his last pitch. Sir Daines Neighland Smythe and Doctor Fyu-men Chew lay with their arms around each other. This was appropriate, Silver thought. During their sixty years of feuding, they'd had innumerable opportunities to kill each other but had always ignored them. Deep down, they were lovers.

Nor would Doctor Sen Sen offend anyone with his breath ever again. It was a question, however, whether it had been a ruptured heart or a broken head that had killed him off. He'd charged Luna Head, who had bent over as he countercharged. Sen Sen's head had rammed into the big opaque metal fishbowl concealing his enemy's features. There had been a loud hollow ringing sound, and both had fallen on their backs, feet to feet. Luna Head didn't look as if he was going to get up either.

Not all the old ones had fallen. The Black Night Owl, wearing dark glasses, was striking his opponents with a white cane in one hand and a tin cup in the other. Donald Diavolo, clad in a scarlet costume, was lashing out with a bullwhip held in his right hand. With his left he was distracting antagonists with magical tricks: an endless scarf, an American flag, a bowl full of goldfish, bouquets of flowers, a rabbit, a flock of pigeons, all from his sleeve.

And there was the Gargler, dressed entirely in battleship gray, masked, striking with the butt of an empty automatic. But there also was Doctor Terminal slipping behind him, a stone axe in hand. Terminal had spent his life trying to destroy civilization, to send people back to the Old Stone Age. He was an idealist who thought that technology had ruined man's spirituality with its materialism. All his murders, individual or mass, had been for man's good, though even he had to admit that he had been able to perform his greatest deeds only because of modern science.

Now Terminal smote the Gargler in the back of his head, though not very hard, since his arms were feeble. The Gargler opened his mouth, and the specially-made plates inside his mouth shot out. These were equipment to change the shape of his lower face when he was in disguise. As a side effect, the plates had made him talk in a weird gargling manner. Now he was down on his hands and knees, groping around among a seaweed-dance of legs for the plates. Doctor Terminal was raising the axe to bring it down on the Gargler's buttocks.

Silver's attention at that moment was attracted by two men on horses that galloped out between two burning buildings down the street. Evidently the Long Ranger and his sidekick, Pronto, had been biding their time, waiting until a critical moment. Each had two revolvers; each was firing them wildly as their stallions raced toward the battle. Silver ducked as a bullet screamed by him. It struck something metallic behind him, ricocheted again, and dropped at his feet. He looked at it, saw it was made of lead, and felt a little sad. The days when the Long Ranger was rich enough to use silver bullets were no more.

Pete Ruse came out of his stupor then. He got to his feet, staggered to the middle of the street, faced the oncoming riders, and shouted, "Halt in the name of the law of Cochise County, Long Ranger!"

The masked man on the white horse shouted back. "For Pete's sake, I'm on the side of the Good!"

"You're an outlaw!" Ruse screamed back, and he emptied his six-shooter at the masked rider. The Long Ranger had used up all his bullets; Pronto couldn't fire because he'd dropped his gun. It made no difference. Lawman and outlaw had missed with every shot.

Just as the Long Ranger ran out of bullets, his horse stepped in a hole created by a bomb. The Ranger flew up, out, and over while the horse stayed behind. Pronto's horse piled into the other horse, and Pronto followed his senior partner. He landed on the masked rider, who had landed on Pete Ruse.

The horses got up, but the three men did not move.

At least, this is one time when the Indian comes out on top, Silver thought.

And here came the Green Llama, the long scarf he used for a whip in his hand. He radiated a bright blue light, since he'd just swallowed the glowing blue contents of a bottle. Now he was charged with several hundred thousands of volts. Just let the enemy lay hands on him!

He advanced gingerly around the edge of the closely packed crowd on his thick nonconducting shoes. He was looking for someone to lash with his scarf, which was also, of course, made of nonconducting material.

A man Phwombly had pointed out as the archfoe of Scorpio shambled out of the crowd. He was Geoffrey Justkid, once known to the police and the underworld under two identities. Sometimes he was compassionate Doctor Headbone, a man who liked to distribute dimes to slum dwellers and turn in wicked welfare workers. Sometimes he was the deadly Headbone Slayer, demiser of criminals. Now he was squinting around, obviously in desperate need of his glasses. He crouched, trying to see between the milling feet of the battlers. Then he shrugged, stood up, and charged head down toward the crowd.

Unfortunately, the Green Llama walked into his path. Probably the Headbone Slayer did not recognize him as a friend. He leaped at him, though not very high or far, and bore him into the crowd.

There was a loud crackle, some smoke from the Llama, the Slayer, and a few near them. And the entire mob fell as one man.

There was a silence except for the crackling of flames. The wind brought to Silver the acrid odor of smoke and the not-so-sweet odor of vengeance requited.

Was anybody left? Was he the sole survivor?

No. There still were the men in the bank and the blimp. And here came two figures from the shell of a general store. Phwombly and Doc Ravage. They were holding each other up, wincing at every step, but headed determinedly for the bank. What could a pair of injured ancients do now? Were they really going into the bank to clean out a dozen armed men?

They were.

As the two disappeared into the building, Silver shouted at them. Then he was running after them. Then he was flat on his face. It took him a minute to find out that his marvelous electromechanical leg had chosen that moment to malfunction. The servomechanisms responding to the neutral currents flowing through flesh and wires to metal and plastic had failed. And his trainers at the hospitals had not taught him to walk with an inactivated limb.

He managed to get to one foot, and he hopped to the bank. The interior was bright and empty. Wreckage filled the lobby. A couple of old men, bearing no evidence of outward injury, lay behind a mound of plaster and wood. Heart failure, probably. He put his head cautiously through the door to the back of the room. The vault door was at the opposite wall, and it was closed. That meant that the two had locked in some of the gang, since the gang wouldn't have bothered to close it behind them. But how many of them were in it? And where were Phwombly and Doc Ravage?

It didn't need any Sherlock Holmes to figure that out. They'd gone up the stairs to the second floor and on up to the roof.

Using his good leg and the banister, cursing modern technology and two stubborn old men, Silver hauled himself up the steps. He had to crawl over several bags of money and their former bearers, snoring away, their jaws a little out of line. Doc Ravage's still mighty fist had undoubtedly been responsible for that.

Then he was sweating to get up the almost vertical ladder. Through the open trap above him he could see the blimp and the car at the end of the cable. The car was two-thirds of the way up, about twenty feet above the roof. It held the Mad Fokker, who was grinning over the side of the car and thumbing his nose.

Silver got to the top of the ladder and stuck his head out. The object of derision was, as he'd expected, Phwombly and Ravage. They were weaponless, and so helpless to do anything now. But they had forced the gang to abandon much of the loot. Bags of money lay in a pile directly behind them.

The Mad Fokker would not have been so happy if he had known what was happening above him. A pair of bolt cutters was extended through the opening for the car, and their jaws were closed on the cable. Above them was a white beard like Santa Claus', a grin like the Devil's, and a sea officer's cap. Surely, that was Blimp Kernel himself, Silver thought.

Since Phwombly and Ravage were directly under the car, they could not see Kernel.

Phwombly screeched, "8-Ball!"

The face of the man in the car sagged, and his mouth gaped. It took him some seconds to recover, and during that time the car had gone a few feet higher.

"How did you know I am 8-Ball?" he screamed down.

"Only I know!" Phwombly screamed back.

That wasn't exactly true, since he had told Silver, but this was no time for nitpicking.

"8-Ball! Don't you know who your leader is, who's hiding behind that fake face and the beard? It's your old enemy, your archfoe, Herr Doktor Krogers himself! He's been using you, 8-Ball, and laughing at you all the time! I've been trying to figure out for some time who Kernel could be, and finally I hit on the truth! Do you know anybody else who could fit the bill? Tell me, 8-Ball, haven't you thought from time to time there was something familiar about him? Did you ever detect a slight German accent in his speech?"

"No! No! No!" 8-Ball shrilled. He reared up in the car and looked upward. And then he screamed.

A thin voice fell down to the men on the roof. "That's right, *verdammenswert Schweinhund*! I'm the man you've been seeking for sixty-two years. At first, I was going to kill you. And then I thought, what a joke if I use the man who foiled me over and over again, the man who was really responsible for my beloved country's losing the war! And worst of all, making an idiot of me, Herr Doktor Krogers, the greatest brain in the world, in the universe, even!"

The old man in the car screamed again, grabbed the cable, and began pulling himself up it toward Krogers, ten feet above him. He had to be in his late eighties, and yet he went up the thin cable like a baboon. That his rear was bare made the simile even more appropriate.

"Vengeance is mine!" he cried once, but thereafter he quit. No doubt, he was out of wind, because a few feet from reaching the opening, he stopped. His gaspings for breath were so loud that Silver could hear them.

"*Leben Sie wohl, Schwaschsinniger!* Have a nice trip!"

Doc Ravage bent over and seized a bag, probably containing silver dollars, by the neck. Agony passed over his face, quickly replaced by his normal stoic expression. But he remained bent over, and it was evident that he'd "caught" his back. He was unable to straighten up again.

Silver, understanding what he had meant to do with the coins, pulled himself out onto the roof. At the same time, he shouted to Phwombly and Ravage to get out from under the car.

"Kernel's cutting the cable!"

Ravage, stooped over, scrambled over the pile. Phwombly dived over the bags, hit his shoulder hard against the roof, and lay there groaning.

Kernel saw the whole thing. He laughed and then shouted down at them. "Look at this *dummkopf*, you *dummkopfs*. You sweat while he sweats. Ho! Ho! Revenge at last!"

Silver, sitting down, pulled his pants off. Then he twisted his false leg a quarter turn, feeling no pain in the connections to his nerves. The minute connections had come away easily.

He struggled to his foot, hoping that Kernel, or Krogers, would be so curious about what he was doing that he'd delay the cutting. 8-Ball, hanging on the cable, was looking down at him, and though Silver was angered by what he'd done, he also felt a twinge of pity. After all, the old guy was insane.

"So what gives?" Kernel screeched down at him. "You are going to do a one-legged dance? Are you an Indian medicine man, you're going to make it rain yet? Only on one side of the sky, ho, ho!"

Balancing on the one leg, Silver swung the false leg back and then hurled it up and outward.

Krogers cried out, and his face disappeared. He'd probably run back to the end of the gondola in a purely irrational reflex, since there was nothing he could do to prevent the leg from hitting the propeller.

Turning over and over, the limb went into the whirring blades. There was a clang, and the leg flew back to one side, still turning, and landed on the corner of the roof.

The propeller faltered for a minute, then resumed its original rate of rotation. If any of the blades had been damaged, they gave no evidence of it.

Silver grimaced with chagrin. He had hoped that the irradiated plastic of the leg, hard as steel but much lighter, would snap off a blade or at least bend one considerably.

The grimace turned into a grin. Though the casting of the leg had failed in one way, it had succeeded in another. While Krogers had been at the stern of the gondola, 8-Ball had made a final effort. He had pulled himself to the opening and was reaching in. Krogers' scream of fury came all the way down to the man on the roof. A second later, he had seized the bolt cutters and torn them from 8-Ball, who had to release them to keep from falling.

Krogers, leaning over, placed the jaws of the cutters again on the cable. His face became red with the effort, but the jaws closed. The cable parted, and the car fell toward the roof. But 8-Ball had grabbed Krogers' leg and pulled himself up just enough to grab Krogers' long white beard. The two fell, screaming, while the blimp, released of the weight of the car and two bodies, soared upward.

The car struck the roof with a loud crash and went on through it. The building, weakened by the blast, fell in. Silver could do nothing except fall with the roof. Something struck him, and he was unconscious.

In the ambulance on the way to the Bisbee hospital, Greatheart awoke. He murmured to the attendant, "Was anyone left alive in the bank?"

"Just you," the attendant said.

"Then I guess they're all in Valhalla," Greatheart whispered, and he passed out again.

"Hey, Jack," the attendant said to the driver. "Where's Valhalla?"

"There ain't no such place in Arizona."

The Return of Greatheart Silver
Or
The Secret Life of Rebecca of Sunnybrook Farm

Nine

The boom of the .45 automatic pistol in the hallway deafened Greatheart Silver.

He jumped back, slamming the door. A hole appeared in the wooden panel, just where his head had been. Stooping, he reached out and locked the door.

But if they wanted him, they could easily shoot the lock out.

They might try to kill him. He was a witness, and he could describe them to the police. After all, he had been with them all morning.

Where could he hide, where run to? The apartment had only one exit, unless he wanted to leave via the balcony outside the French windows. The balconies of the neighboring apartments were too far away to be jumped to. The one directly below was too far down, since the balconies were staggered.

He sat down and rolled up his left pants leg. Should he take off his mechanical leg? It was fitted for just such an emergency. But the anticipated emergency was on a smaller scale. Its power would give out when he was only halfway down, which meant that he'd have a fall of five stories. No. Use it as a weapon if they stormed in.

He gripped the leg where irradiated plastic and flesh met. One slight twist, and the connections between nerves and wires would break. Then, a turn of a half-circle, and the leg would be unscrewed.

If he did that, though, he'd have to go to the hospital for reconnection of the nerve-endings. That would cost considerably more than the twenty dollars in his wallet, all the cash he had.

Hearing no more sounds in the hallway, he decided not to uncouple his leg. He rose and went to the door and placed an ear against the wood. Silence.

They were either waiting for him to show his head again or they would have taken off like antelopes who knew lions were in the neighborhood. It was evident they were kidnapping the young woman whose face he'd glimpsed. Her mouth was covered with a strip of white tape, and her arms were behind her, obviously tied or hand-cuffed. One of the men was holding a pistol to her head. Her eyes were enormous and half-glazed with terror and shock.

There had been three men and two women with her, the entire crew. Like him, they were clad in bright orange coveralls, and on their backs and fronts in big black letters were: "*Acme W-W Cleaners.*"

The woman wasn't the only one shocked. The kidnappers stared paralyzed at his unexpected appearance, and he gaped with astonishment and bewilderment.

He knew the captive. How well he knew her! He hadn't seen her for years, but he recognized her instantly. And she wasn't Lassie.

"Regina!" he cried.

And then everybody had broken loose from their stasis, as if somebody had pulled a switch cutting off a powerful binding magnetic field. One of the women jerked Regina backward. The others stepped forward, raising their weapons. (These, he decided later, must have been concealed in the cleaning equipment.)

At the same time, he saw out of the corner of his right eye a ghostly figure. It—he—was a tall one-legged man, dressed like a pirate of the Spanish Main, leaning on a crutch, a huge green parrot on his shoulder. He was semi-transparent, not quite blocking out the light green wall and the lithograph on it behind him.

The phantom swiftly drew a finger across its throat. The parrot opened its mouth, seeming to screech a warning though no sound issued from it.

"You're a little late!" Silver shouted at the wraiths. "Thanks a lot for nothing!"

The figures began fading, but he was paying them no more attention. He hadn't needed them to be told that he was in danger.

He threw himself backward, slamming the door shut. And then the slugs from the pistols and the semi-automatic rifle had torn through the door. It would be the man who had a burn mark around his left ankle who had fired the rifle.

At the moment, that had seemed an irrelevant thought. What difference did it make whether the rifleman had a scar or not? Now, he knew, though he could not say why, that it was important. His subconscious would not have intruded that thought at such a perilous moment if it had not deemed it significant.

Silver had first seen the scar on the man named Pete while the crew was traveling in the rear of the Acme panel truck. Pete, sitting across from Silver, had leaned over and pulled up his left pants legs. He had vigorously scratched the broad red area on his ankle. Then, seeing Silver's curious look, he had grinned and said, "The mark of my servitude. But I'm a free man now. Forever!"

He unlocked the door as quietly as he could, listened again, and then rammed the door open with the butt of his palm. It swung out and banged against the wall. There was no response. His heart beating hard, he looked around the doorway. The hall was empty. At the end, the elevator indicator showed a car going down. It might or might not contain the gang.

He breathed in air and blew out frustration. What a hell of a mess he was in! If he told the police how he happened to witness a kidnapping, he'd have to explain then what he was doing in this apartment. And he'd be charged with breaking and entering. Justly so—from the law's point of view. His excuse that he was looking for the painting that Lassie had stolen from him would not be acceptable. And it would be in character for that vindictive bitch to press charges against him.

She had a perfect alibi. Her lover, her other lover, had testified that she was with him when the painting had disappeared. Since he was a detective lieutenant, assigned to the burglary division, his word had been accepted.

Why had he come here after all this time? He had known that Lassie must have sold the Copley long before. It undoubtedly now hung in the locked room of some unscrupulous private collector.

He'd been stupid to expect to find it here, but it was desperation that had made him stupid. Also, Lassie, though she had a body that attracted men like moths to a bright light, had a one-half-watt brain. She might just be dim-witted enough to keep the Copley—if it were still unsold—in her apartment.

No time for recriminations. First, he had to notify the police. Anonymously, of course. Then he'd get the hell out. If the police intercepted him before he got out of the building, they would not, at least, have him for breaking and entering. He couldn't deny that he'd come to work with the gang this morning. That would be enough for them to lock him up as a material witness. Especially since old Bendt Micawber would put pressure on to ensure that.

He walked across the big luxurious room toward the phone. The huge mirror on the wall showed a six-foot-four thirty-two-year-old man in orange coveralls. Across his chest in big black letters: *Acme W-W Cleaners*. W-W stood for *wall and window*. Micawber owned the company. Silver had gotten some amusement out of being hired by a firm that had him on its blacklist. But that now involved more trouble for him. He'd given the personnel manager a fake I.D.

The police would have one more reason to hold him. They'd never believe that he could only escape starvation by assuming a false identity. If he tried to tell them the truth, he'd be subjected to psychiatric tests. He'd probably be sent to the state funny farm. Who besides himself, and the conspirators, of course, would believe that Micawber was persecuting him?

"Aha! Paranoia, not to mention schizophrenia and delusions of grandeur!"

And if he reacted violently, which he was likely to do. "Aha! The padded cell for you, my boy! For your own good, of course!"

And old Bendt Micawber, smiling as he smoked a twenty-dollar cigar over a hundred-dollar brandy, would give orders that G. Silver stay locked up forever. For the good of society, of course. Which meant, in Micawber's parlance, for the good of Micawber.

Why, oh, why did Micawber hate him so? Why the excessive overreaction?

He'd blamed Silver for the loss of the two hundred million dollar

Zeppelin, though Silver was not its commander. Surely, firing and then blackballing Silver should have been enough. But Micawber hounded him even when Silver got jobs unconnected with Micawber's holdings. He exerted pressure, secretly, of course, and Silver was suddenly fired again—and again—with the feeblest of explanations.

Micawber was the genuine paranoiac in this situation, the man who should be in the padded cell. However, Silver was a penniless bum. Who'd believe him?

He looked in the mirror as he picked up the phone. No wonder he looked like a skid-row wino. He had no money to get a hair trim, to keep his thick reddish mustache unragged. His cheeks were sunken, and his eyes were red. And the handsome hawkish features had somehow become a starving vulture's.

He punched the emergency police number. Busy. Maybe he should forget it. No. He couldn't forget about Regina's look of terror. If he hadn't known her so well, so intimately, in fact, then he might . . . no, he wouldn't. She was a human being, and he wasn't going to abandon anybody, known or unknown, in that plight. No matter what the cost to him.

He started as, simultaneously, a voice spoke in his ear and sirens screamed through the window. The police were near, which meant that somebody had called them.

"Who is this?" the policeman repeated.

Had whoever called in *seen* enough to put the cops on the trail? Or had somebody just *heard* the shooting? The police needed a good description of the criminals. And Silver might be the only one who could give the license number of the getaway vehicle. In a situation like this, quick action was vital. Possibly, the gang had already transferred from the panel truck to a car.

Another consideration. The police were going to catch him before he got out of the building. He might as well tell all—except for being in Lassie's apartment.

"This is Greatheart Silver," he said. "I want to report a kidnapping."

"You're the kidnapper?"

"No, but that's about what I expected you to say."

Ten

Seymour Sheester breezed into the "interview" room. As always, he was smiling. He threw his attaché case onto the table and held out his hand across it. "How ya doing, baby?"

Silver ignored the hand.

"*You're* my public defender, appointed to *me*?"

Sheester looked down at his hand and then shook hands with himself. "I get it. You've adopted the old Chinese custom, heh? It's spreading like wildfire. More sanitary that way."

He sat down. "But I notice you aren't shaking hands with yourself. What's the matter? Haven't they allowed you to wash your own hands? Police brutality . . ."

"No," Silver said. "I just remember how you handled my case when I wanted to sue Micawber. Forget it, you said. We can't possibly win, you said. Never mind justice, you said. Roll with the punches of reality, you said. So why did you accept my case now?"

"I get paid the same whether I win or lose," Sheester said cheerfully. "So, what can I do for you, however hopeless your case might be?"

"Get me a good lawyer."

"Haw, haw! Still haven't lost your sense of humor, have you? Very admirable! Most men in your position would be thinking about hanging themselves. You got real guts, Silver, though I can't say you're very bright. But God distributes His gifts in ways too mysterious for us mortals to comprehend. The Great Lawyer prepared briefs for us before the foundations of the cosmos were laid . . . speaking of which, how did you ever track down Lassie?"

His big bright eyes glazed in a hot reverie for a minute.

Silver said, angrily, "I *knew* you were having an affair with her while I was your client, lying sick and desperate in the hospital! With you and the cop, and Lord knows how many others! What kind of ethics are those?"

"I admit nothing," Sheester said, coming slowly out of his memories. "Anyway, my personal life has nothing to do with my professional activities. Now, we got to have something, no matter how laughable, as a defense. But the Great Legal Eagle only knows what we can use. How'd you do it, Silver? You put yourself in a situation where they got you coming and going, fore and aft, up and down, sideways.

"Maybe you can beat the kidnapping charge, I don't know. But you forged those I.D.'s. You were concealing an explosive in your plastic leg. Your fingerprints were found in Lassie's apartment, so they got you on suspicion of burglary. She also claims her jewels are missing, and she wants you to pay for a new door and the replastering of the wall. To top it all, the twenty dollar bill in your wallet was counterfeit! They're thinking of charging you on that count!"

"Ridiculous!" Silver said indignantly. "I won the twenty in a crap game by betting the only money I had, a dollar. If I ever find that guy . . ."

"You'll both be so old you won't recognize each other," Sheester said. "Listen, we just have to come up with something. How about permanent brain damage? Battle fatigue? It was like the siege of Stalingrad at Shootout, and what with all those explosions . . ."

Silver saw the door swing open. Four hard-looking husky men came in. They looked around and then arranged themselves by two's on each side of the door. Another equally tough-looking man stuck his head in the doorway.

"O.K.?"

"O.K.," one of the four said out of the corner of his mouth.

A fifth man appeared, framing himself for a moment in the oblong of the entrance. Silver reared up, glaring. Sheester jerked his head around, paled, and groaned.

"Mr. Micawber!"

"Out, out, Sheester, you shyster!" blared the trumpet voice.

Sheester jumped up, grabbed his case, and slunk out muttering. His voice was low to begin with and by the time he passed Micawber his words were wholly unintelligible. Silver caught the initial ones, something about suing for public libel. Sheer cowardly bravado. He knew he stood about as much chance in court with the tycoon as a hummingbird in a typhoon.

Bendt Micawber remained in the doorway, forcing the lawyer to exit sideways, scrunched up to avoid contaminating the great one with his unclean touch.

Silver, trembling with rage, sat down. If he continued to stand, he might give Micawber the impression that it was in respect for him.

For a minute, Micawber stared at Silver without leaving the doorway. He was about five-feet-two-inches tall, rotund, bald-headed, and huge-skulled. His jowly face was streaked with broken veins. His forehead was ridiculously high, like that of the mad scientist so often depicted in the illustrations of science-fiction stories of the 1930s and in modern cartoons. His eyes were big and staring, the irises green with large yellow flecks. They looked like the eyes of a duck who had just heard the blast of a shotgun from a blind, Silver thought. His nose was huge and curved, like a flamingo's. His jaw was massive; his chin, bullet-shaped.

His mouth was peculiar. The upper lip was very full, but the lower was a thin line. The teeth were false, yet the canines were excessively long and pointed. It was rumored that Micawber had ordered them shaped so in order to frighten his opponents. Or for that matter, anyone within seeing range. This gave everybody the impression he was in the first stage of turning into a werewolf.

Full moon or not, Micawber was a wolf, though strictly of the Wall Street species. It was true that he was usually accompanied by a gorgeous secretary, Miss American Virgin of 1984 and American Mother of the Year nine months later. But that was strictly for show. It was no secret that Micawber's virility—and just about everything else—was channeled toward one goal. Money/power.

Everybody, and this probably included Micawber, had been surprised when his wife got pregnant. Possibly, Micawber was also indignant, even outraged, since he had divorced her a year after his only child was born. The settlement, of course, was immense. On the other hand, Micawber could use all the tax exemptions he could get.

Greatheart wanted to force the financial titan to speak first. But he couldn't control himself.

"What're you doing here?" he said. "Did you pay off the United States Supreme Court so it'd give you permission to execute me? And so save the state some money?"

Micawber halted and removed a huge green cigar from inside his coat. A bodyguard stepped forward, whipped out a knife, and slashed, cutting the tip off the cigar. Silver's eyes widened. If the display of savage precision with a knife was supposed to impress him, it had succeeded.

Another bodyguard flashed a cigarette lighter, snapped it, and held it under the end of the cigar. Micawber sucked and puffed, and presently the room was thick with green, richly odorous fumes. Silver breathed in the smoke with pleasure. He hadn't been able to afford tobacco for a long time.

Micawber removed the cigar and stabbed its glowing end toward Silver.

"There's no need to smirch the great institutions of America with your baseless accusations," he bugled. "They're not all rotten, my boy, not by any means. And no, to be specific, no, I don't have the nine old men in black in my pocket. Just about everybody else, yes, but not the incorruptible justices of the highest bastion of the American system. At least, not so far."

He puffed out some more clouds, all shaped like green dragons.

"I'm here to deal with you!" he barked.

"Deal me *out*, you mean?" Silver said.

"Such cynicism! No, by the Lord Harry, I mean *with*! I don't like doing it, I confess, but I'm a realist. You have me by the short hairs, and you can twist them! But I warn you, any twisting, and I'll see that your nose—not to mention other protuberances—is wrung off! Off, I say! Off!"

Silver wondered if the cigar was injected with a drug. He felt as if the room and all in it, including himself, were unreal. What was going on?

"I, like everybody else, at first assumed you were guilty," Micawber said. "Guilty as Satan himself and twice as deserving of eternal damnation! I never assume anything, my boy, never! Well, hardly ever. In this case, I did! So, I accuse myself of assumption in the first degree. And I plead guilty. I throw myself on the mercy of the court!"

"Me?" Silver said incredulously.

"No, *me*! And I suspend, no, in fact, cancel the sentence. Everybody's entitled to one mistake, well, almost everybody!" he added, looking hard at Silver.

"What's the point of all this?" Silver said. He thought, no wonder Micawber was so successful in his personal dealings. He threw up such a smokescreen and gas attack of verbiage that he confused everybody. By the time he did get to the point, he had his hearers reeling. They'd agree to almost anything to shut him up.

It was also no wonder that Micawber had had such a short-lived marriage and long train of mistresses. By the time he quit talking, any potential passion in him or his *objet d'amour* would have been blown away in the storm of talk. What had happened the night his daughter had been conceived? Had Micawber suffered from laryngitis? Or had Mrs. Micawber stuffed cotton in his mouth?

"The point? Points, you mean. With a big S. A very big one. A point is that I know you're *innocent*!"

Silver could only boggle.

"And I alone know that," Micawber said. "Well, my agents do, too, but they don't count. What I don't know, what I don't say, they don't either. If they know where their bread is baked.

"And be informed and believe, Silver, that the police aren't going to know you're innocent unless you agree to my terms."

"How do you know I'm innocent?" Greatheart said. "I presume you're talking about my alleged participation in the kidnapping of Ms. Regina Lear?"

It was Micawber's turn to boggle. His eyes bugged out and rolled, and he almost quacked around the cigar rolling in his mouth.

"You really *don't* know?" he said finally. "Or are you so pig-headed, so utterly rottenly obstinate, that you can't admit to yourself you're guilty? Or perhaps you are afraid to admit guilt because of reprisals from me?"

"I don't understand you," Silver said. "First, you say I'm innocent. Now you say I'm guilty. Of *what*, whichever the case you think it is?"

Micawber jerked his cigar out, and he shouted, "Damn it, man, don't you really know? Don't you know that *Regina Lear is my daughter*?"

Eleven

There is a time to be clear-headed and certain and unruffled. There is a time to be confused and bewildered and anxiety-ridden.

Today was undoubtedly his day for the latter.

"How . . . how . . . how?"

"I know you're part-Indian!" Micawber shouted. "But this is ridiculous!"

"Yes, but how . . . ?"

Micawber jerked his thumb at Silver and spoke to a bodyguard. "Give that man a belt."

Silver said, "Don't think you can beat me up here. This is a police station; you can't . . ."

He stopped. The guard had pulled a wide flat silvery flask from under his coat. He unscrewed the cap and held it out to Silver.

"Oh!"

The brandy fired up his circulation and warmed his empty stomach. But it didn't help to clear his head. Quite the contrary.

He set the flask on the table and said, "If she is your daughter, that explains something. But not a whole lot. For instance, when we were students at UCLA, I was a senior and she was a freshman . . ."

"I know all that," Micawber trumpeted. "So, she never told you her real name was Jill Micawber? Not a hint that she might be my child? Well, if that's true, then you didn't know what you were doing when you split up with her. You didn't, did you, know that she was pregnant? Or that she was still in love with you?"

"I swear . . ."

"I wouldn't believe you if you swore on a stack of my financial records. But then . . . O.K., my boy. Here's what happened, just in case you're as ignorant as you claim to be. You two had a violent quarrel just before you graduated, right?"

Silver nodded so hard he could almost feel the brandy sloshing around in his skull.

"So you left immediately after the ceremony for Friedrichshafen, West Germany, where you entered the officer's academy for the Acme Zeppelin Company. My company. If I'd known then what had happened between you two, I'd have made certain you were booted out on your rear. But I didn't know.

"Jill had her stupid pride, she got it from her mother, and she said not *one word* to me. She was going to have the baby and bring it up by herself, like too many women in this crazy permissive society. But she knew my agents were watching her every move, so she left college and assumed still another name . . ."

"Why did she enter college under a fake name in the first place?" Silver said.

Micawber's face purpled.

"She didn't want people to know she was my daughter! She said people were either awed—after all, I am the richest man in the world—or else they would be trying to get something out of her. I had to go along with that. In addition, she pointed out that criminals had tried to snatch her for ransom a couple of times before. If she went incognito, that would eliminate that danger. So I gave my permission."

"I think she had another reason, too," Silver said. He regretted saying it at once. The brandy was making him indiscreet. But, what the hell. Why should he spare the old curmudgeon's feelings?

"What do you mean?"

"I mean, why did she pick the pseudonym of Regina Lear?" Silver said. "Didn't that strike you as significant?"

"So it's Irish," Micawber said. "I would've preferred a good old English name, since our family was founded by an Englishman, you know. He emigrated to Australia early in the nineteenth century and became a well-known farmer and magistrate. Very respected, even though he'd been in debtors' prison several times in London. Then one of his great-grandsons emigrated to the States, and . . ."

"Lear isn't Irish," Silver said. "It's really Welsh or ancient British. Don't you know what she was trying to tell you by adopting that name?"

"Maybe I don't want to hear it," Micawber said.

"Probably not. But if you've read Shakespeare's *King Lear* . . ."

"There's no profit in spending time on such trash," Micawber said. "Besides, I never went to college."

"Too bad. Anyway, Regina was a daughter of King Lear. Lear abdicated his throne and gave each of his three daughters a third of the kingdom. Two of them turned out to be real stinkers. They kicked the old man out on his ear. Regina was the only one who stuck by her father. But he thought she was giving him the shaft, and he hated her. He found out too late that she was the only one who really loved him. Now Lear was a crazy old man . . ."

"Stop! That's enough!" Micawber shouted. "Silver, I need you! But if you go too far, try my patience too much, you'll regret it. Bitterly! Bitterly, even ruefully, I say! My daughter doesn't like some of the things I do—though I notice she took the money I made from my so-called evil deeds—but she loves me! And I love her! She's the only person I truly love."

"No use wasting time arguing," Silver said. "Anyway, I did write her from Germany, but I never got an answer. So I figured that it was all over, as far as she was concerned anyway."

Micawber coughed violently for a minute. He wiped his eyes with a garish violet-and-orange striped handkerchief.

"I knew nothing of that. Not for a long while, anyway. You see, my boy, my agents were watching her, reporting her every move to me. They were supposed to keep her, ah, inviolate, as it were. They failed. You two apparently were so secretive that by the time they found out you were having an affair, you'd quarreled. And since you were going to Germany, they figured they'd just drop the matter. The truth was, they were afraid to admit they'd failed. They knew my wrath, a righteous one, would be awful."

"Wait a minute," Silver said incredulously. "You mean your men had orders to make sure she stayed a virgin?"

"Naturally! If my daughter had to get married, if she must leave me, then I wanted her to be a valuable commodity. Undamaged. I had several candidates in mind for her—if she insisted on getting married—young men whose fathers had vast holdings."

"What century were you born in?" Silver said.

"In 1925, if it's any of your business," Micawber said harshly. "You don't understand these things, a father's love, the finances involved, mergings . . . you're a penniless bum, Silver . . . no prospects at all . . ."

"Thanks to you," Greatheart said. "Look. We're wasting invaluable time. Tell me what's going on, and spare me the adjectives, the divagations."

"Divagations? What the hell's that? Very well. Briefly, and to sum it up economically, Jill lost the child. Just how, I don't care to know. I belong to the Right to Life organization. After all, the more babies, the more consumers, the more profit . . ."

"Briefly and to the point," Silver said.

"To be short, I didn't find out about all this until I suspected that my agents' reports didn't ring true. I put other men to check on them, and the whole sad, sordid, heart-wringing story came out. I won't tell you what happened to those who had betrayed their trust. I didn't kill them; after all, this is a civilized age, in some respects, that is, in many others . . ."

"You're off the course by ninety degrees."

"Ah, yes. So, to report only the essentials, I had Jill brought to me. She told me the whole thing, and she wept bitterly, bitterly, my boy, and I don't mind telling you that I too shed those pearls of woe as some poet or other . . ."

This scene had taken place the day before the piracy and wrecking of the AZ-8 occurred. Now, Silver could understand why Micawber had been so irrationally vindictive. And why he had hounded him so. It was unfair, unjust, since Silver had not known anything about it. But to expect fairness and justice from Micawber was to expect the impossible.

His heart ached. He had never really gotten over losing Jill, especially since their quarrel, seen in retrospect, had been about a trivial issue.

Micawber knew that he wasn't involved in the kidnapping. His shadows had kept a close surveillance on Silver. Any contact by him with the gang that abducted Jill would have been detected.

It was only the wildest coincidence that he had applied for work at the *Acme W-W Cleaners* that morning. Or perhaps not so wild. A gang of young terrorists, NADA (not to be confused with the National Automobile Dealers' Association), had found out about Jill's new identity and location. How, nobody knew as yet. Even her father was ignorant of her whereabouts. She had quarreled with him again after their latest reconciliation and slipped away. (Which meant that she must be very resourceful and clever.)

As Lotta Shekels (she had a sense of humor, too), she had rented an apartment on the same floor as Lassie Graves'. NADA (Neo-Anarchist Decorticate Association) had kidnapped an entire crew of *Acme W-W Cleaners* as the first step in their plot. When the crew failed to report, the Acme personnel manager had hired the first to apply for work at the shape-up that morning. Naturally, the NADA members were at the head of the line.

But Silver had been there, too, and he was assigned to the crew. The NADA's hadn't liked it, but there was little they could do. They must have planned on getting rid of Silver later. He, however, on finding, to his delight, that Lassie lived in the building to be cleaned, had sneaked away. He'd been trying to figure a way to get into the security-safe building for two days. Now, Fate or coincidence or sheer dumb luck had opened the door for him.

While he was frisking her apartment for the painting, the terrorists had seized Jill.

"O.K., so you know I'm clean," Silver said. "But why are you here? I know you too well to think you just want to apologize."

"Apologize?" Micawber said. "Why would I want to do that? Everything I've done has been for Jill's sake. Sheer unselfish self-sacrificing paternal love. I've given up hours, days even, I could have devoted to business in order to recover her.

"No, I'm here because I want to fully utilize every means to rescue my daughter. I have a thousand agents out now on her trail, a thousand, my boy. Spare no expense is my motto. Anyway, it's tax-exemptible. Though my men and the FBI and CIA (NADA is connected with foreign groups, you know) and the LA police are scouring the city, they are not enough. I need a man who's thoroughly unscrupulous, crooked to the marrow of his bones, heartless, as greedy and as clever as a fox, villainously unconventional . . ."

"I suppose that's your image of me," Silver said.

"I found out you sneaked into the Acme Security Southwest Phoenix office and reprogrammed the NYC computer," Micawber said. "You got the computer to falsify the data on you. You even arranged it so I had seemed to validate your employment. Highly admirable, my boy, and if I didn't hate you so much, I'd make you a general manager of my security outfits.

"In addition, that is, furthermore, you alone survived the Shootout holocaust. That speaks well of your survival quotient.

"But I'm mainly interested, for my daughter's sake, in your detective talents. You were trained by that old man, Phwombly, I believe he called himself. Though his real name was Ken Tallard, something like that. Anyway, he was tops in his field in the good old days, right up there with Doc Ravage and Dick Bendsome the Punisher and Richard Windworthy the Arachnid. So you have the real McCoy, an education millions couldn't buy.

"But you also have something even better. Motive! If you don't track down my daughter, you've had it, Silver! You won't be able to get a job cleaning out a monkey cage. You'll starve to death. And don't think you can always go on welfare. I got connections; I'll see to it that your records get lost time after time after time. And so on et cetera forever amen."

"You don't have to threaten me," Silver said. "I'm eager to save Jill. After all, she and I . . ."

He shut up. It would only anger her father if he heard how he felt about her.

"What about the charges? Will they be dropped?"

"Of course. If, that is, and it's a colossal subjunctive, if you rescue Jill or find her so that my men can rescue her."

"You no-good . . . !" Silver swallowed the rest of the invective. "In other words, if I fail, I go to the big house for a long long time."

"Till death do you part, if I have my way about it. And I will."

"What about the million-dollar reward you offered?"

"That's open to everybody—except you."

"In other words, my only reward will be that the charges will be dropped."

"Exactly and precisely."

"What about reinstating me as first mate on one of your Zeps?"

"Forget it. I'd rather have a chimpanzee there."

"Could you drop the blackball, at least?"

"I'll think about it."

"Which means no," Silver said. "I'll be doing this for nothing; you'll save a million dollars if I succeed. Well, I won't quibble. Jill's life is at stake, yet you bargain like a used car dealer. You don't love her, Micawber, not really. Or else you hate me more than you love her. Okay, I have no choice. But I will need operating expenses. Five thousand dollars, to begin with."

"No trouble, my boy. If you get Jill back for me, it's on the house. If you don't, you owe me five thousand, which I'll have taken out of your hide if you can't pay it back."

"How could a sweet beautiful girl like Jill have been sired by a soulless double-ugly like you?" Silver said. "Are you sure she's yours?"

The veins on Micawber's forehead swelled like snakes force-fed with cyanotic milk.

"I'm warning you, Silver!"

Greatheart stood up. "Give me the money. While you've been blowing hot air, the trail's been cooling off."

Twelve

Showered, shaved, shed of hunger, and sheveled in new clothes, Silver paced back and forth in his room. Though his quest seemed hopeless, he did not feel so. There was nothing like a full belly and a quart of Duggan's Dew of Kirkintilloch to generate optimism. Even the walls emanating the stale muscatel-saturated sweat of three generations, the peeling plaster, the threadbare carpet, the dead flies in the spider's web across the window, the furtive movements of many-footed antennaed creatures under the scarred bureau, did not now depress him.

The two ravens, Huggin and Muggin, looked happy now. They'd been sad-eyed, reproachful-eyed for a long time. The little food he'd been able to give them had been scrounged out of garbage cans. And sometimes he'd kept part of that back for himself. Now they were stuffed with steak, spaghetti, salad, and garlic bread, topped off by a thimbleful of Drambuie.

Silver had a clue. He'd given it to the authorities along with everything in a complete report. He'd held nothing back. Except one thing. The *significance* of the one clue. At first, he'd not revealed its importance because he had wanted something to bargain with if the charges were not dropped. After talking with—or being talked at by—Micawber, he had determined that he wouldn't part with the item. If he did, then the police or the FBI or the CIA would beat him to NADA and it would be just like Micawber to go back on his promise.

His conscience did hurt him somewhat, since Jill's life was at stake. But he salved it by telling himself that one man could accomplish what a horde could not. If an army rushed around, scaring everybody, making a big noise, it would spook NADA. One man, working stealthily, quickly, cleverly, could find them. And would thus make sure that NADA wouldn't panic and kill Jill.

He spoke to the ravens, who sat side by side on the back of a stained and ripped-open chair. "Sorry, boys, but I can't take you with me. You'd be too conspicuous."

The ravens didn't care. They'd fallen asleep. Muggin even sounded as if he were snoring.

He turned the knob of the door. The phone rang. He swore, hesitated, then decided he'd better answer it. Maybe one of the informants whom he'd paid a handsome advance had something for him. More likely, it was from one of his wino buddies. He'd probably heard the news that Silver was flush, and he wanted to borrow money.

The voice from the phone was so sultry and sexy that it had to be Micawber's personal secretary. It was.

"Mr. Silver? Bon-Bon Heisszeit speaking. Mr. Micawber told me to tell you that he got a note from the kidnappers. They want thirty million dollars for the safe return of his daughter."

Silver whistled and said, "Did it say anything about where the money should be dropped?"

"No. It said another note would be sent later. But they did say that if Mr. Micawber doesn't call off the police and all those government agencies, they might send him one or two of Jill's ears to kind of help him do the right thing."

"He wants to call me off, too?"

"No. He says you're to keep operating. But if you, fu—, uh, mess it up, he'll mess you up. However, he says he has great faith in you."

"Thanks," Silver said. "But he's wasting his breath. Not even Micawber can force the authorities to drop the case now."

"He's talking on the phone to the U.S. Attorney General now. Mr. Micawber always goes right to the top."

"Whatever he does, it's not my concern," Silver said. "I just want to be left alone so I can operate without interference or obstacles of any kind."

"The authorities promised Mr. Micawber they would cooperate fully."

Silver hung up. He turned the knob again, then hesitated once more. There was a lot of noise coming through the window from the street below. He'd better check it out first.

He strode to the window and rubbed away the spiderweb and the dust over the glass. The late afternoon sun shone down on the mean dingy street. Normally, it would have been occupied by a few cars passing, a few winos here and there, some women, residents of the neighborhood tenements, shopping, a few kids playing stick ball, and some drug pushers and their customers. The only loud noise would be from the amplifier over the second-hand record shop across the street. Nobody ever purchased the advertised wares, though furtive individuals slipped in and out now and then. Everybody knew it dispensed drugs in the backroom, including the cop on the beat. But he got his share of the profits, so there was seldom a discouraging word heard from the authorities.

Now the street was jammed with cars, and horns blared and honked loudly. The sidewalks were jammed. Down at the corner, a sewer manhole was open, and two men were putting up a barricade around it. Their city sanitation department truck was double-parked, contributing to the stoppage of traffic. Below him, a car was double-parked, its hood open, while two men poked around the motor with screwdrivers.

On his right, down the street, a big delivery truck was being unloaded. Two men were hauling cases of beer into the tavern opposite the truck.

A streetsweeping machine was trying to back into a parking

space that was obviously too small. The driver gave up while Silver was staring at him. With the machine sticking out into the nearest lane, the driver took a cigarette break.

Passing by the tavern slowly, playing an accordion, a blind man walked slowly. His monkey passed a tin cup hopefully, but vainly, to passersby.

Two winos he'd never seen before sat on the sidewalk, their backs against the record shop front. Each had a brown paper bag and spoke now and then to the bag. Once, one addressed the other man. Silver couldn't read his lips, but his actions made it evident he was asking the other to move along.

On his left hand, a huge diesel semi was stopped halfway around the corner. It had a flat tire.

A woman was pushing a baby carriage back and forth, though why she'd pick out this crowded place for a stroll was a mystery to contemplate.

Just then, a group came around the corner to the right. One man was carrying a large TV camera, and two were carrying electronic equipment. Another carried a folding chair, presumably for the director, a tall red-faced man in a checkered shirt and riding breeches. Behind him pressed a horde, technicians, a script girl, a man with a case that probably held makeup, two men with giant klieg lights, two girls and three men who couldn't be anything but actors, and four cops to handle the crowd for the company.

If they were hoping to make a TV commercial or shoot a scene for a movie, they were out of luck, Silver thought. Nevertheless, they looked as if they were determined to stay.

There was a picket line of six men and six women parading back and forth in front of the one-armed hash joint by the tavern. That was strange, since only two men worked in the place in one twelve-hour shift. And it was a family business, run by a man and his son. Yet all the signs bore: "NON-UNION SHOP."

And here came a Salvation Army band, drum banging, trumpets blowing, marching bravely, only to disperse into the crowd that pressed around and among them. The musicians—if they could be called that—continued to play. But their director disappeared somewhere, presumably knocked over and walked on, and presently three different hymns filtered through the clamor to Silver.

One of the vehicles blocking traffic was a catering truck. Its operator had left it in the middle of the street. He was opening the panels on its sides now, preparing to sell coffee, sandwiches, peanuts, candy bars, and hot dogs to pedestrians or passengers alike.

Hearing a faint buzz, he looked up. There was a helicopter circling back and forth about a hundred feet above the street.

He gripped the window ledge. Yes, believe it or not, here came the Goodyear blimp. Yes, it was turning, intending to circle, no doubt, above the chopper.

And here came a troupe of Hari Krishna chanters around the corner. Shaven-headed youths, dressed in orange robes, adorned with caste marks or whatever they were, ear and nose rings, beating drums, jingling tambourines. And there they went, striking the outer edge of the crowd like a tidal wave dashing into a cliff, breaking up into orange clots.

And here came a troupe of blue-clad harness bulls, on foot since the patrol cars would have been stopped blocks away. Their mouths were open, roaring orders that couldn't be heard above the bedlam, their billies raised threateningly but unheeded by anybody not within striking distance. Evidently some citizen, unaware of the true nature of the mob, had called in the cops to break up the jam, to avert what seemed an inevitable riot.

Greatheart ground his teeth with rage and frustration. Maybe he could get out the back way, though he doubted it, He left the room and went down the hallway, passing three men in coveralls. They glanced furtively at him and then went back to their work, which seemed to be repairing the switchbox at the end of the hall. This controlled the lights on the third floor. Yet, the naked bulbs in the peeling ceiling were blazing brightly.

Though he knew it was useless, he crawled through the window at the hallway's end and onto the fire escape. He looked down. Just as he had thought. There was a score of men in coveralls in the court-yard, all busy carrying out the trash and garbage. In fact, there were so many that they had cleaned up the yard and now were forced to bring the refuse back so they'd have an excuse to be present.

The bedlam of blaring horns from the nearby freeway attracted his attention. He looked through the open part of the U-shaped courtyard and down onto the freeway. The nearest lanes, the southward-going, were filled with stalled cars. Undoubtedly, the freezing of traffic on the street outside had spread around the neighborhood. How far, he could not determine. But the off-ramp was two blocks south of the hotel, and the stopping of cars on it had resulted in halting traffic for miles down the freeway.

Silver snorted with disgust and returned to his room. He called Ms. Heisszeit back (Micawber having given him his telephone number).

"I want to speak to your boss. Right now!"

"I'm sorry, Mr. Silver. Mr. Micawber is still on the line. He's talking to the President now. I mean, the President of the United States."

"Very impressive!" Silver snarled. "Look, you tell him he lied to me. He said he'd called off everybody. I was to have a free hand, and I sure as hell wasn't to be shadowed. You tell him I can't even get out of my hotel, there are so many agents out there!"

Something crashed below, and the hotel shook. Silver said, "Just a minute," and he strode to the window and looked out. He whistled. The pressure of the bodies in the street had been so great that all the street-level doors had suddenly burst in. And the plate-glass windows of the tavern, grocery store, and record shop had shattered, too. The lobby of his hotel must be packed with the people who'd been forced into it.

Yet, the discharge of pressure had not resulted in thinning out the population of the street. A horde had flowed in to fill the vacuum. These must have come from around the corner. Silver couldn't distinguish many of them, but he did make out a Good Humor man, three men in the uniforms of ambulance attendants, a TV news crew holding their equipment above their heads, attempting to keep it from being smashed, a white-robed man carrying a sign: "REPENT! THE END OF THE WORLD IS NEXT WEEK-END!" and a man on a horse. The latter (the man, not the horse) was in the uniform of the Royal Canadian Mounted Police. On seeing him, Silver shook his head. The man must be advertising some movie.

Surely the northern neighbor of the U.S. couldn't have sent down somebody to keep an eye on him.

He returned to the phone. Micawber's voice screeched in his ear. "What in thunderation is going on, Silver? I thought you'd be on your way by now?"

Silver explained as best he could. There was a silence—except for Micawber's heavy breathing. Then the tycoon said, "I'll call the governor and get him to send down the National Guard. But it'll take hours to clean up that mess. There's a helicopter watching you, too, you say? Very well. I'll see to it that it lands on the roof of your hotel and drops you off wherever you want it to. And then, my boy, I'll see to it that heads roll! Roll, I say! You see now why I complain so bitterly about government interference. Private enterprise is the only . . ."

"Get the chopper down here," Silver said, and he hung up.

Thirteen

First, it was necessary to clear the hotel roof of forty or so people. Silver roared at the crowd to get out—at once. They seemed reluctant, some even giving him the finger, until he used the magic name of Micawber. Then, slowly, casting vindictive glances, muttering, they strolled to the exit.

A number of times a fit of coughing interrupted Silver. Four separate crews had been tarring the roof, poisoning the air with the heavy fumes, getting in each other's way. There were at least thirty sunbathers, men and women on folding chairs or blankets. These were complaining about the heat and gases from the tar between racking coughs. When their sandals got stuck in the still soft tar, they bitched to the crews. The "workers" shrugged their shoulders and replied that they were only doing their duty. Some suggested that the complainers file their protests at the appropriate agency—in triplicate, of course. Others suggested that a leap off the roof would make everybody happy.

Finally, the roof was vacant except for Silver and a walkie-talkie someone had forgotten.

The chopper landed. Silver, swearing at the sticky stuff on his shoes, climbed in. "Any place in North Hollywood is all right," he said to the pilot. "But don't you dare to tell anybody where I am. If you do, Bendt Micawber will have you fired and then blackballed. You'll never fly a chopper again."

The helicopter swung toward the northwest. The pilot jerked a thumb behind him. "O.K. But I can't help it if they see where I put you down."

Silver looked behind him. The Goodyear blimp was following them.

"Who's in it?"

"Treasury agents. They rented the blimp a few minutes before my outfit got to the field. My boss was really teed-off."

Silver didn't comment. He figured that the U.S. Treasury was on his tail not because of the kidnapping but due to its interest in the counterfeit money found in his wallet.

A few minutes later, he got out on a vacant lot near a big new shopping mall. The chopper disappeared, but the blimp cruised in a circle above him. Silver walked to the mall and went into a men's clothing store. Ten minutes later, he emerged in the garish neck-ruffed, knee-ruffed garments so popular this year. He was wearing a huge white plumed hat with a floppy wide brim.

Restraining himself from looking upward (the blimp personnel must be scanning the area with high-power binoculars), he hailed a taxi.

"The House of Masterpieces."

"You mean the porno publishing outfit?" the taxi driver said. "Listen, it ain't any of my business, but if you're a writer looking for a job, forget it. They're going out of business, from what I hear. Besides, I heard about their working conditions. Enough to raise the hairs on the back of your neck."

"You're right. It isn't any of your business," Silver said.

He got out at 34½ Wonmissin Street and entered the triangular doorway of House of Masterpieces. The receptionist was a disappointment. He'd anticipated someone who'd reflect the spirit of the establishment. A young busty woman with a low décolletage and exuding an aphrodisiacal perfume. Instead, he found a seventy-year-old woman who looked and dressed like a maiden aunt circa

1940. She, it turned out, was Mrs. Roger Beaver, the wife of the publisher.

"You sure you ain't a bill collector?" she said harshly.

"I'm what my card says," Silver said. "*Wellington Q. Hackman, Non-Fiction Author*. I'm doing a book on the specifically erotic industry. *The Last Bastion of Freedom*."

"The last what?"

"Bastion. I'd like to interview the publisher and the president, if I may."

"They're one and the same," Mrs. Beaver said. "He's also the office boy and the janitor. Things ain't been too good the last coupla years. We're having a hell of a time competing with that computer."

"What computer?"

"Let my husband explain," she said. She punched a button. "He'll be along in a minute."

Silver whiled away the time by looking over the wares displayed on the reception room shelves. Apparently, the company had several lines: Brandiron House, Broad Education Library, Ecksex House, all paperbacks. There was one hardback reprint line: Grossman & Downlap, Inc., however.

Silver picked up one by Lorenzo Dummox, *Lust Hounds of Slaverland*, and leafed through it. He couldn't say much for the prose, but the illustrations were intriguing.

A door opened, and a short, fat, bald man hustled into the room. He was carrying a scrub brush, a can of Vanish, and a harried expression. Mrs. Beaver introduced her husband; Silver told his story; Mr. Beaver was gratified.

"Maybe you can enlighten the public," he said. "After all, we are doing a public service, you know. And we could certainly use the publicity. I don't know, though. By the time your book comes out we'll probably be out of business."

"Why's that?" Silver said, following Beaver through a hall and then stopping before an iron door secured with a huge steel lock. Beaver pulled a huge key out of his pocket and unlocked the door. "You first, Mr. Hackman. I'm going broke on account of I ain't got enough money to keep up with the times. The Fokker D-LXIX Press has cornered the market, you know."

Silver stepped in, saying, "No, I don't know."

The room was as big as a dance hall. A broad aisle ran straight from the door to a platform at the other end. On either side of the aisle were rows of desks, six in each, forty rows in all.

"This was once a hive of industriousness," Beaver said. "But, as you see, we only have a few writers now. We had to let many of them go; some died; some went nuts. As they disappeared, one by one, we sold their typewriters. Actually, that's what kept us going for a long time, selling the typewriters."

There were three rows at the far end occupied by men and several women. They typed away feverishly, pausing only to insert new paper and carbon or to drink coffee. A squat shaven-headed man, wearing only a leather apron, stalked up and down the aisle, shouting at the writers. Now and then his long whip cracked out, coming close but never touching the bare skins of the persons behind the machines.

"Yes, I know, it looks brutal," Beaver said in answer to Silver's raised eyebrows. "But they are a lazy lot, and they are *such* swine. Besides, the faster they work, the closer they are to buying their freedom. It's for their own good."

Silver followed Beaver down the aisle. He noticed that the leg of each writer had attached to it a chain and a leg iron.

"Yes," Beaver said. "They're shackled. It has to be done. Otherwise, they'd just disappear, drop out of sight. And they'd never pay us back for the advances on their salary. They have no regard for the sanctity of contracts, you know."

Silver didn't comment. He knew that publishers of this type of literature paid pitifully little and kept all the reprint and movie rights. He hadn't known about this version of the old coal-mine company store. But he wasn't interested in the economics of the business. He only wanted some information.

Beaver nodded at the platform. "Used to have a man there beating a drum," he said. "Got the idea from the movie, *Ben Hur*. But I had to let him go, couldn't afford him after he joined the musicians' union."

They turned right between the rear row of desks and the platform and entered a door. After passing a large room filled with three-tiered bunk beds, all sporting chains and leg irons and exhaling the effluvia of unwashed bodies and despair, they went into Beaver's office. Its walls were decorated with covers from paperback books. *I Was Frocked!: The True Tale of a Nun. While Moses Was Up the Mountain: Extracted from the Dead Sea Scrolls. The Evening Shape-Up*, by Mrs. Brigham Young. *Galilee Gal*, by Mary Magdalene, translated from the Aramaic. *Shiva Chivaree*, by Rambam Thankoomam. *Voodoo Votary*. And so on.

Beaver filled two glasses with a vile-smelling bourbon and handed one to Silver. "That religious line went over great for a while. But some fanatical cult—Temple of the Prince of Peace and Divine Love, I think it was called—threatened to bomb us if we didn't drop the line. So we did. Too bad. It was a great money-maker."

Silver said, "Too bad." He set the whiskey down without tasting it. "Listen. My name isn't Hackman. I gave you a false I.D. so I could get in here. No, I'm not a cop. I'm a private detective. Listen."

Beaver became less agitated as Silver explained what he was after. He looked at the pencil sketch Silver had made, and he said, "Sure, I remember him. Most porno writers are faceless, the miserable wretches. And their personalities are interchangeable. But this guy, Peter Stamboek, was the best writer in my stable. He was a genius; that is, he made lots of money for me.

"He took *Bomba the Jungle Boy*, it fell into public domain, you know. And he wrote, rewrote, I mean, an entire series based on it. First, he wrote a straight heterosexual, *Bomba and His Aztec Princess Feel the Pyramid Move*."

"Aztec?" Silver said. "Bomba operated in South America, didn't he? The Aztecs were in Mexico."

"Yeah? Well, our readers wouldn't know the difference. Anyway, it took place on Easter Island. All those giant stone heads, you know. You shoulda read the scene where this Aztec medicine man brings a stone head to life, and it goes after the princess with . . . well, never mind.

"Anyway, Pete took that book and rewrote it as *Bomba and the Jungle Boys*. That got rave letters from the gay crowd. Then he rewrote it for the lesbians as *Bomba Meets the Amazons*. The sequel to that was *Bomba and the Passionate Panther*. That really rocked the bestialists.

Then he put out *Bomba and the Shoes of the Inca Princess*. The fetishists went wild over that one. Before he took off, he'd written fifty Bombas, not one a bomb.

"The beauty of it was the speed with which he could rap them out. He'd just change the names of the characters and locations, change the sexes, rewrite some passages here and there to adapt it to the theme, twist some dialog here and there, change the title, and presto! change-o! he had another book.

"In the end he was putting out a book a day, each essentially the original book, you understand, with maybe only a few thousand words changed. Man, I tell you . . ."

"That's interesting but irrelevant to my purpose," Silver said. "You say he took off? You mean he escaped?"

"Yeah, the ungrateful wretch. He slipped his leg iron one night, how I don't know. I won't tell what he did to his typewriter, but it took my wife two days to clean it up. Anyway, I found out he'd gone to work for the Fokker D-LXIX Press. Micawber had just bought it up . . ."

"Micawber!"

"Sure. The Fokker Press is a subsidiary of the Acme Zeppelin Company. Anyway, Pete only worked for it for a short time. He was hired to help program the computer that writes all Fokker's stuff. What happened to him after that, I don't know."

"Thanks," Silver said, thinking that the Fokker Press would be his next step. "I'll say goodbye now."

But Beaver wouldn't let him go. He took four books from the shelf behind him and handed one to Silver.

"These are Fokker books. I got some because I wanted to study them. I wanted to find out what makes them so special. You see, it ain't just quantity that's enabled Fokker to run the rest of us out of business. It's also quality. Every one of their new books sells like wildfire. And they go into many reprints. People that wouldn't be caught dead reading porno are buying them, and the big critics are giving them rave notices. All of a sudden, Fokker porno is popular.

"I don't understand it. I've read some of them, and when I read them I think they're great. Real classics. Not just in my field, you understand. Classics that stand up to Tolstoy and Flaubert and Hemingway. Of course, I ain't never read those guys, but that's what the critics are saying.

"But I just don't understand it. The writing is about what you'd expect from a computer. The spelling and grammar are correct, and you sure don't get that from the human writers in this business. So it must be the excellence of the prose. But when I run the passages over in my mind, they don't sound like nothing special. The same old crap in everybody's books.

"Then I read them again, and I'm enthralled, fascinated, spellbound. It's the greatest stuff I ever read. I'd say it's orgasmic. Only don't tell my wife I said that."

Silver put the book on the desk and said, "I don't have time. I have to get . . ."

He stopped. A figure had formed itself out of the air, a semi-transparent man in late eighteenth-century clothes and a wig. It stood in the corner behind Beaver, who thus couldn't see it. Not that it made any difference. Silver was the only one who ever saw such wraiths.

The man was red-haired, handsome, intelligent-looking, and of aristocratic bearing. He pointed a finger at the book on the desk, nodded, and then faded slowly away.

Silver looked around. The appearance of such figures had always indicated an immediate danger somewhere in the neighborhood for him. The apparitions of Long John Silver, of his grandmother, White Spots, and of Sally Hemings, another remote ancestor, had warned him a number of times that he was in grave peril.

But how could this situation threaten him? Beaver was standing there, blinking at him, apparently wondering what was wrong with him. He'd never seen Silver before. He'd have no reason to attack him. Had somebody who was after him, for some reason or another, entered the building? Was he on his way now to kill him?

Perhaps the fact that this particular figure had materialized meant that this situation was different from past ones.

Though he'd never seen the man in the flesh or as phantom, he recognized him. He was Thomas Jefferson, whose portraits he'd often viewed. Thomas Jefferson (1743-1826), third president of the United States, statesman, planter, inventor, coformulator of the Declaration of Independence. And Silver's ancestor.

The descent came through Sally Hemings, the quadroon half-sister of Jefferson's wife. After Mrs. Jefferson had died, Thomas had taken Sally as his mistress. She had borne octoroons, and their progeny in the succeeding generations had become white or black.

Sally had appeared several times before when Silver needed a warning. But this was the first time for Thomas.

Why this time?

He had pointed at the book. Was this because he was a man of high intellectual attainments, and he would naturally be associated with a book? Perhaps he was not indicating danger. He merely wanted to urge Silver not to ignore the book.

Silver decided he should take his advice.

It wasn't superstition that made him change his mind. He did not believe that the phenomena, the "visitations," were actually the spirits of his ancestors. He had long ago rationalized that they were exteriorizations of his subconscious thoughts. He had a peculiar mechanism down there, in the cerebellum, that acted like radar. It picked up things which his conscious mind missed. It scanned the gestalt, the totality of a situation, and signaled to him by means of the "phantoms."

Maybe he did have some sort of ESP. He didn't know and had no way of finding out. All he could do was to react to his inner workings.

The paperback had a garish cover which showed a nude nubile girl running across a meadow. Behind her, obviously out to horn her, was a huge black bull. In the background was a red barn and a farmhouse.

"*The Secret Life of Rebecca of Sunnybrook Farm*," Beaver said. "It's one of the many 'secret lives' Fokker publishes. They got a whole slew of them. Fokker calls them *euphoric classics*."

He snorted. "A high-class name for a ripoff! But they pay off, man, how they pay off! Let me show you why I want you to look at it."

He took the book back, opened it, and handed it to Silver.

"Feel along the outer edge of the page. Notice a very slight thickening? Every page, and the cover too, has that extra thickness. Why? I asked myself. So I took some copies to a friend of mine, a scientist, and he looked at it under the microscope. He also analyzed it chemically. And do you know what he found?"

Silver shook his head.

"It's a spray-on microminiature circuit! Made out of selenium and other elements!"

"What?" Silver said. Then, "But why?"

"I wish I knew," Beaver said. "I just found out, you know, and I've been racking my brains ever since trying to figure it out. It has to be an expensive process, yet his books are sold as cheap as mine. So there's something sinister about it, something sneaky Micawber has up his sleeve. It's something illegal, too, you can bet on that!"

"I'll tell you what," Silver said slowly. "You keep this to yourself. I don't have time to investigate it now. But when this is over, I'll look into it for you."

"I can't pay anything," Beaver said. "As you can see, I'm going down and under."

"I'll do it for nothing," Silver said. "Only, don't let a word of this out. Micawber's a dangerous man."

Beaver turned pale. "You telling me! That's why I've been so cautious! I only told you because I heard about what you did at Shootout, and I know you're a tough hombre, mucho macho. And you hate Micawber's guts, too. So, if you can find out what's going on, maybe, just maybe, we could get Micawber over a barrel!"

His face had regained its normal liverish color, and he was rubbing his hands. Silver could almost see his eyes spinning, almost hear the click, click, click as they stopped, almost see the three cherries in a row.

"Millions!" Beaver whispered gleefully. "Millions!"

"Or cement overshoes in Davy Jones' locker," Silver said. He looked down at the page and read a line. Wow! Wow! Wow!

Suddenly, the book was torn from his hands, and, wide-eyed, panting, he emerged from his trance.

"Do you know how long you've been reading, turning over one page after another?" Beaver shouted.

"Turning the pages?"

"Yes, turning the pages. You've read a quarter of the book!"

Silver looked at the wall-clock. "Oh, my God! A whole hour!"

"Now you see what I mean?"

"I've been wasting time with that trash!" Silver cried. "And Jill . . . listen, I got to go! Call me a taxi, will you?"

"Sure," Beaver said. "But ain't that something? That book, I mean."

Silver shook his head to clear it, and he said, "Yeah! But I have to be on my way. See you later, Beaver. Remember, keep this just between us."

"Yeah. Between you and me and a glorious future."

Fourteen

"Hey, mister, we're here," the cabbie said.

Silver looked up. "What? What?"

"That must be some book, mister," the driver said. "I could hear you panting through the glass."

Silver got out and handed the grinning cabbie his fare plus tip. "Here. You take the book, too."

The cabbie shook his head. "No, thanks, mister. My wife's hung up on them euphonic classics or whatever they're called. They really charge her up, so I ain't complaining. But they're not for me. I don't read nothing but the racing forms."

Silver slipped the book into his coat pocket and went into the phone booth outside the Fokker D-LXIX Press building. He punched Micawber's number. Two minutes passed while the busy signal beeped, then two more before Micawber answered.

"Yes, Silver, what is it?"

"Heard any more from the kidnappers?"

A string of invectives ripped from the phone. Finally, after a series of snorts and choking sounds—like a bull buffalo drowning in quicksand—Micawber said, "Yes; I heard! They want me to deposit thirty million in a coded account in a bank in Minerva! You know where Minerva is, don't you?"

"I read the papers," Silver said. Minerva was a new republic founded on a small island in the south Indian Ocean. It had no extradition treaty with anyone, and its banks were replacing Switzerland's as an untouchable repository for clandestine funds.

"It's a foolproof scheme!" Micawber snarled. "Or so they think, anyway! I deposit the money and airmail the coded book to Minerva. As soon as their accomplice in Minerva reports that the deal is validated, they'll release Jill! But they don't know me if they expect to get away with that! If they think they'll be safe, lolling around in Minerva on my hard-earned money, they're wrong! Dead wrong! I'll find out who they are, and . . ."

"How long is this transaction going to take?" Silver said.

"About six days. Then they'll release Jill somewhere in this area."

"Let's hope they keep their word," Silver said grimly.

"And how much progress have you made? Where are you?" Micawber bellowed.

Silver hung up. A minute later, he was in the splendidly furnished lobby of the building, presenting his card to the splendidly furnished receptionist.

"Ah, Mr. Tulkinghorn, attorney-at-law? I'll see if Mr. Starling isn't too busy. Ordinarily, the personnel manager would be the one to see, but we don't have one anymore. Mr. Starling takes care of all executive functions since we started using the computer."

Silver waited patiently, eyeing the receptionist, wondering if she was one of the "executive functions" Mr. Starling had under his jurisdiction.

A minute later, a door opened behind her. A sharp sallow-skinned ferrety face appeared. It smiled, exposing crooked teeth. Silver recognized him. Rade Starling had been the producer-director-writer of a once famous TV series: *Weird Clime.* His face, such as it was, had been familiar to millions, since he had introduced each show.

Unfortunately, Starling had contracted to write all the shows himself. Finding himself unable to do this, he had plagiarized at least a score of stories and presented them as his own works. Also unfortunately, ten of those ripped off were *Weird Clime* fans. Righteously outraged, they overwhelmed Starling and Taurus-Magnum Production with suits. Though Hollywood had a long history of tolerating plagiarism, it could not forgive getting caught. Not on such a large scale, anyway.

Starling lost the series and was blackballed in the industry. His fortunes sank lower and lower, hitting bottom when he became manager of a porno firm. But he certainly looked prosperous enough now.

He advanced and shook Silver's hand vigorously in a weak grip. "What can I do for you, Mr. Tulkinghorn?"

Silver explained. Starling frowned. "Well, yes, I remember Pete Stamboek. But he hasn't been in our employ for a long time. We got rid of all our writers when we put in DRECC."

"DRECC?"

"Digital Rewrite Euphoric Classics Computer."

"It's urgent, vital, in fact, that I track down Mr. Stamboek," Silver said. "An uncle, a very wealthy one, died and left him a large sum of money. From what I've learned about Stamboek, he would be in need indeed. You would be performing an act of charity, of benevolence, in fact, if you would allow me to see your records.

"Even if, as you say, he left no forwarding address, his records might contain some clues which would enable me to trace him."

"What would your fee be?" Starling said, smiling lopsidedly.

"There's no need to be cynical, Mr. Starling."

"Sorry," Starling said. "I worked in the movie industry, you know."

"Apology accepted. May I say, Mr. Starling, that I thought your series was the work of a genius."

Starling melted. "Well, thank you. Perhaps there would be nothing wrong in showing you the files. They're supposed to be confidential, but this case is urgent, as you say. Step in, Mr. Tulkinghorn, and I'll see what I can do for you. While we're at it, I'll show you the resident genius of the place. We're quite proud of him, you know."

They entered a vast high-ceilinged room, a contrast of brooding shadows and squares and cones of light. The ceiling was upside-down V-shaped, adding to the cathedral effect. At the far end, illuminated by lamps placed in the floor around its base, towered a cylindrical ball-topped structure. The shaft was bluish-white; the onion-shaped ball, a dark red. About five feet from the floor were two round glassy ports, or CRT displays, flashing with pinpoints of bright lights. Below these "eyes" was a triangular opening, the "mouth."

An attendant, technician, rather, shuffled around the vast computer in bare feet. He was shaven-headed and clad in very loose yellow coveralls.

Silver and Starling advanced in the hush. When they were within a few feet of the machine, Starling halted. He spoke softly. "Behold! DRECC!"

"Very impressive," Silver said, almost whispering. "Tell me. How does this . . . this thing . . . work?"

Starling spoke to the technician. "Bons, initiate the gentleman."

Bons bowed and then opened a panel downward, revealing a control panel. He punched a button, and the lights in the ports changed configuration.

"He's stopping the present cycle," Starling said. "After he's shown you how it operates, exteriorly, of course—we can't display the mystery of its inner workings—he'll reset it, and the suspended cycle will resume."

"You really don't have to go to all that trouble for me," Silver murmured. He was interested, but he did not want to be diverted from his quest.

"No trouble at all."

Bons padded to the nearest wall, pressed a button which was almost invisible in the shadows, and a section of wall slid sideways. He reached in and removed a book, pressed the button, and the wall closed. Starling took the book from Bons and showed it to Silver.

"*Glinda of Oz*, by Frank Baum." He handed it back to the attendant. "Bons, epiphanize it."

Bons stabbed a few buttons, turned a few dials, closed the panel, and dropped the book into the triangular hole. Starling looked at his wrist watch. "Sixty seconds at a maximum."

Forty seconds later, a bell chimed within the opening. A book appeared within the shadowy recess. Starling removed it and handed it to Silver.

The dust jacket was bright with colors, mostly yellow and greens. In the background was a city, emerald-green, walled, towered.

In the foreground was a fat elderly man, his clothing torn, riding a galloping sawhorse. Both had a desperate expression, generated by a desire to escape the desire of the woman in hot pursuit of them. She was tall and beautiful, and auburn-haired, wearing only a crown and a flimsy transparent robe. Her physique reminded Silver of Starling's receptionist. He would have bet money that she had modeled for the illustration.

Silver read aloud: "*The Secret Life of Glinda of Oz, or The Good Witch Goes Bad.* By Peter Clydesdale."

In small letters along the bottom was: A Euphoric Classic, The Fokker D-LXIX Press.

Silver riffled through the pages, noting that the outer edges were thicker than the inner. He was careful not to keep his thumb on any page very long, and he avoided reading any of the text.

"Magnificent, isn't it?" Starling said. "What hath DRECC wrought? Well, to put it in basics, another best seller, another forty million dollar profit."

Silver handed the book back and pointed at the attendant. "If it only takes sixty seconds to rewrite and illustrate and print a book, why did you bother to interrupt the cycle of the previous book?"

"Oh. Well, that cycle takes a little longer. We're running through the entire Tarzan corpus, all twenty-four books at once."

The bell chimed, and Bons, at a gesture from Starling, handed him a book, "Volume 1," Starling said. "The first of an assured triumph. *The Secret Life of Jane, or Getting High in the Tree-House.*"

"Very impressive," Silver said. "But I really would like to see Stamboek's files."

"Of course. It will just . . ."

Starling paused. A loud buzzing was coming from somewhere. Starling said, "Excuse me," and walked to the wall. He opened a panel, revealing an intercom box. He spoke into it for a moment in a voice too low for Silver to hear. Once, Starling looked up at Silver. Then, after lowering the panel, he walked back. "I have an urgent call. But I'll conduct you to the files first."

Silver followed him to the southeast corner and through a deltoid, fur-trimmed doorway. They went through a narrow hall and then turned left. The room was large and half-filled with boxes and cartons. "Books ready to be shipped out," Starling said.

The room was used for more than that, however. On his left Silver saw a metal cube extending from the wall. This was about twelve feet high and apparently led into the computer through the wall. Probably, he thought, it provided access to the circuits in case of malfunction. Its door was closed.

No, he was at least partly wrong. Starling stopped before it, took a key from his pocket, and unlocked it. He turned the knob and swung the door open, saying, "After you, sir."

"Are the files in there?" Silver said.

And then he saw, standing beyond Starling, by the corner of the cube, a thickening of the air, a swirling, a swift clotting. And suddenly, semitransparent, his grandmother was standing there, the long straight white hair, the dark wrinkled face, the checked calico dress falling to the ankles, the blanket over her shoulders, the buckskin boots. She pointed at Starling and then beyond Silver and then drew her finger across her throat.

Silver came out of his paralysis and whirled.

Too late.

The attendant was bringing down the butt end of a huge automatic pistol.

Fifteen

He awoke on his back on a hard metal floor. The top of his head hurt. He would have been surprised if it hadn't. The back of his head was on a soft lap, and tears were falling on his face.

"Jill!" he said.

"Thank God you're all right," she said. "But . . . how . . . why . . . are you here?"

"That's a long story," he said. He turned his head, wincing, and looked around. The cube looked as bleak and bare from the inside as from the outside. It was, however, furnished with a chemical toilet, a water cooler, a washbowl on a metal stand, a roll of paper towels, a roll of toilet paper, and a pile of blankets.

He rolled off her lap, groaning, and got to his feet. Though he knew the door would be locked, he tried it: Yanking on the knob drove pain through his skull.

"Did they frisk me?"

Jill was on her feet and wiping her eyes with a handkerchief. Even with a sorrowful expression and no makeup, she looked beautiful. A pang of longing and regret for all the lost years shot through his heart. Unfortunately, the abrupt rise in blood pressure made his head hurt even more abominably.

"They took your watch, wallet, and pocketknife," she said. "Oh, Greatheart, it's been so long!"

She needed holding, and he didn't mind some himself, so he held her for a while and kissed the top of her head. Jill sobbed out her story, most of which he already knew. She remembered nothing between being put in the panel truck and waking up here. One of the men had jabbed a needle into her arm, and she had become unconscious immediately.

He told her what had happened to him since they'd parted at UCLA. It took a long time, but while he was doing it he looked around. He hadn't been altogether wrong about this place. One wall did hold a panel which could be removed so the troubleshooters could get into the computer. It was secured by six large Phillips-head screws.

Jill said, "Do you really think they'll let me loose after Daddy pays the ransom?"

"I hope so," he said. "But more's going on in this deal than appears on the surface. What, I don't know. But that spray-on circuit on the books has something to do with this. Your father's up to no good, as usual . . ."

"Greatheart!" she said. "You can't mean that he's in on the kidnapping? That doesn't make sense!"

"No, I mean that Starling, a genuine Hollywood rip-off artist if ever there was one, is probably after more than just thirty million dollars. He's shrewd, a real coyote, and he must realize the potential of this, ah, euphoric circuit on the books."

Laughter burst out of a wall, maniacal laughter that would have done credit to the Shadow of the old radio show.

Silver leaped, saying, "What the?" and then he groaned. The sudden violent movement had shot pain through his head. It was comparable to the pain felt by a hemorrhoidac sitting down on a tack.

"You just signed your death warrant, you fool!" Starling's voice said. "Yours and that of Micawber's daughter, too! I can't let you go now. You'd spill the whole thing, and it'd be ruined! Ruined!"

Silver bit down on his tongue in an agony of self-reproach, yelped with the pain, and then swore. Somewhere in this cell was a voice transceiver. He should have checked for bugs before he said a word.

"Yes, you're right, you dumbhead! Old Rade Starling has more up his sleeve than thirty million dollars, though that isn't to be sneezed at! It is, however, just something to prime the pump. I'll use the ransom to make a hundred times thirty million dollars. But making money isn't primarily what I'm after. I want power, power such as few men have ever had, maybe no one ever had before.

"And I'll have it. Once I'm in Minerva, I'll start my campaigns, and I'll win them all. I'll buy up a publishing house in the U.S. first. It won't make any difference what kind of fiction it prints. Its readers will get hooked on its books because the euphoric circuit will ensure it. With the profits from that, I'll buy more publishing outfits. And then local TV stations and newspapers. And then I'll take over the national TV channels and cable TV.

"You see, the circuit strips can be used in radio and TV sets, too. All it takes is a much larger circuit; actual physical contact between the circuit and the subject isn't necessary with a large circuit. Its magnetic field can be extended to a range limited only by the power available.

"And then, ah, then, I'll back my candidates for office on the national, state, and local level. One by one until I've got the whole country in my fist. Why, the circuits can even be sprayed on political pamphlets, you know! And their readers will become hooked on the pamphlets themselves but will associate the euphoria with the candidates praised by the pamphlets."

"He's mad, mad!" Jill whispered.

"Which doesn't mean that he won't succeed," Silver said.

"Eventually, I'll have enough power to ruin Micawber! By the time he finds out what I'm doing, it'll be too late for him! I'll expose his nefarious activities . . ."

"He's talking about *nefarious*," Jill said indignantly. "He's the most nefarious person that ever lived!"

"He'd like to be, yes," Silver said. "But he's just dreaming. So far."

"And then," Starling screamed, "I'll buy up the whole Hollywood industry! And I'll fire those hyenas, fire them, hound them, break them. They'll regret having booted me out, they'll . . ."

Starling raved on and on. Silver whispered to Jill, "That's the whole thing. Revenge on Hollywood. The rest is just gilding or afterthought."

He walked around, turning this way and that, until he had located the source of the voice. Yes, just as he had first thought but had not believed.

The voice was coming from the chemical toilet.

Well, that was appropriate enough.

He closed the lid, and the volume diminished.

"I don't think he can see us," Silver said. "We'll find out quickly enough."

He sat down on the lid and rolled up his left pants leg. Jill said, "What are you doing?"

Silver held his finger to his lips and then disconnected the neural-wire endings and unscrewed his leg. Holding the leg in one hand, he rose on the living leg in a sudden movement which practice had perfected, and he hopped unipedally to the door. Balancing himself, he opened a small section in the mechanical leg. A tiny control panel with switches and pushbuttons nestled in a recess.

He gestured with one hand for Jill to come to him. When she was at his side, he said, "Get behind me and balance me. And when I give the word, shove against me as hard as you can."

He removed the shoe from the plastic foot, and then turned a tiny slot on the bottom of the foot. After maneuvering the foot so that the exposed hole was aligned with the keyhole, he leaned forward, pressing the leg against the door.

"Okay, push hard," he said. "This has a hell of a kick."

He flicked a switch. Immediately, a needle-thin jet of flame roared out of the hole. Smoke rolled out, causing them to cough. Jill was so surprised that she almost jumped back. Silver started to go backward. He cried out, "Push, Jill, push!"

She threw her shoulder against his back and strained. The vibrations from the leg rippled through Silver and shook her. The leg oscillated like an air hammer, but Silver, sweat running from his face and staining his shirt, kept the flame against the hole.

Just as Jill thought that she could hold no longer, could feel herself and Silver being moved backward no matter how they resisted, Silver flicked the switch. The roar and the bright light died away.

Starling screamed, "What the hell is going on in there? What're you doing? Silver, I demand that you tell me!"

Silver ignored him. Jill, looking around him, saw that the lock was melted shut.

"Oh," she said, "I thought you were cutting it out."

"I could have," he said. "But we'd never make it out that way. They'll be here soon enough . . ."

He stopped. Somebody was hammering on the door; somebody else was cursing.

"Go get the acetylene torch!"

"That's what I was afraid of," Silver said. "O.K. Phase Two now. Pray that we have enough time."

Jill helping him, he hobbled to the opposite wall. Opening another section of the leg, he removed a screwdriver handle. Then, a quarter-inch Phillips-head screwdriver shaft.

"What else do you have in there?" Jill said.

"You'd be surprised. Normally, I don't pack so much stuff in it. But, like a Boy Scout, I wanted to be prepared. So I used your father's advance to buy everything I thought I might need."

After screwing the shaft into the handle he went to work on the removal of the panel. That done, he entered the dark cavelike opening. With the aid of a small slender flashlight, extracted from the leg, he found the light switch.

The bright lights revealed a two-and-a-half story structure, a maze of girders, beams, wires, circuit boards, plastic boxes, cables, and pipes. Many of the upright beams had rungs leading up to platforms here and there.

Silver moved the flashlight beam around until it lit on several boxes attached to the wall.

"Ah! I was hoping the schematics would be in here!"

He removed the flat bundles and began unfolding them.

"But Greatheart," Jill said. "What are you going to *do*?"

"We'll see. I took enough courses at UCLA and the Friedrichshafen Academy to qualify for an E.E. The Acme Zeppelins were computerized, you know. I could take the computers apart and put them back together blindfolded, had to in order to pass my final examination in electronics."

"But you don't *know* this computer!"

"Don't have to," he said cheerfully. "I just have to locate a few circuits and then do some reconnecting. I hope, I hope."

He sounded more optimistic than he felt. He needed time to study, more time probably then he would be allowed. And even if he got it, he might find that his plan was unworkable.

Jill left while he traced frantically through the schematics. As he was moving his finger through the lines and symbols of the fourth, she returned.

"They just cut a small hole above the lock!"

"Then it won't take them much time now to cut out the lock," he said. "O.K., I don't like to take the time to show you how to operate my leg. But it might buy us a few more minutes."

Standing on one leg, leaning against the wall, he showed her the controls to the flame-jet. Looking grim but determined, she left with the leg.

Silver went to work swiftly then, having found out all he needed to know. Or so he hoped. It wasn't easy getting up the rungs to the platforms because of his handicap, but he had powerful arms and the agility of youth. He also had a powerful motive, the most powerful: survival.

He had to disconnect that, reconnect this, install that, unplug and replug this, reverse the outputs and the inputs of a certain circuit board. Fortunately, there was no rewiring necessary. All the wires terminated in quick disconnects. If he had had to work with bare live wires or use insulation tape, he would have been out of luck. Besides, he didn't have time for that.

Up and down and on his belly, crawling under the platform or the cable assemblies above him, turning onto his back, opening boxes, identifying circuits by their coded numbers, disconnecting, removing, replacing, rerouting.

He was soaked with sweat despite the internal airconditioning; he was panting with the combined exertions and tension.

Ah, now, at last!

He opened a box, examined it, checked it again to make sure. He reached into his coat pocket and pulled out *The Secret Life of Rebecca of Sunnybrook Farm.* He opened it at page ten—that was the sexiest scene in the book as far as he had read and seemed to have a slightly thicker strip than the others. Almost, on looking at the text, almost, almost, he was caught, seized, gripped and snared. But with a wrench of will, he removed the thumb which he had inadvertently placed on the edge of the page.

He tore the page lengthwise, separating the thickened margin from the printed portion. He put the book down, and then he placed the strip on top of the circuit he had reversed in the box.

Positive to negative at both ends.

He had no means to make sure that the contact of the poles would be firm enough. He would just have to pray that it would be sufficient. Wait a minute! His heart and his brain were going too fast. He could put the book down on top of the strip. Its weight would be enough to press the two circuits together.

Which he did.

Jill called from down below. "Greatheart! I did like you said to. I shot the jet through the hole. I must have burned the guy with the torch. He yelled, and the torch clattered on the floor. When I left, they were still talking outside. I don't think they'll try again for some time."

"That's good," he said. "Wait! I'll be right down."

She helped him down the final rungs. Panting, he said, "They won't be held up long. They're bound to have some plastic explosives around. They'll get that and slap it against the door and blow it in."

"I heard Pete Stamboek's voice," she said. "Starling must have called in the NADA gang."

"Yeah, I expected that. Listen, they're going to think about trying a two-pronged attack, if they haven't already. They'll be removing the front access panel in the computer room. And when the back door blows, they'll come in fore and aft. Unless . . . here. Help me up. No time for dignity or pride or all that crap."

Having gotten onto his foot, he said, "I also hope that they don't turn off the power to the computer. If they do, we're sunk. But then why should they? They don't know what I'm doing."

"Neither do I," Jill said.

He explained. When he was finished, she said, "But that's so fantastic! Do you really think it might work?"

"In theory it should. In practice . . . well, we'll find out soon enough. Just remember, the euphoric circuit is only effective when operating in conjunction with the written or spoken word. At least, I think it is. So don't look! Under no circumstances, look!"

"I won't. But what about those men who'll be breaking in from the rear? They'll follow us out into the front, and if they don't see it either, then they'll be able to do what they want to do. Which'll be killing us."

"We'll hold them for a while. Maybe long enough to let us get away. Help me with the panel."

It only took a few minutes to get the panel through the opening. While Silver leaned against it, Jill screwed the panel against the frame on the inside.

"They can blow that up, too," he said. "But it'll delay them for a minute or two. Oh! Oh!"

He pointed through the walkway leading to the front of the computer. Light had appeared at the end of the walkway. First, a thin bar about two feet above the floor. Then, suddenly, a square of illumination blazed, and the legs of a man appeared.

"They'll have to crawl in," Silver said. "But they'll be reluctant to do so. For all they know, we'll be above them, waiting to spray them with the jet. Come on, come on!"

"Come on what?" Jill said.

"The effect! The effect! Oh, oh!"

"What is it?" Jill cried.

"Don't you feel a slight tingling? A tingling that comes and goes?"

"Yes," Jill said. "What's the matter? Is something wrong?"

"It must be even more powerful than I thought," Silver said. "Maybe I connected it to too many step-up generators."

Jill opened her mouth to say something, but a loud explosion made her jump forward into Silver's arms. He fell backward, unable to support both of them with only one leg. As he tilted, he saw the panel bulge under the pressure of the expanding air in the cell.

For a moment he lay on his back with Jill on top of him. The impact of the back of his head against the cement had reminded him that he was suffering from an intense headache. Jill rolled away, and he sat up.

"They've blown the door," he said unnecessarily. "They'll blow the panel next. Hand me my leg, and I'll put it back on."

While he performed an improvised reconnection of his leg, reconnecting it to his stump, she crouched, staring through the front access. "I can't see anybody now," she said. "What do you think they're doing?"

"Nothing, I hope, except enjoying themselves."

He rose, and they walked together to the access. They got down on all fours, Silver in the lead. He hesitated, since he might get his head shot off when he poked it out. But the pulsating tingling over his entire body, strongest where unclothed, was increasing. Maybe it would work. Just maybe, just . . .

The roar of the plastic explosive against the panel at the other end of the walkway propelled him through the opening and sent him sprawling on his face. Jill cried out, and he turned his head to see if she was hurt. If that panel had been expelled with enough force to hit her, it might have injured her seriously. But he could see nothing except smoke pouring out of the hole.

"Jill!" he shouted. He crawled forward into the smoke, and something rammed into his head. He stopped, half-stunned, groaning. His head was a huge sponge soaking in all the pain in the world.

The smoke cleared. Jill was sitting down, holding her head. "We bumped into . . ."

"Never mind! They'll be coming through! If we can get to the front door, we might make it! Come on! Come on!"

He got to his feet and looked around quickly. What he saw would have made him smile triumphantly—under less urgent circumstances. Starling, his receptionist, and three men and a woman he recognized as NADAs were standing there, immobile, their gazes fixed on the upper part of the display panel.

So far, so good. But the waves of tinglings were becoming even stronger, even faster. His fear that the second explosion would shake the computer enough to cause a malfunction had been groundless. But he might have hooked up too many electromagnetic amplifiers in a series. The computer might become overloaded and burn up or throw out a switch. And if that happened in the next thirty seconds . . .

A shaven head protruded from the access hole. Silver leaned over, flicked the leg control, straightened up, and, balancing on his right leg, stuck the left leg three inches in front of the man's face. The three-second delay in activation of the flame-jet mechanism was just enough for him to maneuver the leg. It was not enough for the startled Bons to get out of the hole and onto his feet. The pencil-thin flame spat out, missing Bons' nose by a quarter-inch because Silver had turned the leg just enough to do so. But the heat singed the nose. He screamed and scuttled backwards into the hole.

Silver turned the jet off. It wasn't likely that those inside the computer would venture forth for some time. They would not want to be exposed to third (or even fourth) degree burns. However, there was nothing to stop them from going back down the hallway and then through the doorway in the southeast corner.

"Let's go," he said. He grabbed her hand and pulled her after him. He expected at any moment to hear shouts or shots behind him. The people inside the computer could race around quickly enough to make it to the doorway in the southeast corner if they reacted swiftly.

He stopped and turned the knob of the door.

It was locked.

"Oh, no!" Jill said.

"Starling!" Silver said. "Starling must have the key!"

"Stay here!" he shouted. "And don't look! Keep your eyes straight ahead!"

He whirled, putting his right hand at a slant over his right eye to block out the display panel. He ran back, looking at the southeast corner door as he did so, hoping he would not see anybody come through it, wondering what he could do if he did. The answer: not much.

He skidded to a halt. Starling was standing rigid, vibrating, his eyes fixed on the computer. He had an ecstatic expression which made his face even uglier. Most people with such an expression would look beautiful, transfigured. Not Starling. His features were not built to carry beauty. Ugly is as ugly does.

"Caught in your own trap, heh, Starling?" Silver snarled. Then, for some reason feeling ashamed of himself, he dug into the pockets of the transfixed man. The pants pockets were empty. Silver swore, and the sweat ran down into his eyes and stung them. The shirt pocket was empty, too. What if Starling had given the key to his receptionist? What if he'd given it to one of the people in the back? What if he'd swallowed it?

Ridiculous, Silver told himself. You're getting panicky now.

He forced himself to pause, to simmer down. Where could it be?

Starling's eyes did not waver. They remained glued upon the display panel, upon the two "ports," the CRTs. The CRTs which bore two words. One was a five-letter word; one, a four-letter word. When Silver had programmed the display circuits, he had picked two basic words to be shown on the CRTs. Two words which would hold a multitude of meanings, which would grab right down to the roots, to the bottom, which would reverberate through each person who saw them with their personal interpretations, denotations, connotations, and annotations. Acting in conjunction with the vampirish positive feedback from the euphoric circuit—or negative, if you took that viewpoint—the words had clenched deep into each of the beholders.

"Ahha!" Silver cried.

He'd spied a section of the chain around Starling's neck. Fearful that jerking it off might bring Starling out of his reverie, he lifted it carefully up and around the man's head.

He then sped toward the door, but halfway across the room broke his stride.

Jill was standing with her face upturned, staring at the display.

Like Lot's wife, she had disobeyed the vital imperative. She had turned to look, and now, though no pillar of salt, she was as immobile as one.

He resumed running, at the same time swearing at Jill and expecting to hear the bellow of a pistol behind him. If he would hear it, that is. You never heard the shot from the gun that sent the bullet that killed you.

He inserted the key and turned it, pushed the door, turned to grab Jill's hand, and hauled her through into the hallway. Jill suddenly tore her hand from his and started to run back. Yelling at her to stop, he whirled and ran after her. She almost made it, but he dove and snagged her legs and brought her down with a crash.

She sat up after he'd released her, shook her head, and said, "Listen, Greatheart! You have no right . ! ."

He rose, reached down to get her hand and straightened up. Somebody had shouted, and sure enough, here came the first of the gang through the southeast doorway.

He leaped forward, grabbed the knob, and slammed the door. He leaned down to lock the door, which was a good thing to have done. Two holes suddenly appeared a few inches above his head.

Still bending down, he returned to Jill, yanked her upright, yelled, "Keep down!" and pulled her along. Not until they were around the corner of the lobby did he stop.

Jill said, "Greatheart! I was having the most wonderful . . ."

"Later! Later!" he panted. "We got to get out now! I'll bet Starling planted explosives in the computer. He'd want to blow it up if the authorities, or your father, got too close. He'd blow it up anyway so he wouldn't leave any evidence for the police when he took off for Minerva! If that computer starts burning . . . come on!"

As they went through the door to the outside, he heard shots faintly. One of them was shooting the lock off the door. Which meant that if he and Jill didn't put a lot of distance between them and the building—and also find a hiding place—they'd be shot down. In a very short time.

Still pulling the protesting Jill, he ran out into the streets. Horns blared; tires screamed; drivers cursed at them.

And then, halfway across the street, the world seemed to go up and out.

Sixteen

They were limping down the sidewalk, breasting the tide of people running toward the pillar of smoke. Patrol cars, sirens whooping, lights flashing red, and fire engines, painted red, manned by red-faced firefighters, raced by.

"What do we do now?" Jill said.

"We'll step into that cocktail lounge there," Silver said. "We'll wash up and then we'll sit down and have some booze and some salted peanuts and popcorn. Restore our bodies and souls. And we'll talk about our future."

"How about getting married?" Jill said.

"I thought you'd never ask," Silver said. "Let's do it right after we get things talked out. Although I'll admit I don't feel up to a honeymoon."

"Daddy isn't going to like it," she said. "Not that I care what he thinks. Not at this moment, anyway."

"That old buzzard is in for a shock," Silver said. He chuckled. "I got enough to send him up for life, so I think he'll cooperate all the way. It may kill him—which isn't a bad idea now I think on it—but he can't do a thing except say yes. Yes, yes, yes. I got him where it hurts. It may not be honest, but I'm going to blackmail him. Not for money, you understand. I just want him to give me my rightful job back. First mate on a Zeppelin. With back pay, of course, for all the time I was off.

"And then . . ."

Jill sighed and said, "I hope so. But Daddy's such a rotten person, and he has such power. What can one man do against him?"

Silver squeezed Jill's hand. "Against one man and one woman, you mean? And that woman is his daughter."

Greatheart Silver in the First Command
Or
Inglories Galore

Seventeen

Whom the gods would destroy, they first make sappy.

A more jubilant man than Greatheart Silver on that fine evening probably did not exist. He was captain of the Acme Zeppelin Company Airship AZ-49. It was his first command, won after a long, hard, dirty battle against forces that seemed unbeatable.

Also won, and on board, was his bride, Jill Amber Micawber. Though the captaincy had been squeezed out of her father through blackmail, Greatheart didn't feel guilty. He had overcome the biggest rapscallion and curmudgeon in the American business world. Old Micawber had been defeated on every front, including financial and personal.

Other men, faced with such failures, would have had heart attacks. His father-in-law had come down with a case of piles.

How symbolically appropriate, Greatheart thought, smiling to himself.

Silver looked out of the wide, curving windscreen of the navigating bridge, which was just below the radome bubble in the nose of the dirigible. Seven thousand feet below was the night-blanketed South Pacific Ocean. Above were stars undimmed by clouds.

God was in His Heaven, Silver was top dog of the AZ-49, and all was well with the world.

The zeppelin was making 100 miles per hour on a south-west course. Its nose was turned just enough to the northwest to counter a 10-mph wind. Two hundred miles to the northwest, over the Marquesas Islands, a typhoon was roaring at 110 mph, heading toward the airship. But the AZ-49 would have slipped by its main force by the time it arrived in this area. Nevertheless, there would be peripheral winds to battle against for an hour or so before a calm region was reached.

Greatheart had ambitions to be captain of one of the nuclear-powered air leviathans of the Acme fleet. However, there were no openings. In any event, it was company policy that the chief officer have at least five years' experience in freighters before assuming command of the superclass zeppelins. Not even Micawber could override this. Nor would Silver have wanted to be appointed through nepotism.

He was happy enough. The AZ-49 was a fine dirigible, primarily a freighter, but with accommodations for over thirty-five passengers. It bored through the skies now, a monster of conventional cigar-shape, 1345 feet or more than a quarter-mile long, with a midsection diameter of 224.16 feet. Its giant gas cells held 40,000,000 cubic feet of noninflammable helium. Ten diesel engines could, in still air, drive it at 125 mph. Two were in gondolas, one under the nose, one under the tail. The others were in the middle section, inside the hull, their power transmitted through gears in exterior housings. Their variable-pitch propellers could be swiveled through 180 degrees to assist in hovering or upward or downward flight.

The twin cargo holds in the midsection could each accommodate five stacked modules, each enclosing containers of cargo up to 50 tons.

This trip, the modules enclosed three containers with peculiar contents: liquid methane. They had been loaded with little advance warning at Caracas, Venezuela. The expected cargo had been withheld. An emergency had demanded that the methane be taken posthaste—*hang the expense*—to Minerva. This independent island-nation of the south Indian Ocean needed it as soon as possible.

On top of one stack was another unusual item. This was an irradiated plastic container in which, under the label "HEAVY METALS," was a quarter-ton of platinum and iridium. Silver did not know why the tiny state needed such a large quantity of these, but it was not his place to ask questions. However, he alone had been told the true contents of the container. He understood why this was necessary. The metals must be worth at least $90 million.

Among the passengers, the most distinguished was Dr. Pierre de Rioux, a very wealthy industrialist who could be France's next premier.

With him were his blonde secretary and two tough-looking bodyguards. Though it was normally forbidden to bring arms abroad, the guards carried automatic pistols and knives. The Acme executive office in New York had authorized this. De Rioux was traveling incognito, another secret which Silver was not to transmit even to his wife.

The rest of the passengers consisted of eleven Americans, nine Frenchmen, and ten South American businessmen and their mistresses. None, as far as he knew, were going to Minerva to apply for naturalization papers. You couldn't get citizenship there unless you owned more than $6 million.

Silver made a final check of all stations. Now he was free to go to Jill's cabin, allotted her as the chief steward-person. After spending some time with her, he would go to the captain's quarters, a cabin just above the control rooms. According to regulations, the captain must sleep there alone, even if he were married. Old Micawber had some strange ideas, but he was one who could enforce them.

Before leaving, he checked the navigational bridge. Third Mate Siskatoo, an Alaskan Indian, was standing his watch. The pilot was at the control panel, though the controls were on automatic. The radar man was intent on his scopes. Sparks, sitting in a corner, was busy monitoring his communications set.

"I'll turn in now," Greatheart said to Siskatoo.

"Have a good sleep, Captain." The Indian's dark face split into an ivory grin. Silver had once remarked that the marriage was six months old, but the honeymoon was still going on.

"Watch out for blonde line-squalls," Siskatoo added.

Silver mock-winced. A passenger, Mrs. Katherine Hooward, a tall, willowy, busty, blonde about thirty-five, had given him some trouble. If he hadn't married, he wouldn't have called it trouble. (However, a company regulation did limit the zeppelin personnel in the degree of social intercourse permitted with passengers.)

Jill had commented, laughingly, on Mrs. Hooward's too-obvious passion for him. Mr. Hooward, though he had said nothing, was very cold to Silver. Greatheart found the situation embarrassing.

Silver said goodnight-all and started for the navigation room when Sparks said, "Just a moment, sir. A message from the head office. It says that the navigational satellite is malfunctioning. There's no telling how long it will be down."

Silver looked at the screen in front of Sparks. The message was in large white letters with some alpha-numerical codes in the margin.

"That means we'll have to switch the navigation to the computer," he said to Siskatoo, who already knew it. It also meant that if, by some unlikely chance the zeppelin went down and couldn't transmit messages, its locations would be unknown. Other satellites could pick it up, but only if they were told to do so.

"We can make it on our own. No sweat," he said. "Siskatoo, you'll take care of the computer feed-in."

He left the bridge and went through the navigational and smoking rooms. Beyond was the main passageway, which ran along the main keel from nose to stern. The only one visible was Albert Agocelli, a steward. He was carrying a covered tray, probably a snack for the bridge crew.

Forty yards away, the cabins began. The passengers, officers, and stewards were quartered there. De Rioux, or Corday, as he was listed, was in the first cabin on the left. His two bodyguards slept with him. In the next cabin was his secretary. Jill's small cabin came next and then two cabins down was a large room where the Hoowards were now sleeping. At least, he hoped they would be. At this late hour, Mrs. Hooward wouldn't be waiting to grab him and exercise her not inconsiderable charms upon him.

Whistling softly, he strode down along the passageway, which curved downward gently at this point. His bionic left leg moved slowly. Some of the women he'd known, in the biblical sense, had been disconcerted by the hard, shiny artificial member, but Jill had not been upset in the least. She really loved him. Idly, he wondered how Mrs. Hooward would react if she were confronted with it. Well, he'd never know, not if he could help it.

Silver was somewhat vain, and he could not help thinking what a fine figure of a man he made. His uniform was a tight but crinkly silver-gray plastic. His black knee-length boots were shiny. The only thing he didn't like about his dress was the black silver-banded plug hat. That was Micawber's idea—the silly old ass.

However, his physical attributes more than made up for the hat. He was six feet, six inches high, weighing 245 pounds, broad-shouldered, slim-waisted, and long-legged. His face was, he might as well admit it, handsome, though his nose was perhaps a little too long and curved. The long, shoulder-length, wavy hair, once yellow but now, at the age of thirty-three, a dark brown, and his long moustache made him resemble the late but not necessarily lamented General Custer.

No wonder that Mrs. Hooward craved him.

He forgot about her when he reminded himself to cover the cage containing his two pet ravens. These were in Jill's cabin, since regulations forbade pets in the captain's quarters. Last night, he had forgotten to throw the cover over the cage. He'd been forced to get out of bed when they had made some raucous and deflating remarks. Jill had howled with laughter. Of course, the ravens weren't capable of originating such bawdy language on their own. Jill had coached them.

Recently, he had spent some time with Jill in training the two big birds to attack people if given a codeword. So many dangerous situations occurred to both himself and Jill that he thought this was a good idea. You never knew when they could come in handy. But he hoped that it wouldn't be necessary.

Agocelli passed him. "Good evening, sir."

Silver said, "Isn't it, though!"

At that moment, he saw a figure emerge from the dim light of the passageway. It was about a hundred feet away, and it seemed to have formed from the air, like ectoplasm shaping itself into a ghostly figure. This time, it was Crazy Horse, a tall, good-looking, but ferocious-faced warrior. He held a lance in his hand and he shook it at Silver.

A snake hissed behind him.

He broke out of the cocoon of astonishment. Whirling, Silver lifted up a hand to ward off whatever attacker was behind him. If it really was a snake—*but how could a snake be aboard?*—it would break its fangs if it bit the bionic leg . . .

Suddenly a biting odor filled his nostrils.

Silver's senses flew away like fireflies escaping a spray of bug-killer.

Eighteen

Greatheart awoke with a scream in his ears and confusion and a pain in his head.

He sat up, groaning, as the pain burst and caught fire, like the *Hindenburg* exploding. He was sitting naked in a strange bed in a strange room. Not so strange now that he looked around. It looked much like his cabin except that the photographs of himself in the graduating class at Friedrichschafen and of Jill and himself just after their marriage were missing.

That was not really so, he told himself. What business did an unclothed Mrs. Hooward have in his room? Why was she standing at the foot of the bed screaming? What was Mr. Hooward doing? He was clothed; he was, in fact, dressed to kill. His right hand held a big cane above his head. It seemed to Silver's whirling senses that Mr. Hooward intended to hit him over the head with it.

Ah, he was right. Hooward's thin face was as red as a face could get without exploding its blood vessels. His brown eyes, usually so little and heavy-lidded, were as wide as the gape of a feeding baby vulture. Red veins in his eyeballs seemed to squirm like snakes. His thin lips were like the edges of a bloody knife.

Mr. Hooward was going to break his skull.

Mrs. Hooward stopped screaming, and cried, "Jeffrey! Don't do it! You'll go to jail for life!"

Mr. Hooward stopped. The only sound now was his breathing.

"You shut up!" Mr. Hooward yelled. "I'll give you the same thing in a minute! You put knockout drops in my drink! My own wife!"

Greatheart, croaking like one of his ravens, said, "Take it easy, fellows. I don't know what's going on, but I'm sure there's a reasonable explanation."

There had to be one, but he doubted that he could come up with it.

"Yes, and I know what it is!" Mr. Hooward shouted.

Greatheart rolled swiftly away from the bed and bumped against the bulkhead. No escape that way.

Mr. Hooward yelled, "Die, you filthy animal!"

Silver lunged upward and caught Hooward's wrist in his hand. Hooward struggled, then went limp as somebody banged on the door. Muffled voices sounded.

"You'll pay for this, you sneaking bastard!" Hooward said. Silver released the wrist. Hooward whirled, ran to the door, unlocked it, and snatched it open.

"Come on in, everybody! Take a good look! What do you think of that?"

Dramatically, he turned and pointed a long thin finger at his wife and Silver. Scorn had replaced anger.

Silver groaned and pulled the sheet up over his waist. First came the second mate, James Flaherty. After him—Lord preserve Greatheart Silver—Jill! She pushed forward toward her husband, who cowered in geometric progression according to the inverse cube of her proximity to him. Behind Jill were several crewmen. Then Monsieur Pierre de Rioux, the great French statesman and financier, his secretary, and his two bodyguards. Urging them on in were four of the passengers from Brittany, two Americans, another stewardess, six men who were usually found playing poker in the smoking room, and three cigar-smoking men who only came out of their cabins for meals. Half of the crowd was in pajamas.

"No smoking!" Silver cried. Had that thin, ragged voice come from him?

By then others had jammed themselves in. Jill was propelled forward until her knees were pressed against the edge of the bed.

He did not want to look at her face, but he had to. Silver wondered if he looked as stricken as she did.

"It isn't what you think, Jill."

Mr. Hooward was bellowing then. He'd been forced by the crowd into a corner but had battled his way to the bathroom. Now his head stuck out of its entrance, and he yelled, "Let me at that creep! I'll kill him!"

More people squeezed in. Mr. Hooward was forced out of sight, shoved into the toilet. His voice, calling for vengeance, threatening to tear Silver apart, sounded like a banshee's. It mingled with the gurgling roar of an advertently tripped flush lever.

Mrs. Hooward started shouting, "My clothes! My clothes! Where are my clothes?"

Silver wondered where his own clothes were. Probably on the floor along with hers.

Giving up the futile request, Mrs. Hooward crawled into his bed. "What are you doing?" Greatheart said, his voice ascending toward a screech.

"I won't be naked in front of all these people," she said. She pulled the sheet over her, leaving Silver exposed. He yanked it back savagely.

"It's a little late for that," Jill said.

More people had shoehorned themselves in. Jill was pushed onto the bed. She stood up and bumped her head on the overhead.

"For God's sake!" Silver yelled. "Flaherty! Get these people out of here!"

Flaherty managed to hear him above the babbling and bellowing. Though a short man, he was thick-necked and deep-chested. His Irish brogue rose above the clamor, like the roar of the Bull of O'Bashan. "Ivrybody out a here ixcept the guilty parties, the intimately concarned, and officers of the ship!"

"What do you mean, guilty parties?" Silver shouted.

He looked up at Jill. She seemed to be thinking about a choice. Either she was going to kick him or she was going to weep. Her dilemma was solved by doing both.

Silver said, "Ouch!" and then felt tears falling on his stomach. Though he was absolutely innocent—unless a few fantasies concerning Mrs. Hooward were counted—he still felt guilt. Shame, too. They pulsed through him like alternating currents.

"Damn it, this is a frameup, Jill!"

"I know whose frame you were up!"

"Please, Jill. It *is* a frameup . . . and guess who's behind it all?"

She stopped crying, and her angry expression softened a little. "You mean my father?"

"Who else?"

"You can't blame everything on him."

"Please let me explain."

"I intend to! It had better be good. *Better than* good."

Silver groaned. "I don't *know* what happened!"

"Don't *tell* me you *blacked out* and woke up in here!"

He groaned again.

"We just got caught, that's all," Mrs. Hooward said.

"Don't listen to her!" Silver cried. "She must be in on it!"

"I don't know how she could be an innocent bystander," Jill said coldly, but her voice trembled.

"I am sorry, so sorry," Mrs. Hooward said. "I was just mad about your husband! It was one of those things. He couldn't help himself either. Everything would've been all right, no one the wiser or hurt, either, if only my husband hadn't woken up sooner than he should have. I should've put another drop in his drink."

"You're pretty cool about this, sister," Jill said.

Silver's heart rallied. Maybe Jill might believe him. He was glad he'd resisted the impulse to sock Mrs. Hooward after her last remark. She might say too much, and if she did, she'd be caught in a lie. Jill was upset, but she would be wondering if perhaps her father hadn't arranged this setup. True, Jill had told her father that she'd never see him again if he tried any more shenanigans. Old Micawber had sworn on a stack of Dun and Bradstreets that he would never interfere again.

But conniving, cheating, and double-crossing were among his major genetic features. He had to have been born with them. Otherwise, how account for his head start in crookery? At the age of twelve he'd stripped his own father of the chairmanship of Acme Industries, though through adult collaborators, of course.

"We were swept off our feet," Mrs. Hooward said. "Carried off by a tidal wave of passionate vibrations."

"Shut up or I'll kick you, too," Jill said. "Much harder."

By then Flaherty had managed to bulldoze most of the crowd out. There was a brief interruption when one of the women passengers shrieked out that the man behind her had pinched her fanny. The woman's husband scuffled with the alleged molester until Flaherty and a crewman threw them out. All three complained about the violent treatment and threatened to sue Acme.

One more problem, thought Silver. But it was minor compared to the other.

The first mate, Reynold White, entered, yawning. His black face sagged at the spectacle, and his brown eyes widened. Then he assumed his official expression, inscrutability.

Perhaps he was having some trouble trying to keep from laughing. Silver glanced at him while, wrapped in the sheet and carrying his clothes retrieved from the deck, he headed for the toilet. White's stony face seemed to be breaking up. Mrs. Hooward diverted him. She was protesting at being left uncovered.

"You're no gentleman, you swine!" she shouted after Silver.

"You're no lady," he said, and closed the door. Within two minutes he emerged, fully dressed except for one sock, which he had been unable to find. His artificial leg was unshielded beneath the boot. The other sock had gone on his living leg, but since his artificial leg was equipped with delicate sensors, he felt its contact with the interior of the boots. Well, he didn't have to worry about developing a blister.

Mrs. Hooward was just finishing dressing. Judging from the expressions of the men, the process had been stimulating. Whatever her character, she was lavishly endowed.

The stateroom door had been closed. The occupants included the first and second mates, the Hoowards, and the Silvers. White was telling the Hoowards to put out their cigarettes.

"I'm too nervous not to smoke," Mrs. Hooward said. "Besides, that's a silly rule. Helium can't burn. This isn't the *Hindenburg*, you know."

"It's the rule, anyway, ma'am," White said.

"And what if we don't?" Mr. Hooward said.

"I'll take all your tobacco away from you and forbid you to go to the smoking room," White said.

"Who's the commanding officer here, anyway?" Mr. Hooward said. "Isn't Silver the one who gives the orders?"

There was a silence. White looked at Silver, who knew what he was thinking. Regulations covered just such a situation as this. Silver's status depended now on what the Hoowards said.

White cleared his throat. "We-e-e-ll, I don't know what happened. Maybe you'd better explain. Captain, do you want to speak up first?"

Mr. Hooward savagely threw his cigarette on the deck, where it continued burning. "To hell with it! I'll tell you what happened! My wife, my future ex-wife, I should say, put a Mickey Finn in my drink. She did that so I'd pass out and then your captain—some captain!—sneaked in. I woke up quicker than she thought and caught them in bed."

White looked at Silver. "Is that true, Captain?"

Greatheart looked at Jill. She was leaning forward in a chair. Her face was set and pale, she was trembling, and her gaze was beamed in on his face.

"Partly true," he said. "I don't know whether or not Mrs. Hooward put knockout drops in her husband's booze."

Jill spoke in a shaky voice. "What booze? I don't see any empty glasses."

The others looked around. Mrs. Hooward looked stunned. Then she said, quickly, "I washed them out and put them away."

"You're not the type," Jill said flatly. "You'd leave them for the stewardess to pick up."

"Prove it," Mrs. Hooward said.

"We'll search the cabin and see if you even have any liquor," Greatheart said. He felt better, and Jill looked as if she had been relieved of some doubt.

Mr. Hooward spoke up. "There wasn't any booze. I don't drink because I'm diabetic. Katharine seldom drinks; she prefers pot. I drank a can of sugarless root beer. I don't see it. What'd you do with it, Katharine?"

"Put it in the wastebasket. Look for yourself."

Flaherty reached into the container and drew out an aluminum can. He held it up so that everybody could see the label.

"Slim's Root Beer," Flaherty read out loud. "Sugarless. An Acme Canning Company Product."

"My father owns that, too," Jill said.

She looked at the Hoowards. "I wonder if he owns you two, too?"

"I'll sue for defamation of character and libel!" Mr. Hooward shouted.

"That's enough of that!" White snapped. He turned to Silver. "You were saying . . ."

"The only other statement of Hooward's that is even partly true is that I was in bed. But I don't know how I got there."

He paused and then described exactly what had happened to him. A silence pregnant with disbelief followed.

Greatheart said, "White, call in Agocelli. Flaherty, you get two crewmen and frisk Agocelli before you bring him here. Put a guard over his quarters. Make sure no one leaves it without being searched. Put two more crewmen on a search of his bunk and effects."

"Yes, sir," White said. "What are we looking for?"

"I was coming to that. Based on the hissing sound I heard and the burning odor I smelled just before I passed out, and the headache I woke up with, you'll be looking for a small spray-can. I must've been rendered unconscious by some kind of gas."

Mrs. Hooward said, "That's ridiculous! You're lying to save your own skin!"

White stepped close to Silver and spoke softly. "If Agocelli is involved, sir, he wouldn't be stupid enough to hide the can where it could be found easily. He'd get rid of it."

"I know. But he may not have had a chance to hide it yet. And if it isn't found on him or in his quarters, then it may be somewhere inside the ship. You'll ransack the entire ship if you have to."

From the mate's expression, he knew that would take the entire crew a very long time.

Greatheart said, "You'll look in the garbage disposals, too, of course. And check if any of them have been used recently. The computer will register if any hatch opening to the exterior of the hull has been used."

White, still speaking in a low voice said, "You know that if the captain is accused of a crime by a passenger, he's to be relieved of command until he's proven his innocence. That's a company regulation, sir."

"I heard that!" Mr. Hooward shouted. "I demand that he be relieved of duty according to regulation!"

White shrugged. He said, "I'm sorry, sir. I had meant to give you a break. Maybe . . ."

"Then you should've spoken to me in the passageway," Greatheart said. "Okay. I won't burden you with any trouble from me. I relieve myself. As of this moment, you're acting captain."

"Thank you, sir. Your suggestions will still be carried out."

Jill said, "Could I see you in my cabin for a moment, Greatheart?"

"I'll be along after Agocelli has been questioned."

"I have some questions of my own. For you," she said, and she walked out. Mr. Hooward snickered.

Flaherty left. White used the cabin telephone to inform Third Mate Siskatoo of the situation. Then he gave orders to rouse the entire crew for the search.

Silver waited until White had hung up the phone. He said, "There's the possibility that Agocelli could have slipped the can to a passenger."

"They'd raise a big stink. Micawber would have your head, not to mention other parts. Look, Captain, your suggestion, if you'll pardon me, sounds a little paranoid. I can see how the Hoowards could be in the plot—and it's possible they could bring a third person into the plot. But surely not a fourth!

"We'll look for this alleged can, but we won't disturb the other passengers any more than we have to."

A knock sounded at the door. White opened it and admitted Flaherty, a crewman, and Agocelli.

"I'll sue the company!" Agocelli cried. "I'll sue you, Silver! And I'll register a complaint with the union!"

"That's up to you," White said. "Flaherty, did you find anything?"

"Nothing except Agocelli. He was in the galley eating a sandwich."

White looked hard at the steward, a little man with a weasel face, a thin body, a big belly, and skinny arms and legs.

"Agocelli, I have some questions, and I want the truth."

He paused.

At that moment, men yelled outside in the passageway. Explosions followed. White and Silver raced to the door. The first mate got there first and opened the door. Silver pressed his big body against White's back to urge him out so he could get a look. Something whined; something else went thud. White gave a small cry and fell face down upon the passageway deck.

Nineteen

While pistols and automatic rifles filled the passageway with hellish noise and the Hoowards screamed, two men forced their way into the cabin. Silver backed up with his hands above his head. One of the men closed the door and stood by it, crouching warily. The other man held his GK-3 automatic rifle upon the occupants. He spoke English with a French accent.

"Hands behind your neck. Okay. Now back up to the wall."

"It's not a wall," Flaherty said. "It's a bulkhead."

"For God's sake!" Silver said. "This is no time to worry about terminology!"

The two men were French passengers, ticketed to get off at the island-nation of Minerva. The tall, thin, redheaded man by the door was Jacques-Pierre Mellezour; the other, Robert Calloc'h, was short, massive-shouldered, and big-bellied.

Mellezour turned his head and spoke loudly to make himself heard above the gunfire. "I am Captain Mellezour of the First Corps of the Children of Breiz. Now, Captain Silver, how did you find out about us?"

"Sure, and he's not the captain," Flaherty said. "He's been suspended from his duties. First Officer White—that poor divil of a black lying on the deck outside—he's captain now. Unless he's dead. In which case, me good man, I'm captain."

Mellezour looked confused.

Greatheart said, "No, Captain Mellezour, I'm captain again. Actually, no formal complaint has been lodged against me. The Hoowards have to sign a statement charging me with something illegal and/or irregulatory. Besides, this is an emergency which threatens the ship and its passengers. I'm captain."

"Actually," Flaherty said, "Third Mate Siskatoo is captain. He's on duty in the control room, and the captain is incapacitated. Namely, by you. You'd have to speak to Siskatoo."

Mellezour waved his rifle wildly. "I don't give a damn just now who's captain of this ship! What I want to know is, how did you find out about us? Who set up this ambush?"

"I don't know anything about an ambush," Greatheart said. "I don't even know what you're doing with those guns."

Calloc'h said something in a language wholly unintelligible to Silver. He supposed it was Breton. Mellezour spoke in French. "Traitors?"

The gunfire cut off suddenly.

Mellezour spoke to Calloc'h. Calloc'h gingerly opened the door and peered down the passageway toward the control room. A shot. Calloc'h, apparently cursing, jumped back and slammed the door.

"You are not lying?" Mellezour said to Silver.

"No. What's your game? Hijacking?"

"It is no game, my captain," Mellezour said. "It is the highest patriotism. We are members of the Children of Breiz. Breiz, that means Brittany. Originally, it was the Sons of Breiz, but certain feminist militants threatened to form a splinter organization unless we called ourselves the Persons of Breiz. We compromised on Children.

"Anyway, we have been demanding independence for Brittany, which is presently an oppressed department—province—of France. No doubt even you Americans, who read nothing but the sports section of your newspaper and the comic books, have heard of us?"

"Last time I read about you," Greatheart said, "you had blown up a mailbox in Paris. You killed ten adults and six children."

"That was too bad about the children," Mellezour said. "But you can't make an omelet without breaking eggs.

"We patriots boarded this dirigible at Caracas in order to seize the reactionary financier and potential premier of France, M. de Rioux. We intend to hold him as hostage, to demand the release of six of our comrades now awaiting the guillotine."

"And where were we to be taken after your demands were met, if they were?"

"Ah, the captain anticipates? That is good. You are cooperative, is it not? If our demands are not met, we will throw de Rioux, his secretary, and his two bodyguards into what you Americans call the big drink. Then we will disembark at a certain port of a certain nation of Africa. Where your airship will be confiscated because it has illegally entered. No doubt it can be freed for a certain sum."

"No doubt," Silver said. He was trembling with rage.

Mellezour said, "Two of my brave ones are lying dead upon the floor."

"Not floor. Deck," Flaherty said.

"How would you like to join them?" Mellezour said. "Do not interrupt me for trifles. We were on our way to seize M. de Rioux in his cabin, when people in the control room shot at us. De Rioux's bodyguards also joined in, but they were gunned down. Not only that, somebody fired upon us from the door of the cabin near this one. Two doors down, I believe."

"That's Jill's cabin!" Greatheart said.

"Jill?"

"She is the wife of the captain," said Flaherty, "I mean, he *was* the captain. That still has to be . . ."

The telephone rang. Mellezour and Calloc'h jumped. Mellezour's rifle stuttered, the explosions half-deafening everybody. Though his ears rang, Silver could hear Mrs. Hooward yelling.

"Shut up!" Mellezour cried. "That was an accident. I was so startled, I squeezed the trigger. Nobody is hurt, though, alas!"—he waved at the row of bullet holes in the bulkhead—"there has been some damage."

Calloc'h answered the phone. After listening a moment, he said, "It's the officer of the control room. He asks for the captain."

"I'll talk to him," Mellezour said. Standing sideways, his rifle pointed outward, he talked to Siskatoo. As the conversation progressed, it became evident that Siskatoo was a prisoner. Five armed passengers had invaded the control room a minute before the Bretons had come into the passageway.

"What do they want, these criminals?" Mellezour said. He looked at the others. "The bandit chief himself will speak to me."

The conversation progressed from an icy politeness to furious screaming. Then Mellezour put his hand over the receiver.

"They are American gangsters, Captain," he said. "They have taken over the control room. They intended to hijack your ship for the platinum and iridium, which they say is more valuable than gold. They offer to share part of it with us if we will cooperate with them."

Calloc'h spoke in Breton.

Mellezour said, "Do not be stupid, my compatriot. Of course we will get vengeance for the blood of our comrades. But we will appear to cooperate. And once they are within range of our guns, we will massacre them."

He removed his hand from the phone.

"Your offer sounds tempting, Hooke. I think we can come to terms agreeable to both parties. How will we arrange a meeting where—I hesitate to say this but you understand, it is not?—we will be safe from, forgive me, treachery?

"Also, how would you like to exchange hostages? One of your men for one of mine? You will have to confer with your colleagues first? I also must have a conference with my colleagues. After all, one of them must volunteer to be a hostage."

His face became even redder. "What? I be a hostage? Name of a pig! I am the leader! The heart! The brains! The intestines! My men would fall apart without me. Would you be a hostage? Ah, I thought not!"

A minute passed while he listened again. Then he said, "Very well. I will call my men and I will put forward your so interesting proposal."

He hung up. "Difficulties arise only to be overcome. Now I will call . . ."

His outstretched hand stopped. The phone was ringing. "Name of a thousand devils! Hello!"

He turned once more. "Captain, it's your third mate. Hooke has given him permission to speak to you. But hold your phone out so I can hear also."

Silver walked across the cabin and unclasped his hands slowly from his neck. Calloc'h backed away. Mellezour put his ear close to the receiver.

"Captain? Siskatoo. We're in a hell of a fix, Captain. The robber chief didn't say anything about it, mainly because I hadn't said anything about it. But when these thugs burst in here, the pilot tried to jump them. He laid one of them out, but they gunned him down. He's still alive, though. They also shot up the computer and the teleset. The electrical lighting system, air-conditioning, and telephone systems still are working. So's the radar.

"But, Captain, we don't have any control! The engines have stopped operating, and there's no rudder or elevator response! The backup system is out, too!

"We're drifting, Captain!"

Twenty

Silver asked to talk to the chief of the robbers.

Hooke's voice was like gravel sliding down a chute. "Yeah, what is it?"

"Captain Silver here. Did Siskatoo tell you about the hurricane coming our way?"

"Yeah, he did. What can I do about it?"

"Without aerial control, we won't be able to get away from the hurricane. Also, there may be line-squalls preceding it. They could break up this airship in a short time. The control equipment must be fixed."

"That sounds reasonable," Hooke said. "If this ain't just a trick. So what do you want to do?"

"Arrangements must be made to get some engineers and repair equipment into the control room. At once. We may not have much time."

"You wouldn't be trying to scare me, would you?"

Mellezour snatched the phone away. "Hooke? I don't think he's trying anything underhanded. The danger sounds very real to me."

He listened, then nodded and said, "I comprehend. First we must arrange for hostages? Very well. I will call my men. When we have decided what to do, I will call you back, is it not so?"

He replaced the phone on its hook.

"First, though, how many men will be needed? And where is the repair equipment stored?"

"The chief electronics officer, Moon, and the mate—in both senses, since he's her husband—are enough. I think. Ask her. Maybe she'll need another man. The storage room is off this passageway, near the aft section."

"This had better not be a trick," Mellezour said. "Remember, if these repair people do anything suspicious, we can always knock you off. Or some of the passengers."

Mrs. Hooward gasped; her husband whimpered.

Mellezour reached for the phone. It rang before he touched it, and he jumped. Calloc'h grinned. Mellezour scowled. Calloc'h's grin collapsed.

Mellezour's face turned from red to gray. Muttering something in his native Celtic language, he handed the phone to Greatheart.

Moon's voice crackled in his ear. "Captain? I'm being held prisoner here, in the aft observation room, by four of these Children of Breiz. There are twenty of the crew here, including my husband. Three crewmen got away. These terrorists shot at them, but I think our men got away into the upper structure. One of them knocked down a Breizist and took his rifle.

"But their wild firing tore some big holes in Gas Cells Three and Four. They also punctured some of the containers holding the liquid methane. The helium's coming out of the cells, and the methane's boiling out of the containers."

Silver took a deep breath. He wondered if his color was the same as Mellezour's.

"Okay, Moon. Is anyone wounded? Or . . . dead?"

"No, sir. We're all right, though I did wet my pants when these bandits stormed in."

"I doubt you're the only one who did that," Silver said. "Now, have you warned the Breizists not to smoke?"

"Yes, sir, but they're smoking anyway."

Silver told Mellezour what she had said. The Breton grabbed the phone and launched into a high-pitched gabble. His face turned from gray to red once more. When he handed the phone to Silver, he said, "That's taken care of. I promised to shoot the first man who lights up."

"A gunshot'll set off the methane, too," Silver said. He did not explain that methane was lighter than air. It, like helium, would be rising. But in a short time, the gas might fill the lower levels of the hull. Maybe he could use that grace period.

"Mellezour, those leaks have to be fixed. If the cells continue to lose helium, the ship will become heavy. Also, unbalanced. Eventually, the ship'll fall. The methane will asphyxiate everybody aboard, if it doesn't blow up first."

Mellezour, like a human chameleon, turned from red to gray again. "My God, what kind of mess have you gotten us into?"

Greatheart was too outraged to be able to protest.

The Breizist got on the horn once more and talked rapidly to Hooke. A sound like an angry Donald Duck came from the transmitter.

Mellezour put his hand over the mouthpiece. "He says he isn't sure this isn't a trick on my part."

"What do you care?" Silver said. "You control the aft section. Get the repairs on the gas cell and the methane containers going at once. Oh, yes, some of the crewmen must go aloft and open all the hatches. That's so the methane can escape. The hatches can no longer be opened by remote control from the bridge. They'll be the smaller hatches. The big hatch, used for loading freight, is too heavy to be moved manually."

"Which means my men will have to go along and watch them," Mellezour said. "What are you trying to do, divide and conquer?"

"Mr. Mellezour," Silver said dignifiedly, "my foremost duty is to ensure the safety of the ship and the passengers. I will do nothing to endanger them. I have sworn an oath to put that above everything else."

Mellezour called the aft observation room. In a few words he told Glanndour, his lieutenant, to start the repair work. Some crewmen should be locked in a room as hostages to ensure good behavior on the part of the workers.

Glanndour was a loud talker, too. Silver heard him protest. He could spare only one man to watch the prisoners. That left four, including himself, to go into the hull to watch the repairmen.

"That can't be helped," Mellezour said. "Oh, watch out for those crewmen that got away. They might try something."

"I doubt it," Silver said. "If they don't give themselves up soon, they will be overcome by methane. Of course, they might not know that the containers have been punctured." He paused. "Listen. They're in real danger. Why don't you let me talk them out of hiding? I can use a bullhorn."

"No," Mellezour said loudly. "You stay right here. They'll just have to take their chances."

"But we need every hand we can get for the repairs."

"No. As you say, they'd be overcome by the gas. They'd be three fewer problems."

"But they'll fall through the hull covering. The skin is a tough aluminum-titanium alloy, but it's only millimeters thick."

Mellezour shrugged, and said, "That's what they deserve. And if they do fall, it'll mean just that much less weight for the ship."

The Breton and Hooke held another conference. It was both brief and inconclusive.

Mellezour spoke to Calloc'h. "If only one of us could get to the cabin opposite the captain's wife's cabin, and do it swiftly enough, he might not get shot. Then he could shoot through the walls . . ."

"Bulkheads, damn it!" Flaherty said.

Mellezour paused, glared at Flaherty, and said, "You could spray the walls of her cabin and liquidate Hooke's men."

Calloc'h said, "You started out by saying, 'us,' and now it's 'you,' meaning me. It would be suicidal."

"I don't really think so. The men in the woman's cabin would be taken by surprise. However, perhaps you could just get across the passageway to the cabin opposite this. Then you'd have the correct angle at which to empty a clip into the cabin. If we got rid of those men, we'd be in a better position to bargain. As it is . . ."

"That's my wife in there!" Silver cried. "You'd kill her, too!"

Mellezour said, "I am a humanitarian, Captain Silver. I regret very much spilling the blood of uninvolved people. Not innocent, I say. Just uninvolved. Though, in actuality, there is no such thing as an innocent or an uninvolved person in this complex world. Everybody is either for or against one. One must, even though with deep sorrow, break some eggs . . ."

Greatheart roared, and he swung his left fist. It sank into Mellezour's stomach. The Breton said, "Ouf!" and he folded in the middle. His red face became gray again. The rifle clattered on the deck. Something struck Silver on the head.

Twenty-One

The overhead lights were in his eyes. The headache from the spray was now replaced by a bigger and more painful one. Groaning, he sat up. He was by the far bulkhead, in the corner near the toilet. The other prisoners were all sitting with their backs against the bulkhead. The two Bretons, by the telephone, were eyeing him.

Mellezour said, "I should have shot you, as Calloc'h urged me to do. But I am a kindly man, Captain Silver, and an understanding one. I appreciate your concern for your wife. Your reaction was laudable in one sense, though blameful in another. As captain, you should have exercised an iron control.

"Since you have demonstrated that you're not fully in charge of your emotions, you'll have to be watched more carefully. One more reprehensible move like that, and you'll be shot."

He smiled. "Or perhaps you'll restrain yourself if you know that your wife will be shot."

He picked up the phone and called the aft section.

"Glanndour? Oh, it's you, Luzel. Where's Glanndour? Out with the workers? Well, call Glanndour. What? He isn't near a phone? The incompetent fool! Very well. But if he comes back, have him call me at the captain's cabin. No, you idiot. That's not the number. I meant the cabin where I am. The captain's here, too. Don't call his own cabin. It's held by the criminals."

Silver had by then gotten to a sitting position and moved slowly backward until he was stopped by the bulkhead.

Flaherty whispered, "How's your head, Captain?"

"It feels like the inside of a bell that's been rung once too often."

"Sure, and that's a pity. You didn't even have the fun of getting it. Hangovers and the clap you don't mind . . ."

"No talking there!" Mellezour shouted.

He phoned the control room. "Hooke. This . . . What do you mean, address you properly? You're the captain now?"

He put his hand over the receiver. "What kind of madness have I gotten into? Now he wants to be called Captain Hooke!"

Though it hurt his head, Greatheart leaned over and began removing his right boot. The Breton stopped talking and frowned at him.

Greatheart said, "My feet are sweaty. They itch. Is it okay if I scratch them?"

"Watch him, Calloc'h."

The boot off, Silver removed his sock and began to work his foot over with his fingernails. His face assumed a relieved expression.

"Just to make sure, *Captain* Hooke," Mellezour said, "Have you informed all your men of the exchange of hostages? There will be no gunfire?"

Mellezour nodded, then said, "Very well. My men have the same orders. Actually, nobody can shoot anyway unless he wishes to sacrifice his own hostage. And it is absolutely vital that the control equipment be repaired as quickly as possible. Almost all of my own men are busy with the repair work on the gas cell and the methane containers. So, you see, we must trust each other. Otherwise, we will all die."

His face glowed with a rush of blood. "What? What is that? I assure you that I am not full of what-do-you-call-it? *La merde du taureau* would be the correct translation in French. I do not sully my lips with its American translation, and we will get along better if you refrain from such vulgar phrases."

"Very well. We comprehend each other, is it not so?"

He put the phone on the hook and peered around the corner of the half-opened door. Calloc'h, reluctantly prepared to play the role of hostage, moved by him and out into the passageway.

Cursing under his breath, Greatheart began to take his other boot off. One glance from Mellezour would tell him that the foot was artificial. If only he had been able to find all his clothes. For want of a sock . . .

The Breton was alternating glances down the passageway and at his captives. He took a quick look out of the door, then turned his head to Silver.

"Throw your boots over to me," he said. "Gently. And then roll up the cuffs of your pants."

"Okay," Silver said.

He slid the right-foot boot on its side across the deck and resumed pulling off the other boot. Now he was glad that he didn't have a sock on his plastic foot. He would have to act swiftly, and taking the sock off would have given Mellezour time to shoot. When it was halfway off, he pressed on a button on the inside of the cuff. There was a click, but it would be inaudible to Mellezour.

Flaherty said, softly, "What the divil was that?"

"Don't say any more," Silver said.

He leaned back. He had only one shot, and if he failed he'd be blasted by Mellezour. Maybe he shouldn't be trying this, since his first duty was to the passengers. But he was tired of inaction and of being ordered around.

As the boot slid off, he held it so it would, he hoped, conceal the brown, hard plastic.

It would have to be done very swiftly. Aiming a foot at a target, even at this close range, wasn't easy. However, he had practiced shooting in just such a posture.

His finger poised above the button. One press readied the mechanism within the artificial member, just as the cocking of a six-shooter pistol hammer turned a loaded chamber and brought its load within the radius of the hammer. A second pressing of the button fired the small missile-shaped syringe.

Mellezour had turned his head. Silver released his two-fingered hold on the boot. As it dropped to the floor, he pressed the button on the side of the leg.

Two explosions resulted. Not from his leg. They came from the passageway. Rifles.

So startled was he, he almost missed. But the gray cylindrical missile streaked out with a slight hiss from its muzzle in the bottom of the plastic foot. Instead of hitting its target, the side of Mellezour's hip, it rammed into his neck.

The Breton grunted and dropped his rifle. He grabbed the side of the doorway, grunted again, and pitched forward, his face landing on the passageway deck.

Silver was up and running. After snatching up the rifle, he whirled and threw it to Flaherty. He grabbed Mellezour's ankles and started to drag him inside. Guns banged in the passageway. A bullet struck the door and slammed it against the Breton's legs. Silver dropped them and jumped back. He waited a moment, then, hearing no more shots, cautiously looked out.

Mellezour was full of holes.

Silver pulled the body in and shut the door. With more pleasure than he should have had, he slapped Mrs. Hooward's face. She stopped screaming.

Flaherty said, "Here. You better take this." He handed him the automatic rifle. "I don't know how to operate it."

The phone rang. Silver answered it. A gravelly voice cursed him for a full-minute.

Silver yelled, "What's the matter?"

"You *$%¼&.!" Hooke said. "You double-crossed me! But your own man got it, too, though that ain't much satisfaction to me! I'll kill you, you weasely frog, you!"

"I don't know what you're talking about."

A silence. Then Hooke said, "Say, you ain't the frog! Who are you?"

"Captain Greatheart Silver. Mellezour's dead, killed by your men! It was your men that fired. Wasn't it?"

"Are you kidding? It was *your* men. From the cabin between you and us!"

Silver was astonished. Hooke said, "You still there?"

"No, it wasn't one of us. We thought the men in that cabin were yours. We thought you'd called them and told them to hold their fire while the hostages were exchanged."

"Some exchange!" Hooke said. "They're both dead, leaking all over the floor."

Silver checked himself. He'd almost said, "Deck, not floor." Flaherty was a bad influence.

"Then who are those men in the cabin?"

"Hell, I don't know! What's going on here, anyway?"

"I'll call them and find out," Silver said. "I'll call you back."

He hung up. Flaherty had removed the needle from the still unconscious Breton and was binding him with belts. Hooward was complaining that he couldn't keep his pants up.

"Is that what they was?" the man said. "We wondered why they was coming down the hall. They didn't have no guns on them, none showing, that is. We figured it was a trick so we shot them. Say, just what's going on?"

Silver explained. After a considerable pause, the man said, "So that's how it is? What a mess! Well, it don't make no difference to us. We're still holding Jill Micawber for ransom!"

Silver was too stunned to say anything for a moment.

"Hello! Are you still there?"

"Yeah," Silver said. "So that's why you fired on us."

"Yeah. After we grabbed the Micawber chick, we was going to take over the control room. We was going to demand forty megabucks from her old man. Cheap at the price. And we was going to have the money delivered by chopper while the ship was still in the air over Minerva. Then we was going to have you drop us off at a place it wouldn't be smart to tell you about now."

"How is my wife?" Greatheart said. "Can I speak to her?"

"No, you can't. She's okay. But if you try anything, we'll sieve her."

"Look," Silver said, "if you don't let my engineers by, they can't repair the control computer. This dirigible is going to fall into the sea soon unless all repairs can be made quickly. Of course, before then, we may be smothered by methane. By the way, if anyone's smoking in there, make them stop. Methane is highly explosive."

There was a curse, followed by shouts at somebody named Smith. At the same time, the ravens, Huggin and Muggin, yelled obscenities and Jill's voice came faintly to him.

When quiet came, Silver said, "What's your name?"

"Captain."

"Captain who?" Silver said.

"William Captain. Spelled K-a-p-t-e-n. And don't make no jokes about it. So, what're we supposed to do? One thing, though, we ain't letting loose of Micawber's kid whatever happens. She's our ticket to Paradise."

Silver wanted to yell at him. Instead, he spoke quietly. "That's okay. The main thing right now is to save the ship. We can talk terms later. I'll call Hooke and tell him what's going on. Speak to you later."

"Real bad news?" Flaherty said. "You look pale."

Silver told him. To his surprise, the Irishman burst out laughing.

"Three gangs of crooks all trying for different things but at the same time? Captain, this ship is jinxed!"

"It isn't funny," Silver said. He was wondering if perhaps the jinx wasn't on the ship but on him. He'd been in command of the AZ-8 after its captain was killed, and the ship had been wrecked. It had not been his fault, but he had gotten blamed anyway. Then he was in poverty and trouble up to his ears for many years. That was old man Micawber's doing, but, nevertheless, he had been touched with extraordinarily bad luck. Now he was captain of the AZ-49, on his first voyage as captain, and he couldn't be in a worse pickle. Well, yes, he could. He could be dead.

He shrugged, and called the station just aft of Cell No. 1. Luzel was very angry about the death of Mellezour and the capture of Calloc'h. Silver said nothing until Luzel had cooled off.

"As your leader said, you can't cook an omelet without breaking some eggs. However, we're dealing with human lives, not eggs. Now, Luzel . . ."

"It is now Captain Luzel, if you please."

"All right, Captain Luzel," Silver said. "Here's the situation."

After he had finished speaking, he hung up to let Luzel phone Kapten and Hooke. Occasionally, he tried Hooke, and, when he no longer got a busy signal, he phoned the bridge.

The gravelly voice said, "Captain Hooke! You made up your mind yet?"

"This is Captain Silver. I'm waiting for all of you to get together. Meanwhile, could I speak to Siskatoo? I want a weather report."

"Yeah. I guess it's okay."

Siskatoo said, "According to radar, we're being pushed by the wind at eighty mph on a southeasterly course. My calculations are that we'll be over, or in the vicinity of, Easter Island, I mean Rapa Nui, in about eight hours. The main force of the typhoon hasn't caught up with us yet. But when it does, it'll be bad. There are some very violent air currents preceding the front."

Siskatoo drew in a deep breath, then said, "Captain, when the hell're we going to get things fixed up? The ship's getting heavier. You noticed the deviation from the horizontal? It's about ten degrees now."

"Yes, I noticed," Silver said. "But Luzel says the damage to the gas cells and the containers was worse than first estimated. And the repair crew only have ten oxygen masks. Luzel insists that three of his men wear masks so they can keep an eye on the crew. That leaves only seven men working. It isn't nearly enough. Meanwhile . . ."

"Yes. I know. The methane's filling up the top of the hull faster than the top hatches let it escape. Captain, can't you convince those dummies how desperate the situation is?"

"Who you calling a dummy?" Hooke roared. There was a click.

Silver had wanted to ask how much altitude had been lost. However, though methane did not have the lift of helium, it was lighter than air. Thus, it was giving some buoyancy to the hull.

The phone rang.

"Captain Luzel here. How many parachutes are there on this tub? This female engineer says we don't have any. She's lying, is she not?"

"No, she's telling the truth. Why did you want to know?"

"You mean we got to go down with the ship?" Luzel said. Silver couldn't see his face, but the man's voice was pale.

"All the way," Silver said. "Anyway, if you chuted, you'd just land in the ocean and drown."

He added, "Let me talk to Moon."

"Okay. I'll get her . . . what the . . . ?"

Faint gunfire and shouts sounded. Silver yelled questions, but Luzel had evidently deserted the phone. More shots came. He held the phone to his ear, and cursed. What was going on?

Ten minutes by his wristwatch passed. Ten minutes during which the punctured cells were losing who-knew-how-much helium. Ten more minutes for the storm to reach them. Then Luzel, breathing hard, came back on.

"Those sons of pigs, your escaped crewmen, tried to jump some of my men! One of them grabbed Emgann, and they both fell off a catwalk and went through the hull! Another got a rifle and wounded another of my men. Three of your men, including the one with the rifle, got away. They're somewhere in the hull down at the other end. I think. Listen . . ."

"I am not responsible for their actions," Silver said. "I am not in a position to give them orders, as you well know."

"Yes? That doesn't matter. What does is that more holes have been shot in the cells and in the containers. I would say that all the containers are leaking. I am not letting any repair work be done as long as your men are out there. We'd be easy targets."

"I could call them in with a bullhorn," Silver said. "But, as you well know, I can't leave the cabin. Have you asked Moon to call them in?"

"Of course, I did. And she did. But they refuse to come in. I threatened to shoot some of their crewmates, and one of them shouted back that that was too bad, but they weren't giving up. What's more, they threatened to release the valves on top of the gas cells and force the ship down if *we* didn't give up. They wouldn't do that, would they, Silver?"

"I hope not," Greatheart said. "Our only hope is to come to an agreement on getting the repairs, fore and aft, done as quickly as possible. You've got to strike an agreement with Kapten and Hooke. And quickly! It may be too late already!"

Silver said a few more words, then called the kidnappers and the robbers. After more precious minutes passed, he hung up. He would have to wait until they had discussed the matter with Luzel. Meanwhile, the AZ-49's tail was dragging, getting near a stall condition. Airships, like airplanes, could stall. And it was dropping toward the storm-whipped waves of the Pacific. Once the full fury of the typhoon struck, it would be subjected to violent updrafts and downdrafts. Though the dirigible was better constructed to take punishment than the pre-1989s, it could break up under such sudden alterations in altitude.

A working agreement could have been reached by the three gangs long ago if it were not for distrust and greed. The exchange of hostages had been agreeable to the Breizists and the robbers. The kidnappers, however, had refused. Kapten wouldn't say why, but Silver guessed the reason. There were too few of them. To lose two of their party as hostages might, for all he knew, reduce the number holding Jill to one. They had already lost a man; he lay in the passageway, cut down in that first furious burst of gunfire.

"Captain? Siskatoo. Radar shows we're a thousand feet from the surface. Losing altitude at the rate of a foot a second."

Silver pulled his electronic calculator from his pocket. He worked it, then said, "We now have less than sixteen minutes!"

"Yeah, I know."

Siskatoo did not sound perturbed. Perhaps he was playing the role of the stoic, imperturbable Indian.

Silver called Hooke and told him what must be done. Hooke's voice seemed to break into a sweat.

"Okay. But I sure hope this ain't another trick you've pulled out of your sleeve."

Silver wanted to ask him what tricks he had played, but there wasn't time.

"You call Kapten and I'll call Luzel."

"Captain who? Oh!"

Silver called Luzel. The Breton said, "Whaaat? We're doomed! Fifteen minutes, you say?"

"Less than that now," Silver said with all the calm he could muster. “Relay my orders to Moon. Tell her everything except the cutting lasers, the extra ropes, and the tools must go overboard. She knows why. First, though, the ballast breeches . . .”

“Breeches?”

“The forked bags of water hanging alongside the catwalk above the keel passageway. Ordinarily, in case of emergency, they could be dumped by remote control from the control room. But they’ll have to be discharged manually now. We might have to discharge the big tanks of ballast water, too.”

Luzel almost wailed. “But we can’t! Three of your men, one armed, are out in the hull!”

“I’ll get them to give up. They won’t ignore me. After all, I am the captain, whatever anyone else says.”

More precious minutes were lost while the three parties talked to each other. Then Hooke rang Silver.

“Okay! Those clowns holding your wife say they won’t come out. But they won’t shoot anybody going by their cabin—as long as nobody’s carrying weapons. And we can only go by one at a time.”

Silver said, “Have you gone up the ladder to the cabin above? My cabin?”

“Do you think I’m a dummy?” Hooke said. “Of course I have. I got a man stationed there so them Frenchies won’t sneak up on us from that way.”

“Then I’ll tell Luzel your hostage will leave by that cabin. He can walk to the stern on the catwalk above the main passageway. But you better call Kapten and tell him your man will be walking overhead. If he hears him, he might shoot up through the overhead. Kapten’s very nervous.”

Hooke called Kapten and told him what they’d be doing. Kapten objected. He thought that the robbers, once on the catwalk, could easily shoot down through the cabin’s overhead. Hooke called Silver back to tell him this.

Silver said, “Oh, my God! Jill’d be killed!”

“Yeah. That Kapten’s right, though. It’s a great idea. But I ain’t going to shoot if there’s methane around. Besides, I got my own life to think about. Listen. You’ll be on your own for a while. Don’t think even once about ducking out and trying something dirty, see?”

"Where would I go?" Silver said, and he hung up.

A moment later, he and Flaherty left the cabin. Mr. and Mrs. Hooward were moaning in the corner, holding on to each other. In the passageway, Silver stopped briefly to determine if White was dead. He was. He ran down the passageway. Doors opened behind him, and voices called. He looked back. A number of passengers were cautiously opening doors to see what was going on.

Once in the tail section, he talked quickly to the electronics people. Moon left with a party of four, headed for the storage room. Luzel, an unlit cigar in his mouth and a rifle cradled in one arm, greeted him from the top of a ladder. He looked like the twin brother of Mellezour. Silver climbed up. A Breton handed him a bullhorn.

He opened a hatch and stepped out onto a platform. Its ladder led down to the port catwalk, which ran all the way from the platform to the nose. To his left the visibility was comparatively unrestricted, though there were plenty of crosswires and transverse girders. On his right the massive deep-ring main frames, bracing wires, and the bulging cells obstructed the gaze. The whole was shrouded in a deep twilight; the scattered lights were brave but weak candles in the gloom.

Holding the bullhorn, he went down the ladder and advanced on the catwalk until he was near the port cargo hold. This was a towering structure of girder latticework and shear wires. The bottom girders of the hold were twenty feet above his head. Craning his neck, he could see the rectangular modules stacked within the hold.

Smoke roiled from some of them, the bullets having penetrated both the module sides and the sides of the containers within the modules. The liquid methane within the containers was boiling out through the holes, turning into an invisible gas a short distance from the jets. Not only was it invisible, it was odorless. The natural gas used commercially was provided with a smellable additive in order to warn its users.

A sudden cutting off of oxygen if a man were surrounded by it, or an explosion if a spark were present, would be the first—and last—notice of its presence.

Two of the cells were alarmingly deflated. A landsman wouldn't have thought much of their shrinkage, would scarcely have noticed it. But he saw that the situation was indeed desperate.

His bullhorn bellowed, echoing in the vast hollow between the cell bays and the port hull.

"Williams, Carszinski, Chong! This is your captain. Can you hear me?"

A faraway voice answered, seeming to come from above and to his right. If so, the three were in grave danger of suffocation. They must be far forward, however, since a more central location would have caught them in the upward- and outward-spreading gas. Perhaps a top forward hatch was giving them ventilation.

"Give yourselves up! Come on in! There'll be no retribution! The ship's in a bad case! We have to start repair work at once, and it can't be done until you surrender! Otherwise, we'll be in the ocean in a few minutes!"

"Is that straight stuff, Captain!" Chong's voice rang. "You aren't just saying that under duress?"

"No! This is a number-one emergency!"

"Okay! Tell those %$*@ +!s not to shoot!"

"They've promised they won't!"

Luzel came out onto the platform, a rifle held ready.

"They're surrendering?"

"Yes. They should be visible in a few moments."

He pointed toward the fore section. Far off, a small figure was moving on the catwalk toward them.

"Hooke's man, coming for the hostage exchange."

Luzel said, "Ah, there they are!"

He pointed at three shadowy forms that had emerged from behind the second nearest main cell to the nose. They were climbing a perpendicular ladder used mainly by inspectors and sailmakers.

"Hooke's man doesn't seem to be armed," Luzel said.

He turned and said, "Keriverc'hez!" A tall muscular man stepped from behind the door. Luzel spoke a few words. The man went down the ladder and began walking slowly. Hooke's man had reached the central part of the catwalk and now was waiting for the Breton.

Silver said, "We don't have nearly enough sailmakers to patch the holes in the time we need. The sailmakers will have to use every hand available, supervise them. But we'll need all the gas masks. At that, the patching will have to be done from the bottom up. Helium can asphyxiate a man, too.

"Also I don't want to do this since it increases the danger, but there's no other way—holes will have to be drilled through the module sides and the container sides. The release of the liquid methane will lighten the cargo considerably. That'll keep us aloft much longer.

"Unfortunately, that can't be started until after the lower holes in the cells have been patched.

"Meantime, the laser cutter can begin work on the girders at the bottom of the cargo holds. We only have one laser, which means the work will be slow. The bottom girders will be removed so the modules will drop through. That'll mean a tremendous loss of weight."

Luzel paled. "You can't do that!" he cried. "The laser's heat will ignite the methane!"

"No, the hydrogen and methane will rise. The laser'll be below the leakage."

He added, "Also, I'll have to release some helium from various cells. That's necessary to trim the ship, that is, put it into equilibrium. Normally, I could do that by remote control from the bridge. But the computer isn't working, so the valves must be operated manually. It's a ticklish job, since it's guesswork, and I'll have to run the operation by phone. I can't take the time to run back and forth from cell to cell. Besides, I'm not a long-distance runner.

"The trouble with trimming the ship is that we'll be losing helium we can't afford to lose."

Luzel looked as if he'd like to object. Instead, he suddenly pointed his finger at the three crewmen. These had almost reached the catwalk.

"Your man still has the rifle!"

Silver swore. He should have ordered that the weapon be dropped overboard. That would lighten the weight and also prevent the trigger-itchy fingers of Hooke's or Luzel's gang from shooting. But he had his mind so overloaded with problems that he had forgotten. There was no excuse for it; a captain shouldn't forget anything.

He quickly put the bullhorn before his lips.

"Williams! Carszinski! Chong! Whichever one has the rifle! Drop it! Right now!"

Too late. The two hostages were yelling and dropping onto the catwalk. Flashes of gunfire stabbed from the dim light at the fore approach to the catwalk. One of Hooke's men must have been stationed there to watch, and now he was firing at the crewmen.

All three fell, one landing across the catwalk, the other two bouncing off of it and over the side. With one went his rifle.

Silver remained standing. Luzel dived to the platform deck. Suddenly, bullets were screaming by him and ricocheting off the girders. Silver decided to dive, too.

His face pressed against the metal deck, he cursed and raved. The murders of his men had filled him almost past the bursting point. Hooke's man was out of reach. Silver grabbed Luzel. Silver could have taken the man's rifle away from him then and shot him. Into the aft section he would go, rifle blazing. Wipe them out.

Sanity cooled off his white-hot fantasy. He let loose of Luzel's throat.

"Sorry," he said, though the word choked him. "I just grabbed the first thing that came in reach."

Luzel coughed, then said, "One of us has to get to a phone and explain to Hooke."

However, there was a safer way to communicate. Luzel called out instructions to a man behind the door, and in a few minutes he returned. Hooke had said that the exchange of hostages could now proceed. He did not offer an apology.

The two got up. Luzel was actually smiling. Silver restrained the impulse to knock his teeth out.

"I suggest," Silver said, "that all the corpses be thrown overboard as quickly as possible. That'll lighten the load."

Luzel's smile became even broader. "Perhaps we should also throw the passengers out? They are useless, and their total weight must be considerable."

"That is a logical step," Silver said, "but it isn't humane."

They stepped aside as riggers, carrying a laser cutter and associated equipment, crowded past them. Fortunately, the electrical generators in the tail cone had not been damaged. Otherwise, the ship would be in even greater danger.

The sailmakers and their assistants went by. Some wore oxygen masks, and all carried rolls of patching material and patching "guns." A minute later, the hostage from Hooke came up the ladder. Luzel's man had disappeared into the gangway at the other end.

The hostage was a tall, thin man with a wart on his nose. His face was a pale green.

"I'm Miggleton," he said. "And I'm sick." He rubbed his stomach. "I think I got appendicitis. That's why she picked me to be a hostage."

"She?" Silver and Luzel said simultaneously.

"Yeah, she. Hooke. Why, didn't you know she's a woman? Hooke the Hooker they used to call her in Chicago. Now she's fat and fifty, she's turned her hand to robbing banks. She shoulda stayed in that profession. Hijacking airships ain't turning out so hot."

"Yeah, but that voice . . ." Silver said.

"Ain't that something? She sounds like a truck driver. She was one, too, for a while."

Four of Luzel's men, armed, had gone down to the catwalk to guard the repair crews. Silver wondered if there were any more in the tail section. If so, they were greatly outnumbered. It should be possible to overwhelm them. But some of his crew were bound to be killed or badly wounded. Besides, for the moment, all energies had to be concentrated on keeping the airships buoyant and on regaining aerial control.

Nevertheless . . . he struggled with his wrath, and he won. A captain must be cool at all times.

"Ain't you going to get the doctor for me?" Miggleton whined.

"You can go to sick bay," Silver said. He gave him directions while Luzel, frowning, listened in. "I don't know where the doctor is. If he's in his cabin, which is within shooting range of Kapten's cabin, you're out of luck. It's up to you to phone him; I don't have time. The doctor's name and cabin number are on the ship's directory on his desk."

"I don't know about letting him roam around unguarded," Luzel said. "I'll take him down there."

Miggleton was not so sick that he wasn't curious. "What're all those men doing?"

Silver told him, although Luzel had lifted his finger to his lips to indicate he should not do so.

Miggleton's eyes bugged. "You mean, you're going to throw out the platinum and iridium? You can't do that! They must be worth millions!"

"Yes, and it weighs a quarter of a ton," Silver said. "It has to go."

"You can't *mean* that," Miggleton said. Even more sweat formed on his forehead and upper lip. "Man, that's why we're holding up this ship!"

"Would you rather *swim* for it?" Silver said.

"Hooke ain't going to like this," Miggleton said. "She won't allow the repairs to the controls if you dump those precious metals."

"Tell her it's the metals or her life."

"No, *wait*!" Luzel cried. "That's a fortune! It could be used to finance the operations of the Children of Breiz!"

"You ain't thinking of taking it all, are you?" Miggleton said.

Luzel drew himself up. "Of course not! I am a man of honor, a patriot, not a common criminal such as yourself. I agreed to split the metals with your party, and my word is iron. It is true that it may be necessary to sacrifice it to save our lives. But for the present, we will hang on to it as long as possible."

"That can't be done," Silver said. "The methane containers are all on the bottom. The metals container is on top. It's too heavy to move, so it goes with the rest of the cargo."

"How'd you get it in the freight container structure?" asked Miggleton. "Didn't you use a crane?"

Silver rolled his eyes at such ignorance. "The cargo's lowered into the hold through a big hatchway by a helimp while the freighter is in the air."

"What's a *helimp*?"

"A blimp with helicopter motors."

Miggleton's brow went up. "Hooke's going to kill everybody in sight if you dump those metals."

Silver was unswervable. "If we *don't*, this ship's going to crash.

As it is, cutting the holds' bottom girders will weaken the ship's structure. If it's hit by any violent drafts, it may buckle. Or break."

Silver was exaggerating for effect, though not by much.

Luzel turned gray. Miggleton looked even sicker. Luzel, apparently deciding he didn't want to leave the scene, called one of his men to conduct the hostage to sick bay. This made Silver certain that there were only five Breizists. Luzel, however, gave some additional instructions in Breton to his man.

Silver went into action at once. Using the platform phone to give directions to the crew, he readjusted the helium contents of the bags. The ship resumed a near-horizontal attitude. For a while, there would be no tail-heaviness.

In the meantime, however, the air had become bumpier, forcing the men on the catwalk to hang on for safety. The sailmakers and riggers relied on their belts.

Silver told Luzel, "Since we're without propulsive power, we're drifting. We don't have dynamic stability. We could stall if we get tail- or nose-heavy. Releasing the gas makes the ship even heavier. We *did* gain some buoyancy when we released the water ballast. Now we have to discharge the big water ballast tanks, the fuel, and the slip tanks. The big fuel tanks will have to be emptied, too, and then the tanks'll be cut loose. But first, the cargo must go."

By then, the rigger C.P.O. had plugged in the cord of the laser cutter into a girder connection. His safety belt fastened around a girder, his feet on another, he was moving the tip of the cutter across the girder on the deck of the port hold.

"I hope," Silver said, "that cutting the bottom girders on three sides will weaken the deck so much that the weight of the containers will bend the girders on the uncut side. And the modules will drop through. If they don't, then the cutter has to get underneath and cut the inside ends of the girders.

"Another problem is that we only have one cutter and so we can't cut the decks of both holds at the same time. When the port cargo modules drop, the starboard modules will remain. Their weight will roll the ship so many degrees—I don't know how many—to starboard. Everybody will have to be warned of that. Otherwise, they might be pitched overboard."

He added, "We have to cut some bracing wires, too. That will weaken the ship's framework some. On the other hand the loss of liquid methane has lightened the load. Still, the modules and the empty containers weigh many tons."

Luzel said, "Is that why you sent men to the starboard hold to drill holes in the containers?"

"Yes. The less weight there, the smaller the degree of roll to starboard. Let's hope the containers don't jam when the bottom goes out. It'll be a hell of a job manhandling the modules. We'd have to cut the vertical girders and more bracing wires, and that'd put an additional burden on the framework."

The man whom Luzel had sent with Miggleton reported.

"My captain, the hostage is with the doctor. But the doctor complains that, in accordance with orders, he had thrown practically all his medical equipment overboard. He says the company will have to reimburse him for the loss. I told him that was no concern of ours.

"He is going to conduct an operation, however. But he disclaims any responsibility for fatal results.

"Also, as you ordered, I forced all passengers out, except for the reactionary de Rioux, who refused to leave his cabin. I set the passengers to work throwing the dead men overboard."

Luzel said, "Kapten gave you no trouble?"

"No, he lived up to his agreement. He kept his weapons trained on the passengers, who are, of course, scared to death. The corpses were carried to the observation deck, where they were cast out through the open space left by the removal of a window."

The man grinned.

"One of the corpses was a kidnapper, one of Kapten's men, who had been shot by Hooke's men in the passageway. Only it seems he still had some life. Just before he was swung out of the window, he opened his eyes and he protested. 'I am not dead yet,' he said.

"'Who would take a criminal's word for that?' I said. The passengers holding his shoulders and his feet also protested. I told them that they would eject the kidnapper or I would see to it that they too went out the window. And so he went out. He was doomed to die soon, anyway, and the sooner we got rid of his weight, the better."

"Well done," Luzel said.

Silver felt sick. He had no sympathy for the kidnapper, but the callousness of the Breizists showed what they could do if pressed hard enough. The time might come when they would feel it necessary to pitch the passengers out. And then . . . the crew?

Silver called Siskatoo.

The third mate said, "Our altitude is now fifteen hundred feet. Unless we lose a lot more weight, we'll strike the surface in about fifty minutes."

"How's the computer repair coming along?"

"Moon says it'll take at least two hours to fix it."

Silver ordered three crewmen to go into the main passageway and set the passengers to stripping the cabins. Everything removable, including their baggage, was to go.

The cooks and stewards were to detach the stove, refrigerators, and sinks and get rid of them. All galleyware except trays and glasses was to be cast out. All food except a twenty-four-hour supply would also go out.

During this time, the zeppelin was hit by ever stronger gusts. Silver had to cling with one hand to the phone box to steady himself. Though the air was bumpy, its effect was smooth compared to that an airplane would have experienced. The ship was not moving against the wind; it was moving *with* the wind. Its troubles would come when it encountered violent up- or downdrafts.

Just after Silver hung up, Luzel got a call from Hooke. When he turned from the phone, he was pale. If Luzel suffered any more color changes, Silver thought, he would become a permanent human chameleon. If he didn't die from shock first.

"Hooke insists that we save the platinum and iridium, no matter what happens. Otherwise, she'll stop the control repair work. And she just might shoot some of your men."

"She's out of her mind!" Silver yelled. "Doesn't she realize that if we don't get the motors, rudders, and elevators working, we're helpless? Even if we made the coast of South America, we'll be able to land only by crashing. And we might not be able to pick a good, smooth landing site. How'd she like to end up on top of a mountain with its peak up her . . . ?"

Luzel interrupted. "I told her that. She says she doesn't care. This is her chance to make a fortune, and she isn't going to give it up. She'll throw out the passengers first."

"That means a long delay in the cutting operation! Okay, then, I guess I can't do a thing about it! Tell her we'll save her precious metals!"

"Perhaps," Luzel said, "I could storm the control room?"

"No! The electronics men might be killed. Then where would we be?"

He stopped. A machinist mate had halted before him. "Captain, the chief sent me to tell you that all the methane containers have had holes drilled in them."

"Very well," he said. "Get back to your posts."

He turned to speak to Luzel. "I won't ask for volunteers to unpack the metals. I'll do it myself."

"Why you?" Luzel said suspiciously.

"Because we're shorthanded. Because it's too dangerous."

Luzel narrowed his eyes even more. "But you will have to station men on the ladder to hand the metals down to each other?"

"No. I'll lower each ingot by rope. That'll only require two men. Me and another."

"Go ahead, then," Luzel said, smiling. "To tell the truth, much as I acknowledge the necessity of getting rid of weight, I profoundly regret losing all the money those metals represent. Perhaps we can salvage them and the ship, too."

A few minutes later, Silver, wearing an oxygen mask borrowed from a rigger, climbed up a ladder alongside the starboard cargo hold. Coiled over one shoulder was a long light rope. On his head was a metal helmet to which was affixed an electric lamp. A safety belt was attached to the broad leather belt around his waist. Clips on this held a pair of wirecutters and stuck under the belt was a short crowbar.

As he passed the holes which had been drilled through the module sides and the containers, he heard the hiss of liquid methane evaporating and saw the almost foot-long jets of semiliquid gas. He was surrounded by a deadly invisible explosive. But as long as his mask operated and he made no sparks, he was safe.

Once, halfway up the 150-foot ascent, he looked down. The men on the catwalk were not exactly lilliputian figures, but they certainly looked a long way off.

Toward the nose, the chief rigger, Salmons, was using his laser to cut the bottom out of the elevator shaft. This led from the catwalk to the top of the zeppelin and was used to carry personnel and equipment. Silver had decided that the elevator itself should be dropped before cutting proceeded on the hold decks. Getting rid of it would add to the ship's lift, and the work could be done quickly.

Just below the ladder were Luzel and a crewman with a plastic bucket.

Silver resumed climbing. After what seemed like a long time, he reached the top of the hold. Above was the dark surface of the huge hatch through which the helimps loaded supplies and cargo. At regular intervals, the helimps also picked up crewmen and deposited their reliefs.

There were a few overhead lights, but they were inadequate for his purpose.

He climbed over the top and got onto the top cargo module, which was open on top. He removed the rope from around his shoulder and lowered it over the edge. The crewman at the bottom tied its end to the bucket, which held an electric drill and a long extension cord. Silver hauled it up and then tied the one end of the rope to the horizontal girder forming the top of the hold.

The plastic container stamped "HEAVY METALS" was against the far side of the hold, resting on top of a methane container. Brace wires secured it, preventing it from sliding. Standing well back so the suddenly severed wires wouldn't strike him, Silver used his cutters on them. Then he forced open the lock and raised the lid. It would have been easier to have used a key, but that was in the possession of a man in Minerva.

His helmet light showed rows of forty-pound dull-gray brick-shaped ingots.

After gazing at them for a few seconds, he muttered, "Maybe I can fool Hooke and Luzel. It's worth it to get rid of over 1,100 pounds. More, counting the container's weight."

Using the crowbar, he forced up one end of the tightly packed ingot. Then he lifted it out and carried it to the fore part of the hold. Straight below him there were no girders or wires to deflect the ingot. And he was hidden from the view of those below by the vast, bulging gas cell in the next bay.

Over the ingot went, disappearing into the darkness. It would pierce the hull-covering and hurtle into the storm-torn Pacific.

The next ingot he sent down in the bucket. The third he dropped after the first one.

Neither Luzel nor Hooke knew exactly how many ingots there were. And they wouldn't have time or the means to weigh them. The only scales on the ship had been thrown out during the lightening procedure. Silver had made sure of that.

Working swiftly, he walked back and forth. There was no time to stop and rest, to catch his breath. Back and forth. Up and down. Sweat, pant, gasp, groan. It was just like his honeymoon—minus the pleasure. If it hadn't been for his gloves, his hands would have been burned by the speed with which he lowered the bucket.

In exactly an hour, he had cleaned out the container. Twenty-eight ingots had been disposed of, averaging two minutes and eight seconds for each ingot. That was twice as fast as union regulations permitted.

Sweat running into his eyes, his mask-enclosed face feeling as if he were in a turkish bath using salty water, he dragged the empty container across the top and heaved it over the side. An end struck a wire as it rotated, causing a faint hum.

Twenty-Two

Silver plugged the extension cord of the drill into one of the receptacles along the top girder of the hold. He drilled three holes in the top of each container in the starboard hold, then disconnected the cord and climbed over a girder to the port hold. Here he repeated the procedure. It wasn't absolutely necessary for him to make additional holes, but the more there were the faster the top containers would lose their contents.

The drilling was disconcerting. The moment the point broke through, it was blown back out by the enormous pressure of the escaping methane. He had to hang on to the drill to keep it from being jerked out of his grip and into the air. Moreover, he had to be careful not to let any of the jet touch him. It would have frozen his skin, at the same time giving him a terrible burn.

By the time he climbed back down, he found that the ingots had been laid end to end along the catwalk. There was no time for men to lug them to a safer place. Moreover, the elevator and its cables had dropped through, and Salmons was busy cutting along the girders of the starboard hold's deck. The girders had been severed on three sides of the hold, and he was working on the port hold.

Silver was disappointed in that the weight of the almost-empty containers had not been enough to bend down the girders and let the containers fall through. It would be necessary for Salmons to go between the cargo structures and cut the girders on the inside. If the containers jammed, the horizontal girders outside the hold and perhaps the vertical girders at the bottom of the hold would have to be cut.

That was a very dangerous procedure. If the bracing wires did not hold, the cargo structures could topple over with the containers still in them. Should they fall sidewise, they could—and probably would—tear through the network cording around the neighboring cells and make huge holes. If they fell sidewise, they would wreck the hull framework. In the first case, that of cell damage, the ship would become so heavy it would plunge into the sea. In the second case, the framework might be completely broken and the ship would break in two. If it held together, there would be no way to get the containers out. And Silver was depending upon jettisoning them to keep the AZ-49 aloft.

However, there was some good news. Despite the difficulty in working in the rough air, the sail-makers had patched all the holes in the cells. They had done an almost miraculous job in such a short time.

Heading aft, Silver saw a man running down the catwalk. It was Agocelli.

Agocelli stopped. A Breizist at the far end yelled at him, asking what he thought he was doing. Agocelli shouted back that he was delivering a message from the control room. The third mate had phoned Silver, but he wasn't in sight. So the guard at the hatch, seeing Silver, had told Siskatoo. And he'd sent Agocelli.

Silver, impatient, yelled, "*What is it, Agocelli?*"

"Officer Siskatoo says to tell you that we're about to hit really rough air! Everybody should tie themselves down, if they can, and if they can't, hang on!"

"Is everybody notified?"

"Yes, sir. I gotta go, Captain."

"Before I hit you?" asked Silver. At that moment he was hurled down onto the platform deck. An invisible force, pressing him downward and also to port, perhaps 35 degrees, made it impossible for him to rise. For a moment, the unexpected and violent change of situation scattered his senses. Then they decided to come home. Now he knew what was happening. A terrible updraft was carrying the giant airship toward the skies as if it were a stone ejected by an erupting volcano.

Metal groaned all around him. Behind was a screech that tore at his nerves. Girders were coming apart . . . and then came the twang of shear wires snapping.

The pressure increased. Turning over, holding on with one hand to an upright, he looked back. The electric lights were flickering, but he could see between the girders of the starboard cargo hold.

It was empty.

The bottom girders had broken under the load, precipitating 560 pounds if the containers were completely empty. More if the liquid methane had not completely evaporated.

The sudden loss of weight had made the ship rise even faster in the updraft. And the containers in the port hold must not have fallen. It was their weight which was causing the list to port. This was not so much now, perhaps 15 degrees, but that was far too much.

Slowly, the pressure on him eased. The updraft was losing its hold on the vessel. The gas cells nearest him had swelled. As the altitude increased, the lessening atmospheric pressure allowed the helium in the bags to expand.

He did not know whether or not the ship had been carried above its pressure height. The air seemed thin but it did not seem as oxygen-poor as it would have been if the altitude were 20,000 feet. In fact, it had to be much lower. If the pressure height had been exceeded, he'd have been unconscious by now. And the automatic valves on the bottom of the cells might not have opened swiftly enough to relieve the pressure. In which case, the cells would have burst.

He noticed that the ingots lining the catwalk were gone. Of course. They would have slid overboard when the ship had leaned to port.

So much the better. That meant less weight. But Hooke was going to be furious. Maybe she'd be too scared to even think of her loss.

He stood up and started walking forward to check on the damage. Suddenly, he was floating a few inches off the catwalk. Terrified, he grabbed for something to hold onto. There was nothing to reach, though a wire was only a few inches from his hand.

Once more, he was bewildered. As his feet slowly regained the catwalk, he realized that the ship was now in a terrific downdraft.

His hands gripped the side of the walk. It was well he did, for his grip was almost torn away by a sudden violent jerk to starboard. More yells. A crack of something large breaking. Screams of torn metal.

What else could happen?

That question was answered at once. Something struck the deck in front of him. Something else hit him in the back, causing him to cry out with surprise and pain. Other objects splattered onto the metal in front of him, and his leg felt another blow.

He was so confused that it took several seconds to recognize the orange-sized grayish-white objects, some of which were spread out by their impact.

Hailstones!

He said, "Ooof!" as another hit him between the shoulder blades. One smashed just before his eyes, spraying icy particles on his forehead and nose.

Then it was over. He lay for a few seconds, waiting to be hit again. Quivering, he got to his feet, his hand squeezing an upright.

Agocelli, moaning, ran by him.

Vaguely, he noted that the zeppelin had almost regained its proper horizontal attitude. At least, it felt as if it had.

The catwalk was twisted, curving in two places. Shear wires hung loose here and there, and a transverse ring was definitely out of line with the rest.

Moreover, there were holes in the gas cells again. Ordinarily, the hull and the bags would hold out against any normal-size, normal-velocity hail. But these monsters had come plunging through like meteors of ice. What made the phenomenon so strange, however, was the fact that the ship had been falling when the hail struck. The pellets must have been hurled by a different draft from the one which had pressed down on the ship. Or was that possible?

By then his mental numbness had lifted. Now he knew that the restored lateral attitude of the vessel had to be due to the loss of the modules and containers in the port hold. The bottom girders had snapped.

He continued on the crosswalk to the port catwalk. From the platform, he looked down the length of the hull. The nearest cells displayed some holes; shear wires were dangling; but the port hold indeed was empty.

However, one of the containers, undoubtedly from the topmost module, had somehow been tossed out before the cargo had fallen. The brown plastic cube was on its side, resting against a girder, kept from falling by some wires.

He staggered to the phone, noting on the way that the ship now seemed to be nose-heavy. There were no outside references to determine this, of course, but gravity was definitely pulling him forward.

Siskatoo answered the phone. Frightened voices almost drowned out his. But he spoke calmly, as calmly as if he were ordering dinner.

"We came close that time," Siskatoo said. "Another twenty feet, and we'd have crashed. We're rising now, but we are nose-heavy."

I'll get the sailmakers on the bags," Silver said, "if they weren't all pitched overboard. Now, Siskatoo, everything in the control room goes out. The control computer, the chairs, the radar."

"The radar?" Siskatoo said, shaken.

"Yes! We can't afford its weight, and it won't make any difference if we know how fast we're falling if we can't do anything about it. I'll also send riggers to cut out the equipment in the radome.

"And tell Hooke that her weapons have to go, too."

"She won't go for that."

"Make clear what might happen if she hangs onto them."

He called Luzel, who sounded scared. In as few words as possible, Silver told him the situation. Then he asked for the rigger and sailmaker C.P.O.'s.

Salmons, who answered first, was breathing heavily. Silver ordered him to dump all the oil in the fuel tanks and then cut them loose. After that, he was to cut loose the nose- and tail-engine gondolas. Then the housings and struts for the gear transmission and propellers.

"After which you will remove the mooring bolts of the inboard diesels and all their connections. Then you will muscle the engines overboard.

"Shove them over on alternate sides. The fore starboard engine first. The aft port engine next, and so on. We don't want to unbalance the ship any more than we have to."

"Yes, sir. Only we don't have near the tools we need. Most of the heavy crowbars went into the drink to lighten the ship, or were lost during the drafts. Not only that, we'll have to run back and forth like madmen! My crew is pooped out!"

"Do the impossible," Silver said, echoing the orders of a long line of officers, a line that probably went back to the Bronze Age, if not further.

Viren, the sailmaker chief, got his orders to look for the new holes and patch them. He groaned but said nothing.

Twenty-Three

Silver went into a room in the tail section and down a ladder. Confusion and panic predominated in the main passageway, but work was being done. All the cabin doors had been removed and thrown out. White-faced passengers were carrying out the chairs and beds now. Even the doors to the control room had been removed. Silver, having entered via a ladder in the tail section, could see the lower part of the entranceway through the smoking room, the navigation room, and the bridge. An armed man stood at the doorway of the smoking room.

Walking forward, he found out that one door still remained, that on Jill's cabin. It was opened enough to reveal a short chunky man with a bushy black beard and a fringe of bristly hair around his bald pate. He held a rifle. The interior of the cabin was dark.

"Are you Kapten?" Silver said.

"Yeah. What's it to you?"

"I'm Captain Silver. You've been informed that the ship's in grave danger."

"Sure." Kapten grinned. "That's quite a show you're putting on. You had me fooled for a while. But not any longer. Them bums, the frogs, and that Hooke, they made you do it, didn't they? So I'd get sucked outta here and—blammo!"

For a moment, Silver was speechless. Then he said, "This is for real! We may fall into the ocean any minute! Everybody's got to pitch in and help! And every bit of excess weight *has to be* thrown overboard!"

Kapten spoke, apparently to the men behind him. "Ain't that something? I told you it was all a trick. He sure puts on a good act, though, don't he?"

There was no use wasting time arguing with this man, a splendid example of what Mark Twain called "invincible ignorance."

Jill's voice came from the darkness. "Greatheart! Operation Odin!"

Silver wanted to protest, but he dared not. She had decided to take action that might result in her being killed. Not to mention himself. However, she must have a good reason for this desperate move.

Kapten half-turned. "What's this? Operation Odor? Shut that chick up, Punchy."

Strange cries burst from the room. A black cloud suddenly struck Kapten's head from behind. He screamed and batted with one hand at the thing.

Head down, Silver charged. His shoulder rammed into the door, which struck Kapten and sent him rolling. Silver pitched forward onto the deck, spun on his side, and grabbed Kapten's beard. He jerked with all his strength.

A man, yelling, his head also covered by a black cloud, tried to run out of the cabin. He stumbled over Silver and Kapten and sprawled on the deck, his body halfway out into the passageway.

Kapten, bellowing with pain and anger, was up. Then he was diving for the rifle, the barrel of which was revealed in the light from the passageway. Silver couldn't get to Kapten fast enough, but two clouds, feathers flying, swooped onto him. The beaks and the claws of Huggin and Muggin pecked and tore at him. Kapten yelled, "My eyes! My eyes!" and he dropped the weapon.

Silver yelled, "Huggin! Muggin! Retreat!"

The light came on. Silver, rising with Kapten's rifle, saw Jill standing over a man's prostrate body. An automatic pistol, butt reversed, was in her hand. Beyond her were the two raven cages, hanging from stands on the bulkhead. Their doors were open.

"That was pretty dangerous, Jill," Silver said. "Downright foolish."

"I was desperate," she said.

"Well, it turned out all right." He grinned. "Those birds certainly responded on cue."

As he spoke, the huge ravens fluttered from the edge of the bed and settled down on his shoulders. Silver spoke to them, and they flew back to the bed.

Kapten, holding his bleeding face, got to his feet. Silver told him to get into the corner. The man who'd fallen over him groaned. Silver got him up and shoved him toward the corner. The man from whom Jill had snatched the gun was still unconscious.

Flaherty came in grinning. "Sure, and what's this?"

Silver explained, then said, "Throw their weapons overboard. Get some passengers to strip this cabin. Put these creeps to work."

Kapten said, "You'll pay for this, you jerk! I'll get you!"

Silver whirled on him. "It may come down to deciding who's going to be thrown out so we can lose weight. You'll be the first candidate if you don't cooperate!"

Kapten croaked, "You can't do that! I got my rights!"

"We're in international waters. The only law here is the captain's, and I'm in command."

"Yeah! Tell that to those frogs and that butch!"

"They don't love you either," Silver said. "Jill, are you able to help out?"

"I'm a little shaky, but I'll be all right. I'll take the guns and the ammo and get rid of them."

He paused. "Sweetheart."

Jill smiled wanly. "Okay, sweetheart. I've been doing a lot of thinking. The Hoowards and that steward must've been paid by Daddy to frame you. But I won't really know until they confess, will I?"

"They will. Or I'll wring their necks."

After throwing the captured weapons and ammunition overboard, Silver pushed his way through the mob to the bridge. A man holding a rifle stopped him at the entrance to the control room and frisked him. Silver bellowed for Hooke, who came waddling to the doorway. She was very short, very broad, and looked like Santa Claus minus the beard. Minus also the twinkling eyes. They were mean, tinged with scare. And Santa Claus never wore pistols nor carried an automatic rifle.

"Let him in, Anko."

The windscreens had been cranked down. The electronics crew had gutted the control console and thrown out its contents. They were unscrewing the bolts securing the console to the deck. All the chairs had already gone overboard.

Silver was amazed to find that there were only two robbers left. Ronan, the Breton hostage, sat in a corner, scowling.

Hooke said, "What was that shooting about?"

Silver told her. She looked at him narrow-eyed. "You sure you didn't hide them rifles?"

"I thought about it. But I'm the one who gave the order to get rid of all weapons."

"No, we don't," Hooke said, walking toward him, her belly shaking like a bowl of jelly. "You're going to get this tub onto land. Otherwise, I'll shoot you—if it's the last thing I do."

Twenty-Four

"That'd save me from drowning by a few seconds," Silver said. "And it would be the last thing you'd do. If you're hanging on to the guns because of the platinum and iridium, forget it. They went overboard when the ship rolled."

Hooke looked stunned. Then she burst into tears.

"You mean it?" she said, sobbing.

"Ask Luzel."

"I wouldn't trust that crook. He'd try to keep it for himself."

"No, he's seen the damage and he knows what a mess we're in. Now, get rid of those guns."

"Not me, mister. Not even if Luzel's gang throws their blasters away. If we get to land, we'll need them. Old Hooke ain't going out without a fight."

Silver said, "At least chuck the rifles. You can get by with your pistols. I tell you, every ounce gotten rid of means a few more minutes of life."

Hooke wiped her eyes with a big, dirty handkerchief. "Yeah? You really mean it, don't you? Okay. If Luzel does the same."

Luzel finally answered. Silver told him what had happened, then gave the phone to Hooke.

There was a long discussion, punctuated by bursts of profanity from Hooke. Somebody, Flaherty probably, had ordered the stewards to make sandwiches. Agocelli staggered in under a huge tray holding sandwiches, cookies, glasses of milk, and several bottles of booze and wine.

"This is the last supper," Agocelli said in a shaky voice. "We're throwing the trays out and the cutlery, after everybody eats. From now on, if you want food, you'll have to go to the galley to get it."

Silver said, "I'll take a couple of ham-on-ryes and milk, steward."

Agocelli came toward him but stopped several feet away. His arms shaking under the strain, he held the tray out to Silver. Apparently, he did not want to get within hitting distance.

Hooke snatched two sandwiches with one hand and a bottle of Duggan's Dew of Kirkintilloch with the other. Stuffing half a sandwich into her mouth, she chewed savagely for a minute, then washed the food down with several ounces of the scotch.

"Say, Agocelli," she said, "things ain't turning out the way we hoped, are they?"

Silver said, "What's this? What do you mean?"

Hooke took another massive bite. Mayonnaise streaked her chin and lips.

"No harm telling you now."

"No!" Agocelli cried. "You promised to keep quiet!"

"Aw, what the hell's the use now? Anyway, I ain't taking you with us. The metals're gone; your usefulness is over. Yeah. This little creep sold you out, Silver. He smuggled our guns in for us. Really held us up on the price, too. That's the kind of jerk you got working for you."

Agocelli paled and retreated a few more steps.

Hooke laughed, spewing food down her front. "He snuck the guns in long before the ship took off. Had to bribe a guard to do it, though."

Silver, glaring, said, "Agocelli was working for somebody *else*, too. He was in a frame with the Hoowards to bust up my marriage."

At that moment, the bridge deck tilted up. For a second, Silver thought it was an updraft. It wasn't however. The nose-engine gondola had been cut off by the laser. Now Salmons and his gang would hasten with their equipment to the tail, over a quarter of a mile away, and would sever the support struts of the engine gondola there.

The phone rang. Silver, nearest it, answered. Luzel, panting, said, "What are your demands?"

Silver told him that Hooke would agree to throw away the rifles if the Breizists did the same.

"How would we arrange that so nobody is holding any rifles back?"

"I know how many each party has," Silver said. "I'll collect them. I'm an impartial agent."

"Yes, but what if we gave you our rifles and then she refused to surrender hers?"

Silver sighed, and he said, "A good point. Very well. I'll stand by in the observation deck. Each gun can be brought alternately to me.

First one of yours, then one of hers. No, make that simultaneous. Since there's two of them and five of you, your man should bring in all your rifles and her man will bring her three. Miggleton left his when he became your hostage."

He added, "Then I'll count them and throw them out."

"I don't like it, but I can see the gravity of the situation, no pun intended."

Silver called Hooke to the phone. She talked a minute, then hung up. "Okay, Captain, you get to the observation room."

The transaction took ten minutes. As one of Hooke's men, carrying three clipless rifles, came down the passageway, one of Luzel's, burdened with five, approached from a point equidistant from the control room. Silver took their weapons and cast them out the port. The two, their hands on the butts of their holstered pistols, backed away from each other.

During this time, the tail-engine gondola was cut lose. The dirigible was now close to a horizontal attitude.

The rigger C.P.O. reported that the fuel tanks had been released. Cutting was now being done on the fore starboard transmission gear and propeller struts.

Viren, the sailmaker chief, reported that three cells were completely patched. But he had nineteen holes to go.

"You sound like you're playing golf," Silver said.

The ship's doctor called as soon as Silver hung up.

"I'm sorry. My patient, you know, the hostage, just died. It's not my fault. He was too far gone. And my surgical equipment . . ."

"I know, Doc," Silver said. "Just get rid of everything in the sick bay. And I mean everything."

He hung up. Hooke said, "Who was that?"

Silver hesitated. If he told her the truth, he might be held responsible for her hostage's death. On the other hand, if Ronan were dead, he could be thrown out and the ship would have that much more lift.

He said, "It was the doctor. He wanted to know if he should throw his medical equipment overboard."

Dawn came, bringing light but little relief. The sailmakers had just found two holes in the cells they had unaccountably missed in the first inspection. The vessel was only fifty feet from the waves when the last of the ten engines was jettisoned. The ship responded by rising to an estimated six hundred feet.

Telling Hooke that he was going to see if he couldn't get more food brought in, Silver went down the passageway. Most of the passengers were lying down on the deck of the observation room or in the main smoking room. They huddled together as if for comfort.

He checked on the doctor, to make sure that Miggleton's corpse had gone out. The doctor complained a little about having to drag it out to the tail and rolling it out a hatch without any help. Silver said, "You could stand a little exercise, Doc."

He went to the port catwalk and walked down to a point opposite the big container caught in the wires. He paused to consider it. Should he get rid of it now or wait a little longer?

And then he was lifted up, curving backward and sideways as if he were a diver leaving a springboard. His shoulders smashed into the hard metal of the catwalk. A great cracking noise drowned out any others that might be made.

When he finally regained all of his senses or most of them—some seemed to have been lost forever—he was able to reconstruct what had happened.

Another downdraft had gripped the airship and hurled it toward the ocean. It had also twisted the framework again. He had been launched from the catwalk. As his luck had it—it couldn't be all bad, could it?—he had not been precipitated off the catwalk and so become food for the fishes. Speaking of which, they could not be too far away. Ocean water was lapping against the catwalk, occasionally surging up and wetting his back.

Standing groggily, he looked around. The container was now floating on the water, which was almost washing over the top of the main passageway. The impact of the crash had dislodged it.

He started to groan with pain, but, seeing Jill standing on the platform, he gave a cry of delight. She pushed through the people on it and came down to greet him. They put their arms around each other and wept.

"The crash knocked me out," she said, "but the water rushing into the cabin woke me up. I fought my way up to the tail section. A lot of people got out, though I don't see how."

Greatheart looked over her shoulder through a huge tear in the covering. The sea was comparatively smooth; the sun shone unhindered by clouds; the storm was over.

But their ordeal was by no means over. They were down in the ocean, kept afloat only because of the gas cells. The ship's metal skeleton had been twisted and damaged to such a degree that it might break apart at any time. Though the surface of the ocean, judging from the rise and fall, consisted of long, low rollers, the prolonged action might separate the aft and fore parts.

They had no means of notifying ships or shore stations of their location. Which, in any case, they did not know except in a general sense. If the navigational satellite was still malfunctioning, it could be some time before they were located and help could arrive. By then, they could be under the ocean.

The first thing he did was to check on the food and water. There was enough in the aft section, in the crew's stores, to last them two days. Then he checked on the survivors. Amazingly, there were forty. Four, however, had broken legs; three, broken arms; one, a minor concussion of the skull. All, including himself, were badly bruised and suffering from various degrees of cuts.

Apparently, de Rioux had been among those who'd drowned. His secretary and two bodyguards had been trapped with him.

Siskatoo had not made it out of the control room.

He was not happy to find that Luzel and three of his gang were among the living. Nor that Hooke and one of hers were limping around. All of the kidnappers, except Kapten, had died. Nor was he gratified that the Hoowards and Agocelli looked healthy, discounting their frightened faces, skinned knees, and various contusions.

The only two who had not lost their pistols—wouldn't you know it?—were Luzel and Hooke.

Amey, the doctor, did the best he could for the people with the broken limbs, but it wasn't much.

Silver made sure that the electric generating equipment was still working and that the laser cutter and certain tools were still available.

After this, he got everybody on the catwalk. Addressing them from the platform, he said, "We may drift to Easter Island, that is, Rapa Nui. Perhaps, a ship might pick us up. But we may sink before that happens, and we're short on food and water. So, here's what I propose."

His audience was stunned. Finally, Hooke said, "You must be crazy!" A few echoed her sentiment. The others looked as if they thought his plan was desperate but agreed there was little else they could do.

During the long day, the airship looked like a broken but busy beehive. The riggers used the laser to remove the girders atop Cell No. 2. As these fell, they were diverted to one side by ropes attached to their severed ends. This prevented the thin cover of the cell from being damaged.

Meanwhile, the container was pulled out of the water and gotten onto the catwalk.

The cell was already covered by a rope network. The ends attached to the lower girders were freed. The cell floated up for a short distance, then was held from rising on through the hole by wires placed through the bottom of the rope network. The ends of the wires had been run over girders and twisted around the wires.

Salmons returned to the container and with his laser cut off its upper portion. This was shoved into the sea, where it floated bumping against the side of the catwalk. Salmons then cut a series of holes about six inches below the open edge of the container.

A gang shoved the container into the water, where it was jockeyed around until it was directly below the cell. At this point Silver would have liked to place a circular piece of metal at a point below the cell and then attach the ends of the rope network to it. There was none available, and he had no means of making one. The laser could cut a strip from a girder, and it could heat parts of the strip soft enough to be curved. But the laser could not weld the open ends of the piece together, and the welding equipment had gone overboard long ago.

Instead, the ends of the netting were looped through the holes in the sides of the container and tied.

A length of rope was attached to the automatic valve on the

bottom of the cell. Its free end dangled to a few feet within the deck of the container. If the rope were pulled upon, it could open the valve, an arrangement made possible by Salmons, though undreamed of by its designer.

Though he was exhausted, Silver had enough energy to feel pride when he looked at the completed vessel.

What he saw was, in effect, a free balloon.

It was rough work, but he hoped it was adequate.

Everybody was exhausted from emotional drainage, physical battering, and lack of sleep. He let most of them lie down while food and water were brought out of the crew's galley.

"Eat up. Drink up," he said, giving them an example. "This is the last of it."

After half an hour, a silent time broken only by the moans of the hurt, he got the ambulatory to their feet.

A section of a ladder had been cut, one end tied down to the catwalk and the other end run out over the container or "basket." The riggers carried pieces of metal of varying weight into the basket and arranged them along the sides. They were to be used as ballast.

Next came the badly injured. They were assisted or carried over the ladder or even dragged, not without some complaints, over the ladder and handed down to the riggers. After this, all but two riggers climbed out. The others stayed to help the passengers in.

Huggin and Muggin, the ravens, flew onto the edge of the basket, where they perched.

Meanwhile, Silver had passed word through the crew to line up on the catwalk ahead of the passengers. He took a place in between the two groups. If Luzel or Hooke thought this was a peculiar boarding arrangement, they did not say anything.

This might have been because they were watching each other too intently. At no time did they take their eyes off each other, and they managed to keep a good distance between them. Moreover, their hands never left their pistol butts.

Luzel now stood up at the foot of the ladder to the platform. His men, armed with crowbars and metal saws, stood behind him. Hooke stood on the crosswalk to the right of the platform.

"Okay, Captain Silver!" Luzel shouted. "I have an . . ."

"Just a minute, Luzel," Hooke said. "I got something to do before we take off. Agocelli, you dirty, double-crossing fink! You put the shiv in my back, and what's more you stuck it into Luzel, too!"

"What do you mean?" Luzel said.

"I mean, I found out that he not only smuggled in guns for me and Kapten, he smuggled them in for you, too! He took money from all three of us, knowing we was bound to shoot each other. I call that triple-crossing, not double. What's more, he probably took money from the captain's wife's old man to frame him. So that makes it a quadruple-cross!"

She snatched the pistol from her holster and aimed it at Agocelli. The steward, his ferret face twisted with horror, screamed, "Please, Captain, don't let her do nothing to me! I confess! I confess! I was in on the frameup with the Hoowards! But if you save me, I'll testify in court that you was framed!"

"It'd serve you right if she did shoot you," Silver said.

He spoke to Hooke. "Come on. Put that gun down. You're not judge and jury. He'll get what's coming to him when we get back to the States."

"What do I have to lose?" she cried. "I'll be in the slammer for life if I'm caught, but I ain't going to be. No, I pays my dues, and rat-finks is one of them."

Agocelli backed away, forcing the crew behind him to retreat. Silver was also pressed back. There was no way he could do anything about Hooke except talk to her. She was beyond his reach. Anyway, even if he had been close to her, why should he risk his life by jumping her? He wasn't going to get killed trying to save that piece of slime, Agocelli.

Hooke's gun bellowed. Agocelli, lifted up and spun around by the force of the Magnum .375, disappeared over the other side of the catwalk.

A second later, Luzel's automatic boomed. Hooke was knocked backward into her colleague, and both went down. Neither got up. Apparently, the bullet had gone through both of them. The woman's pistol had flown out of her hand and dropped into the water.

Luzel, pointing his weapon at the crew in front of him, said, "I was waiting for a chance to get her. She was a mad dog, an irresponsible killer."

He backed away. "And now," he said, "comes the denouement. It's obvious that we cannot afford to take you people along. If we get to Rapa Nui, you'd tell the authorities about us, and we'd be jailed. And eventually we'd be guillotined in Paris.

"But if there are no witnesses, then we will just be poor devils who survived the crash of a zeppelin at sea.

"Besides, the fewer there are for the balloon to carry, the more chance it has of reaching land."

Passengers cried out; many wept. Luzel, waving his pistol, shouted angrily. "I do not like to do this! But it is necessary for patriotic reasons! My men and I must not be kept from advancing our great cause! I hope you understand, even if you cannot fully sympathize."

Silver, hidden by the crew in front of him, stood on one leg, a hand gripping a crewman's shoulder to support himself. Jill swiftly rolled up his left pants leg. He lifted the leg, and she turned the plastic member to remove the neural connections. Two complete turns unscrewed the leg.

"I could leave you on this floating hulk so that perhaps you might drift to land or be picked up by a boat . . ."

"Ship, dammit!" Flaherty said.

Luzel glared at the Irishman. "You will be the first to swim for it.

"Now this grieves me, but it is a matter of necessity, of historical pressure, of inevitability."

Mrs. Hooward screamed, "We'll drown! Or be eaten by sharks!"

"Then you can make an existentialist choice of your fate," Luzel said. "Very well. Mr. Flaherty, you will jump into the water and swim through that breach in the hull. Land is due southeast of us, perhaps a hundred miles away. Or so you told me."

"Thanks for the directions," Flaherty said. "You scum!"

"The patriot must expect abuse," Luzel said, smiling. "Go ahead, Mr. Flaherty. I don't want to shoot you. But if I have to in order to set an example for the others, I will."

Silver had by then adjusted controls in a groove on the inner side of the plastic leg. He held the end of the thigh in his right hand while Jill's finger poised above a button.

"Now!" he bellowed, and he threw the leg over the heads of the crowd in front of him.

Spitting a narrow, blue-white flame a foot long, it rotated in an arc, the end of which was Luzel.

The Breton froze just long enough for the missile to strike him. Unfortunately, the thigh-end hit him. But as the leg bounced off his chest and flopped over the catwalk, its flame turned at him. In effect, a hot foot gave Luzel the hot foot.

The Breton jumped back, screaming, and he fired at the plastic leg. By then, Flaherty, head down, bellowing like one of the bulls of Cooley, was charging. The top of his head rammed into Luzel, who folded. His automatic fired twice, but it was pointed away from the crowd. Over he went, Flaherty on top of him.

Close behind the second officer came the crewmen. They leaped over the two strugglers and bulldozed the other Bretons backward.

The battle was furious but brief. Flaherty wrenched the pistol loose from Luzel's grip, and it slid into the sea. The burly Irishman then proceeded to choke the Breton until he became unconscious.

The five Breizists hurt a few of the crewmen, though not seriously. Then they went down under a barrage of fists and feet.

Twenty-Five

Jill retrieved the leg and turned off the flame. Greatheart resecured it and then got things going swiftly. The Bretons were dragged upon the platform and their hands and ankles bound with rope.

"We'll be long gone by the time you work yourselves loose," Silver told the now conscious Luzel. "I don't want you to be able to interfere with our ascent. I won't wish you good luck."

Luzel groaned and spit out a tooth.

"If we reach land, I'll send a ship out for you. Maybe you'd better wish *me* luck."

"Either way, I die."

"Then you have an existentialist choice of your manner of death."

The boarding took fifteen minutes. Silver got into the basket last. He looked around, then opened his mouth to order the men stationed at each corner of the basket to cut the restraining wires. Jill put a hand on his shoulder and said, "Are you really going to leave those men here?"

"I've been wondering if I should," Silver said. "It goes against my grain to do it, but they *are* dangerous."

"Yes," said Jill, "but you've allowed Kapten and his men to come along. And they are just as bad."

Silver looked at the kidnappers, who sat on the deck, their hands bound before them.

"Okay. I was really hoping someone would argue with me about Luzel."

There was another delay while the Breizists' feet were unbound and they were roughly muscled into the basket. Luzel cursed him while this was going on.

Silver said, "Your gratitude overwhelms me. Now, sit down in the middle there and don't annoy me at all. Otherwise . . ."

He made a gesture as if he were throwing ballast overboard.

The wires were cut. The cell, looking not at all like the layman's conception of a balloon, resembling more a wrinkled elephant skin hung up to dry, rose slowly. Some of the passengers cheered; others looked as if they were going to be sick.

The balloon rose straight up until the upper one-third had cleared the hole in the top of the zeppelin. Then, as Silver had expected, it moved forward. And it stuck.

Though the airship was being moved by the wind on the ocean surface, its speed was slower than the air outside the hull. The wind had pushed against the upper part and now only the up-and-down movement of the ship in the waves would free it. Knowing this, he had had the girder ends wrapped in covering taken from a cell.

Some of the passengers asked why the balloon was not moving. Silver ignored them. The balloon would have to free itself; he could do nothing to aid it. If it did not get loose, then it would have to be brought back down. He'd pull the release valve cord, and the balloon would settle back. And they would be back where they had started.

Well, yes, he could do something.

"Throw out two pieces of ballast."

Over they went, splashing in the well below.

Suddenly more buoyant because of the loss of weight, the balloon shot up. Passengers and crew cheered. But Silver, Flaherty, and Moon leaned out over the side of the basket. As the balloon sped up and out, it would drag the basket along. Here came the end of a girder, inserting itself between ropes. The three pushed against the girder just above them, and the basket swung back. Just enough to free it. For a second, the basket scraped against the girder end, tearing off the wrapped cell-covering. But not before Silver saw that the girder had not been thoroughly covered. A thin edge of metal had projected beyond the fabric. There was a chance that the thin skin of the cell had been ripped. If so, it would have been better to have stayed on the AZ-49.

Looking back at the zeppelin, now dwindling as it fell behind and below, Silver estimated the wind speed. It should be around a spanking twelve miles an hour. Number 3 on the Beaufort scale. A gentle breeze.

They were on their way, but to where?

An hour passed. As the helium in the balloon expanded due to lessening atmospheric pressure, the balloon became rounded. It would continue to rise until it reached pressure height, at which point the valve would open automatically. But it could not be allowed to go so high. Everybody aboard would die of oxygen starvation before it attained its maximum ascent. As soon as breathing became difficult, it would be necessary to release some helium with the cord.

After that, the balloon would fall. It would do so slowly, but nevertheless, unless checked, it would descend. Only Silver's skill could keep it up beyond its natural rate of fall. And the situation would be complicated, though possibly improved, by temperature inversions, updrafts, and down-drafts. And by his aptitude at estimating ballast jettison.

"We must be at about ten thousand feet," Silver said. "It's hard to judge."

A few minutes later Flaherty said, "I think I see land. It could be low clouds on the horizon, though."

"If it's land," Silver said, "it could be Rapa Nui. Or maybe one of the islands closer to Chile, Sala-y-Gomez, or San Felix, or Juan Fernandez, one of those islands. Maybe even Chile. I don't know. There's no telling how far that wind blew us since we lost our instruments.

"But if we are at about ten-thousand-feet altitude, and if that is land, then it's about one hundred and seventeen miles away."

A half-hour passed. Silver, using his wristwatch, estimating the distance between wavecaps over an estimated mileage, tried to calculate their velocity.

"I make it between thirty-five and forty miles an hour," he said to Flaherty. "The wind's stronger up here."

"Yes, but it seems to have gotten stronger on the surface, too," Flaherty said. "Look at those waves."

Silver did not bother. He was too intent on his figuring.

"If the wind keeps up, we'll get to that land, if it is land, in about three-and-a-half hours, maybe four. Just pray that the wind keeps its direction. If it shifts, it could blow us to one side."

"The balloon'll stay up that long, won't it?"

"Sure!"

A half-hour passed. The land, or the clouds, swelled slightly.

And at the same time it became evident that the waves were getting larger.

Silver's heart turned over like a cold motor with a weak battery.

The balloon was losing altitude.

He went around the basket, leaning out to look above. The enormous bulge of the semisphere made it impossible to see any holes in the upper part. It was easy to see that the bag was deflating, however.

His inspection finished, Silver said, "That girder must have torn a hole. Okay. Get rid of four of the larger pieces of ballast."

Flaherty did so. The balloon rose again, then started to settle down. Two more pieces went over the side. Since it was difficult to conceal the reasons for the sudden activity, Silver told the passengers not to panic. Some of them went into a fit anyway.

Mrs. Hooward yelled, "It's all your fault!"

"You could have stayed behind," he said. "I told you about the dangers."

He looked around. "Flaherty, untie those men. They're going to need their hands, and they're too outnumbered to give us any trouble.

"Now, everybody throw overboard anything you're carrying or wearing except your underwear. We need all the lift we can get."

He removed his wristwatch and flipped it over the side. Huggin, the raven, left his perch, disappearing from view.

Most of the people obeyed him quickly enough, but Mrs. Hooward and two other passengers seemed reluctant. Silver urged them on. Mrs. Hooward plucked a pearl necklace and a tiny jewel box from between her breasts. Another woman wept as she threw out a diamond necklace and a wristwatch which she had hidden in her bra. A man, scowling, cast his wallet and two jeweled rings over the side.

At that moment, Silver was startled by Huggin's landing on his shoulder. He turned his head to see his wristwatch dangling from the raven's beak.

"He must have dived after it when you threw it out," Jill said.

Silver removed the watch and cast it over again. His left hand held the bird's legs, restraining him from repeating the feat.

"Say, what about the crows?" a passenger said. "They weigh *something*."

The man was right, except about his identification of them as crows. Silver called Muggin to his other shoulder and spoke to the two birds, pointing at the clouds ahead. After some croaking protests, they obeyed. He watched them wing toward the dark mass on the horizon, wondering if they would be the only survivors.

Another half-hour. More and more ballast hurtled toward the sea, which seemed to rise toward them depressingly often. Silver tried to measure out the lost weight sparingly. The higher the balloon rose, the more helium escaped because of the difference in pressure.

Another thirty minutes. More ballast was tossed. Two more hours passed. And the last piece of metal was dropped.

But now, the clouds were not clouds. They were land! *Mountains!* Hills, anyway.

Grinning, Greatheart Silver announced the news. Everybody cheered.

Ten minutes later, his spirits chuted from high to low. The balloon was sinking again and so swiftly that it would be in the ocean many miles from land.

Nobody cheered.

"Okay, everybody. Off with your underwear. Every last stitch."

To set an example, he removed his T-shirt and shorts and dropped them over the side. A few people protested, though not vigorously.

Mrs. Hooward, looking malicious, said, "Off with it, Silver."

"What? I'm not wearing anything, as you can plainly see."

"Your handy-dandy, razzle-dazzle, flame-throwing electro-mechanical member. Your plastic leg."

Greatheart stuttered with rage. "But, madame, I can't walk without it."

Flaherty said, "Logically, she's correct, sor."

A number of passengers seemed to agree.

He shrugged, "All right."

A moment later, he sailed the leg over the edge. His eyes were dimmed with wetness. It was almost like losing a part of his body. Hell, it was just that. He could get another one, but it would put him in debt for years. At that thought, the tears did flow.

By then the balloon was falling even faster. The land was three or four miles away, and the basket would touch water in about three minutes.

"And no more ballast," Silver muttered.

Flaherty said, "Sor, your permission to leave the vessel. I'm a strong swimmer, Captain, and the seas ain't so rough, ayther. I can make it."

"That's a noble thought, Flaherty," Silver said. "But what about the sharks?"

"I don't see any. Anyway, if I don't do it, we'll all be battling sharks soon enough."

"Go, and God bless you," Silver said, choking.

"Sure, I always was glory-happy."

Two minutes passed. "We're almost ready to hit," Flaherty said. "Wish me luck, Captain."

Over the edge went Flaherty. Silver watched him fall feet-first and enter upright. The Irishman emerged grinning, waved a hand at them, and began swimming strongly. The balloon was rising—for the moment.

Twenty-Six

Silver watched, sweating from more than the westering but still hot sun, as the coast slowly drew nearer. The balloon began dropping again. When it was two miles from the surf-pounded beach, it would strike the water. For a little while the wind would blow it along with the basket tilted. Then it would fall to the surface, and water would enter the basket. Eventually, the basket would go under, and there would be thirty-two people in the water. Ten of whom couldn't swim at all.

Then Moon, the chief electronics officer, made the offer. "Captain, I'm not a bad swimmer myself. I'll go next, if the situation demands it."

"God bless you, too," Silver said.

A moment later, she went over the edge, falling about ten feet. Immediately, the balloon rose.

But four minutes later, he felt compelled to call for another volunteer. Sparks said he would go, though he wasn't exactly eager.

"You coward!" Mrs. Hooward said to Silver. "Why don't you volunteer?"

"Madame," Silver said, "and I do mean 'madame,' I'm the captain. The captain is always the last to leave a vessel in distress. It's an ancient tradition."

Sparks sat on the rim of the basket, one hand gripping a rope, facing Silver. "Tell my wife I love her, even if she is hell-on-wheels to live with. And tell her there's a checkbook taped to the back of the Maxfield Parrish picture in the living room. I got a hidden account. Only don't tell her if I make it. She'd kill me."

"I promise. And go with my blessing."

Sparks let himself off backward, like an aqualung diver. The balloon soared up. But not for long.

Jill called up from below. "Are we going to make it?"

Greatheart shook his head.

"I'm going next," she said, "and don't you dare say no. You know what a great swimmer I am, sweetheart. I'm also a coward. I was waiting for someone to volunteer. But I guess they aren't going to."

He squeezed her and kissed her cheek. "You're no coward. I am. I just don't think I could make it, though, and that'd be a useless sacrifice."

"I know. Well, so long, baby. I love you."

Jill seemed to be in no difficulty, and there were no shark fins visible. She'd make it.

A few minutes later he asked for more volunteers. This time, since the coast was only half a mile away, Salmons and four crewmen went overboard. The balloon rose swiftly, and presently it cleared the beach and the low hills behind it by a hundred feet and the higher hills by forty feet. Below it spread a valley strewn with rocks. Some of the rocks, he soon recognized, were the towering carved stone heads which made Rapa Nui so intriguing.

The balloon began to settle again, and the figures at the other end of the valley became more distinct. The large ones were stone heads staring from a hillside across the valley. At the base of one was what appeared to be a sacrificial ceremony. Hundreds of scantily clad Polynesians were dancing around it to the beat of drums and the tootling of flutes. A woman was stretched out on a stone block. By her stood a feathered man wearing a high feathered headdress.

Silver wasn't alarmed at this grim sight. Around the dancers were a number of cameras and chairs for the chief actors, the director, and the producer. Extras stood by; an actress was sitting on a chair while a woman added touches of makeup. Beyond a low hill was an army of tents, vans, and trucks.

Silver called down. "Everybody get to the other end! We'll be landing in a moment. The basket will tip over, so I want your weight to be on that side. Now, don't panic. Just hang onto the rim. The balloon'll drag us a little ways. But thank God there's plenty of help to grab us."

By then the movie company had seen the approaching intruder. They all stopped dancing; the drums and flutes were silenced;

everybody was looking up. A man, probably the director, was running out toward them, waving them away.

As the balloon got nearer, Silver could hear the director's screams. "Go away! Go away, dammit! You're ruining the scene!"

"Sorry," Silver shouted. "We can't do a thing about it."

"It's ruined, ruined! I'll have to shoot the whole thing over!"

Silver could see by now what was going to happen. The basket was going to hit the upper part of the stone head.

"Brace yourselves!" he called out.

The stern weird profile of the ancient rock spread out before him. He ducked. The next moment, the basket struck with a loud noise. He was half-stunned. But he felt the basket tilting, and then he slid forward. Behind him, shrieking, came most of the occupants. He went first, falling out of the basket, scraping off skin against the coarse volcanic stone and landing with a thump that seemed to jar his teeth loose on the ground.

Others fell on him, knocking the breath out of him. And, as he found out later, cracking several ribs.

Through a haze of confusion and pain, he saw the basket, suddenly relieved of many bodies, snap to an upright position, as its edge slid off the statue's chin. And the balloon carried it on past the head and up.

Not everybody had been tipped out. Mr. and Mrs. Hooward must have hung on with all the tenacity of the thoroughly terrified. Their pale faces looked despairing, and their screams rose—along with the rapidly ascending balloon.

Then the director was standing over the scattered pile of squirming, groaning humanity. "I'll sue! So help me, I'll sue."

"You idiot," Greatheart said faintly, just before fainting, "don't you know what a scoop you just made?"

Twenty-Seven

He was right. The movie company—Famous Artists Resplendent Teledramas—sold the films of the landing to the news networks after the story of the AZ-49's ordeal became known worldwide. Moreover, the producer bought the exclusive rights to Silver's personal narrative while Silver was still in a daze, not sure what he was signing. He was shafted on the deal, but he was able to buy another bionic leg with the money.

All this came out later. In the meantime, Silver was joined in the hospital by Jill, Flaherty, and the other crewmen who had swum for it. Both the Silvers were out of bed in two days. They moved into the Hilton Rapa Nui, expenses paid by the film company. Jill phoned her father, who was delighted that his daughter was safe and delirious with ecstasy at not having to pay a huge ransom for her. As for the ship and its cargo, the loss would be covered by insurance.

Micawber had a few painful moments, however, when Jill accused him of trying to break up her marriage. He denied it, of course. Unfortunately, there was no way of verifying Agocelli's confession through the Hoowards. They had been picked up by a ship twenty miles east of the island and taken to Los Angeles. There they disappeared, no doubt assisted by her father.

Jill said, "I really told him off. I swore that if anything fishy like that happened again, I'd automatically assume that he was behind it. And he'd never see or hear from me again."

"That's a fate to chill the blood," Greatheart said. "Come here and warm it up."

Later, Jill said, "Daddy promised me you'd get a new command as soon as you were on your feet. He didn't like it, but he knew what'd happen if he tried to make out that you were negligent in losing the ship."

"That's great," Greatheart said. "After that mess, I'm sure life is going to be one sweet song. I've used up all my bad luck."

Jill looked doubtful.

The Grant-Robeson Papers

Maxwell Grant is famous as the author whose by-line appeared on all but one of the *Shadow* novels. Kenneth Robeson is equally well known for his *Doc Savage* and the *Avenger* series.

The work at hand, Number One of *The Grant-Robeson Papers*, is the first new fiction by Grant since a softcover *Shadow* novel in 1967. "Savage Shadow," however, was written in 1935, four years after the appearance of the first *Shadow* novel. Kent Allard, sometimes known as Lamont Cranston, always known as the Shadow, is not Grant's hero in this tale. Ken Robeson is the protagonist.

In the story by Ken Robeson, to appear in the future, Maxwell Grant is the main character.

Why should these two writers use each other as their heroes? And why should these works, written in 1936, have been unprinted until 1977, forty-one years later?

These stories and others by Grant and Robeson have been in a small safe in a residence on Riverside Drive in Manhattan. Your editor was recently made aware of this when the estate of the late J***** D***, a wealthy manufacturer of safes, was inherited by a cousin, L***** C******. (The names are not revealed because of the wishes of the latter.)

It seems that Mr. D*** was an admirer of the works of Grant and Robeson. One reason for this was that Mr. D*** had been, in the early part of the twentieth century, a fighter against crime whose exploits pioneered the path for Doc Savage and the Shadow—not to mention the Spider.

Mr. D***, a collector in various fields, offered Grant and Robeson a tempting sum to write stories which would be unique items, so unique that only he, aside from the two authors, would know of their existence until after his death. Grant and Robeson were contractually obliged not to mention these stories until after Mr. D***'s death.

Though these two prolifics were busy, they had time enough to write sixteen short stories and novelettes for the eccentric collector. Being good friends, they decided, half-jestingly, half-seriously, to make each other the heroes (sometimes, the antiheroes) of their respective tales.

After the first four stories were written, Mr. D***, who was also a science-fiction buff, asked them if they would transfer the scene of their tales to the future—say, the late 1970s. He was interested in seeing, if he lived long enough, how close their fictions would come to reality.

The two responded to the challenge, but they retained their original heroes. In the stipulated decade, they would have been old men. But the writers arranged for both their protagonists—each other—to travel in time to the '70s. Thus, they were still young vigorous men, able to survive and adapt to the strange conditions of the future. They also agreed to depict a common milieu for their heroes, the same future world.

These "future" tales may appear in the heroic fantasy books of Byron Preiss Visual Publications from time to time.[†] It should be interesting to note how closely these approximate reality while in other respects widely missing the mark.

Mr. D*** also asked that each writer attempt to write in the style of the other. This presented a problem. As the student of the *Savage*, *Shadow* and *Avenger* epics knows, both experimented with different styles during their careers. Even their concept of their heroes changed somewhat over the years.

The two sometimes wrote in one or another of the other's styles and sometimes tried entirely new styles. Mr. D*** apparently did not object.

[†]No more of these stories have been published to date.

Savage Shadow

Maxwell Grant

One

There were no shadows here. Yet the white-haired man insisted he saw one. His own.

Kenneth Robeson, on this cold, cloudy December day of 1932, thought the tall, scholarly looking, middle-aged man must be crazy. He felt sorry for the daughter, a tall, beautiful, bronze-haired woman of about twenty-five. They were standing by the ramparts of the observation deck of the 86th floor of the Empire State Building. Robeson didn't know why they had come here to endure the bone-chilling wind. Aside from himself, they were the only people who'd stayed long out of the warm concession and display rooms.

He was up here to get an idea for a story. For a whole series, in fact. He'd spent one of the few coins in his pocket to take the elevator to this floor. He'd hoped that looking down on New York City might inspire him. But all he'd been able to think of was the Depression which gripped everybody except criminals.

The man and woman had come along about ten minutes later. He'd eyed them, especially the woman. She didn't look like a tourist or a newcomer, the only people who ever came up here. Her clothes were what he imagined the smart set would wear. A graduate of Vassar with money of her own. The man looked like a college teacher, since he wore tweeds and his hair was as wild as an orchestra conductor's. Or an absent-minded professor's.

They'd not been interested in the view. Instead, they gesticulated violently at each other. Thinking that something he might overhear could give a spark for a story idea, he'd edged close enough to hear them.

"You must go back, father!"

"Never! I tell you, they're doing evil things to me!"

That was enough. His mental ears were pricking up and Robeson moved even closer toward them. Writers had no shame about eavesdropping.

A minute later, as he tried to make sense out of their passionate, incoherent dialog, he saw the man jump to one side. He pointed down at the floor and said, "There it is! My shadow!"

His daughter spoke soothingly, though her face showed her distress.

"Now, father, there's no shadow there! It's an hallucination. Admit it, you're sick!"

He saw her suddenly stiffen, and he turned to see what she was staring at. Three men had come onto the platform. Two were shorter by four or five inches than his own six-foot-three. They were chunky and dark-faced and wore long, black overcoats and dark fedoras. The third was almost as tall as he, slim, elegantly dressed, and blond. He was quite handsome, though a scar disfigured his left cheek. It could have been made by a knife. Or a saber.

The blond man smiled coldly on seeing the two by the rampart. He said something to his companions. Followed by them, he strode toward the couple.

A few seconds later, two more men came out. They wore dark overcoats, but the caps and the white trousers suggested they were ambulance personnel or hospital attendants. One of them carried a straitjacket.

The white-haired man tried to run. His daughter called out to him to stop. The tall blond gestured to the two thuggish looking men, and they ran after the fugitive.

Things happened fast after that. The white-haired man tripped and fell. The woman screamed. The blond grabbed the father, rolled him over, and tried to remove the father's coat. The two struggled. Then the thugs seized the elderly man and held him while the coat was taken off. One of them, struck by a flailing fist in the nose, howled. He hit the white-haired man in the belly.

Robeson started forward. The woman ran up to the man who'd hit her father and began beating on him with her fists. The blond pulled a hypodermic syringe out of his coat pocket. The woman staggered back, pushed by the man she'd attacked. He was yelling names at her which no gentleman would use in a lady's presence.

Robeson cut his speech off with an uppercut to his chin. Then he fell into a blackness, only vaguely aware that he'd been hit over the head from behind.

Two

He awoke flat on his back on the cold concrete. The woman and a cop were looking down at him. His head hurt, but not so much he couldn't get to his feet without help. The father, his three attackers, and the two men with the straitjacket were gone. They'd been replaced by the curious from the 86th floor.

"Sure, me lad," the big cop said in a thick Irish brogue. "Are ye all right?"

"I don't think so," Robeson said. "Otherwise, I'd not have gotten into this mess in the first place."

"The blond gentleman said he's preferring no charges." The cop took a pencil from his pocket and held it, ready to write in his notebook. "I'll need your name, occupation, and address. And your version of the particulars."

Robeson gave it to him. The cop's eyebrows went up when he learned that Robeson was a writer. They ascended as far as they could go on hearing his residence.

"Bleeker Street, is it?" Indicating that anyone who lived in that area was of no consequence.

"Ye should go to a hospital and get checked out, me boy."

"I'll be okay," Ken said. He looked at the woman, whose make-up was smudged with tears. "How about you? Aren't you preferring charges against the man who hit you?"

She shook her head. "No. I'm not hurt. It wouldn't do any good, anyway. Father *had* escaped from a sanitarium. I shouldn't have interfered. But they were so *brutal*!"

"They shouldn't have hit a pretty colleen like you who was just showing a natural concern for her father," the cop said. He put away his notebook. "Ye both should go inside where it's warm and maybe drink a cup of coffee."

Robeson watched him walk away. He said, "I'm sorry about your father. It's none of my business, but . . . is there any way I could help?"

Looking utterly miserable and hopeless, she said, "No. No one can help."

"Well, at least you could tell me what it's all about. Maybe getting it off your chest will help."

He felt the blood rush to his face. Even with the coat on, she looked more than full bosomed.

"I mean . . ."

She began crying again. In a minute, they were inside, sitting at a table while the waitress was getting their coffee, and she was pouring out her troubles. Despite the pain in the back of his head and the feeling that he should be working out his series ideas, Robeson listened intently. Anyway, what she was telling him could eventually become the basis of a story, even if it didn't inspire him about the project at hand. All was grist for the writer's mill.

She was Patricia Burke. Her father was Professor Winston Burke, a teacher of chemistry and biology at a small upstate New York college. Her mother had died five years ago. Patricia, "Trish" for short, had taken care of the household duties for her father but had managed at the same time to attend classes at Kanyoto College, graduating in 1928. She'd gotten a job at a high school near Kanyoto, commuting to her father's home and taking care of him.

Then the Depression had come, and she lost her job. In 1930 she had gone to Manhattan to work as a bookkeeper for a friend who was managing a chain of beauty parlors. Her father had tried to make her stay at home, and this had led to a quarrel. Though they wrote to each other now and then, she hadn't visited him for a year. He felt that her duty was to be his housekeeper. Moreover, he strongly disapproved of her living alone in the big wicked city. Some of his letters even hinted that he did not believe that she was living alone.

"He's a very moral man," Trish said. "A real churchgoer. He just can't believe that I can resist the temptations of New York City. Which doesn't say much for his trust in me.

"Anyway, about a year ago I got a very excited letter from him. Instead of preaching to me, as he usually did, he told me that he had been experimenting with a chemical compound which, when injected into people, could force them to be moral. He didn't tell me the formula, of course, nor did he explain exactly how people could be made to act like saints.

"It was then that I began to have misgivings about his sanity.

"Six weeks later I got a letter saying that he had gone to see a big industrialist in Utica. This man, Mr. Bierstoss, was also very active in his church. In fact, he owns a radio station most of the programs of which are devoted to spreading the Gospel. You know, sermons, hymn songs, collecting money for missionaries. Stuff like that.

"Another letter followed. Father was in seventh heaven. Bierstoss was going to finance his experiments. I didn't hear anything from him until a month later. Actually, I didn't hear from him directly. I got a letter from a colleague, Professor Smithton, an old friend of the family. He said that my father had been acting peculiarly lately. I should come right away.

"I got a leave of absence and packed. But before I could get going, Smithton phoned. He said my father'd had a complete breakdown, and he was now in the Restful Meadows sanitarium. That's up in the Catskills. Mr. Bierstoss was paying for the treatment.

"I tried to phone Bierstoss, but I could never get through to him. His secretary said he'd call back, but he never did. So I drove up to the sanitarium.

"Doctor von Adlerdreck met me in his office. He was very nice but firm. My father, he said, was in no condition to have visitors. In fact, he probably wouldn't even recognize me. But he had great hopes that my father would recover completely in time. The doctor said he'd keep me advised. When it was okay for me to visit my father, he'd call me."

Kenneth Robeson gave no sign of his impatience. So far, there was nothing out of the usual in her story. Her father was undoubtedly crazy. He felt sorry for her, but he could do nothing for her. Still . . . maybe he could use her tale as a basis for the first in his series. It would make a socko beginning.

First, however, he had to get his characters outlined, establish their motives, their main purpose. Create a great villain for his hero and his sidekicks to combat.

The big shot at Street & Smith was waiting for him to come up with an idea that would excite him. If he could bring it in within the next three days, and set the big shot on fire with it, he'd be on easy street for a long while—if the series caught on with the public. A novel a month would bring five hundred dollars a month, big money. He could rap out a novel in a week and have plenty of time left to write other stuff, another novel, three or four short stories. Maybe he could bring in fifteen hundred dollars a month. Then, if the series continued to be popular, S & S would raise his rates, and in a year or so he'd be making three thousand a month.

Thirty-six thousand smackolas a year. Wow!

But if he couldn't get an advance within the next three days, he'd be kicked out of his sleazy, cockroach-ridden apartment. And he might have to sell apples on a corner like so many poor devils. Might, God forbid, be in such desperate straits he'd have to hock his typewriter.

He felt himself turn pale at the prospect.

No, he'd starve first.

He came back to his surroundings with a start. Trish Burke was looking at him peculiarly.

"Aren't you listening?"

"Sure. You were saying . . . ?"

"Restful Meadows was supposed to be a high-class sanitarium. I was thankful that Mr. Bierstoss was footing the bills. If it'd been up to me to pay, poor father would have had to go into the county hospital, a real snake pit. But I didn't like the two men that lounged around the doctor's office, doing nothing except making rude remarks and drinking hooch from a flask.

"The doctor was a well-educated man; he'd attended the University of Berlin and a medical school in Vienna. I couldn't understand why those two thugs were around. I questioned him when we were alone for a moment, and he said they were his chief aides. He used them when a patient got violent.

"That seemed rather fishy to me. But I was in a state of grief and shock. So I left. What could I do?

"However, I had found out the names of the two attendants. When I got back, I phoned my cousin, Clyde Burke. He's a reporter for the *New York Classic*."

"A real rag, a notorious example of yellow journalism," Kenneth said.

"Yes, I know. I don't know why Clyde works for it, since he is a very good reporter. Maybe because it doesn't demand much of his time, and he moonlights for other papers. It doesn't matter. Anyway, I asked him about the doctor and the two men with him.

"Clyde said the sanitarium had a good reputation. Von Adlerdreck was said to be a fine doctor, but at one time the FBI had investigated him about his rumored connections with the New York German-American Bunds. But they'd not been able to establish any link.

"However, Clyde was very surprised when I told him the names of the doctor's two associates. He said they were notorious criminals. Both Antonio 'Chips' Bufalo and Roberto 'Eggs' Ovarizi had been members of a Brooklyn mob. But they'd left town suddenly. Not because of the police. They were pro-Mussolini, and the Italian-American gangsters are violently anti-Mussolini. Il Duce had broken the power of Italian and Sicilian organized crime—what do they call it there, the Black Hand? The Italian gangsters here hate him.

"Clyde said that Bufalo and Ovarizi had taken off to keep from getting killed. They'd dropped out of sight. He was surprised to find that they'd holed up in the sanitarium. He said he'd like to find out why they were there, but his main source of information was in France at that time. Maybe he could find out something for me on his own."

Robeson stirred impatiently. "What about this shadow your father sees?"

"I'm getting to that. Late last night I got a phone call in my apartment. It was father. He'd escaped, and he . . ."

She stopped. Kenneth turned to see what she was staring at. Then he rose to his feet quickly, pushing the chair to one side.

Von Adlerdreck and his two swarthy companions had returned. The latter had their hands in their coats; it was evident that they held pistols.

Three

Von Adlerdreck, his thin handsome features pressed into a smile, approached them. He stopped, bowed slightly, spoke in English with only a slight German accent.

"Your pardon, Miss Burke. Professor Burke has been taken in an ambulance to the sanitarium. But it occurred to me that I owed you an apology for the roughness of my men. I've reprimanded them, and they have promised never to act in such a hasty and rude manner again."

He looked at Robeson. "My sincerest apologies to you, too, young man. You were only being gallant when you interfered. I hope that your injuries are minimal."

Miss Burke said, "I don't think that it was necessary to be so rough. But then father was putting up a fight. I accept your apology."

Robeson said, "Which one of you hit me?"

Von Adlerdreck said, "My overzealous assistant, Mr. Bufalo."

He turned and pointed at the slightly taller of the two. Robeson strode past him. Bufalo growled, "Whatcha up to, punk?"

"This." And Robeson delivered a hard right-cross to the battleship-prow chin. Bufalo staggered back, his hands still in his overcoat pockets, and he fell to his knees. Trish said, loudly, "Oh, no!"

Robeson turned away. His fist hurt, and the blow had increased the pain in the back of his head. But he felt satisfied.

Trish screamed. Robeson whirled. Ovarizi had pulled out of his pocket a .45 automatic, a huge, ugly weapon which looked at that moment bigger than a cannon.

Von Adlerdreck shouted, "You fool! Put that away!"

There were about a dozen people in the room. All were silently staring at the group.

Bufalo was up on his feet by now, but he looked as if he still didn't know what had happened.

Ovarizi put the gun back into the pocket. The doctor said, "I suggest you leave now, Mr. . . . ?"

"Kenneth Robeson. And I'm not leaving until I know that Miss Burke is safe."

The German's mouth turned down. But he managed to bring it back up into a facsimile of a smile. "I assure you that I only returned to extend to Miss Burke my regrets for this unfortunate incident. Also to tell her that she can accompany us back to the sanitarium if she wishes. She can stay there with no expense for several days and observe her father. I wish to assure her that he is not being mistreated."

This fellow is too oily, Robeson thought. And he sure doesn't keep good company.

Trish Burke hesitated. She looked as if she wanted some advice from Robeson. Seeing that he wasn't giving any, she said, "Thank you very much, Doctor. I'll take you up on your offer in a couple of days. It'll be a weekend then, and I won't be working. I'm afraid I'd lose my job if I took any more time off."

She smiled. "You know how tough it is to get a job now."

He bowed slightly again, and said, "As you wish," turned on his heel like a soldier, and strode off. Bufalo's eyes had become unglazed then. He started toward Robeson, snarling silently. Von Adlerdreck said something Italian to him in a low voice.

Bufalo said, "I ain't gonna forget this, you punk." But he followed the other two to the elevator doors.

Robeson was shaking with the reaction. He said, "I'll bet those thugs don't have licenses to carry those guns."

He put a hand on her arm and looked into the wide blue eyes. "Listen. Take my advice. Don't go up there alone. There's something rotten about this. It isn't just a matter of a crazy old man."

Trish Burke said, "Why'd you hit him? Not that I mind. I'd like to do the same myself. But why . . ."

Robeson waved his hand. "I had to get my self-respect back. Or maybe I'm just angry at a lot of things, and I took it out on him. I had a good excuse. The thing is, this is too deep for you. You'd better go to the police. Fast."

Trish Burke said, "But I can't get the police interested unless I have something solid to tell them. Will you testify that Ovarizi pulled a gun on you?"

Reluctantly, Robeson said, "Yes. But he can claim it was in self-defense."

He frowned. She was right. The only thing on which the police might take action was the question of weapon licenses. They'd regard her as just a daughter overly concerned about her father, a patient at a respectable sanitarium. He was a penniless pulp-magazine writer—an unrespectable profession—and one who could be charged with battery and assault.

Time was speeding by. Monday morning's meeting with the big shot at S & S was getting nearer every minute. And he still had no series concepts worth considering. Why in hell had he come up here just in time to get involved with this woman, beautiful though she was?

He wanted to leave, but he couldn't. He'd feel like a heel, a coward, if he just walked away from her.

Besides . . . her father's nutty talk about a chemical that could control people's moral behavior! Wasn't that the type of thing he was trying to think of? And wasn't he in the midst of a situation that would make a rattling good story?

Trish said, "I'll call Myra and tell her I'm sick. She won't like it, but I can't just abandon my father because I'm afraid to lose my job."

"Then what?" he said.

She came close enough so he could smell her perfume. It was a very light odor, faint, but it did something powerful to him. Not to mention that beautiful face and huge, imploring blue eyes.

"I have a car. We can go up to Roosville now. They won't suspect we'll be there soon. We can scout around, try to find out what's going on up there."

She had no sense of reality. Maybe she had a touch of insanity, inherited, no doubt. But at the moment he felt as if he was, just by being close to her, receiving some of her determination, her unreasonable resolve to make this a quest of some sort. She was transmitting, and he was receiving. And of course he couldn't receive unless he was on her frequency. In other words, he was as unrealistically romantic as she.

He shrugged and said, "Okay. I'll go."

She didn't squeal with pleasure, but she looked as if she'd like to.

They took the elevators down to the ground floor. Robeson felt the change in his pocket and thought of the three dollars in his wallet. His worldly wealth. If she expected him to pay for her food and the gas for the car, she was going to be shocked. Gallantry only went so far.

They walked four blocks to her car, a rusty 1928 Model A coupe with a rumble seat. On the way he told her something about himself, his boyhood in the Midwest, his sudden resolve to come to New York and write for his living. She looked a little askance at his ambition. It was evident that she had no high opinion of pulp-magazine literature. But she confessed that she'd never read any.

"I suppose it is trash," he said. "Ephemeral stuff that'll be forgotten a month after it's published. But it's a living, and it's a stepping stone to the big league. However, it isn't easy to write for the pulps. You have to have a certain talent for it. Very few can do it. I've sold about a dozen stories, just enough to keep me alive. But I have a chance to make it big now. If I do, the money I make'll give me the leisure to write good stuff. After all, Balzac wrote thrillers in his early days, but he became one of the world's greatest writers."

He was angry with himself for having tried to justify himself.

Why should he appease her snobbery?

They got into the car and shivered in the cold until the motor was warmed up and the heater was going full blast. Trish drove the car down Thirty-Fifth to Broadway, then cut north toward the George Washington Bridge. They were silent during this time, he nursing his wounds over her remarks, she probably thinking about her father.

Then, as they took the highway toward the Catskills, he spoke for the first time.

"We're being followed."

Four

He was sure of it, when, five miles further, he told her to pull over onto the shoulder of the road. The big black car slowed, then stopped about four hundred and seventy yards behind them.

"Ten to one it's von Adlerdreck and his gatmen."

She drove back onto the highway again, keeping the beat-up Model A at its top speed, sixty miles an hour. Oil fumes began to fill the interior, and she eased the pressure on the pedal. "It needs a ring and a valve job bad," she said. "But I haven't been able to afford it."

"Who can afford anything nowadays? Keep going. Don't worry. I don't think they'll try anything until after dark, if then. Maybe they just want to see where we go."

"Just what are we going to do?" she said.

"Play it by ear. You're not tone-deaf, are you? Forget about them for the time being. Now, you said you got a phone call from your father. He'd escaped."

"Yes. He wanted me to meet him. He said that von Adlerdreck would be looking for him to go to my place. So I suggested the 86th floor of the Empire State Building. I suppose because I'd been reading an article on its construction when he called. The talk was very short. He was very nervous, he said he'd give me all the details when we got together.

"When I saw him in the restaurant, he insisted that we go outside. He said he didn't want anyone to overhear us. He seemed to think the place was full of spies. And he kept talking about his shadow. Then . . ."

"Just what did he say about the shadow?"

"He said that it was menacing. Savage. It threatened him."

"How could a shadow threaten him?"

"By making terrible faces at him. It had a mouth, and though it couldn't speak, he could lip-read what it said. It said awful things to him. Most of them unspeakable. I mean, they were so bad he couldn't even tell me what they were. Obscene and profane things. So bad they were driving him crazy."

Robeson thought that the professor had the cart before the horse.

"When did this shadow appear?"

"I don't know. Dad was all right one day, and the next day he went crazy. He woke up and there it was, dancing in front of him, grimacing, mouthing those awful words, leaping at him but never touching him. He went to Mr. Bierstoss, who suggested he go to a sanitarium. Dad refused, but Mr. Bierstoss phoned Doctor von Adlerdreck anyway. That evening the doctor and those two yeggs showed up and took him away in a straitjacket."

"Yeggs?" Robeson said. "A yegg is a safecracker."

"Oh? Well, gorillas. What's the difference?"

"Bierstoss must've known the doctor," Kenneth said. "I'd say there's a link between the two. But it may not be sinister. Maybe von Adlerdreck was recommended by Bierstoss's doctor."

"Maybe, but I don't believe that's all. Do you?"

"No. What do you know about Bierstoss? Aside from his being an industrialist. What does his company manufacture? What's his background?"

"I don't know much except what father told me in his letter. He came over from Germany in 1920 at the age of thirty. He seems to have had some money then. He purchased a garage and a used-car business. After he'd set up a whole chain of these, he sold it and bought a partnership in a small pharmaceutical firm. He also bought a small publishing house that dealt in religious books. His rise was phenomenal. Five years later he was president of a chain of pharmaceutical stores and some more publishing houses. Even the stock market crash didn't affect his businesses too much."

"What about his politics? And his attitude toward Germany?"

"Dad didn't say anything about those."

They stopped to eat lunch and to gas up. Trish insisted on paying for the food. Robeson didn't object. The big black car had dropped out of sight. That meant nothing. If the doctor was in that car, he knew by now where they were headed. Robeson studied the road map he'd taken from the glove compartment. The doctor could have taken a country road a half a mile back and come back out on the highway two miles northwest of them.

Just before dusk, they pulled into Roosville. This was a village which, according to a sign, had fifty-nine friendly citizens. There was no hotel, but the service-station attendant directed them to Mrs. Doorn's boarding house. Trish turned off the ignition and looked steadily at him. He felt his cheeks flushing.

"I have all my small savings in my purse," she said. "I took it out so I could give it to Dad if I decided to help him hide. I have enough to pay for two rooms—if Mrs. Doorn's charges aren't outrageous—for a couple of days. But I'd like to save as much as I can. So . . . I propose we share a room. We'll tell Mrs. Doorn we're married.

"But I want your word you won't make a pass. I'll tell you now that I'll say no. Maybe, if I'd known you longer, if I were in love . . . I'm no prude but I am sensible. I don't give myself away. You understand?"

He hesitated, looked away, then said, "I'll be honest with you. I don't think I could stand it. It's been a long time, and you're so beautiful."

"Thanks. Okay. If I can manage it, I'll get us separate rooms. We'll say we're brother and sister. Which makes me Patricia Robeson. Here, take the money. It wouldn't look right if I paid."

Mrs. Doorn, a tall, fat, red-faced woman of fifty, accepted their story. She gave Trish a room on the top floor of the three-story house, built when Queen Victoria was still living. Kenneth took a small room in the basement, the cheapest available.

"I go to bed at ten," Mrs. Doorn said. "The key is under the doormat if you intend to stay out late. There isn't anything to do here at night except listen to the radio."

Robeson thought it best not to say that they had business at the Restful Meadows. His feeling that he was on an absurd quest got even stronger. What, after all, could the two of them do? And why should they be doing anything?

Though they weren't very hungry, they ate dinner at Mrs. Doorn's well-laden table. Kenneth, after his meager diet of hamburgers, hot dogs, and french fries for the last three months, decided that he had an appetite after all. A big thick steak, mashed potatoes with gravy, cranberry sauce, a salad, and a big slice of Dutch apple pie left him feeling happy but logy. It was worth the trip just to eat here. Especially since he wasn't paying for it.

Well, he was footing the bill in a sense. He was giving Trish his time, a commodity a writer couldn't afford to waste. He thought of the typewriter in his crappy apartment, sitting mute and inglorious on a table, waiting for its master's fingers to type out a pulp masterpiece.

While the landlady was cleaning off the table, most of the boarders went into the parlor to listen to the radio. Robeson went to his room for a moment to go to the toilet. He came up into the hallway expecting to meet Trish there. Instead, he found two of the diners. It was evident that they wanted to speak to him.

Five

One was a very tall, very skinny man about forty named Bill Homer Smalljack. His long thin nose was very red. He wore very thick spectacles, one lens of which was a supernumerary. Behind it was an obviously glass eye, not even matching the hazel of the good eye.

The other was a middle-aged giant, towering, well muscled, his face as long, narrow, and gloomy as the stereotyped Puritan's. His hawk nose was as red as his companion's. His hands looked as big as quart jugs. In fact, one of them held a jug. He'd been introduced at the table as Hans van Rijnwijk.

Smalljack's profession was digging holes in the ground. Wells, graves, basements, postholes. Van Rijnwijk was a mechanic for the local garage, but he also repaired agricultural machinery, clocks, anything mechanical. Nowadays, a person had to quit specializing to survive.

Smalljack said, "Hans and me run a little business on the side. Give him a sample of the wares, big boy."

Hans, who didn't like to talk, silently removed the cork and handed the jug to Kenneth. He smelled the odor rising from the open neck. His eyes watered.

"Good stuff," Smalljack said. "The best white lightning in New York. I should know. I've tasted it all. Guaranteed, too. And cheap. Go ahead, take a snifter."

"I can't do that," Robeson said. "I don't have much money. I couldn't afford this."

"Sure you can. It's only two-fifty a quart. Even if you don't drink, you can resell it in the city. That'll bring you three times as much on Broadway."

The prospect of making a profit interested Robeson. God knew, he needed the money. But if the car was by some chance inspected by the police . . . oh, what the hell! So he forked over the money to Smalljack, thanked them, and took the jug, wrapped in his coat, to the car. He put it in the rumble seat. While he was doing this, the bootleggers came out of the house. Smalljack winked at him as the two got into a 1932 Packard. Business must be good if they could afford that.

He started back to the house but stopped as Trish Burke came out. After they'd gotten in the Ford, he told her what he'd just done.

"I know it was your money, but it's a good investment."

"Investment, hell," she said. "We'll invest it in our tummies, right now. I need a shot of Dutch courage."

Robeson was pleased, since he had expected her to blow up about it. But he told her to wait until they got out of town. They mustn't be seen by the local sheriff. She drove onto the gravel road that led to Restful Meadows, then stopped on the other side of a wooden covered bridge spanning a wide creek. Robeson got the jug out and offered her the first drink. Though her hands and arms were slender, she handled the heavy jug well, holding it horizontally across her upper right arm.

"Wow! That makes you see stars!"

Kenneth took his turn. The stuff burned his mouth, his tongue, his gullet, his stomach. But it wasn't rotgut. It was just powerful.

Trish took another long draught, then said, "I'm ready to tackle a tiger now."

Robeson decided he'd pass up seconds. His brain was already beginning to feel numb.

Then they froze. Headlights struck across the bridge, and they could hear a motor. The black-and-white car slowed as it went by them, and they could see a tall-hatted man, Sheriff Huisman, looking at them. But the car speeded up and disappeared around a bend.

Robeson felt his heart resume beating. "We were lucky. He's out after bigger game. Our two dispensers of tabu juice of the corn, I'll bet. You want me to drive?"

"I never feel comfortable when someone else is driving," she said. "I'm just as good as any man behind the wheel and better than most. And I can drink nine out of ten under the table." She added, "In case you were figuring on taking advantage of my drunken condition."

He chuckled. She sure was a pistol. One of those modern liberated women. Maybe he should have registered them as man and wife. No wonder her father didn't want her to go to New York. Even a permissive parent would have worried about her.

The road was dark, the sky being cloudy. The headlight beams showed patches of snow, dry weeds, tall bare trees, ruined choirs. About halfway to the sanitarium, a car passed them going in the opposite direction. It was the sheriff's, going too fast for the road.

"He might be back," Robeson said. "So we ought to park this buggy where it can't be seen."

"Give me some credit for brains."

She was no longer the seemingly helpless woman he'd met on top of the skyscraper. He doubted it was the liquor causing the change. She played roles, and when she was in Rome she did as the Romans did. Or were supposed to do. This tough capable character of hers, though, was probably her real one.

They saw the sanitarium about five minutes before they got there. Lights blazed from and around it. It was obviously set on top of a high hill. When they got to the entrance, they found a pair of iron gates set in a high stone wall. A ditch ran along the walls paralleling the road. A stone bridge crossed the ditch, on the bottom of which was half-frozen water.

Trish stopped the car but left the motor running. "Maybe we should just breeze on in and ask to see my father."

"Then we'd see what they want us to see. That'd be no more than you saw on your last visit. I think we ought to scout around. Maybe we could even get inside the building and waltz off with your father. But if we're caught, we could be charged with kidnapping. Or illegal entry. It isn't that I'm afraid. It's just that I think Falstaff had something when he said discretion is the better part of valor."

"I really have no right to ask you to stick your neck out," she said. "But you did volunteer, and you know there's something rotten about von Adlerdreck and his two mobsters. Why don't we just walk around outside, get the lay of the land, maybe do a Peeping Tom act? Then we can come back to the car for a powwow. After all, we don't necessarily have to take any action tonight."

Robeson agreed. She drove the car into a road which was more two rutted tracks than anything. This cut through a farm across the road from the sanitarium. Trees and bushes lined the wire fence along the acreage. They could conceal the Ford behind them.

Trish drove the car across the muddy field in low gear. Robeson said, "Oh, oh!" He indicated a long black Packard parked by the cover they'd picked out. There seemed to be no one in it.

"It's the bootleggers!"

"The sheriff didn't see it, so it must be invisible from the road," she said.

They left the Ford behind the Packard. They found that the wire fence had been bent open enough to allow them to crawl through.

"Evidently they use this a lot," Kenneth said. "Well, we'll have to be careful we don't run into them."

They jumped across the watery area of the ditch, scrambled up the bank with muddy shoes, went across the road and the stone bridge. As he'd expected, Robeson found that the padlock enclosing two links of the chain around the gates was open. He removed the lock, opened the gates, and the two went inside. He reached in through the steel bars and put the chain back into the large links. A passerby in the dark would think that the lock was shut.

On second thought, he removed the lock and threw it into the darkness alongside the wall. He didn't want to be trapped if the bootleggers closed the lock when they left.

The gravel road wound around the estate, climbed the hill corkscrewlike, and emerged at the front of the huge cubical building. They started down it, then halted.

"Voices! Over there!" Trish said.

Six

Somewhere deep in a grove of leafless trees a match was struck. It went out, but the ends of two cigarettes glowed like fireflies.

He took her hand, and they walked into the trees. It was easy to take cover, though the unmelted snow under the branches made slushing sounds. When within earshot, they stopped behind a broad-trunked sycamore.

He counted seven dim figures, all standing close together. There was just enough light to see the silhouette of a jug being passed around.

From the conversation it wasn't difficult to know what was happening. Smalljack and Rijnwijk had come here to sell some of the patients their white mule. The latter had sneaked out of the building to rendezvous here so they could get the forbidden liquor.

If people could get out, unobserved, then they could get back in. Which meant that he and Trish might also enter.

There had been enough time for the exchange of whiskey and money. But the bootleggers were hanging around for the party, accepting the drinks from the people they'd just sold the liquor to. Or, perhaps, the patients had urged them to stay because they wanted the company of outsiders. Whatever the reason, all seven soon moved on, one of them complaining about the cold. This was a woman called "Pat," the only female in the group.

Robeson's face became warm when he heard some of the remarks. They were certainly risqué. Trish didn't seem bothered. On the contrary, she giggled.

Robeson considered going up to the building and trying the doors. He presumed that the patients had left by a ground floor exit. It didn't seem likely that they would have come from an upper story window down a string of bed sheets tied together. But the more he listened to them, the less sure he was. They sounded like a crazy bunch.

Which, he told himself, was just what they were. Otherwise, they wouldn't be here.

Trish said, "Shouldn't we be moving on. I'm frozen."

"I don't know. Maybe we ought to follow them. We might overhear something we can use. Also . . . maybe we ought to declare ourselves. They won't turn us in. They can't without exposing their little setup. They might even be willing to help us. In any event, they could tell us something about your father."

Trish didn't think that was a good idea. He argued for a minute, and she finally agreed.

They followed them to a clearing near the wall. In its center was a summerhouse, a rather large round edifice with a platform extending from the front. Possibly a band played here in warmer weather. A concrete path led from it toward the hill on which the sanitarium stood.

One of the group must have had a key. The door swung open, they trooped in, and the door was shut. Presently he could see a thread of light between a drawn blind and the window ledge. A few minutes later, wood smoke poured from a metal chimney sticking from the side of the house.

He and Trish crept up on the porch, and he placed his ear against the door. There were sounds of low revelry: roars of laughter, fast-talking, a sudden scream of delight, or maybe it was protest, from the woman. A radio started blaring the *Maple Leaf Rag*.

Trish was crouching, peeking under the shade. Robeson joined her.

There were Smalljack and van Rijnwijk, still dressed in their overalls and checked shirts. They were consuming their own booze, a testimony to its excellence. Or perhaps they would drink anything.

One of the revelers was even taller than van Rijnwijk. He was about fifty, a hard fifty, broad-shouldered, and he looked as if he might have had an outstanding physique in his youth. He also could have been very handsome once. But dissipation had lined his face, bagged his eyes, and fattened throat and waist. It had also coarsened and reddened his nose. His skin was a sickly yellow and his hair was that sort of brown which youthful red turns into as middle age creeps up. He was chugalugging a jug as the others clapped and cheered him on. Robeson was in awe at this feat. Anybody who could drink that fiery stuff down gulp after gulp, pint after pint, and not burst into flames, was a phenomenon.

The next to catch his eye was probably the most extraordinary looking person there. He was very short, not more than an inch or two over five feet. In fact, he looked almost as broad as he was tall. His arms hung down almost to his knees, and the face was that of a chimpanzee's: low forehead, the most prominent supraorbital ridges he'd ever seen—they would have put an Australian aborigine's to shame—under which were small rusty eyes, a long upper lip, a receding chin. Though he was about fifty, his shock of hair was rusty red, and a tuft of curly red hair spilled out from the top of his open shirt.

He was engaged in drinking and in arguing with a tall, slim, hawk-faced fellow of the same age, dressed as if for a formal dinner. Robeson couldn't believe it. A tuxedo and an opera hat! He carried a cane, no doubt because of his limp. However, it had another purpose. Robeson saw him twist the gold-colored knot at its top and remove it. He upended the cane, out of which slid three glass vials. While talking loudly and angrily to the apelike man, he uncorked the vials, filled them with corn whiskey, corked them, and slid them into the hollow interior of the cane.

The sixth was an anemic-looking, skinny little fellow with a sour expression. His hair was of a peculiar indeterminate color which Robeson could only describe as "pale." He sat in a corner on a bare wooden folding chair, drinking steadily from a glass.

The last member was the woman, a tall, long-legged woman in a tight, red low-cut dress and very tall high heels. Her stockings were fishnet. She looked as if she were fifty but she could have been younger. Robeson guessed that the lines in her face had been put there, not by the natural aging of Mother Nature, but by hard living. Nevertheless, the bone structure showed that she had been a very good-looking woman in her prime. Her long hair was peroxided. Her bosom was huge, in startling contrast to her waist, which, though ringed by puffy fat, still looked narrow.

When she walked, she had the long stride of the professional burlesque queen. The eyes of the men followed her legs and the swaying hips when she walked—except those of the pale runt. And the fact that he looked everywhere except where she was showed that he was intensely interested in her. But he didn't want anyone, including himself, to know it.

Ken Robeson, wondering if his plan to question these people was right, despaired. Obviously, they were alcoholics who'd been sent to Restful Meadows by relatives or the lawyers who managed their estates. They'd managed to circumvent the watchdogs of the sanitarium and gotten into contact with the local bootleggers.

They probably wouldn't even know what was going on in the place.

Yet . . . they had to be sober most of the time, even if they didn't like it.

He watched and listened while he tried to make up his mind what to do. The very tall man, whom the others called "Doc," seemed to be of French origin. Though he spoke excellent English, he had a slight Gallic accent. It was obvious that his companions regarded him as a sort of leader. He might be the person to concentrate on.

"Listen, Trish," Robeson said. "These drunks could help us. Or they might think we're just intruders who'll make so much trouble for them that their source of alcohol could be cut off. What do you think?"

Her face was close to his. Her perfume, mixed with the white lightning breathed on him, was intoxicating.

He thought, How lovely she is!

She said, "They can't tell on us without exposing what they've been doing. But maybe von Adlerdreck doesn't care. Maybe he's just running this sanitarium as a cover-up, and he could care less if his patients are drinking themselves to death.

"Maybe I'm paranoid. But . . . what he's been doing to my father . . . I think he's more than just a doctor who's concerned about a crazy old man. I don't have any real evidence to back up my feelings. But I'm a pretty good reader of character. I could detect nuances in a voice, in an expression. I know von Adlerdreck's concealing something sinister behind that oily smile. Don't smile. It isn't woman's intuition. It's a fine-honed ability to tell what a man is really thinking. A lot of women have it because they had to develop the ability in order to survive in this man's world."

"I'm crazy to go on just a feeling," he said. "But there is something wrong. I . . ."

He should have been looking into the room instead of at her. The door was flung open, and a man stepped outside.

SEVEN

Robeson started to rise. The man, the near giant, reeled toward him, grabbed his wrist, and started shouting. Robeson tried to back away, but he was held in a grip like a loan shark's. He quit struggling. There was no use antagonizing him and the others.

"We'll go in with you," he said. "If you keep yelling, they'll hear you up there." He gestured at the building on the hill.

For a minute, it was impossible to enter. The apelike man and the slim fellow in the tux tried to get through the doorway at the same time. Jammed together, cursing, they writhed and wriggled, then both fell through together. The big man, still holding on to Robeson, stepped over them into the house. Trish followed them.

Inside, he released his hold and closed the door in the faces of the two. They howled and beat on the door until van Rijnwijk opened it for them. And they fell again, sprawling on the floor.

The woman named Pat screeched with laughter. The others stared silently.

"All right," Doc said, his nose almost meeting Robeson's as he stooped down. "What in hell were you doing? Spying on us?"

Robeson felt the concentration of whiskey in his veins soar as he breathed the man's breath. You could get drunk just by being near this man. His eyes were a peculiar yellow color. Jaundice. This man was dying of liver disease, and yet he was hastening the process by consuming enormous quantities of alcohol.

The two clowns got up from the floor and dusted themselves off. They kept up a firecracker series of insults and curses.

Robeson said, "No, we're not spies. If you'll listen without interruption, I'll tell you who we are and why we're here."

Nothing was to be gained by lying. The truth might be of some help, though these people didn't look as if they would be much help for anybody. Including themselves.

After he'd finished, there was a long silence. Then the big man said, "Whash, whash . . ." He paused, struggled to get control of his tongue, and spoke more slowly. "What do you want from us? Help against that . . ."

He paused, swallowed the word he'd been about to use, no doubt in deference to Trish, and continued. "Against that medical Attila the Hun, Herr Doktor von Adlerdreck?"

The apish man exploded. "I'm all for it! I tell you, that so-and-so is involved in something crooked! Otherwise, why would he hire two gangsters?"

The lady called Pat said, "Yeah, and I'll tell you something else that's fishy. Eiderduck gets a lot of mail from overseas and from Washington, D.C. Only the letters don't come in envelopes from overseas or Washington. They come inside other envelopes from a New York address."

"Eiderduck?" Robeson said.

"She means Addledrake," the apish man said.

"We call von Adlerdreck a lot of things," the big, dark, yellow-eyed man said. "Some of which ain't fit for young ladies to hear."

He introduced himself as Doctor Marcel Sebastien LeClerc du Bronce du Fauve. He was, he said, a French Canadian of aristocratic descent.

"He ain't a real doctor," Pat said. "He's a chiropractor, a bone bender. He got into trouble because he was too much a ladies' man with his female patients. So he ducked out and hid here. Not that he shouldn't be here. He's a real rummy, just like the rest of us."

"You got a big mouth, Pat," Doc said. "A healer is a doctor, and I healed bodies and broken hearts. Is it my fault that I am temperamentally unable to resist beauty?"

He bowed to Trish and smiled dazzlingly. She backed away, dizzy with the heavy fumes of fermented corn.

The others were introduced. Pat Coningway was just what Ken had guessed. An ex-stripper. But she'd married an old millionaire who'd died a year ago. "He was vigorous for his age, but his heart couldn't take it," she said, looking smug.

The apish man was Anderson Maypole Blidgett, but everyone called him "Jocko." The man in the tux was Ted Scrooch Creeks, Ted to everyone but Jocko, who called him "Oinks."

Jocko said, grinning at the outraged Creeks, "Oinks is a shyster, an ambulance chaser who got drummed out of the New York Bar Association. I calls him Oinks because he defended a pig rustler in his last case. But he was so bombed the judge threw him in the slammer for contempt of court."

"An out-and-out lie!" Oinks said, waving his cane so close to Jocko's nose he had to step back. "I suffer from diabetes and that morning I had neglected my dosage of insulin. This left me somewhat confused, and the judge refused to accept my defense. He himself was a heavy drinker who had no mercy for those defendants in a similar plight."

"Yeah, tell that to the Marines," Jocko said.

Jocko, it turned out, was a wealthy pharmacist who owned a chain of drugstores. But, as he cheerfully admitted, booze got to be a bigger problem than he could handle. So he'd committed himself to Restful Meadows to dry out. So far, without success.

The anemic squirt with the two bootleggers was Bob Thomas. He'd once been a telephone lineman, but he'd gone into full-time whiskey making with the other two. He lived in the basement of a private house where he worked on his inventions in his spare time.

"When he's sober, that is," Jocko gleefully said. "Maybe if Lunger Tom laid off the juice, his inventions might work."

Thomas, his colorless eyes blazing, said, "Yeah, you throwback to the missing link, you'd drink too if you'd got caught in a mustard gas attack. What's your excuse?" He began coughing violently but got over the fit when he swallowed more of the white lightning.

"That stuff'll cure what ails you," Smalljack said.

Robeson said, "Well, what about it? Miss Burke and I would like to get her father out of here. But it'll be risky for you, since we don't have a legal leg to stand on."

Doc Fauve lowered his huge bulk into a folding chair, and he took another gargantuan swallow from a jug. Smacking his lips, blinking owlishly, he said, "I don't like that arrogant son of a . . . gun. I'd like to stick it to him. Especially since there is some evidence that he's up to no good."

"Evidence which wouldn't stand up in court," Oinks said, swaying slightly. "But, if we were to capture those letters and we could find someone who could read German and Italian, we might find that he and his two thugs are engaged in illicit, perhaps even treasonable, activities."

"Treasonable!" Jocko said. "How do you figure that out, Blackstone?"

Oinks hiccupped, then said, "Anyone but a low-browed facsimile of an orangutan would deduce from what has been reported that von Adlerdreck is an agent of, or at least a sympathizer with, the Germans. And Ovarizi and Bufalo are agents of, or at least sympathizers with, that strutting jackanapes, Mussolini. It's only a suspicion, I'll admit, a hypothesis, but it certainly warrants investigation. In a sense, though civilians, we are soldiers for our country. All of us here, except for our two young visitors, are veterans who fought in the Big One. I even include Pat, since, as I understand it, she was something of a camp follower and materially contributed to the morale of the doughboys, not to mention any number of officers."

Pat growled, "How'd you like this jug jammed up your . . . ?"

Doc Fauve interrupted sharply. "Hold it, Pat! There's a lady present!"

"Why, you drunken, lecherous quack, you mean I ain't no lady? It'll be a cold day in hell before I let you sweet-talk me again into . . ."

Robeson said, "Please! No quarreling! Now, how about it? Will you help us? If you agree to, then we should make some plans now. And act quickly."

"That a boy, young feller!" Jocko said. "I ain't been in a good brawl since just before I committed myself."

"He doesn't mean we'll bust into the place like a band of Comanches, you microcephalic," the lawyer said. "This will take subtlety, silence, organization."

Doc Fauve said that they should take a vote. Everybody held his hand up. Robeson was surprised that the three bootleggers wanted to join in.

The beanpole, Smalljack, said, "Us three fought against the Kaiser, you know. I was a corporal, Van and Lunger Tom was sergeants. If this Kraut is a spy or something, we'd like to get our mitts on him. Ain't that right, boys?"

"Yeah," van Rijnwijk boomed. "Here we fought and got wounded so we could save the world for democracy. And here's the Boche up and back on his feet and making noises again. This time, he ought to be kicked silly so he'll think twice the next time before he goes out to conquer the world."

"I say," said Jocko, "let's storm on up there, kick hell out of the Kraut and them two Sicilians, get the letters, and turn the whole lot over to the Feds. Meanwhile, Robeson and the lovely Miss Burke—you're a real peach, kid—can hustle her old man out of here."

This was voted down, since the gangsters were armed and, for all they knew, some of the attendants might be, too.

Everybody downed some more white lightning, including Robeson and Burke. Then the lights were turned out, and they walked toward the big house on the hill. Before they could get out of the trees, they heard automobile motors to their right. They hid behind trees and waited for the cars to come by on the road. But the cars seemed to be staying at the gateway.

Robeson said, "I'll sneak down there and find out what's going on."

Doc, Jocko, and van Rijnwijk said they'd go with him.

"Maybe it's Sheriff Huisman," the latter said. "He's been out looking for us. He's mad at us because we won't kick in more money for protection."

"You mean . . . ?"

"Sure. You think we could operate like we do if we didn't have some official warning us when the Internal Revenue guys are pussy-footing around? I guess we'll have to up the ante to him pretty soon. But we're making him sweat it out."

His three companions kept bumping into trees and crashing through bushes and falling down when they stepped into depressions. Robeson finally called a halt. "You're all too loaded. They'll hear you a mile off. I'll go ahead. You stay here."

"I'll drink to that," Doc said, and he pulled a flask from his coat pocket.

When Ken Robeson got close to the gateway, he saw two long black limousines on the road just inside the walls. The headlights were turned off, and several men were standing by the front right-hand door of the lead automobile. They were looking up at a telephone pole outside the gateway. A man was up there, faintly silhouetted against the light gray sky. Even as Robeson watched, the last of the wires fell away. The man who'd cut them began to climb down.

Robeson tried to count the number of the party. It was too dark to be accurate, but he estimated that there were twelve.

And then, as someone lit a match to light a cigar, he saw a tough face beneath the brim of a hat. And a tommy gun in the hands of the man standing nearby.

Combining stealth with speed, he turned and made his way back to where the three were. Just as he got to them, he heard the acceleration of motors and the shifting of gears. Through the trees he could see the two vehicles, their lights still out, moving along the road.

"We got company," he said. "Heavily armed troops of some sort. I don't know if they're mobsters or G-men."

They went back to the rest of the group. By then the two limousines had passed the hidden watchers and were climbing the winding road. Robeson told the others what he'd seen.

Trish Burke said, "Then that means we don't have a chance. Unless they're government people making a raid."

"We can only wait here and see what happens," Ken said. "But cheer up. Who knows but this may mean that your father'll be sprung very soon?"

At that moment there was a yell. It came from a distance, but even its faintness could not filter out the despair in it.

Eight

Robeson looked at the building. In its blazing light was a tiny figure running down the hill. Behind it came three others, all shouting.

By now the two limousines were out of sight beyond the curve of the hill.

Trish started forward, crying, "Father!"

Robeson grabbed her arm and swung her around. "Don't let them know we're down here!" He turned to the others. "Duck behind the trees! Get ready to jump Adlerdreck and the Gold Dust Twins. But be careful! They're armed. Rijnwijk, why don't one of you get the car? Have it ready for us."

Van Rijnwijk, swaying, said, "Well, I dunno. We can't all gesh . . . get in our car. Need another."

Robeson said, "Trish, you take off with him and bring your car, too!"

"What! And leave my father! I can't, I have to find out what's going to happen to him!"

He could understand her reluctance, though he thought it was ill advised. He said, "Jocko, what about you? Would you take her keys and drive the car to the gateway entrance?"

"Not me, kid! I ain't gonna run away when there's a good fight coming up! Oh, boy!" He rubbed his big, hairy-backed hands together and hopped up and down like a chimpanzee working himself into a battle frenzy.

Robeson got Trish to open her handbag so he could remove the keys. He offered them to the lawyer, Creeks, who shook his head. "Not me. I like a brawl as much as that monkey there. Anyway, he'd say I was chicken if I took off."

All the men refused on the grounds that they'd be thought cowardly if they left now. Besides, as Doc said, they were spoiling to get their hands on Adlerdreck.

Then van Rijnwijk refused to go on the same grounds.

"Whyn't you go?"

"I will, but I can't drive more than one car at a time!" Robeson cried. "Don't any of you have any sense at all!"

"I do!" the ex-stripper cried. "Theshe dimb bozosh ain't go' the shenshe they was born with—if any. Gi' . . . give me the keysh!"

Robeson doubted that she could even find the car, let alone drive it. But she was a last hope. He handed her the keys to the Ford. She immediately dropped them and was then down on all fours groping for them. Lunger Tom, the pale, sour runt, said, "Okay. I'll bring the . . . hic! . . . limouzhine. I got some shenshe, and nobody'sh gonna call me chicken. No' . . . not after I got gashed . . . gassed . . . in the Big One. Gi' muh the keysh to Trish'sh . . . Triss's . . . car."

But he began coughing violently, and Doc Fauve and Smalljack jumped on him, covering his mouth so the approaching quartet wouldn't hear them. He kicked out, catching Rijnwijk in the groin. The big man howled in pain, let loose of Thomas, and writhed on the ground. Jocko leaped upon him and clamped his hand over Rijnwijk's mouth. Then he howled and danced around holding his hand which the big man had bitten.

Robeson threw his hands up in the air.

Doc Fauve said, "Shomebody's gotta shtraighten em out. All thish noise."

His big right fist cracked three times, and Thomas, van Rijnwijk, and Blidgett were laid out and snoring. Robeson almost went amok then. They needed every man available to overwhelm the three pursuers of Burke, and all of a sudden they were reduced to six, two of them women.

He looked up the hill. The professor was still going strong, almost at the road at the foot of the hill. The others were about ninety feet behind him.

Then he saw the first of the big black limousines come around the corner of the house and pull to a stop in front of it. Men with tommy guns and shotguns piled out of it while the second vehicle stopped behind the first. One of the men must have looked down the hill. He pointed, and the others turned to look. One had a flashlight which he directed toward the four running men.

One of the men from the limousines, evidently the leader, waved his arms and screamed orders. Four men ran into the building, their guns ready. The others plunged on down the hill.

By then Professor Burke was heading toward the woods, wheezing like an asthmatic mule.

"Quick! Drag these guys under the trees!" Ken Robeson said. "Then get ready to jump on the Doc and his buddies!"

"Doc?" Fauve said, swaying. "Whash you wanna jump on me and my buddiesh for?"

"Doctor von Altereddrake!" Robeson said. "Holy cow! You got me doing it! I mean, Adlerdreck and his thugs!"

"Oh! Well, okay. Lishen, Robeshon, don' worry. I'm a chiropractor.

I may be deshpished in the medical profeshion, but I know what I'm doing. Thoshe quacksh are jealoush of ush chiropractorsh. Don' worry about me taking care of thoshe guysh! I know all about presshure pointsh on the human body!"

Robeson had already dragged van Rijnwijk's heavy bulk under the branches of a nearby tree. Pat and Trish, he saw, were carrying off the light body of Lunger Tom. He straightened and said, "What do you mean? Pressure points?"

Doc's gigantic body loomed above him, swaying like the Empire State Building in a high wind. A big hand came down and its thumb pressed on his neck.

"Like thish, shee? I probe, I find the nekshush—nexus—of nerve shentersh here, I pressh, and . . ."

Nine

Kenneth Robeson wasn't unconscious very long. But in the short period Professor Burke had reached them. He must have been startled to find a body—Robeson's—on the cold ground and above it a gigantic menacing figure weaving back and forth. Probably mumbling about the prejudices and persecutions of the medical profession and the pressure points of the human nervous system.

Though he didn't know what had happened while he was out, Robeson could reconstruct it. Burke had veered to one side, but von Adlerdreck and his two colleagues, following him closely, had rammed into Doc Fauve. All three had fallen.

He supposed this was so—he was still in the supposing stage because his wits hadn't all rallied to him yet—since the sanitarium head and Bufalo and Ovarizi were just getting up off the ground.

Then two figures—Pat and Trish—flew out of the darkness. Trish's handbag thudded against Ovarizi's temple. He went down. The long-legged, high-stepping, high-kicking Patricia Coningway—she must have thought she was on the stage—kicked high. The point of her shoe caught Bufalo under the chin. He emitted a glugging sound, and went down.

The tall blond von Adlerdreck didn't even see what had occurred behind him. He was running off into the darkness, shouting something unintelligible.

Robeson got to his feet. Doc Fauve rose a few seconds later. Very dignifiedly, he said, "Offisher, I wassh jusht crosshing the shtreet, with the light, mind you, when thish truck . . ."

He stopped, took a quick look around, and said, somewhat embarrassedly, "What happened?"

At that moment Jocko, muttering something about "Mabel," got up. He stood for a few seconds, crouching, his knuckles on the ground, exactly like a gorilla aroused from sleep. He growled, "Where are they? I'll kill 'em!"

Robeson, restraining his anger, said, "Drag them under the trees!"

Too late. Ovarizi and Bufalo leaped up and staggered off. It was evident from the way they kept running into the trees that they were still dazed. Since they were armed, Robeson decided not to go after them.

Van Rijnwijk, Thomas, and Jocko, all groaning, got to their feet. At that moment, Robeson heard feet thudding. There were so many, it sounded like a buffalo stampede. Before he and the others could hide, they were invaded. Men poked guns at them in the illumination of two flashlights.

Robeson could not see for a moment or so. Then the blinding beam was directed toward the surrounding trees. The two women were not visible. Either they'd fled or were concealed behind tree trunks.

Now he could see the leader. He was medium-sized though muscular, clad in a gray cloth coat with a gray fur collar. His head was bare, allowing Robeson to see a shock of polar-bear white hair and a middle-aged face that would have been handsome if it weren't for its total lack of expression. It looked like the mask of a dead man. Or the features of a man playing dead. Since Robeson was very close to the man, he could distinguish the color of the eyes. The gray of Arctic ice-fields. But under the pale, washed-out flatness was a blaze as if a natural-gas leak has caught fire under the polar icecap.

Robeson recognized him from the photographs and the descriptions in many newspaper and magazine articles.

"Ricardo Bensoni!" he gasped.

"You said it, punk!"

The dead lips didn't move. It was as if Bensoni were a ventriloquist who projected his voice. In fact, the words seemed to come from the open, but still, mouth of a huge guy standing like a wooden dummy by him.

So this was "Il Vendicativo." "The Avengeful." The story was that his wife and daughter had disappeared, and Dito "Finger" Sporcizio's mob was blamed. Dito's protests of his innocence did him no good. Bensoni and his gang had wiped out every member of Sporcizio's organization, including some kids who ran numbers. Then Bensoni had taken over the dead ganglord's territory.

A few months later, a juvenile street gang had made the mistake of stealing the hubcaps from Bensoni's armored Cadillac. Bensoni had burned them out of their basement headquarters and machine-gunned the survivors as, their clothes on fire, they ran into the street. The next day, crime dropped 86 percent in Brooklyn.

One of Bensoni's uncles, who ran a grocery store in the Bronx, was beaten up because he refused to pay for "protection" by Affamato Porco's thugs. Bensoni wiped that gang out.

The police knew who had committed these crimes but couldn't prove it. Only last month Bensoni had been shocked to find out that Sporcizio had been innocent after all. Bensoni's wife had run off with a used-car salesman, taking her child with her. They were last seen boarding a ship in Los Angeles bound for Brazil.

The huge man was Hidtkot Schmidt, chiefly noted for his ability to get past electrical security systems. And now Robeson saw another infamous member of the mob, McMurdoro, "The Murderer." He was a tall Scot with hands almost as big as van Rijnwijk's.

Bensoni did not have the prejudice of Sicilian mobsters against non-Sicilians. He hired only the best help, and if the man wasn't from the Old Country, he did not care.

Il Vendicativo spoke softly to Robeson, asking him who he was and what he was doing here. Robeson was too deep in a state of shock to think of a lie. He told Bensoni the truth.

"If you're giving it to me straight, you have nothing to worry about," the wax-mask-faced man said. "Some people say I got a mean streak, but that's a lie. I'm not vengeful. I just see to it that justice is done."

He turned to Schmidt and McMurdoro. "Get Burke. Don't hurt him. Don't knock off Ovarizi and Bufalo if you can help it. I want to put some questions to them."

A chill ran over Robeson at these words. He could imagine Bensoni's type of inquisition.

All of the gang except a tall, skinny colored man ran into the woods to do Bensoni's bidding. The Negro held a tommy on the prisoners.

Bensoni started to say something but stopped. A wild yell came from the woods, followed by the booming of .45 automatics and the chatter of submachine guns.

Ten

"You bums stay here!" Bensoni snarled without moving his lips. "Otherwise, I blow your heads off!"

He and the Negro ran off into the trees. Robeson called softly, "Trish! Pat! You out there?"

A scream soared above him and through the branches, riding even over the gunfire. It was a woman's voice filled with terror. And it seemed to come from the direction where all the noisy action was.

Robeson ran toward it, shouting, "Where are you, Trish?" Behind him was a thunder of feet, the others stumbling after him. He went perhaps a hundred yards, then dived into the cold, hard ground as streaks of fire shot off into the night and bullets wheeling above his head, smacked into tree trunks, and pattered in the soil around him. Behind him was a heavy thump, his followers hitting the dirt at the same time as if they were a trained ballet group.

The firing stopped. A car motor roared, and tires squealed. Raising his head, he got a glimpse of headlights moving away from him. They flashed on the steel gates and then they disappeared. From the sound of the motor, the car was going full speed toward Roosville.

There was some loud cursing near the gate. Then Bensoni's voice rose. "That does it! #%$&**! Burke got kidnapped! Right in front of our eyes, under our noses! †=%&*@¢#!"

Robeson called out. "Hey, Bensoni! Are the women okay?"

"Yeah! It was on account of them we quit shooting! That #$%&@¢†=&!X Bierstoss used them as shields!"

Bierstoss! Who . . . ? Then Robeson remembered what Trish Burke had told him. Bierstoss was the industrialist who'd financed the professor's experiments. The man who'd paid von Adlerdreck to take care of him. He must've driven up just in time to get the professor. What was he doing here?

"Can we come in?" Robeson called.

"Okay. But with your hands up and slowly."

Evidently Bensoni didn't trust anybody. Robeson didn't blame him. The kind of life he led, he couldn't afford to trust his own wife. *Especially* her.

He got up, then stood still as Bufalo's voice cut through the night. "Hey, Bensoni! A truce! We . . ."

The rest was cut off as the second limousine, occupied by the four men who'd entered the building, roared up. Il Vendicativo told them to hold their fire, and he said, "Okay, what is it, Chips?"

"I was just wondering if we ain't after the same thing. For the same people. How about a truce so's we can talk?"

At that moment someone touched Robeson on the shoulder. Startled, he whirled, ready to strike out. But it was Trish Burke.

She said, her voice trembling, "Oh, Ken! That man drove off with my father! Where's he taking him?"

Robeson didn't know. He shushed her so that he could hear the powwow. However, there wasn't going to be any.

Bensoni ordered his men into the two cars. As he got in, he called, "Chips! You and Eggs! You keep out of this if you know what's healthy for you! Got me?"

The lead car started out with the wheels turning in the gravel, firing stones right and left. The second car followed, tommy barrels bristling from the windows.

Robeson figured that the gangsters were going after Bierstoss and his captive—if Burke had been taken along involuntarily.

Von Adlerdreck and his two attendants suddenly emerged from the bushes on the far side of the driveway. They ran up the hill, evidently making for the garage by the big building.

Ken Robeson grabbed Trish's hand and pulled her after him as he ran for their car. Behind them came the sound of stampede again, the patients and the moonshiners taking off after them, none probably knowing why. When, breathless, he and Trish got to the Model A in the farmer's field, the rest piled into the big Packard. All but Doc Fauve. He got onto the running board of the Ford and shouted through the closed window.

"There isn't any room for me in there! I'll ride here so I can be your lookout! We're not going to miss out on the excitement! Tally ho!"

Robeson thought he was nuts, but if Doc wanted to stand out there and freeze, it was okay with him. The cold should sober him up, though he'd be lucky if he didn't get pneumonia.

Then, as Trish backed the car toward the farmer's road, a figure ran toward them. Crouching, its long arms dangling, bounding in a curious run, it looked like a chimpanzee. Trish straightened the car out on the road and started forward. Shouting, Jocko leaped on the running board, opened the door, and got in.

"They threw me out!" he said bitterly. "That lewd shyster Oinks got kind of familiar with Pat, and he blamed it on me. Wait until I get my mitts on him. I'll tear the wings off that legal eagle!"

There was an explosion, and everybody tried to duck. Robeson banged his head on the dashboard, and the pain in it, which had disappeared during the recent frenzy, came back. Trish said, "That wasn't a shot! My right front tire blew!"

The car was stuck in the gateway to the wire fence. The Packard stopped behind them, and everybody tumbled out. There wasn't time to put on the spare, which was, in any event, as bald as the one just punctured. Smalljack said he'd push the Ford out of the way with his car. Then they should all get into his car. There was some argument between Pat Coningway and Jocko while Robeson and Trish danced with impatience. Finally, Jocko, unable to convince Pat that he wasn't the culprit, said he'd promise to keep his paws off her.

By then the Ford had been pushed over into the ditch on the other side of the highway. They started to get into the Packard. Jocko took advantage of Oinks's unprotected rear and kicked it hard.

That started another brawl. The lawyer swung his cane at Jocko, missed, and slammed it across van Rijnwijk's shoulder. The huge fellow struck Oinks on the shoulder with his great fist.

By the time peace had been restored, and they were all jammed uncomfortably into the car, some on top of others, they saw headlights coming out of the sanitarium driveway. They'd wasted so much time, the doctor and his cohorts had gotten a head start.

Within forty seconds, they were rocketing down the road, the rear lights of von Adlerdreck's car about a quarter-mile ahead. Robeson was never to forget that wild, reckless, dangerous, stomach-squeezing, tire-screeching ride. Smalljack drove like a drunken maniac. Maybe he wasn't crazy, but he certainly was intoxicated. He took the Packard at the sharp turn into Roosville beautifully, however. It only turned around three times while negotiating the curve, it didn't roll over once, and it ended up pointing in the right direction.

It tore through the village of dark houses with rustic sleepers inside. Robeson wondered where Sheriff Huisman was. Fifteen minutes later, he found out. By then their car was only a few yards behind the doctor's. And less than a quarter-mile ahead of it was a red flashing light on the roof of the sheriff's car and the faint wail of a siren lifted toward them.

"Huisman must be chasing Bensoni's gang!" Smalljack said. Holding on to the wheel with one hand, he lifted a jug with the other and drank. Then he passed it through the window to Doc Fauve, who was standing now on the running board of the Packard. Doc drank deeply and passed the jug back to Smalljack, who passed it to the ex-stripper.

She began to drink, then stopped, and, swearing, rammed the bottom of the jug hard against Jocko's forehead.

"You keep your hands off me!"

The pharmacist said, indignantly, "Honest to God, Pat, I never touched you. It's that sneaky ambulance-chaser."

"I can vouch for that," said Trish, who was sitting on Robeson's lap. "I know it wasn't Oinks because Jocko's been trying to feel my leg!"

Jocko swore that he was innocent. He claimed it was Lunger Tom, who was seated next to Trish. Lunger Tom got mad and took a poke at Jocko. Oinks began laughing but Jocko's hand closed around his throat. Van Rijnwijk, in the front seat, turned and roared, "No more of that! How in hell can Homer here drive with you bunch of stupid jerks rousting around back there?"

Smalljack said, icily, "I told you never to call me Homer, Van. It's Bill, and don't you forget that!"

For a while there was comparative peace. For some minutes, Robeson could even close his eyes and enjoy having Trish Burke on his lap. Would that this were so in a less disturbing situation. Would he ever get her on his lap again?

The big question, though, was: Would they survive this ride? A dozen times, swinging around sharp curves, the right wheels had gone off onto the shoulder. Once, they skidded sidewise, and this time Robeson was sure they'd turn over. But Smalljack straightened the vehicle out.

Robeson wanted to ask how fast they were going, but he was afraid to.

After an hour and a half, which seemed like five hours, they roared through a police roadblock. This had been set up at the junction of the county road with the state highway. But Bierstoss had taken the narrow opening between two cars and thundered on through. So did Bensoni's limousines, the sheriff's Plymouth, and von Adlerdreck's. And, emulating them, so did Smalljack.

Presently, there were five State Police cars, lights flashing, sirens screaming, behind them.

After Robeson got his breath back—it had been caught somewhere below his lungs—he shouted, "Why don't we stop and explain the situation to the police?"

"Are you crazy?" Lunger Tom squeaked. "We got all this moonshine, and there's distilling equipment in the trunk, not to mention two rifles, a sawed-off shotgun, and a couple of hot gats."

Robeson shut his eyes again. He couldn't bear to look. He could hear Jocko and Oinks quarreling again. The lawyer was angry because he'd just found out that his swing at Jocko with the cane had broken the glass vials inside it. When he'd unscrewed the gold knob, the liquor had run over his arm and his shirtfront and soaked his pants. Jocko was laughing like crazy, then a sharp sound exploded in Robeson's ears.

He opened his eyes. Jocko was howling with pain and holding his cheek.

Trish said, "Keep your hairy paws off of me!"

"It was an accident, an accident, I swear!" Jocko said.

He hunkered down on the floor, jammed between Thomas's legs.

"See! I'll keep my hands in my pockets!"

"Good!" Oinks said, and he poured the rest of the booze in the cane over Jocko's head.

Robeson expected that the police would set up a roadblock at the George Washington Bridge. But there wasn't any. And the crazy caravan continued at seventy miles an hour down Broadway, then over to Fifth Avenue, with whistles blowing, tires screaming, horns blaring, pedestrians and angry car drivers shouting. And violent bumps as the Packard sometimes detoured traffic and went over curbs and down the sidewalk, Smalljack pushing in on the horn button, it blaring, and Doc Fauve, on the running board, waving wildly with one hand for the pedestrians to dive out of the way.

Then, a block from Thirty-fourth, what Robeson had been praying for happened. The gas tank ran dry.

Smalljack smoothly put the gear into neutral and the car rolled for another block.

Robeson looked out the window. They were right back where they'd started from: the Empire State Building.

Eleven

Bierstoss's Lincoln was parked with its left wheels on the sidewalk. Just behind were Bensoni's two Cadillacs. And entirely on the sidewalk, its front smashed against the side of the restaurant at the corner, was von Adlerdreck's Cadillac. He never did see the sheriff.

All the vehicles were unoccupied.

Doc Fauve, his yellow complexion blue from the cold, was running up—no, shambling—toward the entrance to the building. Trish opened the door and slid out from Robeson's lap.

In the distance came the dismal sound of sirens. The State Police, and the city police who'd joined them, would arrive inside a minute.

Robeson got out. He wanted to tell Trish they should stay here and tell the police what had happened. Otherwise, they were as likely to be shot by the cops as by the gangsters. But Trish was running toward the doors to the skyscraper. He found himself also running, though he told himself that the smart thing to do was to stay put. However, he couldn't let her venture by herself into that place which would soon be no-man's-land.

The lobby was brightly lit. Some kind of festivity was being held; big signs, ribbons, decorations, booths all over the place. The attendants, however, were not in a festive mood at the moment. They were running this way and that, screaming, yelling, diving under the counters of the booths, heading toward the exits, taking protection behind the many stone pillars.

A stench of cordite hung in the air, and one pillar was chipped where bullets had struck. No one seemed to be hurt, though.

Robeson saw Trish going into an elevator. He ran after her but the doors closed in front of him. Trish didn't seem to hear his pleas to keep the doors open.

He grabbed a man by the arm. "Those guys who were shooting? Where'd they go?"

The man, pale, trembling pointed upward. Robeson took another elevator.

But only to the second floor. Swearing at himself for not keeping a cooler head, he watched the dials over the doors. Trish's elevator was one of the two expresses, already past the 52nd floor. She didn't know any more than he did about Bierstoss's destination. She was just going up in a frantic, desperate search. But maybe she wasn't so foolish. Maybe she thought that Bierstoss would, in his panic, go as high as possible. He could be operating on the fugitive's instinct, one inherited from ape ancestors. Get as high on the tree as possible.

He went down the stairs to the lobby. By then it was full of state troopers and New York's finest. They didn't seem to know what to do; they were milling around or questioning people. He took the other express elevator which fortunately wasn't being used. It would go to the 80th floor, as high as any elevator could go in one stretch. When he got out, he went down the hall and hopped over the chain put up to keep visitors out. Then he took the elevator that would carry him all the way to the 86th floor. Nobody stopped it because nobody was around.

But plenty of people had been here recently. There were cigar butts, cigarette stubs, a chewing gum wrapper, and a broken whiskey jug just outside the elevator doors.

When the doors opened, Robeson started to stick his head cautiously out of the exit, He didn't hear anything, but that meant nothing. There might be many men lying silently in wait for all hell to bust loose.

Then, a screaming, arm-flailing, leg-kicking, wild-eyed tousle-haired apparition appeared. It seemed to come from nowhere, but its destination was certain. It struck Robeson, drove him back against the back of the cage, and almost bore him under. He grabbed the crazed man—Professor Burke—and he tried to shout sense into him. No use. The man kept on attacking him, at the same time screaming, "My shadow! My shadow! Keep it away from me!"

His face was scratched and his nose was hurting where it had been struck and Robeson angrily picked up the thin man and shook him. "Pipe down! There isn't any shadow!"

Then he hurled the professor against the wall, and the man, sobbing and moaning, crumpled. Robeson stepped forward to punch the button. He'd take this maniac down to the ground floor, tell the police his story, and let them handle it from there on. Much as he wanted to find out where Trish was, he knew that the logical way was to let the cops do it.

But Doc Fauve's big dissipatedly handsome face, its normal, if unhealthy, yellow hue restored, appeared. He seemed to have sobered up somewhat.

"Robeson? You got him, huh? Listen, von Eiderduck and his

Gold Dust Twins're cornered by Bensoni's men. The former are outside on the observation platform. The latter're inside, waiting until they can get a shot at the former. Or is it the former is the latter and vice versa?"

He frowned, then said, "Never mind. What does matter is that Bierstoss has got the young lady, and he's in the top room of the dirigible mooring mast."

"Where are your buddies?" Robeson said.

"We're in the hallway outside the elevators and behind the concession counters. We got Bensoni's men at a standstill."

"With what?"

"With our weapons, of course. Didn't you see Lunger Tom and Smalljack get them out of the trunk?"

"No. How'd Professor Burke get here?"

The near-giant scratched his head. "I don't know. Must've broken loose and nobody shot him because he's the key to the whole mess. One thing he's good at. That's escaping."

"How'd Bierstoss get hold of Trish?"

"Who knows? Somehow, during the confusion, he got hold of her but the professor took off."

Robeson said, "Is Bierstoss armed?"

"Is Roosevelt a Democrat? Sure he is. I got a glimpse of him. He's got two .45 automatics."

"I'm going to take this poor devil down," Robeson said. "The cops can handle it from there."

Doc Fauve came into the cage. He was carrying a gallon jug, and he proceeded to lighten its weight with four or five swallows.

"Yeah? Well, me and the boys, we're going up the elevator into the mooring mast. And we're going to rescue the damsel from the dragon."

"You'll get her killed!" Robeson said. "You guys are too bombed to know what you're doing. You can't go charging in there. He'll open fire the moment the elevator doors open! You'll be massacred!"

Doc Fauve offered the jug to Robeson, who shook his head.

"Yeah? Maybe so! But we're going to do it anyway. Listen, buddy, there's none of us worth a damn. We all had good prospects;

we could have been something. Decent, respectable, giving something to others, our relatives, families, the community. Instead, we peed it all away. We're all drunks, von Addledrake's patients and the moonshiners. And up there is someone who might be something, a real nice girl who got into a situation she isn't responsible for. We've talked about this among us, and we figure we can atone for what we've done, our wasted life, if we can rescue the girl from that villain, Bierstoss!"

Doc Fauve sat down on the floor and drank some more moonshine. Robeson said, "It's alcohol that's talking. It got you into this mess. One final act of redemption, huh? Nonsense! You'll get slaughtered, and Trish will get killed, and all because your booze-soaked brains and your whiskey-rotten conscience have told you you're no good, but you can redeem yourselves by throwing yourselves away. You understand?"

Doc Fauve began weeping. "You don't understand! We're trying to make up for what we've done!"

"If you were sober and aching for drink, you wouldn't be doing this," Robeson said. "It's strange how alcohol carries the seeds of its own . . ."

At that moment a voice bellowed out. Bensoni's.

"Von Adlerdreck! Ovarizi! Bufalo! We know who you are! We got the goods on you! Listen! This has gone far enough! We've been working at cross-purposes! I didn't want to have to tell you this, but there's no way out!

"Listen, I just found out about you last night. I mean, I found out who you and your buddies were and what you were up to! So come on in, you three, and we'll put our heads together and see if we can work something out without these civilians making trouble! How about it?"

Robeson could hear a voice muffled by the glass windows on the 86th floor. But he thought he heard von Adlerdreck say something about not knowing if Bensoni was lying to him.

Doc Fauve got up. He was no longer crying. He said, "What's that gangster talking about?"

The professor quit whimpering, and he tried to get up on his feet. Robeson pressed him back down.

"I don't know. This has been a very confusing night."

Doc Fauve bellowed, "You guys! Come here! We're going on up and rescue Miss Burke!"

The others appeared and crowded into the cage. Robeson wanted to get out; but the press of bodies prevented him. He said, "Damn it! All right! I'll go with you! But this is idiotic! Bierstoss will murder us!"

"He can't get us all!" Jocko shouted. He punched the button and the cage shot up. "One of us'll get him! Here, Robeson, you look scared! Have a shot of Dutch courage!"

Ken Robeson shook his head. "You damn fools! If you start blazing away the moment the doors open, you're just as likely to shoot Trish!"

"Yes," the lawyer said. "But at least we'll have vengeance! Bierstoss isn't going to escape!"

The cage stopped. The doors, whispering, began to open.

The tall, skinny Smalljack and the apelike Jocko held revolvers. Van Rijnwijk had the sawed-off shotgun. Little Thomas, who was coughing, waved the deer rifle around. Pat Coningway had a knife in her hand.

Robeson said, "Where'd you get that?"

"I keep it in a garter sheath," she said, smiling. "That's to defend my virtue."

"Yeah," Jocko said. "This is the only time she ever pulled it out. And her virtue ain't at stake. How about that?"

"How'd you like this shoved up between your glutei maximi?" Pat said. Jocko broke up, bending over with uncontrollable laughter, slapping his knee, and then "accidentally" ramming his elbow into Oinks's ribs.

Oinks yelled with wrath and grabbed Jocko by the throat. "You Pithecanthropus not-so-erectus! I'll squeeze your throat until your brains pop out! If, that is, you have anything in your skull except a vacuum to squeeze out!"

The doors opened. Smalljack's revolver exploded. Van Rijnwijk's shotgun boomed. Pat, screaming like a Valkyrie, tried to dash forward, her little blade extended. Unfortunately, Doc Fauve was in her path, and the point sank into his back. He yelled and threw his hands out, one knocking Thomas out and the other rendering van Rijnwijk half-unconscious. Jocko's revolver went boom!-boom!-boom! as his eyes popped under the pressure of Oinks's fingers. Fortunately, it was pointed upward, and its bullets smashed harmlessly through the ceiling of the cage.

Later, Robeson was to think how extremely fortuitous it was that Trish Burke wasn't standing before the elevator doors. But she was off to one side, looking down at Bierstoss. He was a short, pudgy man lying on his back, his mouth open, his eyes closed.

His forehead was streaked with red. Trish held a .45 automatic pistol by the butt. She was waiting for him to recover consciousness.

But for the moment, she was frozen with shock at the bellow of shotgun and crack of revolver.

The cage was emptied, its occupants spilling out, most of them falling flat on their faces. Robeson went to Trish. "Are you all right?"

"Yes," she said, lowering the hand holding the Luger. "I grabbed him where . . ." She seemed reluctant to say the exact words. After all, she was a lady. "I mean, . . . you know . . . and while he was writhing on the floor, I grabbed his gun from the floor . . . he'd dropped it because he was in such pain, and I hit him on the head with it."

Swaying, pale, she looked at him with enormous blue eyes. "How's father? Is he safe?"

Robeson jerked a thumb at the elevator cage. "I think so."

Trish's eyes got even wider, a feat he would not have thought possible.

"But . . . the elevator! It's gone!"

Robeson turned. The doors were closed. Somebody, maybe the professor, maybe a person on the 86th floor, had punched its button.

As he stared, too stupefied from all that had happened to react swiftly, the doors opened. And there, in the cage, was the white-haired, expressionless Bensoni. With him were von Adlerdreck, Ovarizi, Bufalo, Schmidt, McMurdoro, the colored man, and a dozen others. All had weapons, tommies, .45 automatics, some revolvers. One man was even holding a grenade.

Bensoni stepped out into the room. He said, in his emotionless, robotlike voice, "Well, this is quite a mess, isn't it?"

He put his hand inside his gray flannel jacket and pulled out a gray wallet. He flipped it open. Robeson got a flash of a badge.

"You're all under arrest!"

Twelve

Kenneth Robeson sat typing in his one-room apartment. He'd been writing since morning, stopping only for obligations of Nature, including a three-hour sleep. By now he not only had the continuing characters, themes, and permanent locales of the series worked out in detail, he had half-written the first novel.

His fingers were flying, the keys spewing out golden words of high adventure and low comedy, when someone banged at his door. Impatiently, he rose and went to the door. He didn't want to be interrupted by anybody, not even by Trish Burke.

He flung the door open and looked up at the yellow face and eyes of Doc Fauve. The near giant looked even sicker. In his hand was a quart bottle, not of moonshine, but of Duggan's Dew of Kirkintilloch. At sight of that Robeson lost his cross expression. He was only a moderate drinker, but this brand of scotch was his favorite liquor. He hadn't been able to afford it for a long time.

"I know you're busy," Doc said. "But I'd like to have a few minutes. This is a sort of farewell visit. A couple of snorts, and I'll be off. But I'll leave the bottle behind as a memento mori."

Ken felt a shock travel through him. Fauve didn't expect to live much longer, and he'd come here so Ken Robeson could pay his pre-mortem respects. And he was paying his way with the gift of scotch.

"Come on in," Robeson said. "Sit down."

He got two chipped coffee mugs and half-filled each. Doc, sitting on the worn and torn overstuffed chair, raised his mug. "Here's success to you in your career. And a wish that you and the young lady hit it off well."

Ken sipped at the delicious, heady liquor. Doc Fauve said, "Our bootlegger friends have had to close down their local stills. Sheriff

Huisman is mad because Bensoni and Bufalo and the feds and God knows how many other agencies put the lid on everything. The word is mum. Nothing ever happened. He can't even talk about the affair, let alone arrest anybody. But he did find and destroy our friends' booze-making equipment. So they're bringing in stuff from Canada until the heat dies off. Lunger Tom slipped me a couple of cases of Duggan's yesterday."

He hadn't taken his greatcoat off. Now he opened it and revealed two more bottles of the priceless stuff in specially made pockets. He removed these and put them on the floor.

"These are yours, too. Whenever you take a drink, think of me. And the other guys, including Pat."

Robeson felt a little embarrassed at the references to Doc's coming demise. He said, "Listen, I'll think of you, of the whole bunch, every time I write a story in the series."

"Yeah. I'm glad you told me about it. I'm tickled. All the boys, and Pat, too, are tickled. It's a sort of immortality, you know.

"But whoever would have thought the other night that things'd turn out the way they did? Bierstoss was a German agent, planted years ago so he could operate as a respectable manufacturer and pillar of the church. And so here comes Professor Burke and his secret chemical formula. Burke thinks the chemical can force people to act morally. Bierstoss sees it as a great thing to make people sort of brain slaves. The formula could be modified, he hopes, to make people think as the German state wants them to think. Of course, he doesn't tell Burke this.

"But Burke goes crazy, poor old devil. The chemical injection brings up all the evil thoughts and repressed desires that are in even the most moral of people. So he sees his subconscious projected as a savage shadow which threatens his inner being. He can't endure it, and he goes insane.

"Bierstoss is upset by this. But he figures that maybe the effect can be used after all. All it needs is experimentation. There's plenty of human guinea pigs available to the Germans. So he sends Burke to Adlerdreck, who's a federal agent posing as a German sympathizer. Bierstoss thinks von Adlerdreck can get the formula out of Burke.

Burke hadn't told Bierstoss what it was; he carried it in his head. But that head was all mixed up. So von Adlerdreck was supposed to catch Burke in a sane moment and get it from him, even if he had to use torture.

"Von Adlerdreck pretended to go along with Bierstoss so he could get a line on everybody in Bierstoss's organization. Including his tie-ups with the secret Italian Fascist cells. He used Ovarizi and Bufalo, who were also double agents."

Robeson laughed. "And Bensoni was another double agent working for another secret federal agency. Like Ovarizi and Bufalo, he'd established himself as a genuine gangster. But he didn't know the doctor and his two cronies were also Uncle Sam's employees."

Doc Fauve lost his smile for a moment. He shook his head. "Yeah. That Bensoni! He got lost in his role. It's all right to knock off rival gangs. But to murder a juvenile street gang just because they stole the hubcaps off his car. The man's a psychopath."

"That he is," Robeson said. "Still, that gang was mugging old ladies and beating up store owners if they didn't come across with protection money."

"I heard he's locked up in a mental hospital now," Doc Fauve said. "Though that may be just a story to account for his disappearance. He had to drop out of sight once his cover was blown."

Robeson nodded. Bensoni had been furious, but he had to tell everybody involved just who he was and what he'd been doing. First, he'd extracted a promise of silence from the people in the mooring-mast floor. Everybody agreed, especially after Bensoni had threatened to throw them in jail on trumped-up charges if they didn't keep their mouths shut. Then, while the elevator was kept from operating, so the police would be held off for a few minutes, Bensoni had revealed all that needed to be known.

Robeson had asked him if the story of his wife's running off with a used-car salesman was a fake, too. Bensoni had looked as if he were going to strike Robeson, and he'd told him that was none of his business.

Doc Fauve emptied his cup and poured in an even more generous portion. "Ah, the stuff that kills!" he said. "I'm glad to see you don't overindulge, my boy. Don't ever do it. It wrecks the brain, the belly, the kidneys, the liver, and isn't too good for the heart. And it causes financial distress, breaks up marriages and friendships, strews its golden path with cripples and corpses. Demon Rum and John Barleycorn! Thy names are Satan! Thy grip is legion! I campaigned for Prohibition, I know, and I'm a member of the WCTU. So much for a weak will and a lust to commit slow suicide!"

Robeson didn't want to get into a long drunken-maudlin scene. He said, "I'll have to get back to work soon. But first, let me tell you what I've done. I got a great concept for the series. It's about a sort of superman who, with his five aides, battles the forces of evil. He's one of the richest men in the world, young and handsome, absurdly knowledgeable, moral, and dedicated. He's been raised by scientists who've taught him all they know, which is about everything except women. He invents all sorts of things to benefit mankind and a lot of gadgets to help him in his battle against crime.

"His headquarters are on the 86th floor of a mid-Manhattan skyscraper."

Fauve raised his eyebrows. "There's only one building high enough to have an 86th floor. And that's the observation floor. Nobody lives there."

"Sure. But how many, including native New Yorkers, know that? Anyway, this is fiction, and I take poetic license."

"So, what's the name of our superhero?"

"Doc Savage. *Fauve* means a wild beast in French. That made me think of Savage. Catchy, isn't it? Has a nice ring—and Savage is also known as the Man of Bronze. In fact, that's the title of the story I'm writing. Doc is called this because his skin is a golden-bronze derived from long exposure to tropical suns. His hair is bronze, too."

Fauve laughed. "Unlike my yellow pigment, huh?"

"Well, one of your family names is du Bronce. That gave me the idea for the bronze aspect."

"And Doc Savage's eyes?"

"Yellow. No, don't laugh. Not bilious yellow, begging your pardon, but golden. Magnetic whirlpools of molten gold."

"You could have named your hero Sauvage. French for savage."

"No offense, Doc, but all the major leads in this series will have to have English names. The big boy at S & S says the readers don't like the good guys to have foreign names. It's okay to use Irish or Scottish names, but English names are surefire. It's the Anglo-Saxon complex.

"So, Hans van Rijnwijk becomes John Renwick. He was only a sergeant in real life, but in this series he's a colonel. The same with the other aides of Doc. They're brigadier-generals, majors, et cetera. And van Rijnwijk is promoted from a garage mechanic to one of the world's greatest engineers.

"Anderson Maypole Blidgett, 'Jocko,' a pharmacist, becomes Andrew Blodgett Mayfair, 'Monk,' one of the world's greatest industrial chemists. And so on with the others. You get the idea."

"What models do Patricia Coningway and Patricia Burke provide?"

"Well, I'll combine them, an ex-stripper and a bookkeeper for a beauty salon chain, into Patricia Savage, Doc's lovely young cousin. She'll come into the series later. She'll own and operate her own very posh beauty salon, and she'll be a scrapper who's always getting into trouble. A real Amazon but feminine. She ought to appeal to the adolescents who'll constitute the bulk of the readers.

"There'll be a lot of science in the series. Pseudo-science, rather. And the stories and the characters'll be bigger than life. A lot of the locales will be in far-off, exotic places. This is the Depression, Doc. The readers don't want grim stuff that'll just remind them of their sorry lot. If they're going to part with a hard-earned dime for a story, they'll only do it for something that takes them into the golden realms of fantasy. Where they can identify for a couple of hours with men and women who're rich, who fight successfully against the evils which make so many people feel helpless, powerless to battle."

"Sounds like a splendid idea," Doc Fauve said. "I wish I was going to be around long enough to see for myself! Oh, well, the others ought to live long enough to read some of the series. If they can stay sober long enough to read them.

"But what about this Ricardo Bensoni, Il Vendicativo? Since you've turned sick alcoholics and small-time rural moonshiners into heroes, what about Bensoni? You could use your inside-out magic on him and his associates, transmute their lead into gold."

"I've thought about that. If this series peters out eventually, I could start a new one. The hero could be Richard Benson, the Avenger. Gangsters do away with his wife and daughter in a vast, malevolent plot. Benson's hair turns white and his facial muscles become paralyzed from the shock. He vows to avenge the deaths of his loved ones, and he does. This gets him into the business of fighting crime—he's independently wealthy—and he forms Justice, Incorporated, an illegal but highly effective tool for laying low the great criminals of this nation.

"I might even use that Negro aide of Bensoni's as a model. But he won't be the type you usually find in pulp fiction, the 'hush ma mouf, feets-get-going' comical type. He'll be college-educated, speak excellent English, and be a genuine contributor to Justice, Inc. I don't know if the reader will accept this type of black, but by the time I get the Avenger series going, maybe readers' attitudes will've changed. We'll see."

Doc Fauve raised his mug. "I like your transmutations."

"They're such stuff as dreams are made on."

Doc drank, then said, "A slight paraphrase of Shakespeare's *The Tempest*, a line from Shakespeare's *The Tempest*, act four."

He refilled the mug and raised it again.

"And this is such drams as stiffs are made on."

Ken Robeson winced, and said, "Well, it's time for you to go back to your world and me to mine."

Skinburn

Author's Preface

It makes no difference in the story itself, but devotees of old pulp-magazine fiction might deduce Kent Lane's identity from his fire opal ring and his name. The surname implies, of course, that his parents were never married. I have plans for Lane, who will carry on his distinguished father's career, though in a less violent manner.

This story is about Love, which means that it is also about Hate. One of the themes that run through much of my work is that for every advantage you gain there is a disadvantage, that the gods, or whoever, require payment, that the universe in all its aspects, which include the human psyche, is governed by a check and balance system.

Your skin tingles every time you step outdoors?" Dr. Mills said. "And when you stand under the skylight in your apartment? But only now and then when you're standing in front of the window, even if the sunlight falls on you?"

"Yes," Kent Lane said. "It doesn't matter whether or not it's night or day, the skies are cloudy or clear, or the skylight is open or closed. The tingling is strongest on the exposed parts of my body, my face and hands or whatever. But the tingling spreads from the exposed skin to all over my body, though it's much weaker under my clothes. And the tingling eventually arouses vaguely erotic feelings."

The dermatologist walked around him. When he had completed his circuit, he said, "Don't you ever tan?"

"No, I just peel and blister. I usually avoid burning by staying out of the sun as much as possible. But that isn't doing me any good now, as you can see. I look as if I'd been on the beach all day. That makes me rather conspicuous, you know. In my work, you can't afford to be conspicuous."

The doctor said, "I know."

He meant that he was aware that Lane was a private detective. What he did not know was that Lane was working on a case for a federal government agency. CACO—Coordinating Authority for Cathedric Organizations—was short of competent help. It had hired, after suitable security checks, a number of civilian agents. CACO would have hired only the best, of course, and Lane was among these.

Lane hesitated and then said, "I keep getting these phone calls."

The doctor said nothing. Lane said, "There's nobody at the other end. He, or she, hangs up just as soon as I pick the phone up."

"You think the skinburn and the phone calls are related?"

"I don't know. But I'm putting all unusual phenomena into one box. The calls started a week after I'd had a final talk with a lady who'd been chasing me and wouldn't quit. She has a Ph.D. in bioelectronics and is a big shot in the astronautics industry. She's brilliant, charming, and witty, when she wants to be, but very plain in face and plane in body and very nasty when frustrated. And so . . ."

He was, he realized, talking too much about someone who worked in a top-secret field. Moreover, why would Mills want to hear the sad story of Dr. Sue Brackwell's unrequited love for Kent Lane, private eye? She had been hung up on him for some obscure psychological reason and, in her more rational moments, had admitted that they could never make it as man and wife, or even as man and lover, for more than a month, if that. But she was not, outside of the laboratory, always rational, and she would not take no from her own good sense or from him. Not until he had gotten downright vicious over the phone two years ago.

Three weeks ago, she had called him again. But she had said nothing to disturb him. After about five minutes of light chitchat about this and that, including reports on their health, she had said goodbye, making it sound like an *ave atque vale*, and had hung up. Perhaps she had wanted to find out for herself if the sound of his voice still thrilled her. Who knew?

Lane became aware that the doctor was waiting for him to finish the sentence. He said, "The thing is, these phone calls occurred at first when I was under the skylight and making love. So I moved the bed to a corner where nobody could possibly see it from the upper stories of the Parmenter Building next door.

"After that, the phone started ringing whenever I took a woman into my apartment, even if it was just for a cup of coffee. It'd be ringing before I'd get the door open, and it'd ring at approximately three-minute intervals thereafter. I changed my phone number twice, but it didn't do any good. And if I went to the woman's apartment instead, her phone started ringing."

"You think this lady scientist is making these calls?"

"Never! It's not her style. It must be a coincidence that the calls started so soon after our final conversation."

"Did your women also hear the phone?"

Lane smiled and said, "Audiohallucinations? No. They heard the phone ringing, too. One of them solved the problem by tearing her phone out. But I solved mine by putting in a phone jack and disconnecting the phone when I had in mind another sort of connection."

"That's all very interesting, but I fail to see what it has to do with your skin problem."

"Phone calls aside," Lane said, "could the tingling, the peeling and blistering, and the mild erotic reaction be psychosomatic?"

"I'm not qualified to say," Mills said. "I can, however, give you the name of a doctor whose specialty is recommending various specialists."

Lane looked at his wristwatch. Rhoda should be about done with her hairdresser. He said, "So far, I'm convinced I need a dermatologist, not a shrink. I was told you're the best skin doctor in Washington and perhaps the best on the East Coast."

"The world, actually," Dr. Mills said. "I'm sorry. I can do nothing for you at this time. But I do hope you'll inform me of new developments. I've never had such a puzzling, and, therefore, interesting, case."

Lane used the phone in the ground-floor lobby to call his fiancée's hairdresser. He was told that Rhoda had just left but that she would pick him up across the street from the doctor's building.

He got out of the building just in time to see Rhoda drive his MG around the corner, through a stoplight, and into the path of a pickup truck. Rhoda, thrown out by the impact (she was careless about using her safety belt), landed in front of a Cadillac. Despite its locked brakes, it slid on over her stomach.

Lane had seen much as an adviser in Vietnam and as a member of the San Francisco and Brooklyn Police Departments. He thought he was tough, but the violent and bloody deaths of Leona and Rhoda within four months was too much. He stood motionless, noting only that the tingling was getting warmer and spreading over his body. There was no erotic reaction, or, if there were, he was too numb to feel it. He stood there until a policeman got the nearest doctor, who happened to be Mills, to come out and look at him. Mills gave Lane a mild sedative, and the cop sent him home in a taxi. But Lane was at the morgue an hour later, identified Rhoda, and then went to the precinct station to answer some questions.

He went home prepared to drink himself to sleep, but he found two CACO agents, Daniels and Lyons, waiting for him. They seemed to have known about Rhoda's death almost as quickly as he, and so he knew that they had been shadowing him or Rhoda. He answered some of their questions and then told them that the idea that Leona and Rhoda might be spies was not worth a second's consideration. Besides, if they were working for SKIZO, or some other outfit, why would SKIZO, or whoever, kill their own agents?

"Or did CACO kill them?" Lane said.

The two looked at him as if he were unspeakably stupid.

"All right," Lane said. "But there's absolutely no evidence to indicate that their deaths were caused by anything but pure accident. I know it's quite a coincidence . . ."

Daniels said, "CACO had both under surveillance, of course. But CACO saw nothing significant in the two women's behavior. However, that in itself is suspicious, you know. Negative evidence demands a positive inquiry."

"That maxim demands the investigation of the entire world," Lane said.

"Nevertheless," Lyons said, "SKIZO must've spotted you by

now. They'd have to be blind not to. Why in hell don't you stay out from under sunlamps?"

"It's a skin problem," Lane said. "As you must know, since you've undoubtedly bugged Dr. Mills' office."

"Yeah, we know," Daniels said. "Frankly, Lane, we got two tough alternatives to consider. Either you're going psycho, or else SKIZO is on to you. Either way . . ."

"You're thinking in two-valued terms only," Lane said. "Have you considered that a third party, one with no connection at all with SKIZO, has entered the picture?"

Daniels cracked his huge knuckles and said, "Like who?"

"Like whom, you mean. How would I know? But you'll have to admit that it's not only possible but highly probable."

Daniels stood up. Lyons jumped up. Daniels said, "We don't have to admit anything. Come along with us, Lane."

If CACO thought he was lying, CACO would see to it that he was never seen again. CACO was mistaken about him, of course, but CACO, like doctors, buried mistakes.

On leaving the apartment building, Lane immediately felt the warm tingling on his face and hands and, a few seconds later, the spreading of the warmth to his crotch. He forgot about that a moment later when Daniels shoved him as he started to get into the back seat of the CACO automobile. He turned and said, "Keep your dirty hands off me, Daniels! Push me, and I may just walk off. You might have to shoot me to stop me, and you wouldn't want to do that in broad daylight, would you?"

"Try it and find out," Daniels said. "Now shut up and get in or get knocked in. You know we're being observed. Maybe that's why you're making a scene."

Lane got into the back seat with Lyons, and Daniels drove them away. It was a hot June afternoon, and evidently the CACO budget did not provide for cars with air-conditioning. They rode with the windows down while Lyons and Daniels asked him questions. Lane answered all truthfully, if not fully, but he was not concentrating on his replies. He noticed that when he hung his hand out of the window, it felt warm and tingling.

Fifteen minutes later, the big steel doors of an underground garage clanged shut behind him. He was interrogated in a small room below the garage. Electrodes were attached to his head and body, and various machines with large staring lenses were fixed on him while he was asked a series of questions. He never found out what the interpreters of the machines' graphs and meters thought about his reactions to the questions. Just as the electrodes were being detached, Smith, the man who had hired Lane for CACO, entered. Smith had a peculiar expression. He called the interrogators to one side and spoke to them in a low voice. Lane caught something about "a telephone call." A minute later, he was told he could go home. But he was to keep in touch, or, rather, keep himself available for CACO. For the time being, he was suspended from service.

Lane wanted to tell Smith that he was quitting CACO, but he had no desire to be "detained" again. Nobody quit CACO; it let its employees go only when it felt like it.

Lane went home in a taxi and had just started to pour himself a drink when the doorman called up.

"Feds, Mr. Lane. They got proper IDs."

Lane sighed, downed his Scotch and, a few minutes later, opened the door. Lyons and two others, all holding .45 automatic pistols, were in the hall.

Lyons had a bandage around his head and some Band Aids on one cheek and his chin. Both eyes were bloodshot.

"You're under arrest, Lane," Lyons said.

In the chair in the interrogation room, attached once again to various machines, Lane answered everything a dozen times over. Smith personally conducted the questioning, perhaps because he wanted to make sure that Lyons did not attack Lane.

It took Lane ten hours to piece together what had happened from occasional comments by Smith and Lyons. Daniels and Lyons had followed Lane when he had been released from CACO HQ. Trailing Lane by a block, Daniels had driven through a stoplight and into the path of a hot rod doing fifty miles an hour. Daniels had been killed. Lyons had escaped with minor injuries to the body but a large one to the psyche. For no logical reason, he blamed Lane for the accident.

After the interrogation, Lane was taken to a small padded room, given a TV dinner, and locked in. Naked, he lay down on the padded floor and slept. Three hours later, two men woke him up and handed him his clothes and then conducted him to Smith's office.

"I don't know what to do with you," Smith said. "Apparently, you're not lying. Or else you've been conditioned somehow to give the proper—or perhaps I should say, improper—responses and reactions. It's possible, you know, to fool the machines, what with all the conscious control of brain waves, blood pressure, and so on being taught at universities and by private individuals."

"Yes, but you know that I haven't had any such training," Lane said. "Your security checks show that."

Smith grunted and looked sour.

"I can only conclude," he said, "from the data that I have, that you are involved in counter-espionage activity."

Lane opened his mouth to protest, but Smith continued, "Innocently, however. For some reason, you have become the object of interest, perhaps even concern, to some foreign outfit, probably Commie, most probably SKIZO, CACO's worst enemy. Or else you are the focus of some wildly improbable coincidences."

Lane couldn't think of anything to say to that. Smith said, "You were released the first time because I got a phone call from a high authority, a very high authority, telling me to let you go. By telling, I mean ordering. No reasons given. That authority doesn't have to give reasons.

"But I made the routine checkback, and I found out that the authority was fake. Somebody had pretended to be him. And the code words and the voice were exactly right. So, somehow, somebody, probably SKIZO, has cracked our code and can duplicate voices so exactly that even a voiceprint check can't tell the difference between the fake and the genuine. That's scary, Lane."

Lane nodded to indicate that he agreed it was scary. He said, "Whoever is doing this must have a damn good reason to reveal that he knows all this stuff. Why would a foreign agent show such a good hand just to get me out of your clutches—uh, custody? I can't do anyone, foreign agent or not, any good. And by revealing that they know the code words and can duplicate voices, they lose a lot. Now the code words will be changed, and the voices will be double-checked."

Smith drummed his fingers on the desktop and then said, "Yes, we know. But this extraordinary dermal sensitivity . . . these automobile accidents . . ."

"What did Lyons report about his accident?"

"He was unaware of anything wrong until Daniels failed to slow down on approaching the stoplight. He hesitated to say anything, because Daniels did not like backseat drivers, although Lyons was, as a matter of fact, in the front seat. Finally, he was unable to keep silent, but it was too late. Daniels looked up at the signal and said, 'What in hell you talking about?' and then the other car hit them."

Lane said, "Apparently Daniels thought the signal was green."

"Possibly. But I believe that there is some connection between the phone calls you got while with your women and the one I got from the supposed high authority."

"How could there be?" Lane said. "Why would this, this person, call me up just to ruin my lovemaking?"

Smith's face was as smooth as the face on a painting, but his fingers drummed a tattoo of desperation. No wonder. A case which could not even give birth to a hypothesis, let alone a theory, was the ultimate in frustration.

"I'm letting you go again, only this time you'll be covered with my agents like the North Pole is with snow in January," Smith said.

Lane did not thank him. He took a taxi back to his apartment, again feeling the tingling and warmth and mildly erotic sensations on the way to the taxi and on the way out of it.

In his rooms, he contemplated his future. He was no longer drawing pay from CACO, and CACO would not permit him to go to work for anybody else until this case was cleared up. In fact, Smith did not want him to leave his apartment unless it was absolutely necessary. Lane was to stay in it and force the unknown agency to come to him. So how was he to support himself? He had enough money to pay the rent for another month and buy food for two weeks. Then he would be eligible for welfare. He could defy Smith and get a job at nondetective work, say, a carryout boy at a grocery store or a car salesman. He had experience in both fields. But times were bad, and jobs of any kind were scarce.

Lane became angry. If CACO was keeping him from working, then it should be paying him. He phoned Smith, and, after a twelve-minute delay, during which Smith was undoubtedly checking back that it was really Lane phoning, Smith answered.

"I should pay you for doing nothing? How could I justify that on the budget I got?"

"That's your problem."

Lane looked up, because he had carried the phone under the skylight and his neck started tingling. Whoever was observing him at this moment had to be doing it from the Parmenter Building. He called Smith back and, after a ten-minute delay, got him.

"Whoever's laying a tap-in beam on me is doing it from any of the floors above the tenth. I don't think he could angle in from a lower floor."

"I know," Smith said. "I've had men in the Parmenter Building since yesterday. I don't overlook anything, Lane."

Lane had intended to ask him why he had overlooked the fact that they were undoubtedly being overheard at this moment. He did not do so because it struck him that Smith wanted their conversations to be bugged. He was keen to appear overconfident so that SKIZO, or whoever it was, would move again. Lane was the cheese in the trap. However, anybody who threatened Lane seemed to get hurt or killed, and Smith, from Lane's viewpoint, was threatening him.

During the next four days, Lane read Volume IV of the Durants' *The Story of Civilization*, drank more than he should have, exercised, and spent a half-hour each day, nude, under the skylight. The result of this exposure was that the skin burned and peeled all over his body. But the sexual titillation accompanying the dermal heat made the pain worth it. If the sensations got stronger each day, he'd be embarrassing himself, and possibly his observers, within a week.

He wondered if the men at the other end of the beam (or beams) had any idea of the gratuitous sexuality their subject felt. They probably thought that he was just a horny man with horny thoughts. But he knew that his reaction was unique, a result of something peculiar in his metabolism or his pigment or his whatever. Others, including Smith, had been under the skylight, and none had felt anything unusual.

The men investigating the Parmenter Building had detected nothing suspicious beyond the fact that there was nothing suspicious.

On the seventh day, Lane phoned Smith. "I can't take this submarine existence any longer. And I have to get a job or starve. So, I'm leaving. If your stormtroopers try to stop me, I'll resist. And you can't afford to have a big stink raised."

In the struggle that followed, Lane and the two CACO agents staggered into the area beneath the skylight. Lane went down, as he knew he would, but he felt that he had to make some resistance or lose his right to call himself a man. He stared up into the skylight while his hands were cuffed. He was not surprised when the phone rang, though he could not have given a reasonable explanation of why he expected it.

A third agent, just entering, answered. He talked for a moment, then turned and said, "Smith says to let him go. And we're to come on home. Something sure made him change his mind."

Lane started for the door after his handcuffs were unlocked. The phone rang again. The same man as before answered it. Then he shouted at Lane to stop, but Lane kept on going, only to be halted by two men stationed at the elevator.

Lane's phone was being monitored by CACO agents in the basement of the apartment building. They had called up to report that Smith had not given that order. In fact, no one had actually called in from outside the building. The call had come from somewhere within the building.

Smith showed up fifteen minutes later to conduct the search throughout the building. Two hours later, the agents were told to quit looking. Whoever had made that call imitating Smith's voice and giving the new code words had managed, somehow, to get out of the building unobserved.

"SKIZO, or whoever it is, must be using a machine to simulate my voice," Smith said. "No human throat could do it well enough to match voiceprints."

Voices!

Lane straightened up so swiftly that the men on each side of him grabbed his arms.

Dr. Sue Brackwell!

Had he really talked to her that last time, or was someone imitating her voice, too? He could not guess why; the mysterious Whoever could be using her voice to advance whatever plans he had. Sue had said that she just wanted to talk for old times' sake. Whoever was imitating her might have been trying to get something out of him, something that would be a clue to . . . to what? He just did not know.

And it was possible that this Whoever had talked to Sue Brackwell, imitating his, Lane's, voice.

Lane did not want to get her into trouble, but he could not afford to leave any possible avenue of investigation closed. He spoke to Smith about it as they went down the elevator. Smith listened intently, but he only said, "We'll see."

Glumly, Lane sat on the back seat between two men, also glum, as the car traveled through the streets of Washington. He looked out the window and through the smog saw a billboard advertising a rerun of *The Egg and I*. A block later, he saw another billboard, advertising a well-known brand of beer. SKY-BLUE WATERS, the sign said, and he wished he were in the land of sky-blue waters, fishing and drinking beer.

Again, he straightened up so swiftly that the two men grabbed him.

"Take it easy," he said. He slumped back down, and they removed their hands. The two advertisements had been a sort of free association test, provided only because the car had driven down this route and not some other it might easily have taken. The result of the conjunction of the two billboards might or might not be validly linked up with the other circuits that had been forming in the unconscious part of his mind. But he now had a hypothesis. It could be developed into a theory which could be tested against the facts. That is, it could be if he were given a chance to try it.

Smith heard him out, but he had only one comment. "You're thinking of the wildest things you can so you'll throw us off the track."

"What track?" Lane said. He did not argue. He knew that Smith would go down the trail he had opened up. Smith could not afford to ignore anything, even the most far-fetched of ideas.

Lane spent a week in the padded cell. Once, Smith entered to talk to him. The conversation was brief.

"I can't find any evidence to support your theory," Smith said.

"Is that because even CACO can't get access to certain classified documents and projects at Lackalas Astronautics?" Lane said.

"Yeah. I was asked what my need to know was, and I couldn't tell them what I really was trying to find out. The next thing I'd know, I'd be in a padded cell with regular sessions with a shrink."

"And so, because you're afraid of asking questions that might arouse suspicions of your sanity, you'll let the matter drop?"

"There's no way of finding out if your crazy theory has any basis."

"Love will find a way," Lane said.

Smith snorted, spun around, and walked out.

That was at 11 A.M. At 12:03, Lane looked at his wristwatch (since he was no longer compelled to go naked) and noted that lunch was late. A few minutes afterward, an Air Force jet fighter on a routine flight over Washington suddenly dived down and hit CACO HQ at close to one thousand miles an hour. It struck the massive stone building at the end opposite Lane's cell. Even so, it tore through the fortress-like outer walls and five rooms before stopping.

Lane, in the second subfloor, would not have been hit if the wreck had traveled entirely through the building. However, flames began to sweep through, and guards unlocked his door and got him outside just in time. On orders transmitted via radio, his escorts put him into a car to take him across the city to another CACO base. Lane was stiff with shock, but he reacted quickly enough when the car started to go through a red light. He was down on the floor and braced when the car and the huge diesel met. The others were not killed. They were not, however, in any condition to stop him. Ten minutes later, he was in his apartment.

Dr. Sue Brackwell was waiting for him under the skylight.

She had no clothes on; even her glasses were off. She looked very beautiful; it was not until much later that he remembered that she had never been beautiful or even passably pretty. He could not blame his shock for behaving the way he did, because the tingling and the warmth dissolved that. He became very alive, so much so that he loaned sufficient life to the thing that he pulled down to the floor. Somewhere in him existed the knowledge that "she" had prepared this for him and that no man might ever experience this certain event again. But the knowledge was so far off that it influenced him not at all.

Besides, as he had told Smith, love would find a way. He was not the one who had fallen in love. Not at first. Now, he felt as if he were in love, but many men, and women, feel that way during this time.

Smith and four others broke into the apartment just in time to rescue Lane. He was lying on the floor and was as naked and red as a newborn baby. Smith yelled at him, but he seemed to be deaf. It was evident that he was galloping with all possible speed in a race between a third-degree burn and an orgasm. He obviously had a partner, but Smith could neither see nor hear her.

The orgasm might have won if Smith had not thrown a big pan of cold water on Lane.

Two days afterward, Lane's doctor permitted Smith to enter the hospital room to see his much-bandaged and somewhat-sedated patient. Smith handed him a newspaper turned to page two. Lane read the article, which was short and all about EVE. EVE—Ever Vigilant Eye—had been a stationary-orbit surveillance satellite which had been sent up over the East Coast two years ago. EVE had exploded for unknown reasons, and the accident was being investigated.

"That's all the public was told," Smith said. "I finally got through to Brackwell and the other bigwigs connected with EVE. But either they were under orders to tell me as little as possible or else they don't have all the facts themselves. In any event, it's more than just a coincidence that she—EVE, I mean—blew up just as we were taking you to the hospital."

Lane said, "I'll answer some of your questions before you ask them. One, you couldn't see the holograph because she must've turned it off just before you got in. I don't know whether it was because she heard you coming or because she knew, somehow, that any more contact would kill me. Or maybe her alarms told her that she had better stop for her own good. But it would seem that she didn't stop or else did try to stop but was too late.

"I had a visitor who told me just enough about EVE so I wouldn't let my curiosity carry me into dangerous areas after I got out of here. And it won't. But I can tell you a few things and know it won't get any further.

"I'd figured out that Brackwell was the master designer of the bioelectronics circuit of a spy satellite. I didn't know that the satellite was called EVE or that she had the capability to beam in on ninety thousand individuals simultaneously. Or that the beams enabled her to follow each visually and tap in on their speech vibrations. Or that she could activate phone circuits with a highly variable electromagnetic field projected via the beam.

"My visitor said that I was not, for an instant, to suppose that EVE had somehow attained self-consciousness. That would be impossible. But I wonder.

"I also wonder if a female designer-engineer-scientist could, unconsciously, of course, design female circuits? Is there some psychic influence that goes along with the physical construction of computers and associated circuits? Can the whole be greater than the parts? Is there such a thing as a female gestalt in a machine?"

"I don't go for that metaphysical crap," Smith said.

"What does Brackwell say?"

"She says that EVE was simply malfunctioning."

"Perhaps man is a malfunctioning ape," Lane said. "But could Sue have built her passion for me into EVE? Or given EVE circuits which could evolve emotion? EVE had selfrepairing capabilities, you know, and was part protein. I know it sounds crazy. But who, looking at the first apeman, would have extrapolated Helen of Troy?

"And why did she get hung up on me, one out of the ninety thousand she was watching? I had a dermal supersensitivity to the spy beam. Did this reaction somehow convey to EVE a feeling, or a sense, that we were in rapport? And did she then become jealous? It's obvious that she modulated the beams she'd locked on Leona and

Rhoda so that they saw green where the light was really red and did not see oncoming cars at all.

"And she worked her modulated tricks on Daniels and that poor jet pilot, too."

"What about that holograph of Dr. Brackwell?"

"EVE must've been spying on Sue, also, on her own creator, you might say. Or—and I don't want you to look into this, because it won't do any good now—Sue may have set all this up in the machinery, unknown to her colleagues. I don't mean that she put in extra circuits. She couldn't get away with that; they'd be detected immediately, and she'd have to explain them. But she could have put in circuits which had two purposes, the second of which was unknown to her colleagues. I don't know.

"But I do know that it was actually Sue Brackwell who called me that last time and not EVE. And I think that it was this call that put into EVE's mind, if a machine can have a mind in the human sense, to project the much-glamorized holograph of Sue. Unless, of course, my other theory is correct, and Sue herself was responsible for that."

Smith groaned and then said, "They'll never believe me if I put all this in a report. For one thing, will they believe that it was only free association that enabled you to get *eye in the sky* from 'The egg and I' and 'Sky-blue waters'? I doubt it. They'll think you had knowledge you shouldn't have had and you're concealing it with that incredible story. I wouldn't want to be in your shoes. But then, I don't want to be in my shoes.

"But why did EVE blow up? Lackalas says that she could be exploded if a destruct button at control center was pressed. The button, however, was not pressed."

"You dragged me away just in time to save my life. But EVE must have melted some circuits. She died of frustration—in a way, that is."

"What?"

"She was putting out an enormous amount of energy for such a tight beam. She must have overloaded."

Smith guffawed and said, "She was getting a charge out of it, too? Come on!"

Lane said, "Do you have any other explanation?"

About the Authors

Philip José Farmer was born on January 26, 1918 in North Terre Haute, Indiana. He grew up in Peoria, Illinois where he spent much of his childhood reading everything from the Bible and books on mythology to the classics by Baum, Carroll, Cervantes, Defoe, Dickens, Homer, London, Swift, and Twain to popular works by Burroughs, Doyle, Haggard, Verne, and Wells.

He sold his first story, a mainstream tale titled "O'Brien and Obrenov," to Adventure in 1946 before he decided to try his hand at science fiction. His next published story, "The Lovers," appeared in the August 1952 issue of Startling Stories, and is noted for breaking the taboo on sex in science fiction, as well as for earning Farmer a Hugo Award for "Most Promising New Talent."

Married and with two children, he soon quit his job to become a full-time writer, but after selling several more stories to the science fiction pulps, his career hit a stumbling block when he "won" the Shasta Prize Novel Contest. The grand prize was four thousand dollars (a lot of money in 1953), but he never received his winnings. Instead, the publisher asked Farmer for rewrites while the prize money was invested in another book, which bombed. By the time the truth came out, Farmer had lost his house and was forced to take up manual labor full time.

Farmer left Peoria with his family in 1956 and moved around the country working as a technical writer for the space-defense industry, eventually ending up in Beverly Hills, California in 1965. All the while he continued to write and sell science fiction short stories and novels, launching his popular World of Tiers series and even winning a second Hugo Award for the novella "Riders of the Purple Wage." Then, just before the moon landing in 1969, he was laid off from his technical writing job, so he decided to write fiction full time once again. This time it stuck.

In 1970, Farmer moved back to Peoria with his family and again his career began to take off, this time with a third Hugo Award win, for *To Your Scattered Bodies Go*, the opening novel in his bestselling Riverworld series. For the next few years, Farmer sought inspiration from the popular literature he so loved, writing novels such as *The Mad Goblin* (a Doc Savage pastiche), *Lord of the Trees* and *Lord Tyger* (both Tarzan pastiches), *The Wind Whales of Ishmael* (a science fiction sequel to Moby Dick), *The Other Log of Phileas Fogg* (the "true" story behind Jules Verne's *Around the World in Eighty Days*), and *Venus on the Half-Shell* (written as if by Kilgore Trout, a character from the works of Kurt Vonnegut). He also wrote two "biographies" during this period: *Tarzan Alive: A Definitive Biography of Lord Greystoke* and *Doc Savage: His Apocalyptic Life*.

The next two decades saw the publication of the Dayworld trilogy, as well as the last installments in the Riverworld and World of Tiers series. Farmer also fulfilled his lifelong ambition to write authorized Oz, Doc Savage, and Tarzan novels with the publication of *A Barnstormer in Oz*, *Escape from Loki*, and *The Dark Heart of Time*. Late in his career, Farmer switched genres with *Nothing Burns in Hell*, a detective novel set in his hometown of Peoria.

After Farmer retired from writing in 1999, new collections such as *Pearls from Peoria* and *Up from the Bottomless Pit and Other Stories* continued to appear, as did new collaborative works such as *The Evil in Pemberley House* (with Win Scott Eckert), *The Song of Kwasin* (with Christopher Paul Carey), and *Dayworld: A Hole in Wednesday* (with Danny Adams)

Farmer passed on February 25, 2009, but his fan base is as ardent as ever, ensuring that his works will continue to be reprinted and enjoyed by readers for generations to come.

Garyn G. Roberts, Ph.D. is an award-winning author and editor of a range of books, scholarly articles and related works. Two of his most celebrated works include *Dick Tracy and American Culture* (1994, 2003), which was a finalist for the Mystery Writers of America Edgar Allan Poe Award, and *The Prentice Hall Anthology of Science Fiction and Fantasy* (2003), which earned the Ray and Pat Browne National Popular Culture Book Award. Roberts is a college and university professor, and was a college Academic Chair/Dean and Department Head of Communications and English. He was presented with the Munsey Award in 2013 for his contributions to, and publications about, the history of the pulp magazines (1896 to 1950).

Meteor House Titles

THE WORLDS OF PHILIP JOSÉ FARMER
Anthology Series edited by Michael Croteau
Volume 1: Protean Dimensions
Volume 2: Of Dust and Soul
Volume 3: Portraits of a Trickster
Volume 4: Voyages to Strange Days

The Best of Farmerphile edited by Michael Croteau
The Philip José Farmer Centennial Collection edited by Michael Croteau

WOLD NEWTON SERIES
Doc Savage: His Apocalyptic Life by Philip José Farmer
Tarzan and the Dark Heart of Time by Philip José Farmer

THE KHOKARSA SERIES
Exiles of Kho by Christopher Paul Carey
Flight to Opar (Restored Edition) by Philip José Farmer
The Song of Kwasin by Philip José Farmer and Christopher Paul Carey
Hadon, King of Opar by Christopher Paul Carey
Blood of Ancient Opar by Christopher Paul Carey

THE PAT WILDMAN SERIES
The Evil in Pemberley House by Philip José Farmer and Win Scott Eckert
The Scarlet Jaguar by Win Scott Eckert

THE PHILEAS FOGG SERIES
Phileas Fogg and the War of Shadows by Josh Reynolds
Phileas Fogg and the Heart of Osra by Josh Reynolds

THE TWO HAWKS SERIES
Man of War by Heidi Ruby Miller

THE DAYWORLD SERIES
Dayworld: A Hole in Wednesday by Philip José Farmer and Danny Adams

SCIENCE FICTION ADVENTURE
The Abnormalities of Stringent Strange by Rhys Hughes
Airship Hunters by Jim Beard and Duane Spurlock

REFERENCE - CROSSOVERS
Crossovers Expanded, Volume 1 by Sean Lee Levin
Crossovers Expanded, Volume 2 by Sean Lee Levin

CHAPBOOKS
Being an Account of the Delay at Green River, Wyoming, of Phileas Fogg, World Traveler, or, The Masked Man Meets an English Gentleman by Win Scott Eckert
The Adventure of the Fallen Stone: Being the First Part of the Account of The Dynamics of a Meteor by John H. Watson, M.D. edited by Win Scott Eckert
Watch Your Back, Mr. Minamoto by Frank Schildiner

www.ingramcontent.com/pod-product-compliance
Lightning Source LLC
Chambersburg PA
CBHW030809310726
48980CB00006B/428/J

* 9 7 8 1 9 4 5 4 2 7 1 6 9 *